The

Th

Tessie Gillis

THE STORY OF TESSIE GILLIS is now well known. She was a woman determined to write, who found the time to write only after she was stricken with heart disease, confined to one room and an oxygen tent, living in rural Cape Breton Island. From there she contacted Evelyn Garbary who became her editor, her friend and, after Tessie's death, her devoted promoter—keeping Tessie's work alive, getting stories read on CBC radio and eventually seeing the work published. Tessie saw none of this. She died in 1972. Since then, her stories and two novels have become established classics—the first Cape Breton writing to dare tell stark stories of hardscrabble life, of rural distances and pain, and of alcoholism and domestic abuse—stories that have realized high acclaim. And now, in honour of the 100th anniversary of the birth of this Godmother of Cape Breton Fiction, Breton Books is proud to offer a new collection of the writing of Tessie Gillis.

The Woman *from* Away

The Collected Writing of Cape Breton's Tessie Gillis

Breton Books

Publisher's Note: Throughout this book, Tessie Gillis has used "ye" to convey the spoken form of "you" as it often sounds in Cape Breton. It is not the "ye" of Shakespeare which rhymes with "glee," but rather a sound close to "yeah," but much shorter. The Gaelic greeting "Ciamar a tha sibh?" ("How are you?") is written here as it often sounds to English ears—"Cummina Hashen!"

This book is a work of fiction, based on the final manuscript by Tessie Gillis, edited with Evelyn Garbary. Portions of some chapters appeared in 1992 in *The Promised Land,* edited by James Taylor, published by Wilf Cude, Medicine Label Press.

Cover Photograph: Joe and Tessie Gillis

Editor: Ronald Caplan
Production Assistants: Bonnie Thompson, James Fader

We acknowledge the support of the Canada Council for the Arts for our publishing program. Canada Council for the Arts Conseil des Arts du Canada

We also acknowledge support from Cultural Affairs, Nova Scotia Department of Tourism, Culture and Heritage. Nova Scotia Tourism, Culture and Heritage

We acknowledge the financial support of the Government of Canada through the Book Publishing Industry Development Program (BPIDP) for our publishing activities. Canada

Library and Archives Canada Cataloguing in Publication

Gillis, Tessie, 1910-1972

The woman from away : collected writing of Cape Breton's Tessie Gillis / introduction by Ronald Caplan.

ISBN 978-1-895415-92-6

I. Title.

PS8563.I513A14 2009 C813'.54

C2009-905849-9

Printed in Canada

To Tessie's daughter, Helena Gillis MacLeod, and to her first editor, Evelyn Garbary, who "loved her talent alive"

Contents

Introduction

Ronald Caplan

I WANT NOTHING TO GET BETWEEN Tessie Gillis's stories and the reader—from the withered yellow breasts and the panic of the bull loose in the barn in her novel *Stories from the Woman from Away,* to the beating of Molly and the fate of farm animals in the wake of a husband's anger in *John R. and Son.* Still, there is something I want to add, something new readers should know.

Tessie Gillis was a person who wanted to write. She was a vibrant, observant, courageous woman from away—brought to Cape Breton by her husband Joe. Not only Cape Breton but deepest Cape Breton—to a tiny, off-trail community of small farms distanced from each other by forest and fields. A knowledgeable ranch girl, raised in Montana, Tessie took up the daily work and worries of wood heat and low water and the snow that further blocked her from the world, and the community.

Joe had found her in New York City. They tore into rural life together. They planted poplars and he put in a huge garden. They adopted two children. And Tessie kept the house and served the community, fought for it—"writing letters to politicians, government officials, newspapers in an effort to provide electricity, telephone service and a snow plough for her remote settlement in the hills," as Evelyn Garbary tells in a fragment of memoir. "She had been successful only in providing electricity."

And Tessie wanted to write.

A letter from her comes down to us, a passionate letter that made it through bureaucracy and landed on Evelyn Garbary's desk at the Arts Service, Adult Education Division, Nova Scotia

Department of Education—Tessie Gillis searching for a way to participate in an adult writing course despite being confined to her home. It's July 31, 1965:

"I would like to know if there is some way I could get lessons they will be giving at the adult course on writing. You see I am practically an invalid with my heart and its resultant artery complications; I have been working as steadily as my health will permit on a novel these past three years.

"I find I could do with more than a few pointers on professionalism, I'm afraid I'm very much an amateur. I have contacted correspondence schools but there is the question of the high costs between us.

"A short course such as you are offering could be, at least, a great boost...if we could find a way so I could take them by correspondence.

"Could *anything* be worked out and how much would it cost?

"Don't just say 'no chance' PLEASE without putting aside the fact the request *is* unorthodox and think it over instead. I guess I'm begging you...but I do want something like this so *very badly.*"

Tessie had reached Evelyn Garbary, perhaps best known today as the founder (with Tom Miller and Sara Lee Lewis) and director of Mermaid Theatre based in Wolfville, Nova Scotia. Evelyn came to Canada as a trained actress. "Before I met Tess I had spent many years trying to find out whether or not I possessed any real talent as a writer...but it seemed to me that no amount of hard work would release a talent that didn't exist.... In the early 'thirties, I was told by a mandarin in the Home Office that I possessed 'extraordinary powers for initiating action.' Perhaps that was my only talent."

Their letters plus Evelyn's occasional notes toward her memoirs reveal a marvelous, if minor, Canadian literary event—two extraordinary women making their own lives, and encouraging and worrying for one another—Evelyn on the run praying for time to sit and edit, Tessie trapped in her bedroom often too depressed to pick up a pen—each warning the other to take care of herself.

Introduction

With two small sons, Evelyn Garbary against all warning–"You can't go there alone with only the kids. They're all old bachelors up there"–entered the backlands of rural Inverness County. It took her two days to locate the home of Joe and Tessie Gillis. "By mid-afternoon, I found the lady; she lived in a small farm house on the side of a hill, high up in Glencoe. She told me she had had a heart attack three years ago in the middle of winter and due to the delay in getting her into hospital a part of her heart had atrophied. There was an oxygen tank beside her bed.

"'Some days are bad,' she said, 'I can't breathe and I can't remember anything, but there are good days too.'

"Her husband and thirteen-year-old son were working in the woods, but her daughter, a beautiful girl of fifteen, was making bread in the kitchen.

"'It's hard on her,' the lady said, 'she has had to mind the house since she was twelve years old.'

"Before I left we agreed that she should send me her manuscripts and that I would suggest revisions. She took me at my word. Within days large envelopes filled with hand-written notes, typewritten pages (not numbered), some written on her 'good days' and some written when she had difficulty remembering, arrived on my desk. And so, our friendship began."

TESSIE GILLIS BROUGHT NEW EYES and created a rare portrait of rural Cape Breton life in the 1950s.

"Try and remember that the reader, or the listener, has to 'SEE' the situation," Evelyn wrote on August 25, 1965. "You must make them almost FEEL the cold, and your pain and anxiety.... You will have to build the tension...and you can only do this with DETAIL...DETAIL...DETAIL....

"Now, you know and I know, how much your deep religious convictions and experiences have meant to you—but you can't expect the average reader or listener to know—and so I think a most subtle approach would be to 'suggest' these convictions and experiences and SHOW what happened as a result...."

September 14, 1965: "You have reached the stage where

you are taking the RIGHT word 'out of the air.' You have learnt to express yourself EXACTLY and not approximately. You are no longer using hackneyed phrases....

"Your next stage, (and this is very exciting,) is when you will use words in a way that no one but you could use them....

"Whenever you can, use EXACT WORDS YOU HEAR SPOKEN. You are doing this already, and I am only telling you this to let you know that you are on 'the right track.'

"Get to work on 'The Funeral'! Keep writing, and try, try and not lose precious time brooding, it's so bad for you, dear, and you just can't write well when you allow everything to get the better of you, it's your magnificent courage that is keeping you working so hard. We all know that, and adore you for it. Pull yourself up, Tessie, by the bootstraps, SWEAR, then get to work. I know, I know, how hard it is not to give way to it all, but don't, you are too big for that. When you write as a MAN, you are tremendous, but when you write as a woman, soft, and with too many adjectives, too many FEELINGS creeping in, you are not as good as any magazine writer. You are capable of writing LITERATURE, and this is why I am so hard on you....

"God bless. Evelyn."

ERNEST BUCKLER WAS Garbary's close friend. He read Tessie's work, writing at some length to her directly and to her through Evelyn. In December 1965:

"Tessie has a very keen eye for the telling detail..., a thorough knowledge of her subject, a lively sense of humor, and a talent for achieving certain striking lines and observations that argue if she can do it once she can do it again...."

"AND THEN," Evelyn wrote, "something happened to Tessie. Maybe it was having her family around her and the Christmas festivities or maybe it was her way of welcoming the New Year, but her indomitable spirit took a quantum leap. She gained confidence. She began to see for herself how she could gently 'manipulate her material' in order that her characters could be none other than themselves; how their clothes and all their possessions spoke eloquently on their behalf...."

At one point Tessie wrote: "I wish I was going to live for years and years, now that I can write all the things I used to think about...."

THE TWO WOMEN REMAINED FRIENDS and work mates until Tessie died in 1972. Evelyn Garbary helped her, befriended her, edited and encouraged, got her work read by others, fought with her and fought for her—and after Tessie died she kept the dream of publication alive. Tessie probably heard Evelyn read her work on CBC Radio but she saw none of her work in print.

After Tessie's death, Evelyn continued to fine tune the work, asking herself: "Was Ernest Buckler right in insisting that [the book] must be a collaboration between the two of us, while I as forcefully insisted that the book was Tessie's, alone...? I was only her amenuensis and the clerk of the spirit that informed her."

Evelyn read in Buckler's *The Cruelest Month:* "Her gaunt face...like a talent, when there is no one to love it alive." In a draft fragment of her memoirs Evelyn wrote: "These words explain why for nearly three years I did not behave like a rational being with frightening responsibilities; who in their right mind would take on the care of an invalid woman, who lived hundreds of miles away...to care for Tess and *love her talent alive*?"

In 1976 "Horses of the Sun" was printed in *Atlantis: A Women's Studies Journal,* and *The Fiddlehead* published "The Innocent" in 1991, nominating it for the Journey Prize. These two stories also appeared in an edition of her selected writings called *The Promised Land,* edited by James Taylor and published by Wilf Cude's Medicine Label Press in 1992. Breton Books published the novel *Stories from the Woman from Away* in 1996 and in 1998 *John R. and Son and Other Writings.* And now, in honour of the anniversay of her 100th birthday, the *Collected Writing* in one volume.

TESSIE GILLIS HOLDS A LIGHT to a portion of Cape Breton

about which few writers before her have dared to speak, certainly from a woman's perspective. It is not only perspective in the sense of attitude, feminine approach and so forth—but more specifically it is a woman informed by the conditions and details of usually hidden women's work, women's information. While we might take doing the laundry for granted, and few have written about it, her chapter "The Day the Men Went to Town" (in the novel *Stories from the Woman from Away*) is a laundry-day song, a revel in the sweetness of cleanliness and the battle with lack of rinse water in the face of shitty diapers—and that's only the context, not the subject, of the story being told. A sound calls her to deal with a bull loose in the barn and the threat to other animals she cares for and on which the family's fragile livelihood depends.

When Tessie Gillis tackles this, she opens the world for us as only fiction can. And to have written a classic tale holds that occasion to the light for all time.

Evelyn Garbary died in November 1994—the passionate, tenacious woman who kept Tessie alive and writing, and then kept the work alive. And we are left with Tessie's stories, fierce and loving details close to the Cape Breton bone.

Ronald Caplan
Wreck Cove

Stories from the Woman from Away

~ A Novel ~

1

Last Chapter But One

SINCE EARLY SUMMER the dust on the roads has been raised by cars with American license plates. There were visitors in every house and callers began their rounds as soon as they had recovered from the previous night's festivities.

Most of the people who called were strangers to me. They called to see Jim. Entertaining was hard work and required a great deal of ingenuity since no one ever went to the grocers more than twice a month. I made endless molasses cookies and threw in oats to take the place of flour. I used stale bread and dried fruit to make puddings no one had ever heard of let alone tasted before. I used up most of my homemade cheese. Meat was the problem. Jim had butchered a cow and a pig for winter, but the barrels had been empty for months. There were only chickens left and they were going fast. I skipped many meals. The children were neglected I know, and there seemed to be no end to the stream of visitors.

Thc Highland Games were on and we had all been invited. Jim had taken the children down to his father's place to make the final arrangements. The house was empty! I locked the door, and placed the washtub in the middle of the kitchen floor. I would take a bath. The first this summer. If only I didn't feel so tired I'd be happy. Thank God there wouldn't be any teas to prepare today. There would be time to talk to the children—to listen to what they had to say.

I gave myself a good soaping...it was lovely feeling so fresh and clean. It was hard to get out of the water. I didn't seem to have the strength to pull myself up. "I look like a plucked chicken—only yellow. It must be worse than I thought." (I had taken to talking to myself for some time now.) I walked over to the sink and took down the little mirror from the nail on the wall. My eyes were hollow, my skin the colour of parchment and stretched taut over pointed bones that threatened to perforate the transparent skin. I had no hips and sagging skin hung in bags where my buttocks had been. I looked down at my breasts. I cupped the bags of empty skin that only months ago had been firm flesh.

"Jim can't have noticed. I'll tell him I have to see a doctor.... The kids are so small. What'll happen to them? I won't tell him today. Today is their big day...and they shall enjoy it if it kills me. I'll tell Jim tomorrow."

I looked across the fields. I had been across those fields all day, yesterday, the day before, and the day before. "It's over-ripe. All the good'll be gone out of it if it isn't cut soon." Two weeks now...for two weeks I've been chasing animals out of that hay. If Jim doesn't fix that break in that fence today I'll go down myself and fix it some way...fifteen for dinner and only six plates and six cups (three without handles)...plenty of tea but no meat. Who ever tried to feed fifteen on two pounds of meat? Cut it small and make plenty of gravy, then fill them up with bread.... No use talking to Jim unless I catch him early in the morning and even then he can't think of anything but his thick head.

"I wish to hell they'd all go home," Jim said as he got into bed that night. "I wuz down the road lookin' today. The hay should'a been cut a week ago, an' the fence is down in the upper corner."

"I know," I said.

Jim had declined an invitation to go to a dance at Beatons' that evening and had found the strength to resist all the pleading and protestations that followed. I slept that night but before dawn a car pulled into the yard. The horn sounded sharp staccato blasts. At first Jim refused to stir, but soon the noise became painful to hear and he leapt out of bed and ran down the stairs in his bare feet. I staggered over to the window. Two young men were seated in a flashy new convertible. They had come to show off their new car. Symbol of success! A golden-winged Thunderbird. Jim didn't invite them into the house or offer them a drink.

"Thank you, God!" I whispered, as the roar of the engine died away and the dust on the road slowly subsided.

Jim stayed up and went out to water the horse. Yes, the hay would be cut today! I was sitting down enjoying a cup of coffee, the children were out playing and the house was quiet when four men drove up the road, past the house, and stopped at the field where Jim was working. I watched them as they got out of the car, opened the trunk and took out a bottle. Two of the men took off their jackets, but the other two could hardly stand up and did not attempt such a difficult task in spite of the heat of the sun.

It wasn't long before Lauchie and Harold Beaton came down the road, and J.J. and Dougall came up the hill. Many more bottles appeared from the trunk of the car. Three staggering figures followed the hay-rack round the field with forks on their shoulders unable to lift a straw. Three slept under a tree at the edge of the field. Somehow the hay was cut and all but the last load stowed safely in the barn. Then I noticed one of the men glance at his watch. I saw Jim shake his head—they all started to plead with him. At last Jim got in the car after leaving instructions with Lauchie about stacking the last load.

THAT NIGHT A HEAVY FROST covered the countryside. Autumn was in the air although summer had barely cast a shadow.

Here and there, in the woods, the young maples turned crimson and blazed a warning no one could ignore. Reluctantly the visitors took their leave of families and friends. Everyone went back to work with relief.

"What makes ye so yellow?" said Jim one evening as though seeing me for the first time.

"Are you just noticing? Didn't you even notice how black I looked in those pictures at the Highland Games?"

"No!" Jim could be terse when reminded of his behaviour in the past, especially when he didn't know what the implication might be.

"I'm sick, Jim. Can't you see how awful thin I am? All summer long it's been all I could do to get out of bed in the mornings."

"Do ye think ye should see a doctor?"

"If I'm going to stay on my feet I'd better see one." I couldn't stop the tears now. "Jim, can't you SEE?"

"All right! All right!" Jim snapped back, but he looked at me for a long while.

All that fall I tended a doctor. He couldn't locate my trouble on the first visit or on the many visits that followed. He would go to his cupboard, look over the rows of bottles solemnly and each time take down a different one.

"Try this, Mrs. Douglas?" he would say and "Come back in two weeks time."

I came to enjoy my visits to the doctor. I made many friends in his waiting room, but Ellen Cameron I came to love. We began exchanging notes. Ellen knew she was taking nerve pills, and I had just been given the same ones. Five of my neighbours had come into town with me. Some wanted to visit the grocer and some the vendor. We had agreed to meet at Ellen's place. While Ellen was getting tea ready I noticed how stiff her body seemed to be and how tightly she clenched her fists as she stood at the range.

"Come on," I said, "we'd better go, it'll be getting dark soon." No one made a move.

Last Chapter But One

"Ye must stay and hev some tea," said Charlie, Ellen's husband, as he put his hand on his wife's shoulder. '"You're all right now, aren't ye, honey?"

A rumble of voices drowned my protests. Ellen made the tea. I couldn't take my eyes off her face. The men were drinking beer and they were laughing. At last I managed to persuade the others to leave. That was the last time I saw Ellen alive. It was Janice Lawlor who brought the news.

"Dead! Ellen?"

Janice rushed over to stop me from falling. She helped me into a chair.

"Someone must have the names mixed up," I whispered. "I was with her only last week." This was all I could say. I couldn't believe it. Ellen was only forty. Five years younger than I was. It was not until I saw Ellen in her coffin that I could believe that she was dead. Charlie couldn't tell me anything. He could only stare before him. There were no tears in his eyes. I grabbed Jim's arm.

"Come on, Jim," I said, "I want to stop at Ellen's mother's place. There is something I have to know."

Jim drove me to the farm where Ellen had been raised. A girl of twelve sat in the rocker beside the stove in the kitchen, a baby on her knee. I drew up a chair and sat down beside her.

"How did she die?" I asked. "She couldn't have been sick long?"

"NO!" the girl replied, "not long. They took her to Halifax."

"Halifax! What happened? Was it sudden?"

"It was to Dartmouth—to the mental home, they wuz after takin' 'er to. Ellen got a pain one night, an' he took 'er upstairs to bed. When Charlie got home he called the doctor. But Ellen wouldn't talk to the doctor, so he gave her a needle and left. Daddy came home and sent Mama down to help." The girl stopped—she remembered she was talking to a stranger.

"Well, what happened then? Please tell me?"

"Well, I'll tell ye all I can. The doctor came ag'in next mornin' with herself after bein' jist like that all night and still not lettin' on she heard anybody at all. Doctor Angus gave 'er another needle an' told Mama, 'She jist won't talk. She could answer questions if she wanted to. It's jist 'er nerves. I gave 'er somethin' to quiet 'er. She'll be all right.' Mama was awful mad. Ellen layin' there, nothin' but skin an' bone like she wuz, an' him sayin' nothin' wuz wrong."

"Then what happened?"

"Well, they took 'er to the mental hospital, only they said it was to a hospital in Halifax she wuz goin' to."

"What did the doctor tell Charlie, do you know?"

"No! But mebbe a week after Ellen took the pain, he told Charlie there wasn't nothin' the matter with 'er, that he could only keep on givin' 'er needles. He said fer Charlie to send 'er, or take 'er up to the mental hospital for a few treatments. Ellen was still layin' in bed. So Charlie took 'er up in the car." The girl shifted the baby on to her other knee. "Ellen let Mama dress 'er, then she walked to the door, not lookin' to right or left, past th' kids an' all. The only time she showed she knowed any o' them was to put 'er hand on the baby's head when she passed by th' high chair. She didn't talk none though."

That was all she knew. I had to wait until the funeral to learn the rest. They had given Ellen "treatment" at the mental hospital. The following morning she ate her breakfast, talked to the nurses and seemed better. Charlie started on the seven-hour journey home. When he arrived there was a telegram for him—"Hurry back. We need your permission to operate." Charlie grabbed a bite to eat and sped back to the hospital. Before he had been admitted to the room Ellen was dead.

THAT WAS LAST YEAR. Another summer has come and gone. We still had many visitors, but now they were chiefly neighbours, their relations and acquaintances. The visits all began the same way. The man would pull a bottle out of his pocket and say he had come to treat Jim, but I was the one they had come to see. I knew that. Their scrutiny made me feel uncomfortable and I tried to escape to the kitchen as soon as politeness permitted. Their warmth and concern were unbearable. Angus and Mary Gillis came out from town; Peter and Jane Campbell from the glen on the other side of the mountain; the MacLeods, the Sullivans and the Kavanaghs from the Irish settlement. I hadn't been near a doctor since Ellen died. I no longer had the strength to finish a batch of bread and the churning was more than I could handle; Jim had to take over the dasher as soon as the butter began to form, and if he went out of the house I had to leave the churn the way it was until he returned. I caught cold.

"I don't know what's the matter, Jim, every once in a while I get an awful pain in my chest."

"I coughed all night meself!" said Jim. "It's goin' around. Everybody's down with it."

The cold left but the cough stayed. Then one night I woke up ringing wet, there were big drops of sweat on my forehead. I sat on the edge of the bed and rested my arms on my knees. Drops of sweat fell to the floor.

Jim took me to a doctor on the other side of the Island.

"Mrs. Douglas, I can't find anything wrong with your heart. You don't need to worry about that. I'll give you some cough medicine, take a tablespoon every four hours."

"Seven dollars for nothing but a bottle of cough medicine," I said to Jim as we climbed back into the truck. "But he did say my heart was good. That's all I wanted to know. Long as my heart is good I can throw anything off."

I seemed to have added strength for a while after that, maybe because of what the doctor had said. I started to clean the house, but my pain didn't go away and my new-found energy didn't last for long. I gave up taking the medicine. When the callers came I could only give them cookies with their tea—no more cakes and pies.

One day Blaze and Peggy MacLellan called. They hadn't been to the house for over two years. I made tea for them and stayed in the room until Blaze and Jim started telling stories, then I escaped into the kitchen. Soon Blaze came out after me carrying his cup and plate.

"Dear heart, thank ye," he said, putting his dishes down on the kitchen table, "I couldn't eat a bite." He came over to me and put his arm around my shoulder. "I'm sorry to see ye under the weather." I tried to edge away but Blaze wouldn't let me move. "I hope ye don't hold it against me for stayin' away so long. I'm sorry."

"Quit worrying," I said. I managed to throw off his arm and staggered into the living room. "Jim, you'd better give Blaze a drink. Get the bottle!"

They didn't stay long after that.

"Don't you think it's funny that Peggy and Blaze looked us up?" I said to Jim, after they had gone. "Making the excuse of going to Mass in the Glen when they've passed us by time after time for two years?"

"What are ye dreamin' up now?"

"Well, Blaze was lolligagging over me in the kitchen. I couldn't make out what he was talking about but he was trying to apologize for something. He kept after me like he couldn't rest until he was forgiven."

"Yer imaginin' things."

"No, I'm not, Jim. And it's not only Blaze but all those people we've had visiting. People we hardly know except to pass the time of day with. You haven't been telling around that I'm sick, have you?"

"I suppose I did mention it, but what's wrong with that?"

"Now I can feel sorry for your poor father."

"What's he got to do with it?"

"Those two weeks before he died. Lying there, conscious, not able to talk, but understanding every word, and people from all over the Island flocking in like vultures. He knew...he knew."

"Knew what? What kind of talk is that? Talk sense if you want me to listen to you."

"Jim! They all think I'm going to die. That's why they're coming. They think I'm going to die."

IT WAS ON A SATURDAY late in February, I remember. The Glen was buried in snow. The winding trail to the highway twisted up and down the hills between high cliffs of snow. Saturdays were always busy days for me, and this Saturday was particularly so. The ladies of the parish were holding a fund-raising card party for the church and I had promised to bake for them. I had the last batch of cakes in the oven when I felt a sharp pain in my back. I thought that a five-minute rest would relieve it, so I went into the other room and sat down in the big old upholstered chair. The pain eased in no time at all.

There was still the churning to be done for I had no butter for the sandwiches. I had only made a few turns with the handle when the pain struck again—this time in the chest. I managed to slide into the nearest chair. Jim was reading the paper before the fire and the children were playing in the other room. Once again the pain almost disappeared; once again I went back to my work, but this time when the pain returned it was like an iron claw—a grappling hook, and it seemed to be pulling outwards as though trying to burst through my ribs. Flames of pain shot up into my throat and down my arms. I tried to call out—but there was no air to breathe. I felt I was breathing cotton candy. I managed to reach the staircase, climb the stairs and reach my bed. Lying down only made the pain worse. I tried to call Jim, but he didn't answer. I tried again.

"What do you want?" Jim answered. I listened for his footsteps on the stairs.

"Jim! Get the priest," I called. This time Jim heard me and came running up the stairs.

"Git the priest? What's the matter? Don't you feel good?"

"It's my heart. Get the priest."

"Mary, ye can't mean that. Ye were all right a minute ago. Lay down on the pillow." Jim tried to push me down. "Rest a while. Ye don't want a priest, do ye? It can't be yer heart...."

"Maybe it's not my heart." I couldn't keep my eyes open any longer. "Maybe it's pneumonia or something."

"I'll go git the priest, if ye want.... It isn't your heart, Mary, is it? Are ye sure? It can't be.... Yer jist tired."

"I guess so."

I couldn't help thinking of the children. I wanted to be with them at the end. After a little while I asked Jim to help me down the stairs. He lifted me from stair to stair. Somehow I managed to reach my favourite chair by the old Quebec heater. The children knew at once that something was wrong. Anne found an old hot water bottle. Sonny brought me a pillow. The pain wasn't so bad when I sat quiet and didn't talk. The steel claws relaxed their hold and the burning ache was almost a relief. But how was I going to convince Jim of the need for help?

There was a knock on the door. It was Dougall come to collect the cakes and cookies for the church party. Dougall did not have to be told. In twenty minutes he had returned with J.J. and his pick-up truck. Jim and the children searched for my clothes, but I could not raise my arms, so they had to throw the coat over my shoulders. Jim and Dougall helped me out the back door and lifted me into the truck.

The school yard was full of cars and trucks. The whole community had gathered for the party. Surely there would be one car fit to drive along the highway! A car with headlights and brakes fit to drive twenty-eight miles.

"I'll be back in a minute," said Jim, "are ye warm enough?"

I nodded and watched Jim as he went over to a car across the yard. The driver had just started up the engine—he was an old friend. Jim bent down and talked to him, then I could see the driver pointing to another car. The pain got worse and I had to clench my teeth to keep from screaming. Jim was lost in the shadow but now it didn't seem to matter.... Where were the children? Were they still in the back of the truck in this wind? I could see Jim running from one car to another. It was the old story, one had no gas, and there were no gas stations open at this hour.... Another's brakes were gone and the roads were too icy to take a chance. The MacDonalds had a car full of passengers and were afraid they wouldn't have a way home. Everyone had an excuse. I could see Jim coming back to the truck.

"No one will go with us," he said. "I've asked everyone I know."

"Let's go home, Jim, I'm cold. We won't get away."

"No! Now we're here I'll find someone." Jim tried to tuck the coat around my neck. "Are ye all right till I get back? I'll try again."

At last Jim understood. In a short time he came running back.

"John Angus is goin' to go with us. Be here in a minute. Gone to tell the crowd he came with to wait at Dougall's fer 'im."

I tried to raise myself up.

"No! No! Don't stir. Ye'd best wait till 'e drives over. Tis bitter cold in the wind."

John Angus was kind and considerate. From time to time I could see him taking his eyes off the road to look at me.

"How are ye?" he said. "Can ye stand it? The roads are rough where th' slush froze in the ruts."

At last we reached the highway and I thought we would be able to make better time, but the plow had only cleared a single track and the banks of snow were higher than a man's head. John Angus drove as though unaware of danger.

"It's not so bad," he said. "If there's a rig com-in' I can see the lights once in a while on th' top of th' drifts."

But the car coming to meet us only had one headlight working and the driver and his companion had been drinking. John Angus thrust his foot down on the brake and waited for the impact. Thank God, the other driver crashed into the snow on his left. I supposed I could only have been barely conscious, for I felt no sense of relief when the danger had passed. We only met one other car in the remaining twenty miles, but John Angus saw it coming, found a turnoff, and waited until it had passed.

It was ten-thirty when we drove up the drive to the hospital and parked beside the doctor's house. The doctor's car wasn't there.

"The doctor's out on a call," his wife said. "He should be back any minute, if you'll wait."

We waited in the car. Soon twin ribbons of light pierced the darkness. It was the doctor. I told him my story.

I HEARD MYSELF scream. I must have been in a deep sleep.... I felt as though my body was crumbling into a fine grain and floating up from my feet into my fingers...into my head. The seeds of life were gathering there...waiting...ready to float away....

"Mary!" I knew it was the doctor's voice. "Mary! Would you like a priest? I don't want to scare you. I'll keep trying. I'll not give up. But if you want a priest, Nurse will call him right away."

"Yes!" I managed to whisper.

"O God! If only I could stay with my children for a few years longer...until they no longer need me...then I shall be happy to go, if it is thy will."

The hospital called Jim that morning at the number he had written on the admittance sheet, but the people who had the telephone lived three miles away and they didn't take the message to him until nine o'clock that night.

FOR EIGHT WEEKS I lay there being fed, washed and tended by nurses, but the pain and the burning ache never went away. "It isn't your heart, Mary, that is causing the pain," the doctor said.

"Your heart is coming along well. The infarction mended well. It's your arteries, you have hardening of the arteries."

That was wonderful news. My heart is coming along well, that's what the doctor said. That is all that matters. The pain will go away if only I could get out of this bed and walk around. Every day I asked the doctor the same question. Every day he would shake his head. After many weeks he looked at me and smiled.

"I suppose I'll be a little weak when I first get up," I said with a laugh, "but I'll bounce right back like a rubber ball, you'll see. I'll just stay here for a few days—go to the bathroom, maybe, then tomorrow I'll go visiting the women in the ward,"

That was the way I thought it would be. But after a week I was only able to take three steps over to the dresser, and I was able to crawl back into bed. It was not until the hundredth day that I had the courage to ask the doctor if I could go home.

"Can you dress yourself, Mary?" he asked.

"Oh, yes, doctor, and I can walk as far as the Nursery. I've been going to see the babies every day."

"Well, maybe you would be better off with your family," he said. "But remember, there'll always be a bed here for you."

That doctor was a fine man.

I went home the next day. The children gave me a great welcome. I told Jim I would have to rest that evening, but I'd fix up the house a little the next morning.

"Are ye crazy?" said Jim. "The doctor said you're not to do anythin'."

The next morning when the children had gone to school and Jim had gone into the woods, I got up and went into the kitchen. I thought it would be nice to make some biscuits. I went into the pantry. What a mess! Dishes were scattered all over the counter. The mixing bowl wasn't in the cupboard, it had been put on a shelf—dirty. The pan wasn't hanging on the wall—it was under a pile of other pans on the floor.

Slowly I went to work. I put more wood on the fire, washed

the bowl and the pan. Then I rested, gripped my chest and tried to breathe deeply. I measured the flour and mixed the ingredients in the bowl. Very slowly I cut the biscuits and placed the pan in the oven and crept back into bed. Jim hadn't gone into the woods after all, he had only gone down to the barn.

"What in the name of God is in the oven?" he said as he opened the kitchen door. "Hev ye been up?"

"I tried to make a pan of biscuits," I said. "Leave me alone, Jim, until this pain goes."

The pain didn't go and I had to go back to the hospital.

"'The cat came back at the hour of four,'" sang a jolly nurse. "Can't stay away from us now, can you?"

Three times I had to return to the hospital before I came to know that there was only one place for me in my own home and that was in bed. All I could do was think, look around—and call the children.

"Anne! Come here and bring the broom. Look at the dust under the table; at the cobwebs over there in the corner. Can't you see? You never saw things this way when I was up. The rest of you act as if you didn't see dirt. Maybe you don't, and I could have saved myself all that slaving just to keep the house clean for everyone. Nobody ever noticed, I guess."

"Oh! Mama!" Anne was nearly in tears now.

"What if I die tonight and the neighbours come to get ready for the wake. Wouldn't you care if the house was dirty?"

Then I would lie looking out of the window and watch the cattle going to water. The old red cow was about to calf. I called Jim.

"Jim, aren't you going to look at that cow before you go to bed?"

"No!" he said. "Why? She ain't gonna calf for two, three weeks yet. You an' them sons o' whores cows!"

I waited for Sonny to come in.

"Sonny! Come here to me," I called. "I want you to take a flashlight and go out and take a look at that old red cow for me."

"What fer, Mama? I don't want to go, she ain't goin' to calf."

"Sonny! Now you take that flashlight and get out to the barn. Take Anne with you if you're afraid."

Sonny slammed out of the room and I could hear him putting on his boots noisily in the kitchen. Then I heard Jim's voice.

"What's wrong? Where are you goin' this time o' night?"

"Oh! I hev to go an' look at that darned cow. Mama made me."

"Her an' them bastard cows. Thet cow ain't goin' to calf for three weeks."

"Thet's what I told 'er, but she made me go anyway."

I heard the door slam behind Sonny.

I KEPT THE BLINDS PULLED DOWN after that. One day I heard the clatter of breaking china and glass. I closed my eyes and put my hands to my ears. The only pieces of glass and china in the pantry were old and cherished. Sonny ran into the room.

"Mama! Anne dropped a whole pile of dishes and broke 'em all!"

"Don't holler so loud, Sonny, I can hear you. What dishes did Anne break?"

"Your good ones, Mama."

I looked at him. His eyes were open wide.

"The red bowl you put the oranges an' apples in at Christmas, an' the little glass dishes with the flowers made right in 'em, an' the big platter."

"I had the bowl ever since my mother died, and she had it long before I can remember." I tried to keep my voice steady. "Anne should have been more careful. I had those things for over twenty years. Some of them were my mother's wedding gifts."

"She's always breakin' things." Sonny looked scornfully at Anne crying in the doorway.

"Sonny, keep quiet. Here, come here, dear." I held out my

arms to the little twelve-year-old girl. "Come now, dry your eyes. But you must be more careful, what will we eat out of when all the dishes are broken? There, there, everything will be all right."

TWO MONTHS PASSED and there were many changes in the house and on the farm. I had learned to accept them all without saying a word. It was like being dead and seeing all I had worked for wasted and destroyed. I was helpless to lift a finger and change anything. Once in a while, maybe on a dry and windy day, my spirits would rally and I would not be able to control myself. It happened when Lauchie told me he would be coming to help Jim butcher the next day.

"What are you butchering?" I had asked the question without stopping to think.

"The brown cow!" Jim replied.

"The brown cow! Are you foolish? She's the biggest cow we have and has the nicest calves of them all. Why don't you butcher one of those runts? Butcher Nellie."

"There wouldn't be enough meat on 'er to bother takin' to town. Besides that brown bastard's goin' through all th' fences."

"Jim!" I couldn't stop myself now. "We had seventeen head of cattle when I got sick, and you've got them down to seven now. What's the matter with you? If you sell that big cow and keep those runts you'll have nothing but runts in a couple of years. De-horn the brown cow—but keep her. She's mine. Your mother gave her to me when she was a calf. Please don't butcher her."

The brown cow was saved, but the cursing and grumbling from the kitchen went on for days. I often cried. I couldn't help myself. At first I thought the children were frightened to see tears in my eyes but soon they became indifferent.

A YEAR PASSED. It was fall again. One night the house was very quiet, but I couldn't sleep. "Everything has gone," I said to the darkness. "Everything but Jim and the children. But who am I to doubt God's wisdom? Who am I indeed?" Shapes began to form in the darkness...words rang in my ears...sounds out in the night became louder...the wind playing tag in the branches of the old willow...a fox barking at some unseen creature. "What does it matter if generations of spiders flourish in the corners of my living room?" I leaned over, switched on the light, opened the drawer in the table beside the bed and took out a writing pad and pencil. Words were tumbling over and over in my mind.... I picked up the pencil and began to write.... Blustering, on the eve of All Saints, winter sheds its first snow, a lace that vanishes overnight. A warning to man and beast to prepare. It asks of man—"Is your harvest in? The oats, the hay, the feed for the herd? The potatoes, the cabbage, the turnips and all? Are they dug and stored in your cellar, warm and dry? Is your house patched up against the wind, and banked round the sills where the cold seeps in? Have you harnessed your horses and gathered the maple, the long white birch and the occasional ash, cut in the hot months of summer against the time when the woods will be waist-deep with snow, and boughs bent down and saddened with their heavy load? Is your barn mended? The roof all patched against the winter when the dampness will try the best it can to seep inside and blacken the hay? Hay that should the animals eat in their hunger, would make them sicken and perhaps die? Have you sawed, chopped, and stacked the winter logs in some sheltered place where drifts won't bury them so deep that only an axe can free them? Have you located your animals every one?"

The animals leave the distant feeding grounds, and by instinct come back to last year's habitation. Chained or roped, with freedom gone, they yet have daily food of sorts there, that quiets the rumble of empty paunches. Here, there is no thirst for days on end with only snow to wet their throats, but clean clear water from a spring at the end of a shoveled path.

"Have you found that heifer that stayed with the green of

the undergrowth in the stand of fir and spruce, and led her home again to the safety of her stall?"

Then the voices of winter, bellowing, raging, mourning and sorrowful, in turn, can do their utmost. You are ready!

Blowing snow, ice-laden branches, giant drifts shifting from place to place, now here, now there, like pebbles skipped by a child on the sea, what do you care? The nights, when the rafters groan and strain and you wonder why they do not split from their studdings. The dawn, cold and forbidding, breaking on a whitened world, when there is no trace of man or beast to break the stillness. Northern windows, darkened by drifting snow, blot out the shrouded, weighted woods, trees bent in thanksgiving....

2

The Road to Elysium

IT WAS SO HOT IN NEW YORK that the leaves rattled on the trees and the city had a dusty look of a house long unused.

"Jim, let's not go back to work right away."

"O.K. If we get fired we can always get work some place else."

"We could take another month off? Let's go where it's cool."

"Let's go home!" said Jim as if his native place had been in his thoughts ever since he left there, twenty years ago.

"Well, don't you think it's time you took me to meet your folks? We've been married four years."

We had only been back in New York half an hour and our suitcases, still unpacked, stood in the middle of the living room.

The Road to Elysium

The journey from Oakville, Montana, had been long, the train hot and airless; but it had been a wonderful vacation, back home—the country—the farm—the animals.

"We'd best take some warm clothing, it's always cool in Cape Breton," said Jim, picking up the telephone.

I couldn't believe it. I dumped my suitcase on the bed and started unpacking.

"Don't bother to tidy up," said Jim, slamming the telephone. "There's not much time."

In less than half an hour we were in a taxi driving under the Hudson River and on our way to Penn Station and looking for a northbound train. We were both over thirty and should have had more sense.

We passed through miles of muslin-covered tobacco fields in Maine and were only aware that we had passed into Canada by the presence of excise men passing along the coaches. It wasn't until we reached Truro, two hundred miles from the border, that I noticed how different the people were. I noticed that I was the only woman wearing high heels and that Jim was the only man bare-headed. The men were wearing long-billed caps, out of style in the south. The women's clothing was sensible rather than fashionable. They either didn't care about their figures or their dieting didn't work. Their shoulders were narrow, breasts skimpy, their hips and legs heavy.

"I have some magazines, would you like to read them to pass the time?" The woman sitting opposite folded her calloused hands primly across the well-worn purse on her lap.

"No, thank you," she said without smiling.

"This is my first visit to Canada. Are you going to Cape Breton?"

"No!"

"The country is lovely, isn't it? Are you going far?"

"No!"

I didn't know which question she was answering. She won't

even bother to find out whether she likes me or not, I thought to myself.

Jim sat there silently looking out of the window of the train, as if he had forgotten the beauty of his native land.

The ninety-seven miles from Truro took seven hours. Few travelled to Cape Breton and the railroad used its oldest coaches on the line. They had straight wooden backs and only the seats were padded. The ladies' room was so dirty that the only convenience I could use was the water cooler. The train stopped at every station. It was raining now. Hunched grey figures in drab coats and shabby footwear stood listlessly on the platform.

I felt alone. Jim was the only person I knew in this vast country and he too seemed to be as remote as the landscape and the unsmiling faces on the platform.

"What's the matter?" said Jim, as I grabbed his arm.

"Nothing really...it's nothing," was all I could say.

Just then the steward came to the door of the coach.

"Last chance for the diner," he shouted, "first car ahead."

"I'm hungry," said Jim, "let's eat."

The diner was empty. There were four tables covered with red and white chequered table cloths. An indifferent waiter sauntered over to our table and slapped down a menu. We had the choice of three courses. Two were fish and the third steak.

"I'm going to have that boiled salmon and steamed potatoes," said Jim, rubbing his hands. "You'd best try it too, never tasted anything till you've had boiled Atlantic salmon."

"Fish!" I couldn't hide my disgust. "I never heard of BOILED fish. I came from cattle people. I'll take the steak."

Jim ate his salmon with relish while I picked at a piece of steak that looked like leather dried in the sun. There were no vegetables.

"Doesn't anybody know about vegetables?" I ventured to ask.

"The only vegetables I had when I was growing up was cabbage and perhaps turnip. Carry-over from way back when the old-timers was too busy growing hay, grain, and potatoes. They didn't have time for gardens, I suppose."

The train began to slow down, we were pulling into a small town.

"Port Hawkesbury!" said Jim, as the train came to a halt.

"We have to change here. No hurry though. Has to wait for the 'up' train. There's our engine passing now." We rushed back to our seats, I fixed my hat (the ostrich feather had survived the journey) and grabbed my coat, purse and the smallest of our three suitcases. The train began to move.

"They're going to pull out!" I said in panic.

"No! No!" said Jim, pulling out our heavy case from under the seat. "They're only pulling up a bit to give the people in the back coach a chance to get off on the platform."

People were streaming off the train leaving their belongings strewn on the seats. The coach was nearly empty.

"Where is everyone going?" I asked.

"To the refreshment room," said Jim. "The train stays here a while."

The sun broke through the clouds as we stepped down on the platform. Our train went on to Sydney but we had to change to the "Inverness Flyer" as Jim called it. The station was crowded. Men and women milled about, the men shaking hands with friends, the women kissing and hugging relations or acquaintances in the waiting crowd. They all seemed to be laughing. Everyone was in a holiday mood. This was Canada as Jim had described it!

"Why wouldn't that woman on the train speak to me, Jim?"

"You'll have to get used to that. When they're ready, you'll find they'll talk. You might as well get used to that now. Come on! Our train's over there. We'd best shake a leg. Don't seem to be too many getting aboard."

On the side track at the rear of the train an engine snorted black smoke; a deep grumbling noise seemed to shake the boiler casting. It sounded like it had been waiting a long time and was now overtired. The tender was piled high with glistening coal. Next came the mail truck and baggage car with its single barred window. Two men sat at the entrance of the open doors, their legs dangling over the side. They stared at every passenger as they licked cigarette papers and rolled their cigarettes. There was no caboose and the train had a curious lopped-off appearance.

The step was high and I looked to see if anyone was watching before hiking my skirt above my knees. I must confess I felt out-of-place in my high-heeled patent leather shoes, neat black suit, white blouse with ruffles down the front and my black hat, feathers and all. So did Jim in his new brown suit with mirror-bright shoes to match. His shirt was glistening white and his wavy black hair shone in the sunlight.

"What are ye stoppin' for?" said Jim."Let's get in where I can put down these suitcases. They're heavy."

The smell from the coach struck me like a blast of hot wind from the prairies. The coach seemed small because it had been divided into two compartments. The seats were placed like pews in a church. Their straight high backs and wooden seats were unpadded; only a penitent nun could find comfort on them. In the centre, a small pot-bellied stove squatted on a square of protective zinc like an overstuffed toad. It bulged with candy wrappers, bottle caps, empty cigarette packages, paper bags, tobacco pouches, and whiskey wrappers. Spider webs hung in the corners from floor to ceiling. Dead flies and candy wrappers (faded dimmer than those in the stove) lay in the aisles and on the sills under the filthy windows. Beyond the stove and facing the last seat a ledge had been placed against the partition to serve as a desk. It was strewn with papers and a gaping satchel. This was obviously the conductor's seat.

"Pretty grim, ain't it?" said Jim. "Never noticed before."

"Hasn't been cleaned since it was built," was all I could find to say.

"It's mostly men who ride the train." Jim nodded towards the partition. "Women don't travel any."

The Road to Elysium

The grain in the oak "pews" had been cut and polished with skill and infinite care. The wrought-iron lamp holder circling the hanging lamp hung drunkenly on a rusty chain from the ceiling, made of wrought iron and decorated with foliage of beaten bronze. Under a film of greasy soot the work of a fine craftsman was as unmistakable as beautiful features under a web of wrinkles on a woman's face. I stood tiptoe and tried to straighten it.

"Look out!" said Jim. "Ye'll get oil all over your clothes. It's still got some on the bottom. Must have been there a long time, judgin' from the colour. It's clear yellow."

"What a lamp!" I said. "I can just imagine it in some elegant parlour, all shined up till every petal of the flowers stands out. Filigree bronze. Why do you suppose anyone would put a thing so beautiful in a dirty place like this old coach?"

"Probably all they had when the railroad came in," said Jim. "Come on now, sit down before the conductor comes and thinks you're trying to steal it, or ye're gone off yer rocker. What's 'filigree'?"

I chose a seat about half way down the coach. Jim dusted the seat carefully with his handkerchief before we sat down. In his own good time the conductor came and took our tickets.

"What did ye say yer name was?" he asked Jim.

"Douglas. Jim Douglas—from up the Glen."

"Oh yeh! Would ye be Austin Douglas' boy now?"

"No."

"Well, ye wouldn't be related to Alex Dougall, now would ye?"

The conductor went back to his place, shaking his head sadly. Jim watched the passengers come aboard.

"Do you think I could take a look into that compartment up there?" I asked.

"No! For God's sake, Mary! That's the smoker. There's men in there now!"

"How do you know?"

"I saw them come aboard."

The Woman from Away

The train lurched suddenly, the engine whistled and we started to rock along the tracks. The voices beyond the partition grew louder. Practiced fingers picked out the grace notes of an old Scottish tune. Feet stomped in time to the music.

"Come back on 'er, Angus!" a voice shouted.

"Good boy, Angus!" another shouted.

"I wonder if that man knows what a good violin he has?" I said. "If only he would put rosin on that bow!"

"Wait till you see how much talent there is up here," said Jim, grinning with pride, "I'll see that you 'take in' some dances."

I thought I had better clean up a little and went down to the door marked "Women." I opened the door and went inside. I looked down at the throne and saw the earth whizzing by between the sleepers. I did what I had to do. The wash basin was decorated with candy wrappers. I picked them up, it was almost a pity to disturb them, and since there was no waste basket, I threw them down the hole behind me. I turned on a tap—no water. I tried the other tap marked "hot"—no water. All I could do was make a face at the cracked mirror and pat my hair with dirty hands. I was very careful not to step backwards.

"Thought you were going to clean up?" Jim was laughing. I didn't dignify his question with an answer. By the time the train came to the next stop we were both laughing.

The train moved with incredible slowness. It took almost half an hour to reach the lonely little shack with "Timinitoul" painted on its side. This was a station. Two milk cans stood beside the tracks but there wasn't a soul in sight when the engine whistled to a stop. Then, like magic, men appeared from nowhere.

"How far are we from Port Hawkesbury?" I asked.

"Five miles, I guess. No more anyway," Jim answered.

"Only five miles! How far is it to the next station?"

"About thirty-five or thirty-eight miles. Ye'd best settle back for a long ride. The train's in no hurry. No schedule to keep. Any time it gets there's soon enough. Only goes to the other end of the county and stays there overnight."

The occupants of the smoker rushed off the train as soon as it stopped, taking their bottles with them. Soon passengers, local residents, conductors, engineer and brakeman mingled on the platform, passing the time of day, news, and bottles around. Each time a drink had been taken, a grimy hand brushed off the bottle top and passed it on to the next man, who did the same. Then someone noticed the little man with the violin.

"Cummina Hashen, Angus! Got yer fiddle with ye? How about givin' us a tune?" Angus needed no encouragement. He took one of the many bottles offered him, raised it to his lips, took a long drink and began to play.

"Give us a step, Duncan!" one of the men called out. A circle was formed and Duncan stepped forward to the rhythmic clapping of hands. After fifteen minutes or so the conductor must have realized the passage of time and shouted, "All aboard!" He shooed the passengers back into the train and dispatched the engineer to the engine.

It was the same at every stop. My seat grew harder. Before long a big, broad-shouldered fellow with sandy hair rocked out from the smoker. He staggered down the aisle with a quart bottle of beer grasped tightly in his hand. When he reached our seat he stopped and stared vacantly at Jim and then at me. I slid closer to Jim and stared back. Apparently satisfied that we didn't concern each other, the man resumed his journey down the aisle to the men's toilet.

"That was a wicked-looking one. Do you know him, Jim?"

"No. What are you afraid of? He was only trying to see if he could place me. See if he should give me a drink or not."

"Why is it they're all up there drinking and dancing and making all that noise?"

"It's on account of the liquor laws, I suppose," Jim answered. "Mabou and Inverness are the only places in the county that have liquor stores. It's agin' the law even to break the seals on the bottles until you get home. But it's a long way home for them. They must've been pretty dry to start so close to town. The conductor himself's in there, too, looks like."

All was quiet in the smoker for several minutes after the sandy-haired man got back.

"He's telling the others we're strangers," whispered Jim.

"Where did they come from back at the station? Out of the trees?"

"They were waiting special for the train. The mail driver was there, and the people livin' close by always come when the whistle blows—for news mostly. They come for a drink too."

At every crossroads and station, neighbours heard the whistle and came out to greet the train. Stops were frequent, and at each one, passengers, conductor, and engineer piled out and went through the same ritual.

"He better open her up," said Jim, "to make up time."

We had been rattling along at a fair speed since our last stop.

"WHAT WAS THAT?" I screamed, and clutched Jim's arm. The train took a great leap forward, gave a tremendous shudder, and stopped short.

"Must be the train gone off the tracks." Jim stood up and looked out of the window. "Used to do it regular in winter. Never heard of it in summer before." He chuckled, "Engineer had the old snail crowding the hare there at the last, did you notice?"

"What'll they do?" I moaned. "I'm so tired."

"Now, don't get upset. Good thing there's a crowd on the train. It won't take long to set her back on. Look out the window. Every man jack on the train's already out there. They'll have her back on the tracks in no time...if they can stand up long enough. Maybe we'd best go out too...I can see two or three of them won't be helpin' none."

Jim was right. Some could barely stand, some could only stagger. Two made it to the shade of the trees and went to sleep.

Angus took out his fiddle and began to play. No one but Jim was steady on his feet, although the conductor and the engineer had been somewhat sobered by the jolt. It was Jim who set up the big jack and directed the use of it. The others (in tune to Angus' fiddle) made a frolic of hoisting up each car and pushing it back onto the rails. The job took an hour. There had been no injuries and there was no feeling of urgency to curb their high spirits.

At last, when we pulled into Jim's home station, I looked at my watch. It had taken us five hours and forty-five minutes to cover thirty-five miles—or was it thirty-eight!

3
The Glen

JIM'S FATHER DIDN'T LOOK AT ALL LIKE the stalwart football type that Jim had described. He was a man of medium height and his shoulders sloped like a pear. His face was stern but his lips drew back into a quick smile when he saw us, though his eyes remained cold and detached. When at last he remembered to remove his long-billed cap I could see that the sandy-white hair only ringed his head. He smiled again, and this time the ice-blue eyes twinkled with devilment. With that smile he won my heart. The greetings over, he beckoned to a tall man loafing against the station shed.

"Come on over, John J. You remember John J., don't ye, Jim? Still lives across the river. Spoke to him to come and meet yez soon's I got the telegram in the mail."

"How've ye been, John J.?" said Jim, holding out his hand.

"Goot! Goot!" nodded John J. "Are them all yer t'ings? Ye ready fer to go now? Best get started. There's no lights on the car."

John J. Campbell stood six feet three inches tall. His hair was red; his eyes a watery blue that contradicted the smile on his lips; and although his face was flabby it could not be called weak. His trousers were held up by a rope which made them ruffle round the waist. The length of his legs explained the ruffle. No standard-sized trousers could accommodate the length of his legs and his waist measurement in the same garment.

John J. opened the door of an old Chevy and motioned to us to get in. Before we had time to take our seats a man, who must have been over seventy, detached himself from a group of men loitering on the platform. Although the day was warm he wore high rubber boots and carried an old yellow raincoat on his arm. A battered felt hat sat on the top of his ears and a wide red handlebar moustache covered his upper lip. The moustache looked so heavy on the thin pallid face that I half expected it to fall off.

"Cummina Hashen!" he called, running towards Jim. "Welcome home!"

"Sean MacLellan! You old so-and-so," said Jim, pumping the limp hand. "You still around?"

"Aye! They can't kill me...."

Mr. Douglas had taken his seat beside the driver and John J. was impatiently accelerating the motor.

"Ye'll be out home before they go, Sean?" said Mr. Douglas. "John J. wants to git goin' now. Don't forget, drop over."

I WASN'T ABLE TO SEE MUCH of the countryside as the glass in the two rear windows had been replaced by corrugated cardboard. The springs in the seat defined the thin upholstery and spiralled up under me until I felt like a Jack-in-the-box. When at last we pulled up at Mr. Douglas' home, Jim leaned over and in his anxiety to get out wrenched the handle off the door. The door fell off its hinges.

"What have I done?" said Jim, his face red with embarrassment. "I pushed hard but not that hard. Wuz it broke?"

"Twuz only stuck in there," said John J., throwing out our bags, "think nothing of it."

Mrs. Douglas, Jim's stepmother, stood at the front door waiting for us.

"Cummina Hashen!" she shouted, grabbed my hand and planted a wet kiss on my cheek. Clemmie Douglas was at least twenty years younger than her husband; her movements were quick and her hair black.

"Cummina Hashen, Jim! How have you been?" she said, pumping Jim's hand with vigour. "I s'pose yez are hungry. Come in...come in...."

"Wait, John J." said Jim, trying to free his hand, "I've a drink somewhere's in this junk...."

"Never mind that now, Jim," said John J., "Molly and me'll be over."

We went into the house. Clemmie herded us all into the big kitchen-dining room.

"Yez can just sit anywhere at all," she said, making sure that her husband secured his proper place at the head of the table.

"Dougall came over and I gave him tea. I ate too. No tellin' when the train would git here." Clemmie laughed, but there was no warmth in her laughter. "You know Dougall, Jim? He gives Daddy a hand with the chores. He's got his uncle's place, ye know, on the MacTavish Road, but he ain't there much."

The smell of baked beans filled the air as Clemmie placed a large bean crock before us. I was just about to help myself when I noticed that no one else had moved. I looked around the table. Everyone sat with bowed head. I drew back my hand and waited. Mr. Douglas raised his hand and blessed himself. I hastily did the same.

THERE WAS A PARTY OR DANCE every night. Sometimes they were in a neighbour's house and sometimes in a barn. The farm machinery was taken out and long planks laid on logs along the walls as seats for the onlookers. At the far end a small stage was hastily nailed together for the fiddler. He alone occupied this important place, erected perhaps in gratitude and in the hope that he would play till dawn without payment.

I had never been to a dance like this before. Young men danced with old women, and no self-respecting girl would turn down a set with a white-haired old man. Everyone danced for the sheer love of dancing. Dancers of seventy and over got thunderous applause when, after no more than two or three calls, an old man stood up and danced a "solo a'fore" as they called it. No one asked the fiddler for special music. He knew what to play. Old as some of the dancers were, they never missed a step and the watchers laughed and clapped their hands like children. Old Mr. Douglas asked me to dance.

"Oh, no! I couldn't!" I said, finding myself the centre of attention. "I used to dance back home when I was young, but the dances were different."

"Who cares?" shouted Clemmie. "Jim'll dance with me in the same set. Don't worry, we'll see you through." She pushed me to the floor. We danced the set to gales of laughter and no one minded my mistakes.

"It's swell," I said when I found my breath.

When the older folks had had enough of dancing, and the sips the women had taken made them as mellow as the men, the young folk had the dance floor to themselves. The old and the very young went into the house to listen to storytellers. Every man had his own story to tell. Stern faces broke into smiles. Old men seemed to hypnotize the children with their antics.

Then a woman's voice called on Peter to sing. Peter, a lanky man with a bald head, waited until many voices joined in, then he picked up his chair and carried it into the centre of the room. He nodded to his son who struck a chord on his guitar before starting what must have been the longest ballad ever written. It had been a long dirge of about sixty verses, yet no one seemed bored and the applause was sincere.

One by one the guests were urged to perform; many had brought instruments and played without having to be coaxed.

"Mary!" Clemmie whispered. "Come along with me. Old Bill MacMillan, over there, looks like he's lost his last drink—I'll make ye acquainted."

"Cummina Hashen, Bill!" said Clemmie, shaking the old man by the hand. "See ye've got yer pipes. Ye goin' to give us a little tune tonight? This is Jim's wife from the States, she's never heard the pipes."

"Be glad to," he said, thrusting out a gnarled hand and clutching mine. "Glad to make your acquaintances, Ma'am. Welcome home!" Then gathering up his pipes, he blew two or three times into the bag and tried a few notes. Satisfied, he walked over to a corner, turned his back on the audience, and began to play. The sound in the small room was deafening.

"Did ye smell it?" Clemmie whispered.

"I smelt something, what was it?"

"Th' pipes. Old Bill made th' bag himself out of an old ewe's belly...didn't let her cure long enough."

"What a wonderful old man," I whispered. "Did you hear what he said to me? He said—'Welcome home!'"

NOW THAT JIM HAD LEARNED to manipulate John J.'s car door, the trip into Port Hood was very pleasant. The cardboard box-ends that had replaced the glass had gone with the rain and I found a cushion to cover the loose springs in the seat. Jim sat beside John J. and I sat with Clemmie in the back. The men had business in town and Clemmie and I went visiting.

John J. pulled the old Chevy up to the back door of a spotless house on the edge of town. Clemmie led the way towards the kitchen door and the men said they would call for us later. A big raw-boned woman pushed a kettle over the fire as soon as she saw us and held out a calloused hand in greeting.

"Peggy, I want you to meet Jim's wife," said Clemmie, darting cat-and-mouse glances between us. "Jist up from the States. Mr. MacLellan and Jim was in school together, Mary."

"It's nice meeting you, Mrs. MacLellan," I said truthfully.

"I'm Peggy," she answered. "When you say 'Mrs.' makes me feel ye might be the man fer the rent. Glad to know ye. Sit down, sit down, while I get the tea."

It was obvious that Peggy MacLellan had been expecting us, and it was obvious too that she would have been hurt if we hadn't called. What a tea! There was loaf bread, biscuits, pie, two kinds of cookies and shortbread.

"How d'ye like the Glen?" said Peggy, but before I had time to answer Clemmie spoke for me.

"She says she loves Down East. She thinks there's no place like it, don't ye, Mary? And ye should see her with the cows, and herself knows all about chickens, says her father raises 'em."

"Wonder if she'd be liking it so well after the winter," said Peggy, with a laugh. "As far as I'm concerned, any farm's a bad place. I'd rather live on me hands and knees scrubbin' floors or beggin' me way before I'd go back."

"Peggy was borned back of the church in the Glen," said Clemmie. "I'll show ye the house."

"I FELT LIKE A QUEEN," I said as we drove away, "waited on hand and foot. Is it the same in every house?"

"Pretty much," said Clemmie, puffed up like a courting partridge. "I s'pose ye feel as ye never want to see another piece of bread. That waz a big tea. Seven kinds o' bread, I counted 'em."

John J. turned off the highway and up a narrow road.

"It's really beautiful down here," I said, looking up at the trees arching over the road, "the air even smells different."

"You like down here? Why don't ye make a deal with Dougall?" Clemmie whispered.

"A deal with Dougall?" I whispered in reply. "What for?"

"To buy his place."

"Why do you think he'd sell?"

"What does he want with it? He's never there. It takes money to run a house and the two hundred an' fifty acres that goes with it. If it wasn't fer Daddy he wouldn't have it in the first place. Why not ask him anyway? Jist for fun. Ask him what he'll take for it."

"I always loved the country back home. Do you really think he'll sell? How much do you think he'll want?"

"He'd let it go fer little or nothin'. I'm sure of it. Only cost him seventy-five dollars in the first place. He paid up the taxes."

"SEVENTY-FIVE DOLLARS! For a house and over two hundred acres of land!" I couldn't keep the excitement out of my voice.

"Charlie Lawlor wanted to take it out on taxes hisself fer his oldest boy who was getting married, but Daddy got wind of it and asked Dougall why it waz HE didn't git it—him being next of kin and all. He had first chance, if he paid up the taxes before the sale. Daddy helped Dougall find the money." Clemmie leaned forward and tapped Jim on the shoulder.

"All around here wuz afire, Jim, couple of years back. Started with a spark," said Clemmie, sitting back in her seat, "one little spark from the train, passing on the track. It wuz a windy day, it wasn't no time till the whole Glen looked like she wuz going."

"Any places burnt out?" said Jim.

For a moment Clemmie was silent. I looked at her; she was biting her lip.

"I couldn't say," she said tersely. "John J.'d know. He wuz there."

"Did she burn for long?" said Jim.

"Burnt as far as ye can see fer seven days and nights before the rain came," said Clemmie, as though sure of her ground again.

"The heat wuz something fierce close by an' ye could smell the smoke strong, back home.

"Ye hauled water with yer truck, John J., ye can tell it better'n me."

"Yisss!" hissed John J., "me and the boys wuz just after getting back from Sydney, and they didn't want us to go home. Yisss! They wanted water right then and there. But being we was hungry and I had groceries fer Molly on the truck, we went home first."

"Listen to 'im!" Clemmie whispered behind her hand. "Ye should've seen 'em that day. I guess it wuz something fierce. Not one of them with a leg to stand on. John J. had a couple o' bottles on him and cases of beer in the back of the truck. Gitting directions all mixed up about where to go fer water and where to take it...which part of the line, I mean, and him that stubborn they had to drag him out to the truck to go back over to the fire. John J. was the only one with a truck, ye know."

"Used a lot of gas that time," said John J., pushing his old cap back on his head. "So many trips, and ye had to go seven miles... fourteen to a trip, and a barrel was gone in a minute. Had about fifteen men on that bucket line. Yisss! And maybe more...."

"Look, Mary!" said Clemmie, gripping my arm. "John J., stop a minute, will you please?"

John J. brought the Chevy to a standstill at the side of the road. We had reached the top of the ridge and the whole Glen lay before us.

"This is as good a place as any to see where all the neighbours live," said Clemmie, sitting up on the edge of her seat. "Ye can see every farm from here. The last farm we just passed, well, that was where Dougall wuz brought up. His father lived there with old Angus, the coffin maker. He's made seventy-two boxes and he's still smart. Wasn't for old Angus, Dougall and the rest of the family would have starved to death when the old lady died—that would be Dougall's mother. Now, see the river below?" said Clemmie, straining to see between John J.'s and Jim's shoulders. "Down there, on the right, is

John J.'s place, ye can just see the roof, and a little past is where old Jennie lives, her old man died last fall. She washes the remains of the women around. See where the bridge crosses the river and the house beside it? Well, that's Ronald the Bridge's old home; nobody's there now. The next place up the road is Daddy's."

The few scattered houses were spread out like shoes on a giant spider. There were seven houses, and of the seven only two were painted, the others were grey and weather-beaten.

"The big house up on the hill, to the left, beyond the fork is old Charlie Lawlor's. He's a slink of a Tory, never get him to vote Liberal," said Clemmie with disgust.

"What a beautiful place!" I said, admiring the gleaming white house and the neatly hedged fields. "It only goes to show it can be done!"

"It ain't HIM does it!" said Clemmie with a snort of indignation. "It's them twelve kids of his. He puts every one of them in the fields soon's they're big enough to walk."

"But how did he manage when the children were coming and were too little to help?"

"He had poor Margaret out there then. That was before I come."

Clemmie couldn't find a good word to say for a Tory.

"The road keeps on up the hill between them trees," Clemmie went on, "and on the top ye'll find the farm of old William Barnes, on the right. The best built house around, got two brick flues, must be a fireplace in the parlour."

"Yeh!" said Jim interrupting his thoughts, "ye should've seen it when the old man was alive, and it was kept up. Painted white with green trimming...got a big basement. The dining room and the parlour was PLASTERED! I guess the old man intended to plaster all the walls, but the First World War came along...and when he lost his two sons he just gave up...."

"Old Willie got the place from his uncle, ye know," said Clemmie, breaking the silence. "He's rich, got all kinds of money, and he's deaf as a post and queer in the head. Won't buy groceries for himself and that starving dog of his. Keeps the dog out in the winter and the summer; not another living creature on the place. The old dog makes the rounds for handouts every day then goes home and lays there on the doorstep."

"The other road at the fork, where does that go to?" I asked, leaning over Jim's shoulder.

"That's the MacTavish Settlement Road," said Jim. "The big barn just up a piece is Dougall's place, the house is hid beyond the barn. The MacTavish farm is a good three miles up, and beyond, another half mile is the Beatons. Ye can't see them."

"There's five bachelors and one spinster living in them two places," said Clemmie, with a giggle. "Used to be a whole settlement of them. None of the boys would be after taking a prize for beauty except maybe Lauchie MacTavish—when he was young. He was away for years, come home a while back when the old folks died. I guess the boys wrote him they wouldn't take care of Dave—he's the dummy—said they was going away. Course it was only an excuse to git him to keep them all."

"Can see the fire tower," said Jim pensively.

"Where? Show me, Jim?" I said leaning forward.

"Up there, to your right, on the top of the mountain at the head of the Glen. You can just make it out, standing like a pencil against the sky."

"That's a job I wouldn't care about having," said Clemmie, giggling again. There was no mirth in Clemmie's giggles. "Up there, with no one to talk to all summer long. In years gone by there was over sixty families living on that mountain; they built a church and all, but they're all gone now."

"Yes!" said Jim, "I suppose that church must be a hundred and twenty years old and more. All the studding and beams held together by wooden pegs. The boards was hewed by hand and wider than you'd ever see around now. No tree big enough now, all second growth."

"And all painted," said Clemmie, "inside and out. White and pure as the Blessed Virgin herself. There's many a story about that old place."

We sat in silence for a few minutes.

"Ye remember the story of the Protestant girl, Jim?" said Clemmie. Her voice was quieter now. "She ran away from home to be a nun and followed the blaze marks on the trees to git to the coast to catch a ship to Montreal. When it got dark she couldn't see the marks no more and would have been lost for sure if she hadn't come on the little church in the clearing."

"Aye!" said Jim. "I remember. She made herself a bed with spruce boughs and fir on a rock, there in the graveyard. Then made her way to the coast in the morning."

"Aye!" continued Clemmie, "and her Daddy caught up with her there and took her back home. She tried again a couple of years after and they didn't catch up with her that time."

"Couldn't have been any bachelors living up there in them days," hissed John J., "or she'd niver have got by."

Clemmie's loud laughter woke me from my daydream. That night I wrote to my father. "Daddy, I have found Elysium...."

IT WASN'T LATE when I came downstairs the following morning yet I knew that Clemmie had been waiting for me.

"What did Jim say about Dougall's place?" she said without waiting for me to speak. "Did you ask him?"

"Yes, I did," I replied, wishing I didn't have to share my excitement with Clemmie. "Jim didn't want to give in. I wish we had more time, it would have been better if I could have suggested it to him and let him think it over for a few days. Jim's kind of stubborn and likes to think he has thought things out for himself."

"I know just what you mean," said Clemmie pushing a cup of tea across the table to me. "Have to do that meself with Daddy. But did he say 'yes'?"

"He did. But he said that I'd have to do the dickering, he won't have anything to do with that."

"What are ye going to offer him?"

"I don't know. I haven't an idea. What do you think?"

"He'd jump at a hundred...'specially if he'd seen the cash."

I replied, "O.K.... I'll offer him a hundred the first chance I get."

MASS WAS HEARD at the little church in the Glen on the first Sunday of our visit. The farms were so scattered and the priest had three parishes to serve, so Mass was only heard every other Sunday.

Jim harnessed the mare and brought the buggy round to the door and we all got in. The little mare took her time climbing the hill past Charlie Lawlor's driveway and spruce-hedged fields. From the brow of the hill the land sloped gently down to the church sheltered behind a grove of trees. It was a clear sunny morning and the countryside looked newborn. We passed William Barnes' fine house standing in the centre of fields rank with weeds.

"That's Ronnie and Christina's place," said Clemmie, pointing to a house nearly as large as William Barnes' that stood listless in the morning light. It had never been painted. "Ronnie's family settled the land, ye know, and that's where he took Christina as a bride. She don't help him none. Won't go into the fields or nothing. Ronnie plows, discs and seeds all by hisself. Big place too. Too bad he married that one."

We drove past Ronnie's rich land; many cows and calves grazed contentedly there. When we reached the church Jim tied the mare to the fence that surrounded the graveyard. Then everyone descended on us to bid us welcome and when the priest drove up we all followed him into the church.

The main west door opened into a little vestibule. On the right a flight of stairs led up into the balcony where a wheezy old organ was playing. I dipped my fingers into the Holy Water and followed Clemmie and Mr. Douglas through the swinging doors into the church. In the centre of the nave stood an ancient wood-burning stove, its flue held precariously by wires suspended from the roof. A statue of the Blessed Virgin stood on the left of the altar.

Clemmie nudged me and pointed to a pew next to the altar.

"That used to be old Archie Mac's but he died last month. You and Jim take it."

Little did I know then that this pew would be our own for all time. I wasn't very pious during Mass though the beads dangled through my fingers. I couldn't help thinking about my neighbours.

"For Gawd's sake, Mary, sit still," Jim whispered, "everyone's looking at ye."

When Mass was over I counted fifty adults and God knows how many children. I knew the records of the church must have the names of every member of every family back to the original settlers, and the connections between one family and another, for all would be related, in one degree or another.

I could see that the families living near the church were a little more prosperous than the families living in our Glen. It had been the coming of public utilities that had given them their prosperity. The parish spread over seventy-two miles of farm and wood land. Only the families living near the church had persuaded the power and telephone companies to extend their lines as far as their homes.

"Aye!" said old Mr. Douglas, "everything stops at the church—the power, the telephone, and the snow plow turns at the gate in winter...the gate to the graveyard...."

WHEN WE WERE ALL SETTLED DOWN at the dinner table I had to ask the question that had been plaguing me all morning.

"Jim, I've been thinking about Dougall's place. Any chance

of you taking me up to look round after dinner?"

"Are you crazy?" said Jim, putting down his knife and fork, "that's the last thing ye want to do if ye want to git it."

"He'd never sell if he caught ye snooping around," said Clemmie, "that's for sure."

"Best ye stay away," said old Mr. Douglas solemnly, "if yer set on gittin' it. Sure to make Dougall mad, then he'd not sell fer Gawd's sake."

"Seems like we're taking a chance," I said, "buying without seeing the house. I'd like to get an idea what the rooms look like... I'd like to measure the floors and windows...."

"Jim can tell ye that," said Clemmie, "he's been there often enough. It's kind of run down now, but before Dougall's uncle moved out, ye couldn't ask for a better place to go visitin'."

"Aye!" said old Mr. Douglas, stirring his tea, "and a'fore when the old people was living."

"How many were there in the family?" I asked trying desperately to get some idea of the size of the house.

"They had eight kids"—Clemmie giggled— "and the old people before the oldest boy got married; then his wife and kids lived there too; course by then the girls was married and leaving but there was still plenty room left."

"Dougall's father used to be phooey 'bout people traipsin' over his place," said Clemmie, scraping the plates and throwing the scraps to the dog. "Dougall comes by it honest. The old man used to hunt everywhere's he pleased—even in the neighbours' grain fields and them ready for reapin'—but just let anyone go near HIS place! The old 'bodach' had ears like a cat and I swear he stayed awake night and day.

"I remember one time my eldest brother got wind of the old man hunting on our land and taking our deer without even a 'by yer leave' and then chasing him every time he went by his place with a gun...an' one night he went up to old Dougall's place figgerin' to git a deer he'd seen coming to an old apple tree on the edge of the meadow. It was four in the morning, mind ye, when the deer came in. My brother shot him, dressed him all out an' had started draggin' him to the road, and who came out wavin' his rifle an' yellin' like anti-Christ but old Dougall. The slink had been laying there waiting, just waiting till me brother had done all the work. D'you know the old devil took the deer away and told me brother if he ever came back on his place hunting again it would be his last time."

"Aye!" said Mr. Douglas, nodding his head, "if ye want that place it's best ye stay away."

Clemmie finished clearing the table in silence. Jim pushed back his chair and walked over to the window and stood there looking out over the field. "What ever happened to Willie MacSween?"

Clemmie threw her wet dishcloth down on the table so hard that it sounded like the crack of a rifle.

"Willie MacSween?" she said. "He's dead an' wandering."

"Died in the fire." Mr. Douglas' voice was very quiet and it seemed difficult for him to say the words. "Him and Martha, no one knows exactly. He went by Sean's yellin' 'fire' and Sean and his brother Frank took off across the river. John J. found Willie after, or what was left of him and the mare...harness rings and the wheels. Looked like he was in the wagon heading out. Martha wasn't with him. John J. found her halfway to his place. Willie must've left without her. Maybe she took too long gitting started...."

"Maybe she did," said Clemmie, "God rest her soul."

IT WAS MAIL DAY. Clemmie started shining up the house early in the morning. The neighbours came early and stayed to gossip. After greeting each person Clemmie expertly stripped each one of what news they had. But it was different with Christina, a tall, thin, black-haired woman. As soon as she arrived Clemmie whipped the coat off her shoulders and led her over to the settee.

In a flash Christina had a cup of tea in her hand and Clemmie one in hers and the two sat huddled together, whispering.

At last, when the cups had been returned to their saucers for the last time I saw Clemmie run her tongue swiftly over her lips like a cat after a dinner of goldfish. She followed Christina to the door and without drawing breath continued, "Christina says that Anne Margaret, over at MacLaughlins', is going to have a baby—she's one o' them at the Home in Sydney, ye know. She says it's been somethin' awful to see all the young fellers hangin' around there. She's the one to be tellin', the slink! After all she done to poor Ronnie."

"Christina makes me feel nervous," I said, "those black eyes of hers seem to see through my skin and I begin to feel that my face is dirty."

Clemmie didn't have time to reply for the door opened and Dougall ambled into the kitchen, sat down on the settee and began rolling a cigarette.

"Himself says we'd let the hay go till next week and I thought I'd get the boys at John J.'s to mow me place tomorrow. Git her in in half a day easy, place is run down so bad it's only short."

I caught Clemmie's eye and she signalled me to speak up.

"Dougall!" I said, hoping my voice was steady. "Would you think of selling your place?"

"Why? Ye thinking of buyin' her?" Dougall's eyes never left the cigarette he was rolling.

"Well, I thought it might be nice to live here. Would you sell?"

"Weeel nooow!" Dougall drawled cagily, "I just don't know that I want to sell."

"I'll give you a hundred dollars CASH!" I said quickly.

"Wouldn't sell for no hundred, if I WAS gonna sell."

"How about a hundred and fifty?" I said, trying to keep him from stalling. "Jim said that's as high as I can go."

"Weeel nooow, ye see, it ain't the money so much...exactly. I might as well tell ye...I might be after gitting married meself one o' them days and I'll want the house meself."

"That's different," I replied, trying to hide my disappointment, "if you're getting married...."

"MARRIED! YOU gittin' married?" screamed Clemmie, "and who is it ye'll be marryin'?"

"Well, I ain't asked 'er exactly...just yet, but I was thinking of asking Olive."

"OLIVE!" Clemmie couldn't believe her ears. 'Ye haven't wrote her, have you?"

"No!" said Dougall, pausing to light the cigarette dropping from his lips, "but I'm thinking about it."

"Where is Olive?" I asked impatiently. "Could you write and get an answer back in a week? We have to go back to New York next week."

"Weeel, all right then! I'll git a letter away t'night." And with that Dougall got up and went outside to join the men.

"Olive!" said Clemmie, as soon as we were alone. "Where did he pull that one out of? Must've been in that tobacco. He never went out with her in his life. She wouldn't even look at him before she went away, and he thinks she'll marry him? Thinks she'll be ripe for plucking, I s'pose, after being in the Unwed Mothers Home. Three days old now.... Ronnie and Christina are gonna take it."

A week went by. Two mail days passed and no letter came from Olive.

OUR VACATION WAS OVER. Tomorrow we would be travelling back to New York and still Dougall refused to make a decision.

"Have the cash handy," Clemmie advised. "He'll likely stall around, but if ye show him the money he'll take it, ye'll see."

The next time Dougall came into the kitchen I didn't waste any time.

"Well, are you going to let us buy your place?"

"Weeel noow! I just can't say. P'raps I'd best wait till

herself comes home, then I can talk to her."

I reached for my purse and held out a fifty-dollar bill and five twenties under Dougall's nose.

"Here it is, Dougall, all brand new American money. One hundred and fifty dollars, and you can get the benefit of the exchange. It's your last chance."

Dougall's little eyes followed the bills like a cat watching a fledgling bird.

"Weeel nooow! It would have to be without the hay. Ye'd have to leave the hay for me...being I put her in...or there ain't no deal."

"All right, you can take the hay. Is it a deal then?"

"Could be naaw, could be!" Dougall turned to Clemmie. "Ronnie says Olive is coming home next week. No need for no rush. I'll have to talk to her." Dougall quickly left the kitchen.

That night there was a little gathering at the house in our honour. Before dawn it had turned into a regular party. Jim and I were to leave on the afternoon train but we couldn't make it. John J. hadn't arrived with the car. Late that afternoon Jim went over the river and between him and John J. they decided it would be best to get the night train from Port Hawkesbury.

The rain had become a deluge by the time John J. drove up in his truck. The back was now covered with tarpaulin like a prairie schooner. Sitting on the seats hastily constructed with stumps and cross-boards were Dougall and four men.

"These fellas want to get to the vendor," said John J., oblivious of the mud he was tracking into the kitchen, "and I'm dry meself. Maybe Jim, if ye and the Missus be ready, maybe we could go now.... If we hurry we'll catch the vendor."

"What on earth would we be doing in Port Hawkesbury all that time between six o'clock and the train time?" said Jim indignantly.

"Molly's got people there, we'll find something to do. Andy MacTavish has his fiddle with him in the back."

"Jim, ye'd best go," said Clemmie, drawing Jim into the pantry, "John J.'s not the most responsible man in the world, and if ye let him get away on ye, he might not come back for a week."

We got into Port Hawkesbury as the manager of the liquor store reached up to pull down the blinds. The door was still opened and every man went in. Jim went in with the rest of them. In a few minutes he came running out and threw open the door.

"If ye want Dougall's place ye'd best give me the money. He'll sell!"

We drove over to the railway station and parked in the yard. It was too late to get the deed of sale drawn up but that could be sent by mail for Jim's signature. No one was around and it was raining so hard that we were not afraid of getting caught by the Mounties. Jim, John J. and I crawled into the back of the truck with the others. Andy played his heart out and Dougall got up and danced a solo.

When the train came in I helped Jim into the car, found the tickets in his pocket and handed them to the conductor. Jim never heard the farewell tune Andy played for us on the station platform in the rain...he was fast asleep.

4

Our New Home

WE HAD SCUTTLED OUR SKIFFS! We were back in the Glen with all our worldly possessions covered with a tarpaulin on the back of a shiny new truck. We no longer had our apartment or our jobs in New York City. The Glen was our home.

I couldn't help feeling frightened when I realized what we had done. We had driven through teeming rain for hundreds of miles, but this morning the truant sun broke through the clouds and the air was sweet and warm. After dinner we sat outside and talked. Jim was tired and wouldn't say very much even to his father.

"We got the wire with the money ye sent," said Mr. Douglas, as he stopped to pick up a whittling twig at his feet. "And we fenced the bottom field. We had to make a bush fence along the river. Too much brush to clear for wire fencing. Can't see her from the road nohow."

"Good!" said Jim, livening up a little. "How much do I owe you and the boys?"

"Yez'll stay here a while. The house ain't fit," said Clemmie, drying her hands on her apron.

"Sandy ain't doing nothing right now," said Mr. Douglas, holding his whittling twig at arm's length so his far-sighted old eyes could see better. "I suppose he's about the only one ain't busy... he'd be too, if it wasn't for he's after getting shaky. His work beats most o' them around here. It's just that he's getting slow."

Our New Home

"Well, we'd best see what needs doing," said Jim stretching his legs. "Get an idea where to start. How about it Dad? Feel like taking a walk?"

"Let's all go," I said jumping up. "I'm longing to see inside the house. It's been terrible having to wait so long."

We walked up the narrow road cut through the forest for about half a mile. The grass between the wagon tracks was still damp from the rain and cool to walk on. The tall spruce sheltered us from the heat of the sun until we reached the boundary of our property. Now I could see the wire and the freshly peeled fence posts gleaming in the sunlight. I looked up at Jim, hoping to see that he was sharing my happiness, but his face was stern. He was looking down at the soil. I noticed then how thin the grass was. Even the daisies were scrawny. They barely had enough strength to keep their heads up.

"Might as well plow the works," said Jim. I felt he was talking to himself rather than to me. I slipped my arm through his.

Our house and barn stood on a rise above the road, and our small fields were the only cleared lands to be seen on this side of the river. On the far side I could see John J.'s pasture cut like a giant swathe through the trees. We turned up a grass-grown track dividing our fields above the road. We couldn't see our house until we passed the gaunt unpainted barn. It was a small low house, with one window on either side of the front door, and an extension tacked onto one end like a pan handle. The builders had neglected to include a window or adequate supports for the roof, which sagged like a sway-backed horse.

"They must have had a frolic to put up that house, and everyone must have been cockeyed by the time they reached the windows." My remark was greeted with silence. No one else saw anything funny in those two front windows tilting towards the door like a deaf man straining to hear. I ran up to the door and waited for Jim to unlock it.

"What are ye waiting for?" said Clemmie. "It's not locked.

Nobody around here locks doors. Ye'd never know who'd come by needing shelter."

Jim stepped up beside me, turned the knob, and pushed open the door. We walked inside and found ourselves in the front room. There was no porch or hall. The room was empty, the floor covered in dust, but I could see that the boards were wide and worn thin with constant scrubbing with hard soap. The knots stood out like warts on a toad's back. A pile of bricks lay on the floor where a fireplace had once stood. In the rear wall, facing the window, were two doors no more than three feet apart.

"This was the guest room in days gone by," said Clemmie, opening one of the doors. "Many's the one slept here."

There were three articles in the little cell-like room: a small nail keg, the rim and sides stained with yellow scum, a rickety old rocking chair, and a filthy blanket thrown over it. I turned to the second door.

"I want ye to see the kitchen," said Clemmie, blocking my way. "We'll see that room after."

As soon as I stepped into the kitchen I could understand Clemmie's enthusiasm. It was a bright sunny room with two windows, one opening on the front of the house and the other facing west to the sway-backed shed. The floor boards groaned and sagged under our weight and there was a gaping hole under the front window where rain had seeped through the twisted frame and rotted the boards. In the centre of the room a wood-burning stove stood on three legs, covered in rust and surrounded by bricks from a fallen flue. The only furniture was a small table and a chair that had lost its rungs and stood as uncertainly as a new-born calf. There were no water taps, no sink, not even a pump.

"Have to get water down below," said Clemmie, reading my thoughts. "Tis a good well though. Never goes dry winter or summer."

"She means a spring," said Jim, knowing I wouldn't understand. "I remember it. Water cold as ice all summer long." Jim turned to his father. "Is she dug out?"

Clemmie didn't give his father time to answer. "Oh yes! We've been pasturing our cows up here. Daddy kept her open for to water them."

"Is this the pantry?" I asked, pointing to a door at the back of the room.

"No!" said Clemmie, breathing down my neck. "That was the old folks' bedroom."

It would take more than a name to give that narrow little room the dignity of being called a bedroom. I did not dare cross the threshold. The floor sagged in the centre and in places had rotted completely away. Through the window I could see a tumble-down shed surrounded by weeds and rusty farm machinery.

"This will have to be the pantry," I said firmly. "The carpenter can build shelves along the wall and a bench and cupboards below. There'll be just enough room left to work in. I'll have to have a pantry." I closed the door quickly and nearly tripped over an iron ring set in a loose square of flooring just behind me.

"That's the cellar, such as it is," said Mr. Douglas, holding out his arm to steady me. "Best take a look, Jim."

Jim bent down, grasped the ring and lifted the trap.

A dank mouldy smell seeped into the kitchen. In the murky light I saw a ladder leading down into the darkness below. Jim replaced the trap quickly.

"What's upstairs?" said Jim looking around. "Where ARE the stairs?"

"Back there, some place," said Mr. Douglas, leading the way into a room beside the old folks' bedroom.

"This was the dining room," said Clemmie, "and that door beyond goes into the front room."

"It's no bigger than the pantry," I said, deciding not to worry about what Clemmie would think.

"Here's the stairs," said Jim, pointing to a ladder in the corner that led up to a trap in the ceiling.

"And that was the pantry," said Clemmie, her face twisted

into a smile. She pointed to three narrow shelves under the ladder laden with three chipped soup bowls and an ancient condiment set.

"How in heaven did they manage? You said there were eight children, and the old folks?"

"Yeh! And they was lucky to have it!"

"Come on!" said Jim, climbing the ladder, "let's see what's upstairs. I'll soon get some light down." Jim pushed up the trap and let it rest on the floor above. Mr. Douglas and Clemmie followed. I reached the top step and looked over. A flimsy partition of boards divided off a large room over the kitchen from the rest of the attic. Rafters, braces and studs stood uncovered. The only door, without knob or catch, sagged on its only hinge. Lacy cobwebs hung from the rafters to within inches of the floor and filtered the sunlight pouring in through a window in the western gable. The only furniture was an old iron bedstead with hammock springs. It had been painted many times with different colours, but it was hard to tell which colour had last been applied. The mattress was made up of bags of oat straw placed three abreast over the springs, and ancient straw dropped from jagged holes in the burlap. Then one of the rags moved, and from deep inside I heard squeaking.... Rats! I fled down the ladder. Clemmie wasn't far behind me.

"Take the whole shootin' match outside, Jim," I heard Mr. Douglas say. "Make one big fire, bag and all. It's the only thing."

I reached the kitchen safely, but a huge rat, at least a foot long, ran across the floor right in front of me. I screamed and ran out into the yard.

Jim and Mr. Douglas got rid of the rats. They could carry only one bag at a time down the ladder. The burlap was so rotten that it required both hands to hold it together. I was terrified that something more than straw would fall out of those bags. Then the men went down to the barn and came back with shovels. Jim struck a match and started the fire. Fanned by a light breeze the flames roared upward. Then the squeaking began. I covered my ears and turned away. I didn't uncover them until Mr. Douglas and Jim had stopped circling the burning heap and the flames had died down. Not a single rat escaped.

So this was to be my home. A house occupied by insects and rats. A house in need of a roof, floors, and a chimney. A structure without a single straight wall or window, and in need of gallons of paint. But it was our own. Our only home. It was beautiful!

THE FOLLOWING DAY was Sunday, and the Sunday for Mass. It was useless asking old Sandy to start work until the following Monday. As it was, it took Jim most of Sunday evening to coax and wheedle the old man to work at all. It was only after Jim promised to drive him to and from work that he agreed. The arrangement suited us very well. We couldn't let the old man sleep in the house the way it was. Goodness knows when the old range would be delivered, and the nights were cold.

Old Sandy was a man in his fifties. His head was thatched with sparse sandy hair. His chin and neck sprouted bristles in abundance, which lay like mown hay on his transparent skin. The apex of Sandy's head was not his bald pate but the tip of his Roman nose. The rest of his head receded from that point and gave him the appearance of a large mouse. His head wobbled up and down without ceasing.

It was a hot day, but old Sandy wore a flannel shirt of faded green plaid, buttoned up to the neck. His hands, small and finely moulded, shook in all directions as he grasped a board and laid it across an improvised bench. He picked up the saw and held it poised and quivering in the air. I waited breathlessly for his next move. It came suddenly. The saw plunged unerringly and swift as a hawk on its prey. With one movement, a deep cut was made. Sandy did not stop until the ends fell apart. He held the ends up for inspection, and with a grunt and many nods of the head, measured the smaller piece with his rule. When he came to rebuild the flue, there was the breathless moment before the mortar or the brick came down into exact place.

Old Sandy shook his way through room after room. He repaired the floors, straightened the windows, tore down the wall between the dining room and the little guest room. Slowly and meticulously he made a hallway and stairs that I could use with comfort. He made me a pantry with cupboards and shelves, and hung sheets of plaster board to cover the walls.

Now that the rats had gone and the new staircase was built, I could explore the rest of the attic. Through the cobweb curtains I found a butter tub made by Jim's grandfather, who was a cooper and had never been known to use a nail, and parts of a spinning wheel. The tub was a little pile of staves surrounded by two hoops. Jim picked it up.

"I'll take it down and put it together," he said. "Be just as good as ever when I soak it in water."

We found from the beginning that water would be a problem. The spring down in the field was pure, but the incline was steep. And after a few trips with brimming buckets, we decided that for washing and cleaning we would depend on a natural basin in the ground near the house that gathered and collected surface water. We bought galvanized buckets and set up a washstand on a homemade bench in the kitchen. One bucket was designated drinking water, the other cleaning. We had plenty of money when we chose our range, but no idea how little it would prove to be before we had established our home. With hopes in the sky I decided against a stove with a reservoir for hot water. I had planned on a large tank attached to a waterfront in the stove. Now I found myself with no way of heating water but the tea kettle, until I found, on one of the back pages in a catalogue, a five-gallon blue enamel pot suitable for canning. I sent for it immediately.

It was Clemmie who suggested we ask Sean, the water diviner, to find a place for us to sink a well. Neither of us thought to ask whether Sean had ever found water. And at the time, it didn't seem strange to find Sean was free or that, with a water diviner in the community, everyone lugged pails of water up steep hills and over long distances.

The first day Sean showed up for work, he came into the kitchen for a cup of tea and a smoke. A strange man! His ghostly white skin was startling enough, so thin that the veins showed through like cobwebs on a ceiling. Clemmie had told me that Sean wore every stitch of clothing he owned, winter and summer. It was nothing, she said, to find underneath his flannel shirt another flannel shirt, and under that still another. On his feet, high black gumshoes, a full size large to accommodate all his socks, were kept tightly laced against the snow in winter, and for no reason at all in summer. It was joked—"Sean washed his feet t'other day and found a pair of socks been lost since a year."

His tea finished, Sean took his tools out of the gunnysack he carried over his shoulder and unwrapped each drill from its individual wrapper and spread them out in the sun to glisten. He then covered them with the gunnysack and came back into the kitchen for another cup of tea before going home for supper.

Sean was back before breakfast the next morning. He pulled a forked alder from some place under his coveralls and explained at great length the infallibility of his "machine" when he wished to find water near the surface. Jim, of course, had work to do outside, but I was delayed a full hour from my work while I learned the great mystery.

Sean, with his alder firmly grasped in both hands, forked prongs pointing down, walked all around the house. I peeked out now and then from one window or another. Sean was always there, no matter which window I stood beside. He came in for dinner.

"Found a place just outside the porch door," he said, indicating the door to the sway-backed shed. "Fork jumped near out of my hand. Start drillin' tomorrow." I watched him go.

Just in time for dinner, three days later, I saw Sean coming round the barn. I put out another plate. Sean and Jim came into the kitchen together.

"Where was ye?" said Jim. "What happened?"

Sean grinned and took off his coat.

"Was ye longing?" was all he said.

Not a sod had been turned when Sean came in later looking for his tea.

"Well, the drills be all rigged up. Start the drilling now," he said, when he finished his tea.

I heard sounds of shipping shortly afterwards. Sean worked until suppertime.

After supper he went home, and Jim called me out to see what he had done. Sean had been lucky. He had been drilling in sand, and his drill was down four feet.

"Do you think we'll ever be able to pump water out of that little hole?" I asked. Jim shrugged his shoulders and covered the drill.

Sean didn't come back for eight days. But on the ninth, he came just after sun-up. At ten o'clock he found an excuse to go home.

"Run into rock," he said. "Me drills are all dull, have to get them sharpened. Be back tomorrow."

By now there was a little path circling a hole two feet in diameter. Jim measured the depth. Sean had gained another two feet. This time neither of us spoke, but Jim was not so careful about covering the drills and leaving them exactly as he found them.

A month later Sean showed up again. Then, to justify his appearance, he went out and began drilling. It wasn't long before he was back in for his tea. He talked and talked until I served supper, and only stopped talking long enough to swallow his food. At last, in desperation, Jim offered to drive him home.

"Ye're welcome to stay if we had the other bed up," said Jim, a little ashamed of himself. "But we only have the floor to offer. I'll take ye home in the truck, if ye'd rather."

"Might as well," said Sean, draining his glass. "There's nothing to be done till ye dig where the cave-in is."

This was the first we had heard of any cave-in.

"Yisss!" Sean went on, "she caved in today. Couldn't get the drill down at the last of it. Ye dig down and open her up, and I'll be back when ye're finished."

That was the story of the hole outside the door to the sway-backed shed. Sean never did come back. His drills lay out under the snow all winter.

GETTING STOCK FOR THE FARM was no problem. Everyone had a cow or a calf for sale, or had a friend who was looking for a buyer. We bought an old cow named Star. She was a good milker. Jim knew how to milk, but we had made a deal that I would milk if he built the morning fires. I had to learn, and old Star gave two full gallons of milk twice a day—and two five-pound lard pails as well.

Clemmie had a ten-month-old bull calf that she offered as company for the cow. I soon discovered that all bull calves were left with full potency until they were butchered!

"Mary, I s'pose ye're like the others around here. Foolish over calves," said Mr. Douglas, who walked up the road to see how we were getting along. "Feller over to the church ships cream. Gets rid of his calves. P'haps he got one now. If he hasn't, there's others over there shipping too."

At my urging Jim took his father to the church and brought back a pair of week-old calves.

"They're broke to drink from a bucket, no trouble," said the old man. I felt he was proud to have done his part in helping us stock our farm.

"I don't know how we'll feed them come this winter," said Jim. "And we'll have to get a horse."

"Yell get a few ton of wild hay off the place," said Mr.

Douglas. "Not much good, but better'n nothin'. And John J. has hay for sale most years."

Mr. Douglas made a special trip to tell us about Silver. His owner had three horses, and because the other two worked as a team, Silver had to go. She was a lovely haughty grey mare and looked more like a quarter horse than a farm drag. Everyone offered us cats to keep down the rats, and Clemmie's old dog had pups....

I ordered day-old chickens from a hatchery in Truro, with instructions that they were to be sent to the station for collection. Jim was fencing the day they were to arrive, so I took the truck and stopped to pick up Mr. Douglas to save him going to pick up the mail in the buggy. The train had just left when we arrived at the station. There was no sign of a box of chickens.

"You're sure?" I asked the station manager. "A notice came in the mail telling me the chicks would arrive today."

"Nothing come off the train but what you seen here," he said pointing to the three skimpy mail bags Mr. Douglas had picked up. "Come to think of it though, Ben, the wagon man did have chickens in the car...I heard ' em yeepin'."

I ran to the truck, started up the motor, and turned down the road to town.

"Hi! Where do ye think ye're goin'?" said Mr. Douglas, grabbing his hat.

"The chickens are on the train!"

"Foolishness!" the old man grumbled and braced himself for the bumpy road. He hung on to his hat, pushed his feet against the floorboards, and glared at the road.

"Nope!" said the station manager, at the next stop. "No chickens here."

"I'll have to catch them," I cried, "the nights are cold. They'll die in a station with no heat if they're left overnight."

"Might be ye could catch the train. She's only 'bout five minutes ahead of ye."

I took the right turn into the main road. Incredulity, followed by amazement and finally anger, swept over Mr. Douglas' face. He was speechless. He bumped, clutched, and braced himself all the way to the next station. The chicks were still on the train, and the train still five minutes ahead of us. There was nothing I could do but drive on to the end of the line—seventeen miles away. The old man didn't say a word.

The chicks were at Caithness station, and the station manager was very happy to deliver them. On the way home, Mr. Douglas never stopped talking.

"I s'pose ye know them chicks might be after costing me me job."

"How, Dad?" I asked, unaware of the depth of his anger.

"What's the bondsman goin' to think? Me chasin' all over the county with Government mail. Like as not they'll pull their names off me bond. And it'd be no more than right."

"Who's going to do that, Dad?"

"Everyone. Like as not, it's all over th' county by now."

"Oh! Come now. It's not as bad as that. They won't be mad when they hear that the chicks would have probably died by morning."

"The postmistress...all three of them will be having fits. All them people sittin' round their kitchen at mealtime waitin' for their mail." The old man was more relaxed now, and his voice was gentle.

"I'll take the blame," I said. I stepped on the accelerator.

"Whoa there! Take it easy! We're better late than going on another ride...the last, maybe!"

5
The Children

IT WAS MAIL DAY. Clemmie Douglas was busy sorting.

"Git yerself a cup o' tea, Mary," she said. "I'll soon be done. And bring one fer me." She picked up a letter and looked at it for a long while before putting it between her teeth. Then she went on with her sorting. When she had finished, she sat down and tore open the envelope.

"Mary, read this!" she said. "It came in the mail."

Mary read the note quickly and felt tears springing to her eyes. Then she read it again, more slowly, until the hot sensation in her throat subsided. She lifted a perfectly composed face to Clemmie. "Are you going to take her?" she asked.

"I can't," Clemmie answered. "Joe'd have a fit. He ain't got the patience no more. Gittin' too old to have little ones around. But I thought maybe you and Jim...."

"Poor, poor, little girl! It would be wonderful. What's she like?" Mary was eager for children.

"She's a little over three, maybe four. Red hair. Blue eyes, round as dollars! Fat, and laughs all the time. Nobody'd ever be sorry for takin' that one."

"I know! I know! I'm sure Jim will say yes. How come she's that old and nobody took her?"

"Her mother took a pain and died one night. Left a whole bunch of kids. Some went to the Home, but the Gillis family took this one. Now Mrs. Gillis is sick herself and can't have the care of her. If ye should want, ye can get the papers, ye know."

LITTLE ANNE FITTED into the lives of Jim and Mary Douglas as if she'd been born to them. They were playing on the floor with her one evening before bedtime, when Jim became suddenly serious.

"She could have a wonderful time with a little brother."

"Oh, Jim! Wouldn't it be nice to give a little boy a home. The way it is, we aren't using up half our hearts."

"When ye married me," Jim teased, "ye promised I was to have all yer heart."

Mary wrapped her arms around her husband and kissed him. Jim blushed, as he always did when she made a display of affection. Ten years of marriage had not altered his essential reticence.

"A little boy," he laughed, untwining the fingers laced around his neck. "A son. Be nice if we could get him b'fore Christmas."

"I don't know, Jim." Mary was serious now. "Maybe the Home wouldn't even have a little boy for adoption that soon. Of course, he'd have to be for adoption. I couldn't bear to give him back—I just couldn't do that."

"No," said Jim gently. "He'd have to be really ours. We'll manage. Maybe we should ask Clemmie about it?"

"Oh, no! I'd just as lief not ask Clemmie," said Mary. "I think maybe sometime Clemmie would like to take children for herself, but she says your father'd not have the patience to put up with them. Anyway, she'd always be thinkin' she had a right to be tellin' us how to raise him. We'll go to the priest. We'll have a thanksgiving Mass said for Anne. That'll give us an opening."

Jim nodded his assent.

On Sunday, after Mass, Jim picked up Anne and walked with Mary to the altar rail, where the three knelt to say a prayer. Then Jim carried Anne over to the creche in front of St. Joseph's shrine. He held her close to the spruce boughs so that she could look into the tiny stable and see the animals, the shepherds, Mary and Joseph, and the Infant Jesus lying in the manger.

After a few moments, they found the courage to go into the vestry, where Father Phil was removing his vestments.

"You're new in the parish, aren't you?" he said, extending a hand to Mary, though he knew very well who she was.

"Mary Douglas," she answered hurriedly. "And this is my husband Jim."

"You're Joe Douglas' boy." The priest's voice was comfortably familiar. "I know your people. Good to have you home again."

Jim said it was good to be back and shook the priest's hand, but was too uncomfortable himself to say any more.

"Thank you, Father." Mary was a little breathless. "We're going to be in the parish from now on, so you'll be seeing a lot of us. This is our little Anne. Her mother died last year. We got her through Jim's people. That's what we came to see you about. We just love her. We're so happy God gave her to us. We'd like you to say a thanksgiving Mass for us." Mary took out the five-dollar bill that was folded in her pocket and offered it to the priest. The usual Mass offering was two dollars, but she wanted to give the appearance of prosperity before making her request.

Father Phil took the folded bill and slipped it into his pocket without once looking at it.

"Is she all that nice?" he smiled, putting a finger under Anne's chin, but looking at Jim. "She brings you that much happiness?"

"Yes, Father." Jim had recovered his composure. "She fills our days. And while you're at it, Father, could you slip in a few words about—maybe— a little brother fer her. Mary and me thought perhaps...fer Christmas?"

"Of course, of course!" said Father Phil, as if their request was the most ordinary thing in the world. "I'm a good friend of the sister in charge of infants at the Home. I'll get in touch with her this week."

Father Phil smiled approvingly on the couple.

The Douglases felt their hearts lift with relief.

There was hope!

Word came the very next mail day. Mary's hands shook a little as she opened the envelope, which contained a short note and a picture of a solemn-faced little fellow. The note read: "We are enclosing a picture of a little boy we have here who is available for adoption. He was left in my charge. He is a very bright little lad, perfect for any home. If you find him satisfactory, you can arrange to call for him on Tuesday, the 12th. We can take care of the papers here, as he has not yet been turned over to the Welfare Services." The note was signed: Sister Frances Theresa.

"TUESDAY!" Mary's mind raced. "That's tomorrow! We'll have to tell Jim's father and Clemmie." Mary knew that any letter with a Sydney postmark left Clemmie bursting with curiosity, but one to her stepson's family simply had to be explained.

"AIN'T THAT THE LITTLE DARLING!" exclaimed Clemmie, when Mary showed her the picture. "Who is he?"

"We're getting a little brother for Anne," Mary blurted. "It's his picture."

Jim's father looked at the picture without comment and passed it back. His eyes had a fixed stare, and his lips were drawn into a thin line. Jim squirmed in his chair, shuffled his feet, and looked to Mary for help. She could think of nothing to say. She was helpless before this stern silent man. She shook her head and stared at her feet. She and Jim had told no one of their plans or problems. She knew how hard it was for Jim to explain himself.

"Dad," Jim's voice was reticent, cautious. "We have to go to Sydney tomorrow to get the boy. Ye'd best take the day off and come along. Do ye good."

The old man's face softened instantly. The awkward moment

was over. Jim felt the change and was glad of it, but now he had a problem with Clemmie.

"It'd be nice if you could come too," he said, looking at his stepmother. "But the truck'll only ride three in the seat, and with four, the Mounties'd sure as hell pick us up on the highway. And we have to take Anne along." Jim's voice trailed off.

"That's all right! I couldn't go anyway. Mrs. Lawlor'll be coming down to help me set the cheese." Clemmie was vexed and her words were very clear and a little clipped.

The next morning, at about eight, Jim and Mary drove down to pick up the old man. He was ready and waiting.

"Look, Jim," he whispered. "I've got a little of that—stuff—out back. D'ye think 'twould be safe to take 'er along?"

"Oh, I think so," said Jim, without thinking.

The old man sauntered around to the outhouse and came back with a bulge in his pocket. But he was still not completely confident.

"Yer sure, now? I wouldn't take 'er if ye thought there was any chance of us gettin' caught. Ye could lose yer license, y'know. Maybe even the truck." He peered earnestly at Jim through his heavy grey eyebrows. "Yer sure, now, it's all right?"

"I still got my U.S. license plates," Jim said.

"And everybody says the Mounties don't bother cars with foreign plates much. I don't think we got any real worries."

The old man climbed into the truck. They waved to Clemmie standing in the doorway, and were on their way.

"Perhaps we'd best have a taste before we get to the highway," the old man said. He pulled the package out of his pocket and unfolded the newspaper he'd wrapped the bottle in. Jim took a swig, and Joe Douglas took a longer one. Then he replaced the cork, rewrapped the bottle, and returned the package to his pocket. He felt happy, free but guilty, like a boy playing hooky from school.

"Why don't we take the short cut?" he suggested cheerily. "We'll cut off twenty mile if we go as the crow flies, and the road is not bad at all. Bumpy. But yer truck'll handle 'er easy. Less chance o' runnin' inta the Mounties."

The road was so twisty and bumpy that Mary had a hard time keeping little Anne balanced on her knee. They all got a little giddy as they counted the number of times their heads hit the roof or nearly did. It was after a particularly bad bump that Mary caught the smell of liquor. At first she thought it was only the men's breath in the stuffy cab, but when she shifted Anne to her other knee, the one nearest Jim, the smell became overpowering.

"Do you smell anything?" she asked, glancing at the men.

"Smell anything?" asked Jim. "Like what?"

"Like something a Mountie might like to investigate if he opened the cab door."

"MOONSHINE!" Both men yelled at once.

Jim took his foot off the gas pedal. "Oh, fer God's sake, Dad! Are ye sure ye got the cork in that bottle tight?"

"I banged 'er in with the butt o' me hand. Ye seen me do it, Jim," the old man said, shifting backwards in his seat to raise his buttocks and reach the bottle.

"STOP!" he roared suddenly. "STOP! I'm soaked!"

In his hand, still wrapped in the newspaper that now dripped like a wet blanket, was the bottle of moonshine. He tore off the paper. "My God, Jim! The road must've bumped 'er loose. No more'n one drink apiece. We'd best finish 'er right here. The smell's strong. No tellin' what might happen once we git t' the ferry."

He opened the window, threw out the newspaper, and passed the bottle to Jim.

"Please, Jim," said Mary. "If Sister Frances Theresa smells liquor on your breath, she might think we're not fit parents."

"If she gits one smell of me, that'll fix it." The old man chuckled as he explored his trousers. Then he finished off the rest of the bottle.

"It'll evaporate before we get there," said Mary. "And if it doesn't, you can stay in the truck."

They arrived at the orphanage just before noon. Mary was still concerned about the impression they would make, but she was also eager to make Jim's father feel comfortable in her company and not to have him worrying about the accident.

"Are you coming in, Dad?" she asked anxiously.

"No," he said. "It's best I stay here and dry off a little more. I smell like a distillery. I'd only be causin' ye trouble."

Mary was pleased to hear the cheerful note in his voice. Relieved, she arranged her own dress and little Anne's hair. Then she gave the child to Jim, and the three of them walked up the steps to the Home.

Sister Frances Theresa greeted them warmly and looked over Mary's shoulder.

"Who's that in the truck?" she asked.

"Oh," Mary hesitated. "That's Mr. Douglas... Jim's father." She looked to her husband for assistance and added, "He said he'd rather wait in the truck till we're through."

"Come on in!" Sister called out to him, but the old man merely shook his head.

Reaching around to catch the end of her veil so that it wouldn't blow up around her head, Sister Frances ran out the door and was at the cab of the truck before either Mary or Jim could stop her. She opened the door. Jim looked sick.

"Come in! Come in! Don't be shy," she coaxed. "Nobody's going to sit outside here. The girls have made little cakes, and they have a nice lunch ready for you all. Come on, now, Mr. Douglas. It's not right to disappoint them."

Nobody could resist Sister Frances Theresa.

During the lunch, Mary was uneasy, and Jim nearly dropped his plate. The old man kept his eyes constantly on Sister Frances, and tried to stay as still as a mouse. Once his cup tipped and its hot contents spilled over his trousers. Mary saw him wince and clutch his groin, but Sister seemed to notice nothing. She kept up a friendly chatter, pausing now and then to urge more tea and cakes on her guests, or to entice little Anne to try a soft drink. At last she got up.

"Well, now," she said. "I suppose you're anxious to see your new little boy. You finish your tea, and I'll get him."

When the door closed behind her, Jim let out a long ragged sigh and passed his hand across his forehead. The old man subsided into his chair, and Mary's knotted hands relaxed in her lap. They had been wondering if the delay in producing the child had any meaning, and had shared a silent concern about the clinging aroma of moonshine.

When Sister reappeared with Sonny laughing in her arms, everyone forgot about the smell of moonshine. The child's smile faded suddenly, and he looked at the room's occupants with solemn interest and curiosity, showing neither happiness nor fear. Mary walked over to him and held out her arms. He smiled and went to her straight away. She hugged him close and felt the familiar stinging in the back of her throat, as he wrapped his little arms around her neck and hugged her back. She buried her face in the front of his clean-smelling little shirt until the hot tears had subsided. Then she handed her son to her husband's waiting arms.

Sister beamed. "He's so right for you people! I knew he would be. Look, Anne, dear." She picked up the little girl. "That's your little brother. Would you like to talk to him? Wouldn't you like to say hello?"

Sonny grinned, put out his hand, and laughed out loud.

Anne smiled.

"What kind of soap do you use on the babies, Sister?" Mary asked, as they walked to the door. "Sonny smells so sweet and clean. I'd like to get some while we're in Sydney."

"I don't really know," Sister Frances smiled at everyone smiling around her. "We get it wholesale, and as far as I know, it's just called Baby Soap. You know," she smiled again, merrily this time, "I'd forgotten it had such a nice scent. I have these growths in my nose—polyps—or whatever they call them. I guess it's time I had them removed. I'm missing so many wonderful smells."

SISTER FRANCES THERESA WATCHED as the truck pulled away from the Home. Then she closed the door and leaned against it, laughing softly to herself.

"So Joe Douglas is still drinking the moonshine!" She laughed again, remembering her father's comment on the old man. "He's jist doin' what the fancy folks do, but he ain't givin' the government a cut. And who can blame him? He's got little enough for himself." Her father had worked with Joe Douglas years and years before, when they were both young men working on the buildings at the Sydney steel plant. She wondered if she'd done right in not telling the old man who she was. She'd been only eleven when she'd last seen him.

Sister Frances shrugged and sniffed. Her nose did feel stuffed, but she could still detect the sweet smell of moonshine clinging in the room. She opened the window to let in the sharp December air, adjusted her veil that had been loosened in the wind, and went into the chapel for a quick prayer.

6

Our First Christmas

I WOKE WITH A START. The bedroom was full of shadows. A few hours ago, when I blew out the lamp, it had been pitch dark. Now I could make out the shapes of drawers and even the clothes rack across the room. Heavy clouds had hung low over the Glen all week, dumping their cargo of white snow. But the clouds had gone away while we slept, and now the moon hung high in the sky and the countryside was bathed in light. It seemed like a miracle.

I heard footsteps on the landing.

"Jim," I whispered. "Wake up! The kids are up. I'm afraid Sonny might fall on the stairs. Those stairs are dangerous." I found myself shaking my head and mumbling. "We'll have to find the money somewhere for a banister."

Every day since the children had come I'd worried about the stairs, and I used to like how narrow and steep they were.

"What time is it?" said Jim, shaking off my arm. "What's the matter with them?"

"It's Christmas, remember? They are looking for the presents Santa brought. It's four o'clock. You'd better hurry if you want to see their faces."

The floor was ice cold. I'd have to get the fire going right away.

"Be right there," said Jim, as he jumped out of bed and pulled on his trousers.

Together we tiptoed down the stairs, through the kitchen and into the front room. Two small figures in long flannelette nightgowns stood silent and still before the Christmas tree. The moonlight reflected from the ornaments and the tinsel on the tree created an aura about them.

"Angels!" Jim whispered.

I lit the lamp with shaking hands. The tree Jim had chosen was much larger than the ones we used to have in our little apartment in New York, and the decorations we'd bought with us were too few for such a large tree. The stores in Port Hood didn't carry anything so frivolous, and it was too late for a mail order when we came to decorate the tree. But Anne and Sonny couldn't see anything wrong.

"Look, Daddy!" I still pretended to be surprised. "Doesn't this big doll look like Anne? Do you suppose Santa meant it for her?" Anne's eyes were like blue whirlpools.

"I don't suppose Santa would leave a doll for a boy, now, do you princess?" said Jim lowering himself on his hunkers and putting his arm around her.

I took the doll from beside the tree and held it up. Anne chuckled with laughter, held out her arms, clutched the doll and held it close. It was nearly as tall as she was. I looked at Sonny.

"What did Santa bring for my big boy, I wonder?"

Sonny wasn't listening. He was looking at the tree.

"Look, Sonny, look! A fire engine! All for you. A big red fire engine!" Still Sonny paid no attention. Then suddenly he put out his hand and touched a golden ball hanging from the nearest branch. The ball quivered for a moment, then crashed to the floor, and shattered into tiny pieces. The corners of his mouth began to droop. But before Jim or I had time to speak Anne threw down her doll, grasped a blue and silver bell, threw it down on the floor, and danced up and down with glee.

"Anne! You musn't touch," I gasped, drawing her away. "They're not toys to play with. You musn't touch the tree. Just look at the pretty things."

With two of the biggest ornaments broken, our poor tree looked bare and forlorn. Jim took Anne by the hand and led her over to the armchair. He pointed to the bulging stockings hanging from either arm. I grabbed a small bear that stood guard over Sonny's stocking and held it close to his face trying to block his view of the tree. Slowly his eyes began to sparkle through the tears. Then holding out his little hands he took the bear and held it close to his chest. He laughed. This was the first time I had ever heard him laugh. The fire engine lay unnoticed under the tree. I got up from my knees and touched my man-child on the head. Then I made my way out into the kitchen.

DURING THE WEEK BETWEEN Christmas and the New Year every family in the Glen went visiting. Every man had to treat his neighbours to a drink. We would have to make at least two excursions—one up the road to the Beatons' and the MacTavishes' and the other down the road to Jim's father's place, Dougall's, J.J.'s, then up to Lawlors', and Ronnie's place over the hill. Jim thought we should start our visiting down the Glen. He harnessed Silver to the wood sleigh while I collected the old coats and comforters we had and piled them on behind. While I put on Sonny's coat Anne had taken one of the last ornaments left on the tree and insisted on hanging it on Silver's bridle. Jim waved away my protests and we took off in a whirl of snow. The mare was well fed and eager to run. As we turned off the Settlement Road we could see that there was no smoke coming from the chimney of Jim's father's house. They too must be visiting. We continued on our way down the river until Dougall's house came into view. No smoke came from his chimney either and there were no children playing in the yard.

"We'd best turn around and go back up to Lawlors'," said Jim, "they're all over at J.J.'s and drunk by now." He turned Silver around in the next gateway and we retraced our way up the hill and on towards Lawlors'. Our call at Lawlors' was a duty call, for Charles Lawlor was the big man up our end of the Glen. His house stood well back from the road and guarded by a carefully clipped spruce hedge. It was painted white; the only painted house for miles around. We swung in past the painted high-barred gate into the driveway. Silver took the turn with a burst of speed then slowed down to a walk up the steep slope to the house. Soon we heard singing. A Gaelic song—I knew the tune..."They had neither pole nor paddle So they could not cross the stream." Then a man's voice rang out, more heartily than melodious, describing the hero's frantic efforts to cross the water to the accompaniment of clapping hands beating out the rhythm. Then once again many voices joined in the chorus.

Margaret Lawlor met us at the door. She clasped the children in her arms and swept us into the parlour. She was a gentle soft-spoken little woman with twelve children of her own. We had barely time to take off our coats and rubbers before glasses were pressed into our hands. At Lawlors' each guest was given an individual glass. In the kitchen a gleaming stove hot from anthracite coal, and the air was filled with the aroma of spices from trays of cookies and cakes cooling in the pantry. Plates of turkey and pork sandwiches were laid out on long tables under the window. I was overwhelmed by the joy and hospitality around us. It was as if the framed blessing and prayers on the walls had all been brought to life. It was hard to believe, looking at Charles Lawlor now, that he could silence any one of his children, grown man or child, with a look.

The front room had been cleared for dancing. There was no musical instrument, but that didn't deter the dancers. As soon as a set finished, a voice started a faster tune, and before eight bars were sung the rest of the group joined in. A big strapping youth was pushed into the centre of the floor. He started a series of intricate steps. His feet moved like quicksilver, but his body remained rigid and his arms stiff. Soon our little Anne was jumping up and down trying to dance, and young Charlie Lawlor, a hefty lad in his early twenties led her on to the floor. She didn't know any of the tunes, but she had a good sense of rhythm. I was so proud of her. She looked so pretty, and her red-gold hair gleamed as her partner held her up and spun her round and round. I was so glad that I had been extravagant and made her a party dress especially for Christmas. It was blue velvet with lace collar and cuffs.

No one seemed to get tired, and no one got drunk. Three times we tried to leave but Margaret Lawlor wouldn't hear of it. At last I managed to convince her that we would have to be on our way. The whole family came to the door to see us off. They jammed the porch, waving their arms and calling out..."Merry Christmas! A Happy New Year!"

"Wasn't that something?" I said, as Silver took off at a sharp trot.

"Aye!" said Jim. "Stayed longer 'n we should have."

"What a fuss Margaret made when I wanted to leave."

"Awful nice people," Jim replied.

We had one more call to make.

"It'll have to be hello and good-bye at Ronnie's," said Jim. "Sun's losing her heat and it'll soon be dark. Don't want to be stumbling round in the dark feeding cows."

Jim pulled Silver's rein sharply to the left of the road. The mare knew her way home and wanted to turn the other way. Reluctantly she climbed up to the brow of the hill. At the crest we could see Ronnie's house.

"Look!" I cried. "They're all out in the snow."

"Fightin'," said Jim. "Must be the Roosters. Christina's people."

"The Roosters?"

"Aye! The Roosters!" said Jim with contempt. "When they're around, there's feathers flying. There's a whole settlement of them down the road from the church. With no one around to fight, they fight they selves...and with anything that comes handy...fists, chairs, clubs, hair-pulling, anything at all."

"Let's not go in, Jim. We can wave from the road and turn around at the church. They'll never remember."

"No!" said Jim. "Can't do that. And I don't want to make another trip over—special. Get it over now."

Inside the house, everyone was drunk, even the women. There was no sign of tea or any food. The men stopped fighting long enough to take the drink Jim offered them. One was passed out on the floor. We hadn't bothered to blanket Silver, and we left as quickly as we could.

"None of them will remember we were there," I said petulantly. "We should have gone past."

"WE know," said Jim, firmly.

"Do we have time to run in and give old William Barnes a drink?" I said, looking at the tall gaunt house that hadn't a single light shining through the windows. "It's Christmas, and that poor old man probably won't have any callers at all."

"We'll do that," said Jim. "We'll stay long enough to give him a drink, and that's all."

The children were fast asleep and warm. I went into the house while Jim tied up the mare. The old man didn't hear me enter the kitchen. He sat huddled over the stove, wrapped in an old ragged coat, a cap pulled down over his ears, and his booted feet in the oven. The whole room was hazy with smoke that poured from a crack on the stove top and a loose connection in the chimney pipe. The window was shrouded with limp shreds of curtaining that showed traces of having once been crisp and gay. An unlit lamp, the bowl empty and the funnel caked in soot, a grimy glass of water, and a flickering lantern stood on the table. The old man neither heard me, nor seemed to see me as I moved around.

"Don't shut the door," I called out to Jim when I heard his steps in the porch.

"Why the hell not?" Jim called back. "Want to freeze everyone out?"

"Leave it open. Just for a minute to let the smoke out."

As the air cleared, Jim looked around. I saw him looking at the place beside the stove where marks on the wall showed that wood had been stacked there in days gone by. On the floor lay a single piece of wood, about two feet in length and an inch in diameter. I raised the lid of the stove and motioned Jim to look. Inside, a half-burned chunk of wood encrusted with mud lay smouldering. Jim bent down and shook the old man gently, then took the bottle out of his pocket and held it up for him to see. The old eyes grew wide with excitement. He drank thirstily, but when we shouted "Merry Christmas," he only laughed foolishly, his eyes blank and without expression.

"He doesn't know he's alive," I whispered.

"He don't have any wood," Jim whispered. "Must be some, some place."

"Doesn't he have any relatives?"

"There a nephew or cousin or something in the village, but they don't pay him no mind. Never come out to see how he's doing. I'll take a look around and see if I can find wood for tonight."

Jim stopped at the door.

"Now we can't take him home, so don't try and be a Florence Nightingale, or something. Tomorrow, maybe, we can do something else...even if he is so mean that he wouldn't give his mother a nickel, and her starving to death."

"But we can't leave him to die alone at Christmas!" I protested.

"Now you stay here. I won't be a minute," said Jim, as he went out.

I picked up the lantern and found the pantry. The shelves were bare. There was no bread, nothing in the house. Jim soon returned with an armful of odds and ends of wood.

"Make him a cup of tea," said Jim, throwing the wood into the stove.

"I can't, Jim. I've looked everywhere and there isn't any food in the house. Not even a pinch of tea. It's too late to go home and get some, but we can leave the fruitcake and apples that are in the shoe box on the sleigh."

We left the cake and the apples with old William. Silver needed no urging, she was anxious as we were to get home. The sun had just disappeared over the far hills, and the light was fading fast. Jim would have to feed the animals by lantern light.

We heard the sleigh bells ahead before we saw Charlie Lawlor, standing spraddle-legged on his sleigh, towering over his mare. Jim hailed him, and reined Silver to a halt. We told Charlie what we had seen.

"Hmmm!" said Charlie. "D'ye think if I took him some potatoes and turnips, he'd have the sense to cook 'em? I'd best take a run up anyways."

"Well, that's our good deed for today," I said, as the sleigh moved off.

"If the neighbours are true to form, by the time Charlie makes his rounds tonight the old man'll have everyone in the Glen calling with their hands full before the week's out," said Jim, giving Silver a flick with the reins.

"What makes you think that?" I asked.

"Oh! Guessin'!" said Jim with a broad smile. "Margaret Lawlor'll make it her business to see that the relatives find out that the neighbours are feeding poor William, and they'll find a way of getting him away—him having all that money. I didn't see hide nor hair of his old dog. He must've breathed his last."

IT WAS GOOD TO GET HOME. I was cold and tired. What a Christmas it had been! I put the children to bed while Jim unloaded the sleigh and fed the animals. I soon had the fire going and the kettle singing on the stove. I looked out of the kitchen window. There was a full moon, and the snow was bathed in golden light. I could see Jim's lantern moving inside the barn.

"Mary! Come here!" It was Jim calling. "I got something to show ye!"

I pulled on my coat and boots, and ran out into the barn.

"Look!" said Jim, pointing to a heap of straw.

There stood a newborn calf, as frisky as a speckled trout. As soon as he saw me he darted over to his mother, old Star, who stood there, placid and content, chewing her cud.

"No need to ask is she all right," said Jim, throwing her an extra ration of hay. "Been a while since that feller came. Must've happened an hour or so after we left."

"Oh Jim! Isn't he a beauty! He's the best Christmas present I ever had. But I have something better than any gift this Christmas, Jim."

"An' what's that?"

"It just came to me now. Here we are, with our own home, our own land, two lovely children, good health, good food and good neighbours. This is the best Christmas I ever had. Ever, ever, ever!"

7

Gothic Neighbours

WHEN I FIRST CAME TO THE GLEN there had been seven members of the MacTavish family living up the Settlement Road. Lauchie, the eldest, Joe, Andy, John, deaf and dumb Dave, their only sister, Rose, and her twenty-year-old son, Dan.

Joe and Andy were the first to leave. One day they came home sick, hungry and dirty after four days drinking, and Lauchie told them to go and earn their own keep.

Then there was Francis; who his parents were no one knew, but curious neighbours made it their business to search him out. They never got close enough to see more than a face at the loft window, a fleeting shadow with snowy beard and a mane of hoary silk disappearing into the woods. Sure of their ground now, they went to the priest and pounded out the carpet in the vestry behind the altar. The next day the good Father drove out to the MacTavishes. It took a big man to hold Francis, the wild one, now forty years of age or more, while the priest gave him his blessing and cleansed him of original sin.

There had been many stories after that. One dark and stormy night (so it was said), poor Francis took a pain and expired and so his mortality had finally to be recognized. Reluctant to share his knowledge with his neighbours, Lauchie approached a man he felt committed to keep his secret—a cousin, Matt MacInnes; besides, Matt had a truck! Late that night, wringing wet and trembling, Lauchie arrived at Matt's house, across the river.

"I thought he must be drunk or something, him walking and

it storming like it was." No one could stop Matt telling the story after a couple of drinks. "But he said Francis had died, ye know, and he had to get a box to bury him in. He wanted to know would I take him to Sandy's the coffin maker over in Glen Murray. I wasn't even dressed, but I put me clothes on and went with him. He didn't say no word till we got to the top of the hill, then he said, 'For God's sake, Matt, don't let on who it is we're gitting the box for.'"

When Rose gave birth to her first illegitimate son—she had three—her father accused old Henry MacLeod. Old Henry "the Dirty" as he was called, acknowledged his guilt, raised the boy, and when he died willed his farm to him, now only an overgrown clearing in the woods. Rose gave her second son, whose sire no one had a mind to guess at, away to foster parents; last of all came Dan, whom she kept and named Dan Beaton, letting it be known that Harold Beaton was the father. Harold denied having any part of it, but Dan remained a Beaton until he was old enough to know better, at which time he renamed himself Dan MacTavish.

It happened this way. Rose had hidden Dan's bottle of bush whiskey while he sat in a drunken stupor. His long hair fell down across his forehead almost into a string of mucous that hung from his nose, left there unattached after a sneeze.

Dan always sneezed in his stupors and wet himself until pools formed underneath his chair that filled one mop at least, and sometimes two or more. Dan had never been known to shout, argue or use his towering strength against man or beast in the whole of his twenty years, but when Rose lost her temper and told him what she thought of him, and who his father was, he grabbed her throat and tried to bash her brains out against the steel bowl of the cream separator. Rose was not small and she struggled with all her strength.

Out in the barn Dave finished his chores and sauntered back to the house and the warmth of the fire. Pushing open the door of the back porch he saw Dan, gripping Rose's throat with a ferocity that whitened his fingers. Then with the fury of a plucked peacock Dave, slim and feather-light, threw himself at Dan in such a frenzy that Dan's grip relaxed. Rose took to her heels. Her time was seven minutes to the half-mile end. There at Beatons' she told her tale, and with the help of Harold, Joe, and the buggy she made her exit from the farm and from the Glen.

8

Dave

MARY COULDN'T BELIEVE how anybody could think that Dave wasn't an intelligent human being. His own brother, Lauchie, always spoke of him as being stupid and senseless but Mary had noticed, on many occasions when there was a problem to be solved on the farm and neighbours came to offer their experience, that it would be Dave's ingenuity and energy that found a solution. To put a man such as Dave "a-hide" as if he were some penance cast upon his parents and family seemed inhuman to Mary. She knew that there was nothing wrong with Dave's hearing. She had heard him tap his toes rhythmically to the radio or scamper to a window minutes before anyone else heard a sound, sometimes to identify a rig going along the road and find out whether it was going on up to his place or turning into the yard. He would utter ugly little sounds but Mary reasoned that since he could hear so well he could also be taught to speak.

One day, Lauchie decided to take a trip into town and he left Dave at home alone. Mary had just seen Lauchie and his rig go down the road when another figure, coming from the same direction, walked up into the yard. It was Dave. He knocked at the door and made signs that he wanted an egg. Mary called him in and cooked him eggs and gave him tea; but when he had finished he made no sign of wanting to leave and since he looked so lonesome, Mary left her washing and sat down at the table beside him. She soon exhausted the small number of signs that she knew and in a very short time she and Dave found themselves staring out the window. Then Dave idly fingered a pencil Mary had left on the table when she had finished writing the laying records of her hens. Suddenly aware of what his hands were doing, he took an empty envelope torn open from yesterday's mail and, bending down until his face almost touched the pencil, he began to move his fingers laboriously.

After several minutes and beaming with pride, he passed the envelope across to Mary. On the envelope Dave had written... DAVE MACTAVISH— the outline of each letter clear and strong. Mary had no difficulty in showing her surprise or in giving her praise. Once more Dave grasped the envelope and with more relaxed and sure movements he began to write numbers—all of them from one to a hundred. After writing each he raised a corresponding number of fingers on his left hand. A closed fist stood for ten, so three jerks of a closed fist followed by three pointed fingers meant thirty-three...and so he counted until he reached one hundred and then he began to really show off!

Without ever standing upright, his shoulders still bent as they had been over the table, he crossed the floor to the clock. He showed the time Lauchie had left home and when he was expected back; the time he himself had left—which was ten minutes later; and the time he had spent on the road. Having elicited astonishment and admiration from Mary, he again crossed the floor, his back still bent, to a calendar hanging on the wall. He pointed out all the Holy Days of Obligation for the entire year and the compulsory confession and Communion that preceded each day, which he explained by drawing his hand across his throat to indicate a clerical collar then moving his jaw to mime the movements of eating. He went still further, he turned the leaves of the calendar, and pointed out the Fast Days. No one could doubt the meaning of his fingers to the lips, the negative shake of the head, and no one could doubt Dave's knowledge of his subject.

Mary knew that Dave always carried a rosary in his pocket for she had watched him strike off bead by bead as though he knew the prayers for every one. But Dave had not finished his demonstration. He showed Mary that he must receive Communion twice yearly, at Easter and Christmas, or he would die. Whether it had been Rose, his mother, before she left for Boston, or his grandmother who had taught him, Mary didn't know; but it was not for her to correct their teaching.

Dave's absolution and blessing were obtained in a very simple way. Lauchie (now that Rose was gone) would go first into the confession, explain Dave's affliction to the priest, then send in Dave directly. After receiving absolution, Dave would kneel at the altar and receive his Host, his mind at peace until the next Day of Obligation.

IT WAS PAST NOON on Easter Saturday. Lent was over and Mary was preparing for Easter. The smell of baking pies filled the house. Cookies, cakes and spicy pies were cooling in the pantry and four golden loaves from white flour stood on the rack; now, all she had to do was bake a raisin bread, left to the last until the pans had cooled. She stood before the kitchen window patting the raised dough into rounded loaves...outside the sky was dark, and for an hour or more there had been sheets of drenching rain falling....

It wasn't fit for a man or beast to be out and yet advancing with great strides towards the house was a hatless figure and between the long strings of drenched hair she recognized Dave's tragic face. He bounded through the door without a knock or any sign of apology. He stood before Mary, his eyes deploring his affliction—he darted to the calendar and back again, his hands and fingers moving in grotesque gyrations, sounds sludged through his trembling lips.

When her first terror had passed, Mary stood waiting for her pounding heart to subside. Then she gently grasped Dave's arm and smiling, made him understand that he must calm himself if she were to understand what he was trying to tell her. Gradually the frenzy, the fire left his eyes and in place of fire were ashes, that spoke more eloquently than words for this soul's tribulation. By nudging Dave on slowly from one gesture to another Mary made out his story.

Lauchie had been celebrating the coming of Easter for a week, and he showed no signs of being sober for the solemnity of Easter—he was, at this very moment, fast asleep in the kitchen. Dave made frantic signs of blessing, and then pantomimed a priest standing over an open grave.... Dave believed that he would die physically as well as spiritually if he did not receive Communion on Easter Sunday!

Anger came over Mary like a torrent; she threw on her coat and ran to the barn to find Joe, but he had no comfort to give her.

"You'd better keep your nose out of it," he said. "Lauchie will think you have a hell of a nerve buttin' into his business. Can't you tell Dave something different?"

"I'm going back with Dave whether you come or not, come and see for yourself the state he's in."

"No, I'm not going," said Joe, without moving a step, "and I don't think you should either."

Joe understood the minds and the ways of his people better than Mary.

Next morning the worshippers had filled the altar rails again and again but among the last to come forwards was a swollen-faced and watery-eyed Lauchie and a smiling Dave.

9

The Raid on the Promised Land

IT WAS AN APRIL SUNDAY—a bright day with just enough crust on the snow to make good sledding—a perfect day, said Jim Douglas, to visit Lauchie MacTavish up the Settlement Road. The old folks had died a few years before, and the boys, all of them bachelors, had sent for Lauchie to come home. They wrote that there was nobody to look after "The Dummy," unless he'd come home and do it. Of course, it was only an excuse to get him home to look out for them all. But he did come, for the sake of his brother Dave, born deaf and condemned to a world of gestures and his own brand of sign language, though Dave was wiser and cannier than most of his brothers.

And now Lauchie was getting just like the rest of them, and just as likely not to get married. They were none of them much to look at.

Jim liked his Sundays with Mary and the kids. They gave him a break from the barn and a chance to tell her old stories about the Glen and its people. He knew she felt strange among them, an outsider among the women—and that she often found it easier to get along with the men. They all called her "the woman from away," until they got to know her. Then she was just Mary.

On their way to Lauchie's, they passed a splendid stand of pine and maple, the trees so huge and towering that Mary wondered aloud why they had never been cut.

The Woman from Away

"That's The Promised Land!" Jim chuckled.

"The Promised Land! What does that mean?" asked Mary, pleased at the prospect of another story, another piece in the history of her adopted community.

"Well," began Jim, equally pleased to tell the story. "For years there's been a running feud between the Beatons and the MacTavishes over that strip of land. It's maybe three generations ago that old man MacTavish was sent foolish by a fit of good humour—likely brought on by his latest brew. Anyhow, he announced that he was giving that strip as a bridal gift to his daughter Sarah, who was going to marry one of the Beaton boys. The wedding took place all right, but the girl died with her first baby. Old MacTavish then claimed that her death invalidated the transfer of the land. But Old Beaton claimed just as stubbornly that a gift was a gift.

"To add insult to injury, young Beaton took himself a new wife, Millie Doyle, an outsider from three glens away. Well, the Doyle girl was a little luckier. She had three boys, one right after the other, before she followed Sarah MacTavish to the grave. Poor Beaton was in rough straits. It was hard enough to find a wife, but three kids and his record—nobody at all would bite.

"The last straw was the sewing machine. The MacTavish girl took her sewing machine with her over the brush fence, but when she died, the sewing machine stayed over. Time after time, Old Man MacTavish claimed that since there was no woman in the Beaton house any more, they had no use for the sewing machine. But the machine stayed. With his dying breath, Old Man Beaton told his sons to keep it and lock it.

"Now, it's still in the place where she put it, locked up tight. But the key to it's lost. And there's The Promised Land. You see it yourself—virgin forest, wonderful trees that nobody'll cut because nobody'll agree on who owns them. It's kind of a legend here. But they share it. Now nobody cares so much who owns it. They run moonshine in it—often together."

Jim looked at his wife with a wry smile.

Mary laughed at the story. She liked her husband's tales about the old days. Usually he was too busy or too tired to talk at all. Sunday was her favourite day of the week.

WHEN JIM AND MARY ENTERED the MacTavish house, they nearly tumbled into a gaping hole in the kitchen floor. Lauchie's black head popped cheerfully out of it to greet them. "Take a chair," he said. "I'll be through an' up with ye in a minute. Jist after gittin' some potatoes fer beer."

His eyes were gleaming in a way that told its own story. In the Glen, there were three stages in drinking—"wasn't sufferin' any," "feelin' good," and "full." Lauchie wasn't sufferin' any.

Mary looked around. A queer thing on the table caught her eye. She picked it up. It looked like a home-made curry comb for an oversized grizzly. Rows of nails had been driven through a piece of wood about a foot long, and bristled savagely on the other side. She held it up to Jim in bewilderment.

"It's a scraper for potatoes," he whispered.

She looked more puzzled.

"Fer moonshine." Only his lips moved on his indrawn breath.

Lauchie's shoulders and torso followed his head up from the cellar. He heaved a bucket of potatoes onto the kitchen floor. Then he climbed up the ladder and covered the hole with a square of flooring. Satisfied that the hole was safe again, he picked up the bucket and sat down at the table.

"I got the 'credentials' at the Co-op yesterday," he said. "Dan and John drunk the last the day before, yeast and all, when I wass in town, and it still workin'. That near finished it." He waggled his head at Mary. "I wassn't gonna make any more, but then I like a little sip now and again, an' it costs too much to buy. Too bad ye didna git here a minute sooner." He slid his thumb up his finger, measuring the depth of a good drink, and grinned roguishly at them. "There wass that much left, but I jist finished it 'fore ye came in."

"When you make the run, could I watch?" Mary blurted, taking care not to look at Jim, who was confounded by her breach of good manners and rose red-faced and spluttering apologies for her. Women never went near a still, and men didn't ask to watch.

Lauchie seemed not to notice Jim's embarrassment. "Sure," he said. "Why not? Just hand me the scraper, would ye?"

He was about to drag a potato across the bristle of nails, when he stopped and grinned foolishly. "I s'pose I'd best rub some of the dirt off 'fore I do that," he said.

He went into the pantry and brought back a battered white enamel dishpan, half full of water. He threw in as many potatoes as the pan would hold, and washed them, without brush or cloth, sloshing the water like a miner panning for gold. When he finished them all, he picked up the scraper and this time scraped potato after potato until he had a bucket full of blackened pulp.

"Might as well git goin'," said Lauchie, picking up the bucket. "You bring the molasses, will ye, Jim?"

They followed him down behind the barn to a tiny clearing in the woods which was cut by a narrow, fast-moving brook. On its near bank stood a squat, thick barrel—empty. To the right of the barrel, a ring of dead ashes blackened the snow.

Lauchie started to gather kindling and wood for the fire.

"The dry stuff iss best," he said, dropping a heavy chunk that was too green. "Wet stuff makes a hell of a smoke. Hangs low over the trees. Like a black flag. Sign fer the Mounties to come checkin'."

Once the fire was blazing, Lauchie filled a big blackened pot with brook water and set it on a steel contraption that stretched across the fire between two rocks. The water was boiling in no time. Lauchie tipped the pot into the barrel, added the potato pulp, and tested the temperature of the mash on his wrist. It was right. He took five cakes of yeast from his pants pocket, crumbled them between his fingers, and dropped them into the mash. Then he crossed the clearing and brought back a sturdy maple branch, smooth and stained from frequent use. This he plunged into the barrel and stirred until the ingredients were well mixed. He poured in the black molasses and stirred again. Satisfied, he draped an old feed bag over the barrel and shovelled wet sand on the fire, stirring it well into the ashes. Then he arranged twigs and leaves over the barrel until it looked like a tree stump.

"There! Beer's set," he said proudly. "We'll move 'er into the stable tonight after dark. Keep 'er warm till she's done."

Lauchie ran a hand over his head. "Well," he said, "that's all we can do now for a week or ten days, till she quits workin'."

Mary and Jim left for home.

THE FOLLOWING SUNDAY, they were on the road before dawn. Lauchie had stopped by Saturday to say the beer was ready and he'd be doing the run about daybreak. The crust on the snow was still hard and the coral sunset of the evening before had promised a warm day. As they pulled the mare up at the MacTavish house, Dave darted from the door and jumped on the sleigh, grinning just like Lauchie. He gave the rein a sharp tug. The mare about-faced and retraced her steps to The Promised Land. Dave signalled to stop. Then he leaped from the sleigh to the edge of the road and poked around the sodden undergrowth.

Jim jumped out after Dave and searched the snow for tracks. He found none. Dave nervously checked up and down the road again and fished a long plank from the undergrowth. Then he grabbed Jim by the shoulder, pointed up and down the road, put his hand to his eyes, slapped Jim on the shoulder where an RCMP badge would be and marked out the position of the Mountie's strap. Jim understood his assignment exactly.

With another cautionary glance up and down the road, Dave picked up the plank. He laid the near end of it on top of a flat boulder, well above the snow at the edge of the road, then aimed the other end at a huge tree stump. Gently, his face full of sober concern, he let it down. Again he made worried signals. They understood. They had to walk along the plank—and very carefully.

"Taking no chances, are they?" said Mary.

"Gonna make damn sure no Mountie'll catch 'em," Jim answered. "Not by followin' their tracks into the woods, anyways."

Dave was as solemn in his care as a penitent receiving the last rites. They filed in behind him, obeying his urgent signals. As soon as they were across the plank, he positioned it again, while they stood waiting on another stump. Once more they stepped to the end of the plank, and once more Dave positioned it. And so they proceeded, again and again, until they were deep into the woods and completely screened from the road.

Dave grinned and pointed to a well-travelled path. Jim turned to follow it, but once more Dave seized his arm. Using both hands, he mimed the driving of a horse until Jim nodded his understanding. Then he swung his arm in the direction of the MacTavish house and pointed at the sun just rising over the dark trees. Jim nodded again as Dave turned in a circle until his arm pointed straight up, indicating that he would be back at noon. He grinned and pointed at the path into the woods. Then he picked up the plank, and left.

Jim and Mary hadn't far to go. Soon they smelled smoke, and shortly afterwards they saw the fire. It was in a clearing, quite a sizable clearing, but the thick woods and giant trees made it seem small. They saw Lauchie approaching the crackling fire with a bucket of water in either hand. He nodded, emptied the water into the barrel next to the fire, and turned to them.

"Ye didna have trouble understandin' Dave, did ye? Shoulda told ye the lay-out yesterday. I fergot."

He was making polite chat, and both Mary and Jim knew it. The location of any still was kept as secret as the sins of the confessional.

Harold Beaton came up behind Lauchie with two more buckets of water. He was unshaven and a little shaky. His Saturday night had not been dry, and his rumpled trousers looked slept in. But he nodded affably to Jim and Mary before he sloshed the water into the barrel. An unwritten law dictated that any man near a still had to take a hand in running it. Harold was familiar with his job and needed no instructions.

"John and Jim Beaton iss off gittin' dry wood," Lauchie grinned. "Wanna give a hand makin' some dough to plug them holes. More iss go in' up in steam than iss goin' down through the worm."

Both men set off towards the woods, leaving Mary to stare at the contraption over the fire. She had never seen its like. An old copper washboiler had been positioned on heavy steel bars. A round hole roughly six inches across had been cut in the centre of the lid. Soldered to this was what Jim had described as the collar, into which tapered a copper elbow. The fogs of steam escaping from the soot-blackened boiler made the contrivance look like a devil's cauldron.

Lauchie and Jim came back with fistfuls of flour and water dough. Steam was still rising from every joint. If Lauchie was going to save his moonshine, those leaks would have to be doughed up fast. Lauchie started patching the joints where the steam was escaping, and Jim kept handing him gobs of sticky dough, all the while joking over the number of cracks and holes that had to be patched.

"Ach! Well!" said Lauchie. "It iss good enough. There's so many cracks in it the Mounties'd be thinkin' it's only fit fer boilin' water in fer scaldin' hogs when yer butcherin'. Truth iss, it's hardly tight enough even fer that." His little eyes crinkled with laughter.

Mary stepped closer and peered into the water barrel. There the straight tubing narrowed to a one inch copper pipe that spiralled all the way down through the water. This was the coil or "worm" she'd been told about. The steam in the coil condensed as it wound through the cold water. Then it dripped from the bottom, where a hole had been bored in the barrel to allow the end of the coil to come out. A feed bag wrapped around the copper spout kept the barrel leak to a slow drip. Beneath the spout itself, a clear pungent liquid trickled steadily into a dipper that was filled to the brim and beginning to overflow.

"Lauchie, you'll lose some if you don't come quick," said Mary. "Should I empty it?" She was eager for a job.

Lauchie dropped the urgent task of doughing to pick up the full dipper. He replaced it with a handleless china cup, so that not a drop should be lost while he emptied the dipper into a gallon jug. Then, realizing that Mary had wanted to do it, he tried to make amends.

"Would ye be after tryin' it?" His eyes blinked merrily. "Ye first, Jim. And ye too, Mary. We've been havin' a little taste each time we changed the cup. T'iss not bad! Me grandfather got the recipe out of an old Temperance book, y'know."

"A book!" said Mary. "Imagine that! Would you bring it down to me sometime. I'd like to see it. This stuffs good!"

"Mary!" Jim shook his head. "Fer Pete's sake!"

"She iss jist kiddin'," chuckled Lauchie. "I'll bring it. I know jist where it iss. That's all right."

When the whole job was done, Lauchie held up a quart bottle half full of the last drops.

"Don't know what I'm botherin' to save this fer," he said. "It's a cinch I won't be usin' it."

"Why not, Lauchie?" Mary laughed, feeling warm from the moonshine.

"They're tailin's to start the next run with. But I won't be makin' it though. This batch'll do me." His speech was getting blurred, and he carefully placed the bottle beside the jug under a silver birch and eased himself down for another little sip.

Lauchie saw Dave coming into a clearing and shied like a skittish horse. He fumbled for the gallon jug, hastily stumbled to his feet, and stood in front of his brother grinning. Dave's eyes moved from one man to another with a grin of his own, then stopped on Mary. He clucked his tongue and drew circles at his temple with a forefinger. Everyone laughed heartily at the silent comment. Mary joined them.

Lauchie knocked the fixtures loose from the coil. Dave emptied the blackpot and took off with it in another direction. The fire was doused. Barrel, metal grill and buckets were whisked out of sight. When they started back to the sleigh, Lauchie had trouble walking straight; and he twice staggered off the path into the snow. Dave was frowning deeply by the time they reached the plank.

There, quick as a cat, Dave pounced on Lauchie and carried him, jug and all, across the first plank—and across every succeeding one. Lauchie's arms stopped flailing after the first. At last they were all in the sleigh. The snow between the road and the blackpot was still not cut.

A very dry and sober Lauchie kept his promise and brought Mary the Temperance book later that week. It was very old, its faded green cover marked and ringed. But there, on page twelve, right after a sermon on the perils of tobacco, wine and ribaldry, was a complete guide to the distillation of hard liquor from molasses and potatoes. Mary had been the first woman in The Promised Land, indeed the only one to see a "run." And then Lauchie said he was "going on the wagon."

THE STILL WAS PASSED OVER to Lauchie's brother John, who looked enough like "The Dummy" to be a twin, but lacked his sense. John calculated that the washboiler wasn't big enough for what he had in mind, so he went to Mac, the blacksmith in the next village, and got him to rig up a forty-five-gallon steel drum. Together they cut a round hole in the top and soldered the connecting parts steam tight. Both were "full" when the job was done, and Mac lurched home to his wife. The "pay" he'd accepted was sweeter going down than coming up; and for two days he cradled his head, while his wife scrubbed up the messes and railed at his stupidity and the evils of moonshine.

Lauchie was giving Jim Douglas a day at the threshing when John borrowed his horse and wagon to cart the drum the twelve miles to The Promised Land. On the way home, he picked up enough yeast cake and molasses to start his business. John was figuring his profit and counting the friends he could expect as customers as he let the horse carry him home. His figuring ignored the blacksmith's wife, who had watched his retreating shape with taut lips.

Lauchie grinned when Jim said cautiously, "He's into a hornet's nest there. She's death on liquor. She'd squeal in a minute."

"He took my rig t'git that damn drum. They'll all be thinkin' now it's me that owns it." Lauchie stuck a straw between his teeth and chewed. "I s'pose we'd be obliged to warn him though."

"Too bad he won't ever give a fella a sip," said Jim.

"He iss meanin' t'sell it." Lauchie's voice was dry.

ONE SOGGY DAY that September, in spite of the clay that clogged the wheels of every moving vehicle to their hubs, a Mountie turned at the crossroads and slogged his way down the Settlement Road. Twice in a week, he braved the deepening ruts, and both times he stopped to talk to Jim Douglas.

"What did he want?" asked Mary.

"Nothing much," said Jim.

"Well, I hope he got it then."

"I don't know if he did or not," Jim chuckled.

The next day Jim took Mary and Lauchie to town for groceries and got the truck stuck to its axles in mud.

"Damn it all!" he growled. "The Mountie got through yesterday."

"Yiss?" Lauchie cocked a curious eyebrow. "And what time was that, Jim?"

"Two—maybe three o'clock."

"We thought he might be looking for John's blackpot," said Mary.

"The slink!" Lauchie grinned, then frowned.

The men were collecting stones to put under the truck's tires.

"When I can't get through with the truck," Jim fumed, "I don't see how he made it with that car of his, and it so low."

"They got good cars," said Lauchie. "The best they make."

"Ye'd best tell John, so he'll know."

"*Y* can't talk t' John. Too pig-headed. Y'know how he iss. Jist rollin' his makin's and smokin', and doin' whatever suits him. Never givin' a thought to the Mounties bein' after 'im."

"Tell 'im anyways," said Jim.

"I had an idea something wass up," said Lauchie, collecting more rocks. "Dave wass gabblin' somethin'. Thought he seed tracks at the gate, but I figured he wass seein' things. Musta been that Mountie. Wass there just one in the car?"

"I couldn't see very good." Jim was cursing the road and the mud. "But I think there was only one."

"I wonder what took 'im up." Lauchie pondered, shoving another rock under the wheel. "Ye didna see 'im go back?"

"Damn well, he didn't come back over this road." Jim was furious and getting muddier by the minute. "We'll have to cut a pole to lever up that axle if we're gonna git out today."

By the time the truck was under way again, both men were mud-caked to the knees, and splattered all over. Only the back of Jim's shirt was the clean blue plaid he'd set out in that morning. Neither man had forgotten the Mountie.

WHEN THEY GOT BACK FROM TOWN, Lauchie went home on foot, and Jim went to the barn to check on a cow that was due to freshen. He heard the grumble of a motor and ran to the dung window to get a clearer view of the car and its driver. The Mountie, confident as a rooster, was managing the ruts, but with less ease than before. Jim could hear the tires growling. He snickered quietly to himself as he went back to shovelling the stable.

In the house, Mary was getting supper ready and feeding the children; but she too was watching the road and saw the Mountie's car come struggling through the mud.

When Jim came in to eat, he said, "That fella'll be stuck before long, and he'll be after help from the MacTavishes—or me. A little more mud on my clothes mightn't be a bad investment fer him to leave us be."

After supper, Jim waited expectantly for a knock. He read the paper while Mary darned mitts.

Outside, the night was black as a hobo's pocket. No sound broke the rain's steady rumble.

"Let's go to bed, Mary," Jim said at nine o'clock.

Upstairs Mary lay half awake, listening to the rain and her husband's snoring. Suddenly she heard pounding on the door.

Startled, she looked at the time. Ten o'clock! Who would drag people from their beds at this hour?

She nudged Jim. He stopped snoring and rolled over. She got out of bed and ran down the stairs.

A harsh voice stabbed the night.

"Open up! I'm the RCMP. My car's stuck up the road and I want Mr. Douglas to pull me out."

Jim came running down the stairs in his sock feet, still buttoning his fly.

"Be with you soon's I get my coat," he called out. To Mary, he whispered, "I figured he'd get stuck, but at the last, I thought he must've made it or got the MacTavishes to give 'im a hand."

It was three hours before Jim came back.

"Where was he stuck?" asked Mary.

"In a bog up between here and Lauchie's. He said he'd been stuck there the whole time."

"Did he mention his business?"

"Somethin' about a report there'd been sheep stealin'.

Balls! Nobody up there with sheep!"

"What a night to be stuck so long!"

"Must be hellish anxious to get that blackpot—if that's what he's after. Said the Department would pay me and asked me how much. Then 'fore I could git a word out, he said they only paid three dollars, and that I'd get a cheque." Jim was peeved. "I wouldn't turn out this time o' night for ten dollars, but what can ye do? Law says you have to help 'em."

"Did you get the money?"

"NO! I have to sign a paper."

"Where was the bog he was stuck in?"

"Up by The Promised Land."

"The Promised Land! The cheapskate! You were gone three hours in this downpour!"

"I know! I know! Let's go to bed."

TWO DAYS LATER, the Mountie was back, on foot, looking for Jim's signature. He stayed for an hour at the barn. Mary watched him from the window waving his hands. He looked to bc talking about ruts and car wheels, and all the while Jim held the paper, ready to sign. Then she saw him take the pen and the paper from Jim and walk away. Later Jim told her that he never once mentioned the MacTavishes or the Beatons or the stolen sheep.

Jim Beaton and Lauchie drove up at sunset with the mare and wagon. They were on the way to pick up their mail, and offered to get Mary's and Jim's too.

"Mountie was here agin today." Jim told the whole story. "He's after John, sure'n hell. Ye better tell 'im."

"I told 'im already, and he won't do nothin' but smoke." Lauchie leaned back on the kitchen chair. "Too cocky, he iss. Says he'll not get caught in the rain, 'cause the roads iss too muddy fer the Mounties nor nobody else t'git through."

"Well, I'm tellin' ye," put in Jim Beaton, "there's somethin' in them woods. I could tell by the mare. When we come by, she jumped and shied t' the other side of the road. Jenny don't git scared like that fer nothing." His head snapped down, forcing his chin even further into the folds of loose skin above his collar. "That Mountie is up in them woods right now."

"John's makin' noises 'bout doin' a run in the morning." Lauchie looked worried. "I told him t' leave it alone. Jist not t' go near at all. Tellin's iss one thing. What he'll do iss another. He's got big ideas, and it's hard t' change his mind."

"Well," said Mary, "tell him about this. That Mountie's after John, and he won't stop till he gets him. You never got so much attention before, not from the Mounties."

"He's determined all right," Jim agreed, shaking his head. A grin was starting to twitch at the corners of his mouth. "Reminds me of Father Murphy. Remember him, Lauchie?"

"Remember him!" Lauchie laughed aloud. "It's me that does."

"He used to be at yer place a lot. Ever catch you?"

"Oh, yeh!" Lauchie was enjoying himself. "Came out once with—what's his name, now?" He snapped his fingers as if to pluck the name from the air. "You know his name, Jim. The Mountie—"

"Lynch?" offered Jim.

"That's him! Lynch! Drove up one Sunday, and the yard full of rigs. Yer old man was there, and mine too."

"And did he git anything?"

"Noooooo! Everything got cleaned up the minute we seed 'em turnin' in the gate. They couldna find even a smell. When they wass leavin' the Father told me—'Yer not foolin' me, Lauchie, I'll get ye yet!' But he never did."

The men laughed.

"Remember old Lexie MacQuarrie?" asked Jim.

Lauchie looked puzzled.

"Lived up on the ridge. Remember? Her husband was Angus, and they had a whole raft o' kids."

"Yiss, yiss," Lauchie grinned. "I remember them now."

"And did ye hear what she told Father Murphy about Angus's blackpot?"

"Must've heard. Yiss, I remember somethin'. But what was it?"

"Father Murphy went to the house and old Lexie came to the door. Him and the Mountie'd been searchin' the woods lookin' fer Angus's blackpot. Lexie knew about them bein' on the farm soon's they set foot on the place. When the Father asked where Angus was, she said she didn't know. Then the nosey old bugger up and asked her right out, 'Well, where's Angus's blackpot, then?' Old Lexie, she didn't care fer nothin' y'know. She jist said—'*Ye* wanna see Angus's blackpot, Father? Well, then! Whatta ya know!' An' she put on that awful grin, whirled around, bent down, her skirt clean over her head, and stuck her big fat arse right in his face. 'There's Angus's blackpot fer ye, Father!' "

The men laughed aloud, then fell silent.

"Ah, yiss," Jim Beaton chuckled. "Yiss, yiss, I remember now."

"Anyways, I told John," said Lauchie. "And if the stubborn mule won't be payin' no mind at all, I can't help it."

"But he will when you tell him about tonight," said Mary.

"Nothin' he can do," said Jim. "If the Mountie's there now."

"No, not much," Lauchie spoke up quickly. "But I'm gonna tell 'im strong to let that beer alone—stay away altogether. It iss all worked out, ye know, and ready to run. John iss after braggin' about the money he iss gonna make. By God!" Lauchie jumped to his feet. "He might be tryin' to run 'er now."

"But how did the Mountie get up in the woods?" asked Mary. "His car didn't come by here."

Nobody said a word, but Lauchie's agitation worsened.

"We best git a move on," he said, pacing to the door. "Maybe John'll git wise if he knows he iss headin' fer a trap. Maybe it's not too late to talk some sense into 'im."

Jim saw them to the yard, and returned. "We'd best git to

bed ourselves," he said to Mary. "Lauchie wants to be in town early in the morning."

"In town for what? He just got groceries."

"Lauchie's cagey enough," Jim chuckled. "He's gonna give John a real strong warning tonight. But he ain't gonna be there to git nabbed in the morning. That Mountie's likely found the drum with the mash in it. Can't hide a thing that size, even in The Promised Land. Lauchie figures the Mountie's been watchin' fer around a week now. But he's got to catch somebody red-handed 'fore he can lay any kind of charge that'll stick."

"Why?" asked Mary.

"Because the way it stands, that mash could be the Beatons' or the MacTavishes' or anybody's at all. He'll not be able to prove a thing until he catches somebody tryin' to run it."

LAUCHIE AND JIM SET OFF for town before sunrise the next morning. At about nine-thirty the sun weakened, the sky grayed, and cold air blew in. Flakes of snow spiralled silently down until the sodden earth was covered. September was early for snow. It would be a long winter. Mary kneaded her bread and stared out the window as the heavy flakes levelled the fields, and the little brown hillocks whitened into strange mushrooms.

Her hand was raised to give the dough a final slap when she saw him—bounding towards the house. John MacTavish! His thin hair, matted with snow, fell in a fringe from forehead to twisted lips. His drenched clothes outlined his bones. His reddened hands jerked like flippers by his sides. He threw himself into the kitchen and leaned against the door gasping.

"Where iss Jim?" His voice cracked with terror and cold.

"In town with Lauchie," Mary's voice was calm and soothing. "They went early. I'm expecting them back any minute. But John, where's your coat and cap? You must be chilled to the heart. Sit down, and I'll make you some tea."

"Did ye see the Mountie go up?" John stayed standing.

"No!" said Mary, too loudly. "Is he up there?"

"He iss! I seed him through the window! Goin' into the barn carryin' the worm on his arm."

"Well, how did you get away? Weren't you with Dave? Did you leave Dave on his own? Where is Dave?" Mary's own voice cracked—with concern for Dave being left on his own and his mute attempts to deal with the Mountie's questions.

"Dan iss with him. Dan wouldna wake up. So I runned out the front door and comed through the woods. I thought Jim might be home and drive me somewheres."

Mary made him sit at the table and gave him tea.

Just then Jim's truck went past.

"There they go now," said Mary. "I wonder why they didn't stop for tea. Lauchie usually does."

"I gotta git outa here fast," squeaked John, jumping up and slopping tea on his shirt.

"Oh, sit down now. What would a Mountie want here?"

John tried the tea again, but he couldn't stop shaking.

Again they heard Jim's motor.

"There's the truck, now," cried Mary, relieved.

John jumped so suddenly he sent the cup flying across the table.

"I hafta git outa here." His face was ashen.

"It's stopped at the gate!" said Mary. "There's something the matter. Here! Get out the back—take this cap and jacket."

She closed the back door on John, just as Jim came in the front. He was out of breath.

"Where's John? Is he here?"

"No! Not now. What's wrong? Did you run into the Mountie?"

"Yes!" Jim dashed to the window. "If John is anywhere around, get him the hell out. I know he came here. His tracks are plain as day. Can't think why the Mountie didn't spot 'em. He's in the truck now. Gotta take him back to the station. And the evidence with him."

"But what ev—?"

Jim waved off Mary's question.

"Told him I had to let you know where I was goin'. Tell ye about it later. Gotta go! He'll be gettin' suspicious. He's hellish cranky now."

JIM CAME BACK AT ONE O'CLOCK, and Lauchie joined him minutes later to mourn the day's mishaps. Gloomy over their failures, they needed to commiserate.

The Mountie, disguised in muddy wet mechanic's overalls and thoroughly peeved, had been waiting hidden inside the barn when Jim, hurrying back from town, drove up with Lauchie in the truck.

"What's your name?" he'd snarled at Lauchie, jerking open the door and thrusting his unshaven face into the cab.

"What iss it to ye?" Lauchie snarled back. "What the hell's yer own name? And what's yer business in my barn?"

"That's not for you to question." The stranger was cocky, sure of his ground, demanding answers. "Where have you been?"

"Who in hell d'ye think ye are?" Lauchie's rising fury propelled him from the cab to stand facing the trespasser, fists curled.

"I am Constable Charles Adams of the RCMP, and I am looking for John MacTavish to arrest him." The Mountie spoke stiffly, biting off each word. His lips were blue. His outrage would have been obvious to a blind man. The legal situation was also obvious, but it had to be stated.

"What iss the charge?" Lauchie'd decided to tough it out.

"Distillation of liquor for the purpose of sale." The Mountie held up the coil and the bottle of tailings that had been in the barn for months.

"I knew we wass licked the minute I seed that bottle." Lauchie was shaking his head sorrowfully, unable to believe his bad luck. "Remember?" he turned to Mary. "I left 'er in the barn on the windowsill. Never went near ’er after the spring. Got too busy with the farm.”

Mary nodded.

“He got the little funnel that joins the worm and the arm,” said Jim. His voice was gloomy as Lauchie’s. “Found it in Dan’s pocket. He was asleep. Seized it fer evidence.”

“But the damnedest thing of all wass—he took my horse and wagon! He asked whose it wass. I said it wass mine and he seized it. Said it wass evidence.” Lauchie’s outrage was muted by the defeat in his voice. “He jist did that to be dirty!”

“How could he connect your rig to the mash? You weren’t even home when he was searching?” Mary spoke with unusual heat.

“Last thing I told John ’fore I left the house wass to stay away from that rig,” Lauchie muttered. “I knew that Mountie wass around, an’ more ’n likely he’d spotted the place already. But, no, John iss too smart, y’know. He gits Dan to hitch up my horse—MY HORSE!—and take Dave with ’im to move the mash. Wouldna go hisself—sent them. Now there iss a man fer ye! The Mountie’d been watchin’ the mash all week—waitin’ fer it t’ finish workin’.”

“Dan was caught too?” Mary gasped.

“Yi—sss!” Lauchie’s hiss told Mary that Dan had been drunk. So blissfully drunk that he hadn’t known what was going on.

“I hit every bump between here and town,” said Jim. “But do ye think that arm or worm’d move. Oh no! Any other time, everything on the back would be flyin’ into the woods. Not this time. He’s got the evidence!”

“But, Jim, how did he get up there?” Mary was bewildered, and her questions tumbled out. “He never came by here after the night he got stuck and you got him free. And where was his car that you had to drive him to town?”

“He was in a sleepin’ bag in The Promised Land the whole damn week. That night he said he was investigatin’ the complaints about the sheep stealin’. Well, he was stuck in the bog just below where the little river runs across the road from The Promised Land. And he was sayin' likely whoever stole the sheep had gone up the river with them.

"Well, I knew he was tryin' to put one over on me, beingst I knew nobody up here had any sheep. So I just said that the thief would have a long way to go, since there wasn't a soul livin' near the river between here and Cromarty, and that's twenty miles up. That guff about sheep-stealin'! And it the middle o' the night in a downpour! But I shoulda been sharper.

"I never figured with all the rain that the river'd be high enough fer him to drive up to Cromarty and float a dinghy down to The Promised Land. It never got that high before, near as I can remember. But down he came with a little pup tent and a sleepin' bag, and enough grub to last him the week. He had lots o' time to look around. I never in my life seen a Mountie that determined before."

"My horse and wagon?" Two deep lines furrowed Lauchie's forehead. "I had no part in it. Can he seize my horse and wagon?"

"I wouldn't think so," said Jim. "But I don't know."

THE LAWYER IN TOWN knew well enough. Transporting Illegal Intoxicating Beverage was the offence. Dan was charged; Dave was too, though there was little chance of making him appear in court. Lauchie got a doctor's letter excusing him, just to make certain.

The Mountie got a conviction.

The blacksmith's wife wasn't summoned. John had disappeared, and she could testify only against him.

The horse and wagon were sold. Lauchie bought them back, but that was small comfort.

Jim got the forty-five-gallon drum, John's blackpot, and had it sawn in half. One half he used for watering calves; the other, for butchering hogs.

And so the matter ended—but not without lasting echoes. Another legend had been born. The MacTavishes made no more "runs."

John left the Glen and never came back. Mary wondered about the truth in the superstition that women around a still bring bad luck. And for years, the week of John MacTavish's blackpot, the week the Mountie had watched the still from his sleeping bag, remained a landmark for people to date happenings from. A kind of A.D.

The Year of Drought in The Promised Land.

10

The Day the Men Went to Town

WINTER WAS ANGRY even by Island standards. Ever since the first flurry of snowflakes in November, the winds had been busy shifting the drifts into strange shapes and forms, but it wasn't until after Christmas that winter really began. I hardly took the time to tie my shoes in the morning before rushing to the window to see what new pictures the night winds had drawn.

It was barely dawn and already Jim had shovelled his way out of the house, cut a path to the barn, the chicken house, the toilet and to the spring. In places the drifts had been higher than a man's head.

Jim sat now, taking long draughts of tea and staring at the list of groceries I had left on the table.

"Best get your pencil and start cutting," he said. There was no trace of resentment in his voice. "The Beatons and Lauchie must be out o' groceries, and your list will fill a whole sleigh."

"I can't cut much," I said, picking up the pencil.

"We'll have to have flour—a hundred pounds, then with the potatoes and vegetables I canned we won't go hungry—as long as the meat holds out...we're out of baking powder...I can cut the rolled oats...lard? I suppose I could render some of the fat off the salt pork...matches...both kinds of soap...the dry beans can be halved, macaroni too. Ten pounds of sugar won't last for long, but I suppose it will have to do...salt...I can't cut any more. Heaven alone knows when you'll get out again. I'd better put tobacco and the papers down too, or you'll forget them." I pencilled in "one bag of candy," Jim could put that in his pocket. Jim never forgot to bring candy for the children, still it wouldn't do any harm to remind him.

"Bells!" said Jim jumping up from the table. "They're coming. On this of all days they have to come early. Must've started at midnight."

"Why are you in such a dither? Don't they always come early?"

"Yeh! But I ain't got that end of the road open yet."

"So what! They're early, you're late. There's no harm done."

"That ain't the point! I DIDN'T GET THE ROAD OPEN YESTERDAY!"

Jim's face was flushed with anger. "Time I got through with that whore of a shovel it was milking time."

"But there was a storm—you had a good excuse. They didn't come down on account of the storm."

"Cut it out, Mary, will ye!"

Yesterday had been a bad day. The blizzard had lasted for nearly two days. The temperature had fallen to five below zero. Jim had managed to cut a path to the spring to water the animals when the trouble started. The first bit of the shovel went deep into four feet of snow that covered the spring, but when he tried to pull it out heaped with snow, the handle broke just where it joined the spoon. Frost had made the wood brittle. By the time he had taken the stub out, taped the handle and set it back in the spoon, it had been time to feed the animals and clean the stables. It was too late to start opening the road. Jim had been ferocious. His hands had been stiff with cold, his frozen mitts had stuck to the metal shovel.

"Jim! Look! Harold's mare is in a drift," I shouted from the window. "They're all around him."

"Jesus! Jesus!" said Jim, fumbling with his jacket. "The only day in a month I missed opening the road, they have to come early. I'll be the shit of the Glen after this."

"Cut it out, Jim. A person would think the world was coming to an end all because you didn't open the road. Tell them about Silver. They'll not think it's your fault...."

"NO! They'll know damn well it IS my fault. Where's me mitts? It would have to be on MY stretch of road. Hurry! 'Fore they'll be telling everyone I sat in the house and wouldn't give them a hand!"

It was only last week that Silver had buried herself in a drift. I had never seen a frightened animal before. I watched the little mare writhe, her body covered with foam. I saw the spasms that shook her withers and her eyes full of tears. We took Silver home and led her into her stall. Billows of steam rose from her body; her eyes rolled with hysterics as Jim tenderly rubbed her down. I stood beside her talking gently into her ear as I stroked her foaming neck. It seemed hours before the drops of saliva stopped flowing—drops that turned to ice pellets before reaching the ground. Then we covered her with a blanket and bedded her down. Ever since that day I knew Jim would be reluctant to take Silver out after a storm.

Jim was running down the yard. Harold had calmed the mare with his petting. Jim started shovelling like a madman. In a few minutes the mare was free, and the little procession turned up the short road into the yard. Harold Beaton came first leading his pigeon-toed Queenie, straining at the huge stump hooked to the "swing" that packed the snow down hard and cleared a wider path than a log would have done. Queenie was the best snow horse on the Settlement Road because she was wise enough to stop and wait for Harold to shovel her out when the snow was too deep. Close behind her came Jennie, Joe Beaton's much-loved mare. Small, black, sway-backed, she drew a long log wrapped in logging chains. Last of all came Lauchie's big grey mare. Head up, nostrils flaring, proud and haughty, as though she pulled the fanciest of carriages instead of a homemade wood sleigh. "Them wood-sleds! Coldest things on earth. I'd be warmer walkin' in me shirt sleeves than bundled up riding on one o' them," Jim always said.

The men would be looking for tea! I prodded and turned the damp sticks in the range, trying to coax them to burn. I put out the cups and saucers and cut the bread. They were putting Jennie in the stable. Lauchie and Harold Beaton took their horses to the fence, tied and blanketed them there. "They must be taking two sleighs today," I said to myself.

The men pushed open the door and lumbered over to the stove. They took off their mitts and stood rubbing their hands in what little warmth they could find. There was little to distinguish the three men. Their long-billed caps with the fur-lined ear flaps hung over the collars of their jackets and their heavy woolen trousers ballooned out over their tightly laced boots like sausages.

"Devil take this place," said Jim as he closed the door behind him. "No phone, no lights, no plow, no nothin'.... Nova Scotia, the place God forgot!" Jim clasped his lips together as if he dared anyone to defy him.

"That's not true, Jim! The place God REMEMBERS is more like it. Next winter we'll have the plow. I've written to the Minister and to the engineer, and we'll have electric light and a telephone too, you'll see."

"That'll be the day!" said Jim, throwing off his coat.

"Breaking roads, now that all them farms is empty," said Lauchie, trying to cover up for my breach of good manners in "answering back" my husband. "Takes all a man's time in winter."

"They have to be opened," said Harold. "A single track anyway's, else it's 'good-bye.'"

"Going to town is an all-day job, all right," added Joe Beaton, taking his place at the table. "Even when there is a track." The men ate and drank in silence.

"Thank ye for the tea, Mary," said Lauchie, pushing back his chair and crossing over to the back door where their dripping jackets hung on a row of nails. He turned to Joe Beaton. "Ye be after going on my sleigh, Joe?"

"Me? Naw, I'll wait down at Dougall's. Harold'll be needin' a hand when he gets back. Thought I'd wait there."

Jim stopped and turned to me as he buttoned up his coat. "I don't know when we'll be back. Never mind the stables." Then he followed the men out and closed the door behind him. Jim knew, and I knew, that the stables would be cleaned before he returned.

I HOPE THERE WON'T BE ANY CALLERS. I have so much work to do and the day will be gone so quickly. The sun is a stranger most days now and it is a shame to miss a good day's drying. Will I ever be able to get the big wash and Sonny's diapers done as well? Not with all the outside chores...still I must try. It is a blessing that Joe Beaton is going to spend the day at Dougall's and not here, in my kitchen like he usually does. I hate washing diapers in front of a bachelor. How many times have I had to gather everything up in a rush and hide them in the pantry—any place to get them out of sight, when one of the Beatons or MacTavishes calls unexpectedly.

How shocked my sisters would be if they could see me now! A pile of dirty diapers on the floor—and they aren't all diapers either; many are pieces of worn-out undergarments salvaged from the ragbag. My crooked old washtub standing on two chairs facing each other, seats touching. The family chamber pot in the centre of the room ready for the diapers after their first rough wash.

I put the washboard in the tub, then half fill a smaller tub with cold water, carry it over to the stove and pour in boiling water from the kettle. I balance it carefully on the edge of the stove and test the water with the other hand. It is just hot enough. Then I put it down beside the chamber pot and I kneel down. The little ones are playing quietly now in the other room, thank God! I wonder if Lauchie and the Beatons will stay the night? It will depend on how early they get back. If they stay, there will be four for cards and I won't have to play. I don't care much for playing cards, I'd rather watch, and when the time comes for tea I won't have to jump up between dealings to get things ready, or to keep the fire going. It's nice having company though. I get tired listening to the radio every night...the batteries are nearly gone, too...I'll have to order new ones on the budget plan...the bill at the store is too high to add any luxuries...if the weather doesn't break soon so that Jim can get into the woods for pit timber the store might stop our credit...but if the weather changes we'll be all right. God is good! How pretty Anne looked in her pink blouse...I was right... the colour brought out the pink in her complexion. "Pink wouldn't look right with her red hair," Clemmie said. But what does she know? Anne has the roundest, the bluest eyes I've ever seen... they dance with mischief and make you want to be a part of her fun—her laughter...Anne loves everything and every one... and Sonny is so smart! Talking already...walking and running everywhere...no single steps for him...no single words either...from the very first it had been sentences...he is wise beyond his years, and it shows in his grey eyes...his little face must be startling to strangers...Sonny is so different from other children.

I get up and stretch, to relieve the strain from crouching on the floor for so long. I'll have to dry some of the diapers on the line over the stove. I pick up the little tub of brown smelly water and carry it over to the door. I don't bother to put on my coat. It will only take a few seconds to throw the water out into the snow. That done, I pick up the big kettle of boiling water and stagger over to the tub. I pour the water, slowly at first, so as not to splatter and scald myself. I don't really mind washing, it gives me a kind of buoyance. I can feel the rhythm of the rubbing on the washboard... and my hands bobbing in and out of the water—it feels like part of a dance. The slapping together of the wet clothes, the swirling movement of the water, and the splatter of large drops when I lift a garment to cool, sounds like rain on a stagnant pool. I wish my back wouldn't ache so, and why should streaks of pain dart into my shoulders? No suds! And after using a whole bar of soap! The water is silent and dead; even with a tub of hot water I can't get a single bubble, the water is so hard.

I watch the last drop fall from the diaper; I twist it and stack it on the chair like cord wood. I swish my hand round in the water. There is nothing left to wash; my hand catches the side of the tub. That place is dangerous. Tubs don't last long around here. There are too many uses for them—Saturday night's baths, the washing and butchering. Jim had used this one to catch the entrails of a steer he butchered for Christmas. That is when it got bent. It will have to last until spring.

I don't know when the silence started. All at once everything is stifled, smothered, as if there had been a fall of goosefeathers so thick that I can't breathe. Silence in a house with children? That means mischief. I had learned that long ago. I kick off my slippers and tiptoe to the door and peer in. There they are, the two of them, sitting on the floor close to the back wall; sitting in a circle of pieces of wallpaper—Anne's little hand grasping a frayed end still clinging to the wall and gently ripping it off the plaster board. I wanted to burst out laughing. Spanking them is hard but I have to do it or we won't have any paper left on the walls. I didn't really hurt them and they soon forget all about it and go on playing with their toys.

It had been fun to wash at home in Montana where clothes

came out of the water gleaming white, but how can I get clothes white when the water is brackish and there isn't enough of it? Jim warned me to go easy because the water hole is going dry. He doesn't think there will be enough for the cows for another week, and Clemmie told me that she remembers when the people who used to live here had to take the cows down to the spring near the river in cold weather—and that is a whole mile away. The snow had to be cleared away before the cattle could reach the water and then someone had to stand by until they had finished drinking. Sometimes if a heavy frost followed a thaw, the cows couldn't cross the ice to get near enough to the spring to drink.

THANK HEAVENS! Only the rinsing to be done. I stretch my back again. What was that? A racket in the barn? It's noon already. No wonder the cows are complaining. All animals make a fuss when they are thirsty. I had better take a look. They'll have to wait for their hay until I feed the children and settle them down for their nap.

I put on my coat and rubbers and run down the yard. I throw open the door to the cow stable and brace it to the wall with a big stick, and step inside. It isn't until my eyes have grown accustomed to the half-darkness that I can see the burning eyes not two feet away. The bull! He must have broken out of his stall. And there he is standing behind the cows with a length of frayed rope round his neck. I can feel a constriction in my throat. My mouth is dry. I can't speak. I can't move. My senses come back slowly. I feel the pounding of my heart. Slowly I step back into the open doorway and quickly kick the prop aside and slam the door. What am I to do? I can't leave him there. Most of the cows are heavy with calf; they are wrenching at their chains, trying to free themselves. What can I do? I must try to get him back into his own stall beside Silver and across the threshing floor. I'll have to get behind him. But how? The only way is to crawl through one of the cows' feeding bins. Making sure that the door is secure, I run over to the "little people's door" cut in the big double doors that are only opened for the haymaking. The bull hears me and turns. Then he stands still and glares at me for a moment before pawing the gutter. Oh, God! Joe Beaton has stabled Jennie in the stall beyond Silver's, and if the bull passes his own stall and Silver's and reaches the mare, he'll gore her or she'll kick at him. Jennie'll kick at anything. She even kicks the boards of her own stall for want of something to do. I'll have to build a barricade of some kind to stop the bull passing his own stall, that is, if I can get him back that way at all.

There's a pile of old boards that Jim has left stacked in the corner. I pull out board after board. Thank goodness! Some of them are long enough to stretch from the wall to the end of the stall. But how am I going to support the boards? There is nothing but an old puncheon. I push and haul the puncheon over and use it as a brace. I slant some of the boards so that they slide in between the rails of the bull's stall. Perhaps the puncheon will keep them in position. It's heavy enough. Jennie is getting restive now, pulling at her halter and stamping her feet. Then she kicks with both of her hind legs. The beating of hooves against the walls of her stall sounds like thunder, but my barricade holds in spite of the shaking posts that anchor them. Now I'll have to reach the far side of the bull. How can I manage that? I could go outside and climb in through the little dung window...crawl through on my belly and then drop to the floor. No! I couldn't do that! There's another way. I can crawl through into a feeding bin in front of one of the cows, slide past her to reach the gutter. I walk down the length of the barn, passing each cow. Which stall shall I try? Star's? Poor gentle Star. Jim says she's so gentle that "she'd feel terrible if she even bumped ye!"

I open the clapper and look in. There's Star, but her eyes are now fiery and her nose so huge that a piece of paper couldn't be squeezed past. Perhaps I can get past one of the calves. Their horns are shorter. I run down to the other end of the barn. A pitchfork would be useful! I had better take it along. I can use it to drive the bull—if I ever reach him. I open a clapper to the calves' stall. Calves these animals might be, but they are spring calves, half grown, and now they look as big as elephants. I drop the clapper and look at my watch. The men have only been gone a few hours, and it might be seven or eight o'clock before they get back. I lift the clapper again. "Talk! Talk! Talk!" I say to myself. It will keep your teeth from chattering...take a deep breath...stand still until you stop shaking. Now! Open the clapper, stick the fork through first... leave the handle sticking out so that it will hold the lid up a little...now, first one leg...that's it...up and over...now bend down and put your head in. Quick! Squeeze your body through...hold your breath... there isn't much room but the calf's as far over as he can get...he looks frightened...he's in shock...but watch him... watch him. Why didn't I put the button on the clapper to hold it up...too late now... MOVE...keep going...look out! The calf! He's coming out of shock...quick...grab the fork...hold it before his eyes...go on...go on...the other foot...keep looking at the calf...he's getting bolder...he's getting MAD! Hurry! Hurry! Your feet are dangling...what's caught? Oh, Lord! His eyes are rolling now... I can't move...it must be my coat...take your mitts off...they're too thick, darned too much...I can't feel anything...the calf is edging nearer...Oh, God! If only this awful noise would stop...my hands will have to work...all those cows bellowing like cattle driven to the stockyards back home...that's got it! I'm free! Oh...the fork is stuck in a board...my weight must have driven it in...it's jammed... the calf is coming nearer....

I can't remember how I pulled the fork free and got through the stall. My memory didn't start working again until I found myself in the gutter with the bull. As soon as I passed him the calf started a wild twisting tantrum, pulling at his halter and roaring. Another second and he would have killed me. Now Daisy is frisking! I should have remembered that Daisy was due. It was she who brought the bull over. If only I had remembered I could have left the door opened, untied Daisy and driven the two of them out into the yard. They wouldn't have bothered anyone. It's too late now, I can never crawl back past that calf.

Holding the fork before me I inch my way along the gutter behind the twisting bellowing cows. The bull turns his head and looks at me. I jab the fork straight at his rump. He jumps and turns to face me. I jab again, this time at the neck, but in order to get a straight jab, I have to back into Daisy's stall because of the length of the fork handle. Daisy is incensed and lashes out with her hind leg. I feel pain tear through my knee...again I strike the bull. Slowly and very independently he turns and moves forward in the direction of his stall. Once he starts, he keeps going until he reaches the treadway at the end of the barn and without prompting turns onto the threshing floor. I follow close behind, jabbing him every now and then to keep him moving.

Reaching the centre of the threshing floor, he becomes aware of the space around him, or perhaps because he doesn't like being pushed around, he turns suddenly and faces me. Fortunately the manure shovel stands within my reach. I grab it with my left hand and by holding it near the heavy end I find I can manage the fork in one hand and the shovel in the other. Still jabbing with the fork I raise the shovel before the bull's eyes...he moves forward... I sidestep...he moves forward...I jab again...I don't want to give him time to think or brace himself for a charge. At last I have him facing in the direction of his own stall.

Then without warning he lets out a wild roar that shakes the barn to its foundations. He lowers his head and begins dragging his hoof slowly across the ground. With a crack like a pistol shot he strikes his own belly. I watch him helplessly. Without thinking I drop the fork, scoop up a pile of hayseed from the floor and throw it into his eyes. Then I pick up the fork and run across to a short ladder that leads up into the hay loft. The bull is quiet now. He shakes his head and blinks his eyes. I pull off my coat and drive the fork through the collar again and again, pleating the cloth to prevent it from slipping off the prongs. Then I lower it and the coat, fluttering like a pirate's flag in front of the bull at the entrance to his stall. For a moment he looks at the fluttering coat with indifference, then, as if he had just found his enemy, he lowers his head and charges. As I had hoped, the momentum of his charge carries him into his own stall. I drop the fork, scramble down the ladder and grasp the shafts of the hay rake that stands at the head of the threshing floor. I pull the unwieldy machine across the entrance to the stall. The cows are safe!

I kneel down and crawl underneath the hay-rake to retrieve my coat. I am shivering now, and exhausted. I lie there for a minute to rest, until my breathing becomes more regular. I soon find the machine over me oppressive, and besides, my nostrils are full of dust. I crawl out, brush the hay from my clothes and put on my coat, then I close the barn door behind me and walk up the yard towards the house. The children are still playing quietly, they haven't even noticed that I had left the house. Thank God, I only have the rinsing left to do.

10

The Funeral

"BELLS," SAID JIM, HIS FORK POISED between his mouth and his plate. "Got both teams by the sound of it."

"It's Harold Beaton and Lauchie, and they got Dave with them," said Mary, pulling back the window curtain. "Maybe they're goin' to the wake and they'll take me along with them."

"You've been sulking all afternoon," said Jim. "Can't see why you're so set on freezing yerself to death, for the life of me.

It's not fit for a woman to be travellin' all them miles." Mary pretended not to hear.

"That grey mare of Lauchie's won't let him tie her," she laughed, "keeps nibbling at his arm looking for attention. He's got her spoiled. Can't be staying long, that's sure. They're tying the horses instead of stabling them. I'd better get the tea ready."

"Good evening," said Lauchie as he pushed in the door.

"Cummina Hashen!" It was Harold Beaton, right behind him. "She's cold. Snow comin' down till ye can't see a hand ahead of ye, an' pilin' up."

Dave touched his cap and nodded to Mary as he closed the door behind him.

"Did ye have any trouble gettin' down," said Jim. "I was up to the wake yesterday, never seen so much snow."

The men took off their mitts and stood over the stove rubbing their hands. Except that Harold Beaton was taller than the MacTavish brothers, there was little to distinguish the three men.

"Ye wouldn't have any t'bacco, would ye?" said Lauchie, looking hopefully at Mary, "all of us 'up' are out." Mary smiled and took down a packet from the shelf by the stove.

"We thought, maybe, if ye was goin'," said Lauchie, "we could take the three teams, Jim, but I suppose being ye was there yesterday, ye won't be going tonight? Travellin' would be easier with the three teams."

"You can't get HIM to go again," said Mary. "I've been trying all day to talk him into taking me up. I baked a whole ham shoulder and other stuff, special, and now I can't get them over. I wanted to stay the night with the remains, too, for old Sarah's sake, poor old soul! She's going to be lost without Tom. They were close."

"I've been tellin' her she's crazy, in this weather," Jim shook his head. "Be different if it was summer, but to go all the way there on a sleigh? She'll freeze, mebbe be stuck in a snowdrift two, three hours. Sarah won't be expectin' her in this weather...."

"Nooo!" said Lauchie, slowly. "I don't s'pose they'll be expectin' many." He took a quart bottle of bush whiskey from his hip pocket. "I've got a little sip here. If yell git a little glass, Mary, ye can put 'er around. Ye're welcome to come with us, being we're going."

"Thanks, Lauchie," she said.

Mary filled the glass three times, standing before each man until he had swallowed his drink. Then sat the bottle and the glass down on the table. "I'm goin' to get Dave a cup of tea and get ready," she said. "If you fellows want any more, help yourselves."

When Mary returned the men's voices had grown louder. They were discussing the weather.

"You remember, don't ye," said Lauchie, "winter b'fore last, when Dan held up that long strip of guts from the pigs and said there'd be no snow to speak of."

"He musta been lookin' at the wrong end," said Harold. "I remember the old man up used to hit her every time."

"That's only a story the old-timers made up," said Jim. "Didn't Dan hold up the gut and say we'd have no snow till March the year he butchered here? The next day it started snowing an' never let up till April. You remember, Mary?"

"I didn't see it. I never go near when there's butcherin'." Mary dropped an armful of blankets on the floor.

"I'll guess it'll be pretty rough gettin' to Tom's," she said, tying a scarf over her head. "Didn't they tell ye at the wake, Jim, that the man on the plow told Father Mac he wouldn't take the plow out for him?"

"Got real nasty, they said." Jim nodded his head.

"He'll not be sitting on that plow next year," said Lauchie. "Ye can bet on that! Father won't be taking no guff from the like of him. Did they get the road open?"

"Father Mac called the engineer," Jim went on, "but the plow didn't show up before I left yesterday. Father went up on Willie MacDonnell's sleigh. They broke road most of the way with Willie's double team. One time the horses went in up to their necks, I gucss, and Father and Willie had to work like bastards to get them out."

"Every one in the parish should write that engineer. Wake him up. You think! Refusing a PRIEST, and talking disrespectful to him's bad enough, but not even opening the road for to save a poor man's soul. I wouldn't want to be in that feller's place. No sirree!" said Harold.

"If she's that bad travelling, we'd best get moving," said Lauchie, looking at Mary. "Ye ready?"

LAUCHIE'S MARE, a cool-headed animal, good in snow, took the lead. Harold kept his sleigh close behind at first, then let his pigeon-toed mare, Queenie, make her own pace. She lacked the endurance of the grey. Mary travelled with Harold. They hardly spoke. They watched the mare straining in the traces. Ahead, Lauchie had reined in and was having a drink.

"Best get off and get your blood stirring," he said, as they drew up. Mary's hands and feet were so cold that they ached to the bone. In a moment they were all dancing little jigs and flapping their arms like wounded doves. But there was no time to lose. Soon the lanterns would have to be lit.

As they turned the bend in the road, Lauchie's mare plunged into a drift and sank up to her shoulders. The mare looked back at them, and Mary shuddered at the terror she saw in the animal's eyes. It was Harold who reached her first. He started to dig furiously. Lauchie threw himself at her neck and wrapped his arms about her head, like a hen straddling a nest of eggs. He cooed and caressed her as if she were human. Dave was shovelling so fast that his movements were blurred.

"Here, let me hold her head and keep her quiet," said Mary, pushing her way through the drift. "You can shovel faster than I can." Mary's voice threw the mare into a frenzy.

"Get away from her, Mary!" Lauchie shouted, "that mare's

scared of ye. She ain't never heard a woman's voice a'fore. For God's sake! Look at her. Froth foaming from 'er mouth and her gasping. She's near gone!"

"If ye can shovel, Mary, grab that shovel of Lauchie's," Harold yelled, "and try to get her side cleared there. Perhaps she'll calm down some." Mary was strong, and she shovelled with a will.

"Get off her head," Harold shouted, "let her see she's near freed in front."

"There, there, girl," Lauchie cooed, as he rubbed his coat sleeve across his eyes and slid down her back. He snatched the shovel from Mary and pushed her aside. The mare, sensing her freedom, strained forward and back. Then, as if by magic, her eyes were calm and her breathing easy. She stood quiet and rested.

The men dug feverishly, trying to release her hind legs before she tried to free herself again, but the mare, feeling the snow loosen, shied, then lunged forward. She tore off down the road dragging the sleigh behind her. One of the traces broke under the strain and waved like a streamer in the breeze. Lauchie moaned as he watched her, too stunned to make any effort to follow.

"Come on!" Harold yelled, "jump up. We'll get Queenie through the drift in the grey's tracks. Come on! Get up!" Lauchie crawled aboard like a sleepwalker. There wasn't even a drink to give them. The bottle was on the other sleigh.

About two miles up the road they caught up with the mare. She had run herself out. Lauchie looked her over carefully, and gave her a few strokes and a pat, then went over to the sleigh for some whiskey. Disregarding his manner, he pulled the cork and tipped the brown jug into his own mouth, then passed it to Harold. Then the two set about mending the trace.

"There's a halter rope by the shovel on my sleigh, Mary," said Harold, "will ye get it?"

"Perhaps she'll hold as far as Tom's. We'll do an all-right job on her there."

"No moon tonight," Harold observed. "We done good to get here when we did."

THEY REACHED TOM'S PLACE shortly before nightfall. The men went at once into the little room and knelt beside the coffin. Rising from their prayers, they turned to old Sarah, who sat, beads in hand, in an ancient rocker at the head of the coffin. Her gentle face bore no mark of tears or agitation, but the handkerchief in her hand had been squeezed into a tight ball. Solemnly the men approached her.

"Cummina Hashen!" said Lauchie, "I'm sorry fer your trouble, Sarah." The old lady looked at them gratefully. A smile touched the corner of her mouth, but she didn't speak.

"Cummina Hashen!" said Harold in turn, "I'm sorry fer your trouble." Dave grasped the old hand, crossed himself, sucked in a long breath, then nodded respectfully and followed Harold and Lauchie to the wooden bench placed along the wall.

"Good night!" said Lauchie, addressing Sarah's three nephews, seated beside him, "bad weather we're havin'."

"Yeh!" one answered, "hev to bury the old man tomorrow, no matter what. We was thinking perhaps some of them would get home. First thing after we heard they couldn't make it the weather got bad. Almost a week now. Good thing she's been cold. How'd ye find the roads?"

"Well, now, she'll be jist hard enough, getting the remains to the church," said Harold, looking over to the bench along the opposite wall where Hector Baines sat beside Dan MacTavish. They were settled for the night.

The small table at the foot of the coffin had been draped with a cloth of fine lace. In the centre had been placed the family Bible in silent petition to the Almighty for the repose of Tom's soul. The brown leather cover, encrusted in an intricate floral design and etched in gold, caught the flickering light from the candle standing in a tall white holder. Ranks of Mass cards covered the rest of the table, standing like supplicants and open for all to see the names of those they represented.

The coffin was open. The body lay in state. The hands were folded across the chest and clasped a prayer book entwined with a rosary. A tall crucifix stood at the head, and at the foot a small kneeler covered with worn carpeting. Father Mac had brought them on Willie's sleigh. The lid of the coffin stood like a silent sentinel against the wall behind the crucifix. The odor of death weighed the air.

"Hello!" said Dan. His eyes were so heavy he could barely look up from the floor to greet his uncle.

"Ye been here long?" said Lauchie.

"Got here last night, me and Hector come on the wood sleigh."

"Cummina Hashen!" Hector stood up and pushed himself between the brothers, throwing his arms about like a spider trying to overpower a fly, his black eyes unfathomable under his heavy black eyebrows.

"Ye old son of a whore! Ye wouldn't have a little drink, would ye? Me and Dan is near dead," he concluded in a whisper.

Lauchie's face flushed as he glanced at old Sarah. Sarah hadn't heard a word.

"What makes ye sick?" asked Lauchie non-committally.

"Young Tom, there, had a jug. We drank her last night between the three of us...ain't had a bit to eat today. Me and Dan's been too sick to look at anything. Ye got just one little taste?" Hector coaxed.

Lauchie didn't bother to answer. He shook off the encircling arms, bent down and whispered to his nephew. Dan's face lit up like a child's on Christmas morning. Together they left the room. Hector followed uninvited.

MARY LEFT HER BOX OF FOOD in the kitchen, took off her coat, put on an apron and came in to pay her respects. Tears came to old Sarah's eyes as she saw Mary kneeling beside the coffin.

"Mary, Mary, 'tis good to see you," she said, holding out her arms to the younger woman.

"I'm sorry for your trouble, Sarah," said Mary, clasping the thin veined hands in her own. "I was talking to Annie in the kitchen. She said she arrived last night...were you surprised?"

"Yisss!" old Sarah smiled, "I was that happy to see her. Don't know how we could have managed if she didn't come. Jennie MacNeil, beautiful soul that she is, come and stayed over...we'll never be able to do enough for that woman."

It was said of old Jennie that a touch of her hand and a willow'd stop weeping. She smiled at Mary, showing her few scattered teeth, as she busied herself preparing the tea. Her straight grey hair was drawn back so tight into the bun at the nape of her neck that it seemed hard for her to close her eyes. Jennie didn't walk; she glided silently about on the hem of her dress. She was always barefoot— winter and summer. She possessed three dresses, all cut from the same bolt of coth—navy blue cotton with an all-over pattern of pink roses. The tight bodice, securely buttoned up the front, seemed to apologize for the voluminous skirt which reached down to her ankles. The grey shawl, which she wore outdoors, lay carefully folded on the back of her rocker. Many years ago she had spun and woven the cloth herself.

"I'm staying the night, Sarah, least I can do," Mary said. "It'll give Annie a chance to rest up for the funeral tomorrow. Jennie's staying too. I'd best get back to the kitchen, but I'll be back."

MARY HADN'T FOUND IT EASY to reach the kitchen. The men had gathered in the hall. Sean had arrived!

"Look, Mary," said Hector holding one of Sean's snowshoes in his hand. "Ever seen Sean's snowshoes? Ten-twelve miles from your place, ain't it, Sean? Wearing out the only snowshoes in the county, an' two horses in need of exercise, gittin' stall fed in the barn. Scared they'd mebbe be losin' their shine? Sean keeps 'em shined up all the time."

"Gimme that snowshoe!" Sean's eyes were blazing. "Set me back twelve dollars. NEW. Ye'd best be mindin' yer own business, if ye have any. Legs is made for walking. Yez're all jealous of that team of mine. Way some of you treat yer horses ain't fit for a dog. Taking them out in all weathers, burying them in drifts and driving them till they looks like calves that's been after sucking and the froth still slobbering out of their mouths. Git outta my way!"

"Someday," Hector snapped, "they're gonna pick ye up in one of them snowbanks and them horses home won't be after eating oats then!"

The men stood back and let Sean go by to pay his respects. Not one smiled until he had gone through the doorway, then they all burst into a roar of laughter.

After allowing time for Sean to say his prayers, Lauchie went into the room, took him by the arm and led him out for a drink. The incident was over and forgotten.

The little parlour was dark now and Annie brought in a lighted lamp and placed it on the table beside the candle.

"We'd best be gitting under way," said Lauchie signalling to Harold, "the wind's comin' up, and she's dark."

"Ye can't go yet!" said Annie, "supper's on the table. Ye can't leave without a bite to eat. C'mon, Mama, there's room fer all." Annie led the mother out into the kitchen and sat her down at the head of the table. "The rest of ye just sit wherever ye find a place," she said.

"Will ye be stayin' the night, Sean?" said Mary as she placed his tea before him.

"I suppose me old legs ain't likely fit for to carry me another twelve miles this night." Sean had a twinkle in his eye. Sean always stayed.

"Guess Dave'll be staying too," said Lauchie, who had overheard, "least ways that's what he was tellin' me in the room."

"You and me, Mary'll, stay up with 'em," said old Jennie as she filled the cups.

"There'll be just four of them," Mary answered, "Sean, Dave, Hector, and Dan, and there's plenty cooked. All we'll have to be getting them is breakfast."

"Well!" said Lauchie, pushing back his chair, "I guess we'll hav' to do like the beggar, and get going...no moon at all."

"Did ye bring lanterns?" said Sarah, her voice quivering with concern. "I hate to see ye leaving on such a wild night."

"We'll be all right, Sarah," said Lauchie, grabbing Harold's arm. "Come on, we'd best say some more prayers and git under way."

The two men hastily left the room. Hector, Sean and Dan gulped down their food and followed. Lauchie and Harold were just leaving. Dan grasped Lauchie's arm and whispered in his ear. Lauchie didn't look too pleased, but nodded. Without bothering to fetch his coat Dan followed him out into the yard. A few minutes later he returned, shivering with the cold, but smiling. Hector mouthed a question. Dan nodded his answer, and both men went happily into the little room to watch beside the remains.

"Will somebody lead the rosary?" said Annie. "Mama's tired, and all of us are going to bed, so's to be rested for tomorrow." Then turning to one of the nephews she said, "Young John, will you lead?"

"Ach! no Annie," he mumbled, "git someone else. I'd come out two or three beads long or short, and I don't know the mysteries."

"I'll lead, if you want me to," said Mary.

When the lumbering sounds of kneeling men, clearing of throats and coughing had ceased, Mary began. When it was all over old Sarah took a last look at the coffin.

"Good night," she said softly. "If any of you get cold or sleepy during the night, there's a cot in the store room across the passage. Look and see if there's a blanket, Annie."

"Quit worrying, Mama," said Annie, tugging at her mother's arm, "there's a blanket. Come on to bed, now."

Soon the family had all gone to bed and only the night-watchers remained downstairs. Old Jennie threw herself down on the bench beside Sean. It was the first time she had taken a rest that day.

"So!" she said, "ye walked all the way over in yer snowshoes, eh? First thing we know ye'll be after getting yourself a wife." Sean squirmed, then smiled.

"Far's that goes, I could probably show these young fellers a few tricks yet." And he raised his arms as if to hug Jennie.

"I'll just bet you could, too," said Jennie drawing back, "I wouldn't chance ye anyhow. Would ye, Mary?"

"Oh, if I come around, just once," Sean bantered, "Jim and Angus might as well pack their suitcases...the two of ye'd never look at them again."

"What've ye got, Sean," said Jennie, "must be yer hiding it!"

Sean moved his hands towards his fly, "Ye really want to see?"

The woman's screams and laughter roused Dan and Hector from their own conversation.

"You'd had best watch out," Hector said, "Sean's a gay old dog. I heard say as how ye had the girls all following ye around in your day, that right, Sean?"

Hector didn't wait for the laughter to subside but threw his arms around Dan. "C'mon, Comrade Comfy, open her up! Open her up! Where's ye have it?"

"I have it in the storeroom beyond," said Dan, brushing off Hector's embrace. "Didn't wanna bring her in with the others around."

"Get her, man! Get her!" Hector pushed Dan up from the bench.

"Have ye a glass, Mary? A water glass. Them little devils don't hold a taste."

"Ye'd best be careful with that bush whiskey," said Jennie

sternly, "be something fearful if Sarah got up and ye was all after passin' out."

"Ye'll likely be laid out with the remains, come mornin'." Mary laughed as she left the room.

"Well!" said Jennie, looking down at old Tom, "Mary an' me don't wanna be sittin' up alone with no remains, I'm tellin' yez. What's ye think of old Tom? Looks good, don't he? Except maybe he's got small."

"Fell away 'til there ain't a pick on him," said Sean, his eye on the door, "looks like an old dried-up herring in a cart box."

"There's a cot in the storeroom across the hall," Jennie said, quickly changing the subject, "with an army blanket spread over it. There's a bunch of junk in there, everythin' piled here and there, so ye'd better take a lantern—if one of ye wants to sleep."

"You put her around, Jennie," said Sean rubbing his hands when he saw Mary coming in through the door, "take one yerself and give one to Mary."

Jennie and Mary accepted the customary woman's sip.

"Now, make her a good one," said Hector, as Jennie filled and refilled the glass until they had all had a drink. "Dan, we'd better have another, hadn't we," said Sean, lowering his drink as if he were in a desert. "Can't walk on one leg y'know."

The glass was passed round at five-minute intervals four times again. Dave fell asleep immediately, and Sean began his first story.... "Speaking of the remains...had a jug of that old black rum we used'ta get for a dollar a gallon...every one was after feelin' good, an' lookin' for some devilment for to pass the night...sittin' up with Harry and the Rooster's remains he was...."

MARY LOOKED HELPLESSLY AT JENNIE.

"No need us listening to them. She's cold in here. Let's you and me get to the kitchen where it's warm." The men didn't seem to notice the women's departure. Out in the kitchen, Jennie turned the lamp down and drew her chair close to the fire.

"Put yer feet in the oven, Mary, get them out of the draft. We'd best get some sleep," said Jennie, pulling her shawl close about her. It was midnight.

"Get's creepy in the middle of the night, doesn't it?" said Mary shivering. "Sitting up with a corpse."

"Your first time?"

"Yes!" said Mary peering into the shadows. "Awful quiet."

"Yeh!" Jennie yawned. "Not even a pigeon cooin'."

THE WARMTH OF THE FIRE was comforting: against her will, Mary began to feel drowsy. She woke with a start.

"Jennie! Jennie! Wake up! Did you hear that noise?"

"What's up?"

"I heard a door banging or one of them fell down, had I better take a look?"

"One of the guys steppin' out to take a piss most likely," said Jennie, shifting her weight in the chair. "Sit still or ye'll be having 'em on our necks the rest of the night."

Mary made no comment when she heard other noises in the front of the house, and very soon both women had fallen asleep. It was Jennie who woke first.

"Mary! Wake up, it's three o'clock. It's time to make the tea. The men'll think we're fine housekeepers. Funny they haven't been lookin' for it!"

"They don't know if it's night or day by now," said Mary, stretching herself.

"Let's take the tea in to them, if they come here and see the fire we'll be listenin' to their gab till breakfast time."

"Suits me," said Mary, picking up two mugs of steaming tea and a plate of bread. Together they filed down the narrow hallway into the parlour. They looked round the room.

"Where's Dave?" said Mary.

"Gone over to sleep in the cot more'n likely. Maybe that's what ye heard before." Neither thought to wait for one of the men to answer. Hector wasn't in much shape to answer anyway. He held his bread in an unsteady hand and spilled the tea. Dan was fast asleep. But Sean's eyes were as alert as ever. He took his tea without mishap and ate hungrily. Returning to the kitchen the women washed and put away the dishes, put wood on the stove, and again drew up their chairs to the fire.

"We'll have to wake them up after a while," said Jennie, as she put her feet back in the oven. "Father Mac'll be here for prayers at seven sharp...came as far as O'Donnell's last night."

"Let's not wake 'em earlier than we have to," said Mary, trying to snuggle down into her hard wooden chair, "that Hector'll drive me crazy. He thinks all ye has to do is say some magic words and there'll be a drink for him in your hand. If there's vanilla or shaving lotion around we'd better hide it before waking him."

IT WAS FIVE-THIRTY when they woke. Jennie jumped up with a start.

"Mary! Ye awake? We'd best get the men from the room and feed them. Perhaps they'll go some place and sleep while we fix the room."

"You're right," said Mary pushing back her chair. "It wouldn't be nice for Sarah to see Dan asleep in there and maybe a puddle under him, and heaven knows what shape Hector is in by now."

Together they went down the hall.

"May the Good Saints preserve us!" said Jennie on the threshold, blessing herself hastily, "will ye look at this!"

Cigarette butts, tobacco, chewed out tobacco cuds covered the floor. The puddle that the women knew they'd find under Dan's chair reached the rim of Sean's hat. Sean lay full length on the floor, his hat pulled well down over his ears. Dan was unconscious, but Hector had the brown jug tipped over his head, his mouth stretched wide, trying to catch the last drop. At the sound of Jennie's voice Hector let the jug fall with a crash to the floor. Then he too passed out.

"We'll never get this straightened out without help," said Mary, grabbing Dan by the shoulders and giving him a good shake. Dan muttered, crossed his legs, and slept on.

"Old Tom would turn over in his casket if he could see this mess," said Jennie, stepping over Sean to reach his feet. "You take the other leg, Mary, and we'll haul him out." Both women pulled with all their strength, but they couldn't move him.

"I'll fix him," said Jennie as she left the room. Mary sank onto an empty bench and surveyed the scene with desperation. Jennie returned from the kitchen with a pitcher of water.

"That'll fix him," she said throwing the water over Sean's head. At that moment young Tom came running down the stairs. "What's goin' on in here?" he said, looking around the room. He did not wait for an answer.

"We'd best get Sean out to the fire afore he freezes. Can ye walk, Sean? Come on now." In spite of Tom's wheedling, Sean got to his feet only long enough to fall down again on a bench. He refused to go any further.

"Leave him, Tom," said Mary, "we can work around him. I'll get the mop and the water." Young Tom strode angrily out to the kitchen. One by one the family came downstairs. Old Sarah came down last of all. It was now half-past six.

"C'mon," said Annie, "Mama wants us all to say a prayer. Mary will ye start them off?"

Slowly they all filed into the little room and everyone but Sean and Hector knelt. The women reverently closed their eyes. The men stared ahead as if afraid it might appear effeminate to close their eyes.

"Our Father...," Mary began, "Who art in Heaven...." She got no further. A wild scream froze the prayer in Mary's throat. Dan leapt to his feet and was out the door before the echo of his voice merged with the howling and wailing of Young Tom and his cousins who followed as though swept up by a hurricane. The only men left in the room were Sean and Hector, both sound asleep.

"Heavenly saints!" Annie's voice was strangled in her throat, "is it that I'm losing my mind?"

Every woman in the room seemed to be turned to stone. In silence they watched a hand slowly rise from the casket, stop a moment, then slowly grasp its edge. They watched the skin whiten over the knuckles. Then slowly the top of a man's head, his forehead, and then the face. Annie reeled to her feet.

"Papa!" she whispered, and fainted.

It was Dave. The expression on his face told its own story. Dave thought he was dead. It was Sarah who grasped his shaking hand. There was no anger, no vestige of fear on her face. Her eyes were full of compassion for the poor fellow. She helped him scramble out of the coffin. It was her voice that calmed and reassured him. Slowly the fear left his face. Mary led the old lady back to her rocking chair and she calmly picked up her beads where she had left off. Mary turned to Dave.

"How'd you get in there? Do you remember anything?"

But Dave only grinned, hunched his shoulders and let them fall in bewilderment

"Twas Dave, dear," whispered Jennie, as Annie returned to consciousness. "Everything all right. Best sit beside Hector a minute."

Still uneasy on her feet, Annie sat down on the bench with a thump which upset Hector's balance, and without waking he slowly slid onto the floor.

"What have they did with the remains?" said Jennie, suddenly grasping all the implication. "This is awful. We'll all be after going to hell. Belittlin' the dead like this."

She turned on Dave. "Did ye wake up after ye went to sleep at all?... Oh, what's the use. You don't know nothin'. It's them two slinks!"

Dave grabbed Mary's arm, and began making frantic signs.

Mary couldn't make out what he was trying to say but nodded 'yes' and pointed to the door. Dave grabbed his cup from the floor and made for the door.

"I think Dave's gone for the men," said Mary, "now for those two hellions." She began to pummel Hector. "Come on you... Hector...wake up...come on now!"

"I'd best get after this old 'bodach,'" said Jennie, giving Sean a shake, "the old anti-Christ." She grabbed the pan of water she had brought to revive Annie and poured it over Sean's head. "There! That should fetch him, he's drenched good now!"

"Oh, me head!" moaned Sean. "What's wrong with ye women, leave me be!"

"Tell us where 'twas ye put the remains and ye can sleep forever," said Jennie harshly.

"Remains?" Sean blinked his eyes. "What remains?"

"Ye know what remains. Old Tom's, that's who we mean. No need ye sayin' ye don't know. Ye was telling about the night of the Rooster's wake when Mary and me left ye. Now where'd they hide that body?"

"Quit yer cacklin'," Sean's face became wrinkled with misery. "Me near dead with me sore head and all ye can do is rage about remains. Remains is in the box, far as I know."

"Wake up!" Jennie grabbed his shoulder and shook him, thumping his head hard against the wall. It was enough to make a "well" head sore. "We'll not leave ye till ye've told us, ye know."

Mary noticed that Sarah had finished her beads and had been listening ever since her hands became idle.

"Take your mother out for some tea," she whispered to Annie, "it'll do ye both good. No need for her to be hearin' all this."

"I don't know what we'll do." Jennie was near hysteria.

"I'll get some strong tea," said Mary, "that should do something."

"Bring a whole pot, Mary, an' we'll pour it down his neck till she's pourin' out his ears."

"The men's comin'," said Mary as she returned with the tea.

"Thet's somethin' anyways," said Jennie, taking hold of Sean's chin. "They can get Hector off the floor and search for the remains. Ye get on that other side, Mary, and hold his nose."

They poured one cup down Sean's throat and were starting on the second cup.

"Stop feedin' me that slop!" Sean spluttered, "ye're only making me dizzy and sick. Never remember like that."

The men came into the room.

"Put Hector back on the bench, fellers," said Jennie without looking up, "then spread out and try to find that body. Did ye see the clock when ye was in the kitchen, Mary?"

"It's half past six!"

"Mother o' God, Father Mac's due any time now. Get going." The men obeyed with unaccustomed docility.

"C'mon, Sean," Mary wheedled, "try to remember. Do you want the priest to see you like this?"

"Honest, I can't," Sean was almost in tears. "Good God! Woman, do ye think I'd hold her back if I knowed? An' the priest coming and all!"

"More tea," said Jennie sarcastically.

"NO!" Sean jerked his head clear of Jennie's grasp. "Please, Mary, if ye can get me a drop so's I can get me mind off me head, maybe it'll come back."

Sarah, beginning to show signs of anxiety, followed Mary back into the room. She had a pint bottle in her hand which she handed to Mary. Sean grabbed the bottle from Mary's hand and tipped it up. When he had half finished its contents Jennie snatched the bottle from his hand.

"All right, now, Sean," she said, "let's have it!"

"Holy God, Jennie, a man can't walk on one leg...'sides I didn't get enough to wet me throat good."

"That's every drop there is in the house," said Mary, going

down on her knees. "We'll be hearing Father Mac's sleigh bells any time now."

"WHERE DID THEY HIDE THE ROOSTER'S BODY?!" Jennie was desperate now. Mary snatched the bottle from Jennie's hand and gave it back to Sean.

"If this don't do it, I'd hate to be in his shoes."

"What in God's name are we goin' to do?" wailed Annie.

The sound of running feet and banging of doors came in from the yard, breathlessly the men entered the house and shook like sheep in a pen, huddled at the threshold. They shook their heads.

"I remember! I remember!" Sean said excitedly. "Me and Hector got the blanket from the storeroom and wrapped him in it. I recall almost dropping him a couple of times...kept slidin' on us."

"Yes, yes, but what'd ye do with him?" said Mary breathlessly.

"We took him across the hall to where the cot was."

The women looked at the men, who shook their heads.

"Ye didn't!" screamed Jennie, "the men looked. O God! I can hear Father's sleigh bells."

Slowly Mary rose to her feet and picked up the teapot and cup.

"Best get these things out of here, anyway."

Annie stood over the empty coffin wringing her hands. Old Sarah once again picked up her beads.

"Good God! Women!" said Sean. He was in his dignity now. "Have ye got time to doubt me word? If ye'd let me talk instead of giving up and acting silly. The remains is there alright. Behind the door." Sean cleared his throat, "There's about a foot between the hinges and the wall, just enough as no one can tell when the door is open...now we stood him up...."

No one waited for Sean to finish. The sleigh bells rang out clearer now.

The Funeral

"Get goin'!" yelled Jennie.

"Mary! Look!" Queenie was near hysteria. "Dave tore the lining when he got out.... Jennie, get me a needle and thread, the lining has to be pulled together...the rip is where it'll show."

"Father Mac's at the gate," said Young Tom as they laid the body on a bench, still wrapped in the blanket.

"Stall him!" said Jennie as she hustled Tom out of the room.

"Hurry! Hurry! Get the blanket off him.... Sean, for God's sake, sit down some place," said Jennie, shaking her fist. "Tis prayers ye'll be needin' after this stunt."

"It'll have to do," said Annie, breaking the thread with her teeth, "bring him over and lay him in. Lookout! you've got him feet first...turn him around!"

"Quick! Quick! Father Mac's at the door!"

The men turned the body round clumsily. Mary held the sewn edge down as they laid the body in the coffin. Annie straightened her father's tie and replaced the rosary and prayer book in the folded hands. The door opened.

"Cummina Hashen!" Father Mac said as he entered the room.

"Everyone is ready for prayers, I see." The priest smiled. "Well, we'd better get started. It's a long way to the church." Everyone knelt. If some of the silent prayers were of thanksgiving and not those for the dead, the good Father never knew.

The six pallbearers walked beside the coffin every step of the six miles to the churchyard. The horses went down so many times that no one bothered to count the number. Old Tom was taken to his final resting place in his sleigh—the horses had been his too. The gravediggers, digging since daybreak, were still digging when the procession—horses and sleighs of all kinds—came round the bend, and the sun, weakened and weary, clung indifferently to the western sky.

4 Stories

The Innocent

WILLIE MACSWEEN SWUNG his bony legs over the edge of the bed and reached down to pull the pants from under his feet. Shivering in the chill of the morning, he buttoned the three fly buttons, then ran a hand around the tail of the shirt he'd slept in. He opened the top button and tucked the tail into his trousers.

"Ye gonna stay in bed all day?" he said, bending over to shake his wife. "Git up woman! Git my tea. I'm goin' to town after chores."

"It's still the middle o' the night," Martha moaned. "The stores is not open yit."

"Night or day, no difference 'round here. Can't sleep no how with that old bastard sister o' yours hollerin' and screamin'. Don't know how it wuz I let meself be talked into takin' in her and her brat in the first place. Ye said she wouldn't be givin' me no trouble. Ye said she had the money to pay her way. Well, I ain't seen no money, nor I ain't seen a decent night's sleep since she took sick. Git up! And stop her from screechin'. I'm gittin' out soon's I can."

Martha heard the outside door slam as she buttoned her dress. She crossed to the window, as she did every morning, to take a look at the sheep in the top field. She did not have to count them, so accustomed were her eyes to seeing their exact number. When Willie came in from the barn, she had the fire going and his porridge on the table.

There hadn't been time to quiet the screaming from the bed in the covered porch that served as a bedroom off the kitchen.

"Oh, Sweet Jesus!" a voice rang out. "Please, please, dear God, spare me this agony—. 'Our Father who art in Heaven, hallowed be thy....'"

Martha looked toward the little man she had married so long ago. He had his hands over his ears. His eyes squeezed tight and his nose wrinkled up until his heavy gray moustache bristled. His face was ashen with leashed rage.

"A man can't even have his breakfast," he shouted, jumping up from the table. "Where's them brats we've been feedin'? Git 'em up! Ye'd think I was runnin' an orphanage. Good ol' MacSween! Simple-headed of MacSween! Takin' in everybody's brats and bastards."

"Willie, your own flesh and blood," Martha's voice was barely audible. "Show a little mercy to your own at least!"

"Git them up! I'm goin'!" Willie MacSween pulled his old gray cap down over his ears and stormed out of the room. The screams from the porch drowned the banging of the door. Martha hurried in to her sister.

"Is there anything ye'd like me to do fer ye, Helen?" she asked, kneeling down beside the bed. "Ye had a bad night last night, didn't ye, dear? I wisht Willie would git the doctor fer ye, and the priest. Might as well be talkin' to the wall fer all he cares to listen."

Helen screamed again. Her eyes were open, but there was no recognition, no expression in them.

Martha ran to the foot of the stairs.

"Larry! Sadie! Gretta! Git ye up and git down here! Helen's took a turn, and Himself is gone to town."

Then grabbing her old shawl, Martha ran down to the riverbank and shouted to Jennie. Her friend's house was only yards away, and the women always called back and forth to each other. Large stones made the crossing easy, except during the spring floods. In spite of her age, ol' Jennie could ford the river with ease.

"WE'LL SAY THE BEADS FER HER. There ain't time to git the priest," said Martha, starting back up to the house.

"Is it dyin' she is, then?" gasped Jennie.

Martha nodded.

The house was quiet now, and the children stood silently around the stove, afraid to move.

"I'd best take a look," said Jennie, throwing down her shawl and going out into the little porch.

"Come on. Sit down and eat yer porridge," said Martha, pushing the kettle over the fire. "Sadie, ye'd best clean up the table when ye're through, and sweep up a little. Gretta'll give ye a hand."

"Is Helen bad, Grandma?" asked Larry. "Is she gonna die?"

Martha nodded. "Git on with yer breakfast, child. There's chores to be done."

"Fetch me the lookin' glass, Marthie!" Jennie cried out. "I'm thinkin' she's gone."

Martha reached for the cracked mirror over the sink and ran to the porch. "Git yer beads quick," she called to the children.

Jennie took the glass and held it to the dying woman's mouth.

"She's goin' fast, but she's makin' a smudge. We'd best git the beads started," she said, taking her rosary from her dress pocket.

Silently, the children crowded in and knelt beside the bed.

"Will we be started in time?" asked Martha, bending down and trying to see if any breath clouded the mirror.

Jennie nodded and started rattling off the beads as though she were running a marathon. Martha and the children could barely keep up with her.

"Git me water in the bowl, Marthie, so's I can wash her," said Jennie, rising to her feet. "No need to worry 'bout her soul.

If she don't git to Heaven, none of yez stands a chance. God rest her soul!" she said, crossing herself. "Poor Helen's done her penance here."

"She's all right now," Martha said gently, crossing herself as she rose from her knees. "Now ye kids best go find somethin' to be doin'. Jennie'll be after washin' her now, and she won't be needin' ye to watch. Twas a blessing God took her, poor soul. She's suffered plenty." Martha brushed the tears from her eyes. "May she rest in peace," she whispered.

With bowed heads the little procession filed out of the room. The children stopped to whisper in the kitchen, but Martha continued on her way out into the yard, past the barn and the outhouse, till she reached the sheep pen. The pen was empty now. The sheep were out to range. But in the quiet of this place that housed the animals she loved, there was comfort.

"I been lookin' fer ye all over," said Jennie, holding open the back door. "There's somethin' I gotta tell ye, and there's no use the children hearin' it to repeat."

"What is it, then, Jennie?" Martha's voice was steady now.

"Look, Marthie, I don't mean to be buttin' in on any of yer business, but didn't Helen have some money?"

"I can't say. Why do you ask?"

"Put on yer thinkin' cap. It's not on straight right now. Helen was away t' the Boston States a long time, and her workin' every day she was there. She didn't spend any money to speak of after she came back here."

"Jennie! Don't talk so—" Tears filled Martha's eyes.

"If ye think I'm buttin' in where I've got no business, just say so. But listen first. Now when Willie gits home later, he'll have to go all the way over to Dan Angus's to git him to make the box fer her, and to git the arrangements made fer the funeral. And what is it Willie'll be thinkin' about? It'll be did Helen have any money. And if ye keep standin' there thinkin' how ye'll be desecratin' the dead or some other such foolish notion, YE won't get it. HE

WILL. Soon's he walks in that door after makin' the arrangements. Mark me words. Yell not be seein' any of it then."

Martha wiped her cheek with the back of her hand. "Poor Helen!" Her thin words seemed pulled by her ragged breath. "She worked so hard to earn the money, if there is any, and sufferin' so—I still can hear her screechin'. It just don't seem right to me. But I guess maybe yer right."

"Think, Marthic," Jcnnic went on. "Would it be you Helen'd rather be havin' the money, or would it be Willie?"

"Well, puttin' it that way—"

"Come on, then. The kids'll be here in a minute, and you don't want anyone knowin' what's what, then tellin' Willie soon as they take a spite 'gainst ye fer somethin'."

"I don't think the girls or Larry'd tell 'im," said Martha, coming to the defence of her grandchildren.

"No use takin' chances though," said Jennie, as she led the way into Helen's bedroom. "No tellin' what kids'll do sometimes, nor growed up people either, fer that matter. Let it slip out, and them not meanin' to tell at all. We'll start in here."

Jennie threw open the door to the room where Helen lay. Catching a glimpse of the body covered by a sheet, Jennie put her hand to her mouth. "Oh, Marthie," she moaned, "I forgot! I couldn't git Helen's legs straightened out by myself. And you was gone. Could we...?"

"Oh no!" Martha cried. "I couldn't! Leave her be! Willie can do it when he comes."

"Don't ye think she might be after gittin' too cold by then? And we daresn't call anybody yit." Jennie's voice rose in desperation. "We've got to find that money! The kids are comin' in now. Find a chore fer them."

NOT UNTIL LATE AFTERNOON did Martha remember Helen's trunk stored in the attic. It was easy to get at, and Jennie was in no mood for wasting time. The trunk wasn't locked. Jennie threw open the lid, pulled out the contents and strewed them on the floor. Martha stood by, wringing her hands and blessing herself. Her lips moved in silent prayer.

Jennie's wrinkled old eyes snapped with excitement.

"If I didn't know it was forgiveness ye was prayin' for, Marthie MacSween, I'd be thinkin' you was prayin' fer me to find somethin'," said Jennie, as she sat back on her heels. "And I have!" She grinned and held up a worn pocketbook.

Martha's eyes lost their look of resignation. The pocketbook was crammed with American bills. Slowly she sank down to her knees and watched Jennie as she counted the money, passing each bill lovingly through her fingers.

"EIGHT HUNDRED DOLLARS!"

Martha was stunned. Never before had she seen so much money. The girl's voices from the kitchen brought her back to reality. She whipped the bills off the floor and stowed them safely in her bosom.

"I'll see ye git a share, Jennie, soon's we're alone again," Martha whispered. "What on earth will I do with all that money! Wisht I could buy some baby lambs, but like as not Willie'd catch on and take a spite on them maybe."

"SHEEP!" Jennie snorted. "Ye needs new curtains, and ye could use a new church dress."

"Yes, but if I bought things at the store, Jennie, even if Willie'd let me come along, he'd ask where I got the money. And I couldn't lie, Jennie."

"The catalogue, ye fool!" said Jenny, forcing her voice into a whisper. "Send away fer them. It's you takes care of the mail. Ye'll see. Willie don't notice curtains or such things. And if he do, ye can say yer cousin Frannie sent another parcel from the States. No need to say they was in it. Git the idea!"

The women smiled and hurried down the stairs.

NEAR SUNDOWN, the big gray mare trotted smartly into the

yard. Larry rushed out to meet his grandfather, to be the first with the news.

Willie didn't give the child time to speak. "Well, don't stand there with yer eyes buggin' out! Git the harness off this animal and put her in the barn." He threw the reins at the boy, and for the first time saw the expression on his face.

"She's gone, then, is she?" he said.

The boy nodded.

"So—she finally died!" Willie squeezed two tears from his eyes and set his face in an expression of benignity.

"Sooo—." Willie got no further. Over his wife's shoulder, he saw ol' Jennie. He bowed his head. "Oh, hello, Jennie. The boy's been tellin' me poor Helen's after leavin' us. Poor soul! She suffered the tortures of Hell this last while. She's lucky to be shed of all the pain." He frowned. "God rest her soul," he added as an afterthought.

"Ye'll have to be goin' to see will Dan Angus make her a box, Willie," said Martha, "and see can ye git one of the boys up there to see the priest about a Buryin' Mass."

"I s'pose so," Willie mumbled into his moustache. "Best git a bite to eat. Haven't ate since mornin'." Willie marched to the table, sat down, and waited for his dinner to be placed before him.

"Tell that feller to throw some hay to the mare, so's she'll have ate, time's I's ready to leave," he grumbled, apparently to the food on his plate.

The girls came in to fetch the milking buckets.

"Granny," said Sadie, "the cows was way up by Lawlors. We called in to tell them 'bout Helen. They said they'd be down as soon as they got the chores done."

"All right, then," said Martha. "Now, best ye git the milkin' over and git back fer prayers when they come."

Two hours passed before the Lawlors arrived. Willie came in soon after they were seated. He accepted their condolences and went directly upstairs to the attic.

"Well, I s'pose we'd best say a few prayers," said Jennie. "I washed her, and bein' there wasn't any man to help, we thought it best to leave her be."

Martha led the way into the little bedroom. The sound of Willie prowling overhead punctuated their prayers. They heard him tramp down the stairs.

"Would ye care fer a drop, Charlie?" he asked by way of greeting, when the devout had returned to the kitchen. "I have to keep her ahide, or she'd be gone."

"And who but yerself would drink her?" said Martha, stating the truth with no trace of anger in her voice.

"When did it happen?" asked Charlie unexpectedly.

"This mornin'. Right after Willie left fer to go to town. Jennie and me was with her."

"She went so fast there was no time fer to call anybody," said Jennie, hoping to avoid further questioning. "We just got to our knees in time fer the beads. Willie bein' away, I said to Martha here to git cleanin' and fix things fer the wake. I was here, and there weren't no use puttin' other people out to help clean the house."

"I know it weren't anywhere lately she went," said Charlie. "She's after gittin' stiff already. If I was ye, Willie, I'd git her outta that bed and straighten her legs. She won't be fittin' in any box the way she is."

"I thought of it," said Willie, "but fer about a month now, the rheumatiz's been botherin' me right arm, and havin' nobody around but the boy fer to help...." Willie's voice trailed off.

"Is that so?" said Charlie. "I could've given a hand around the place. I had no idea yer arm was botherin' ye."

"Well now, seein's yer here, we'd best git her outta here," said Willie, as if he had just thought of it himself. "We'll catch the ends of the sheet and bring her in, sheet and all."

Willie took the head and left Charlie to manage the feet as best he could. Helen's knees were drawn up under her chin. They tried to pass through the door into the kitchen, but had to turn this way and that, and finally turn her over on her side to get her through. They laid her on the table and threw back the sheet to expose her twisted form in its long flannel nightgown.

"Ye'd best not plan to keep her long," said Charlie, looking around to make sure that Martha wasn't near. "She's smellin' perty bad now."

"That ain't from bein' dead," Willie answered. "She's been stinkin' fer a long time now. Herself says it was cancer she had. I couldn't say."

"She musta suffered something terrible," said Charlie, shaking his head. "Look at them legs. Doubled up like a fence staple, and that stiff! Bear down, Willie. See if we can git the knees straight."

The men tugged and pushed. Willie complained at every move. But the legs were set. They would not move.

"Larry!" Willie yelled. "Go out into the barn and git that two-by-four standin' against the door in the horse stable and fetch her here."

"What'll ye do with the two-by-four?" Charlie asked.

"Put it across the legs and bear down. The boy'll help. Gotta git them down fer the box lid."

MARTHA AND JENNIE were in the pantry making tea.

"What did ye shove me for at the stove?" asked Martha.

"To stop ye from tellin' how long we was, givin' out the news," said Jennie. "Turned out the truth was best. When old Charlie said she was stiff, I knew how close he'd come to catchin' us. I can just hear the valley buzzin' now, if ye'd paid me any mind at all."

"Jennie, I just don't feel right about takin' that money," said Martha. "There's Belle. Shouldn't she be told?"

"Belle!" scoffed Jennie, sputtering with disgust. "Marthie, are ye after gittin' queer? When was it ye last heard from Belle?"

"Never heard from her since she left," Martha answered sadly.

"How can ye give her money, then?"

"I could git her address all right. Are you sure, Jennie? Are ye sure it's not wrong what we're doin'?" Martha was pale.

"Tell ye what," said Jennie, closing the pantry door behind her. "Tell Father MacGillivray—about everything, just like it is. Everything now, mind ye, and see what he says. Trouble is, he'll want a chunk of the money fer somethin'."

"Helen was a lot of care for over a year now," Martha sighed, as she took the roll of notes from her bosom. "I guess I have this comin' to me. Here's fifty fer ye."

"No!" said Jennie firmly. "That's yers. I only want ye to keep it." Jennie pursed her lips. "Poor Helen's troubles started with that Belle of hers. Wouldn't leave her in the Home. Oh no! Paid fer her sins with the rest of her life. She gave up everything fer that baby. If she didn't have Belle, she could've found a good man and got married. Then fer Belle to run off as soon as she could make her own way and leave you to take care of her mother. Didn't even have the decency to write. If I was you, I wouldn't even bother to tell her Helen was dead."

"But Helen cared fer her." Martha shook her head.

"And how do ye know?" Jennie was not to be stopped now. "Helen didn't see her in years. Ye took care of her after she come back. Ye put up with Willie grumblin' and hollerin'. I heard him from over home, rantin' and carryin' on."

"Jennie, I want ye to take this fifty," said Martha, trying to change the subject. "I wouldn't feel right if ye didn't."

"Well, if it'll make ye feel any better. I didn't expect it, mind ye." Jennie stowed the bills safely in her bosom.

"Ye've always been a good neighbour, Jennie," said Martha as she finished buttering the biscuits. "I'd be after goin' foolish by now, only fer ye."

"Will ye be all right now fer a while? I mustn't stay no longer. The ol' man'll be after blowin' the top of his head, bein' there's no supper fer him. We'll both be back after we've ate," said Jennie, as she put on her shawl.

THE DAY OF THE FUNERAL PASSED. And day after day, Willie searched the house. He tore the bed apart, he emptied boxes and drawers. Martha often caught him looking at her with his mouth shut tight and his eyes almost closed. The search went on.

Martha bought new dresses for the girls and one for herself. She hung new curtains in the kitchen. A parcel came from her cousin Frannie down in the States, with the usual things all too large or too small for the children. Martha hid the contents and disposed of the box. She felt safe now.'

Then one day the silence was broken. It was on a Sunday, and they were in church. Willie reached across his wife to drop his envelope into the collection basket, and out of the corner of his eye, he saw her new dress. Martha watched his eyes sweep over her and on to the girls at the end of the pew. Between her "Hail Mary's" she whispered to herself, "Here it is—here it is." Willie's jaw was set hard.

After Mass, they all got into the rig for the journey home. Willie flicked the horse with the reins; and leaning over so as not to splatter the rig, he spat a brown stream of tobacco juice into the light snow.

"New dresses ye and the girls got on?" he asked.

"Yes."

"Frannie sent a parcel?"

"Yes."

They drove home in silence.

That night after supper, Martha pulled her shawl over her head and waded the river to Jennie's place.

"Jennie," said she, almost in tears, "I believe Willie's caught on."

"How?" asked Jennie, lowering herself into the comfort of her old rocking chair for support.

"The way he looks at me, when he looks at all. And he noticed the dresses—and he asked about them. I was lucky. Frannie'd sent a box, and when he asked about it, I said 'Yes.'" Martha shuddered. "What if he'd not asked just the way he did?"

"What d'ye mean?" asked Jennie. "Which way did he ask?"

"He just said, 'Frannie sent a box?' What if he'd said, 'Did Frannie send them things?' What would I have said then?"

"Yeh! Ye and yer conscience!" Jennie went over to the stove to get the teapot. "Twould only have been a white lie if ye did say yes. Ye're the one as should get the money anyway. That shouldn't be no sin. If you said the Act of Contrition right away."

"He'd know I was lyin'." Martha left her tea untasted. "I was never one to lie. I just couldn't do it. Oh! I'm after wishin' I never started this thing at all."

"There, there, now, drink yer tea and quit worryin'. Perhaps he'll not be after askin' ye more questions at all."

Jennie was wrong. At dinner next day, Willie loaded his fork with herring and potatoes and pushed it into his mouth.

"Them curtains," he said, with his mouth still full. "New, ain't they? And the kids' overalls?"

"Yes," Martha answered.

"Sooooo, Frannie sends all new things now?" Willie grabbed the backbone of the herring, scraped off the flesh and threw the bone down on the table. "Musta come into money. Couldn't be Helen's money bought them now, could it?"

Martha didn't answer.

Willie didn't expect her to.

WINTER STORMS CAME EARLY that year. Within two days the snow was well over three feet deep, and it kept on falling. Martha looked out at the sheep. Their wool was long. They seemed to love the cold. She watched them come out of their shelter to feed at the rack, to eat snow, and to mill about. When the storm abated, she put on her warmest clothes and went out to talk to them and stroke their heads. Willie watched her from the window, but turned his back when she entered the kitchen. Willie stalked through the house from window to window, cursing as he went. He shovelled paths that filled in behind him. Martha crouched over her catalogues. She bought for everyone. Willie's gumshoes showed holes through the patches. Martha bought him new ones. She made heavy woollen pants for him to wear in the woods, and a cap with earflaps. Willie accepted everything as if it were customary. He did not even blink when he saw new coats on the women folk.

Storm followed storm. Groceries ran out, and when it was possible to get to the store, everything was bought on credit. In the spring, when the timber was hauled out of the woods and the trucks loaded for the mill, the bills were paid. But when this spring came, the storms never abated. And spring held no hope, for there was no timber cut for loading.

For a long time past, Willie had taken his bed privileges without word or warmth. More than once, Martha had been on the point of telling him about the money and comforting him that all was not lost—that they could meet their bills. But she found herself unable to speak.

Martha spent most of her days with the sheep. It was lambing time.

"Cummina Hashen," said Jennie, leaning over the sheep pen. "I thought this would be where I'd find ye."

Martha smiled. "There'll be a storm for sure with ye comin' out," she teased. "Come on in. I been out here day and night since the little lambs started comin'." She held up a newborn lamb. "He wasn't breathin' at all at first. He came round though," she said, stroking the baby lamb gently.

"Martha," Jennie called. "Come and give me a hand. Seems I've hung me big arse up on a barbed wire."

Martha set the lamb down and hurried over. For the first time in months, she laughed. "If you only knowed how funny ye look there in them wires, both arms swingin' like a lobster, yer feet hardly touchin' the ground, and yer rear end hoisted up in the air like a straw tickin' out fer airin' in the spring."

And they laughed until they could laugh no more, and wiped their eyes.

"She was a bad winter," said Jennie. "The ol' feller nearly drove me outta me mind. In the house all the time, pickin', pickin', pickin'."

"I know what ye mean," said Martha, with a sigh. "Willie's after buttonin' hisself up inside fer nearly two months now. Talkin' to no one except when he has to, or to give someone the what for." She picked up her latest lamb, and they started toward the house.

"Ye didn't tell him anything, did ye?" asked Jennie, peering into her friend's face.

"Ye old fraud, ye!" Martha laughed. "That's what's been on yer mind since ye came. No! Not that I hadn't a mind to tell him more than once. Just to see if he'd come out of it, knowin' the bills could be paid. But every time I started, he'd look at me as if there weren't nobody there, and I got tongue-tied. If he keeps on like this though, I'll have to tell."

WITH THE AID OF LARRY, Willie repaired the ravages of winter. They spread manure on the fields and put in new fence posts. The shearers came and garnered the wool crop. Willie piled the bags of wool onto the truck-wagon, took Martha's list of groceries, and went to town.

"It's good Willie's gone to town," Martha said to the children. "Pray God he'll be after comin' back in better cheer."

That night in bed, Martha felt that Willie turned to her for more than hasty relief. She ventured a question.

"Why didn't ye manure the plowed field?" she asked.

"How?" Willie answered in an icy voice.

"Won't it be too late if it's put off much longer?"

"NO!"

"No? How's that, Willie?" Martha insisted.

"No need breakin' me back manurin' a field there's no seed fer."

"Won't the wool buy the seed?" Martha could feel his body

stiffen, but at last she had him talking and she intended to keep him talking.

"There's bills, woman! How is it ye're buttin' into man's business?" From Willie, that was enough. Martha lay quiet. But Willie did not seem anxious to let the conversation stop there.

"Course, there's one thing more I could do."

"Why don't ye, Willie?" said Martha eagerly. "Twould be a sin to let the field lie fallow."

"That's right. And it plowed and all. I'll do 'er tomorrer."

"Do what? What is it ye'll be after doin' tomorrer?"

"Gittin' a buyer fer the sheep."

"THE SHEEP!"

"Yeah, the sheep!" There was no mistaking the smugness in Willie's voice.

"Willie, how much d'ye have to have? Fer the seed, I mean. Perhaps I could git the money, and you'd not have to sell the sheep—" Martha's voice broke. "The wool crop each year is a big help, and the little lambs...."

"It's meself that knows how much of a help the wool and the lambs be each year, but a man can't leave his horses and cows to starve either. I'll be goin' to town again tomorrer to see about a buyer."

"Willie! It was meself that got Helen's money! Ye could have it. No need to sell the sheep!"

"I know ye had it, woman, all along. How much?"

"Ye didn't ask me before."

"Didn't have to. How much have ye got after the spendin' spree ye've been havin' all winter?" There was no softness in Willie's voice.

"There's six hundred left. That should pay up everything and be enough over fer the seed." Martha waited.

"Git the money and give it here!" said Willie, striking a match and lighting the lamp beside the bed.

"Right now? In the middle of the night?"

"Course, now! It may be I'll be after leavin' afore ye gits up, come mornin'."

Martha leapt up from the bed and went to her ragbag in the corner beyond the old chest. Out of its depths she took a knotted rag and handed it to Willie. In the flickering lamp light, she watched him count out five hundred and eight dollars. Martha smiled secretly. What did money matter? She was free from guilt now, and her sheep would be safe.

WILLIE WAS GONE BY DAYBREAK.

At about ten o'clock, Jennie came over the river. "Well, I must say ye looks happy this mornin'," she said, sitting down in her usual chair. "The ol' fella sleep with ye last night?"

Martha blushed and Jennie chortled. "Ye're blushin', Marthie. Ye know, I ain't sure it ain't a downright sin fer a woman yer age to be still as pretty as ye are, when ye blush."

"Ye're an old fraud, Jennie." Martha threw her head back and laughed. But Martha was not accustomed to laughing, and it seemed as if the sound of her voice startled her. "Don't know if I could stand things if ye and yer jokes wasn't around to put some life into the world."

"Why? What happened?" said Jennie. She wasn't teasing now.

"Ye're gonna take me fer a fool, but I gave Willie what was left of the money. He was gonna sell the sheep!"

Willie was back by noon. He had never returned from town so early before.

"Give the horses a drink," he shouted to Larry, "and some feed. Then git the harrow out. I'll be needin' ye, so don't go away."

And Willie went in for his dinner.

Martha took up the food she'd left warming in pots at the back of the stove, and sat beside him with a cup of tea, watching him as he ate.

"Ye had a quick trip, then," she said.

“No need fer talk with all the work that’s to be done.”

“Ye got the seed with the money?”

“Yeh.” Willie was in rare good humour. “Seed and some fertilizer. New stuff. S’pose to sweeten the land.”

Martha watched him as he walked down to the barn. She saw the loaded truck-wagon and turned to her work. There was no one in the house to hear her singing. Willie had bought apples and some raisins. She’d bake him a pie. Apple and raisin pie was his favourite. Might as well make nice fresh biscuits too, long as she was at it. Martha’s nook of a pantry was tiny and without a window. What light there was came in through the doorway. The flour barrel furnished a stand for her breadboard, and the three small shelves above held her spices. She neither saw nor heard the men arrive. They didn’t come any further than the barn.

WILLIE AND THE CHILDREN talked all through supper. Willie praised the children for their help. He praised Martha for her cooking.

“Marthie, ye’re a wonder! Me favourite pie! Guess there ain’t no one can make apple and raisin pie like yer granma, kids,” he said. The children smiled nervously. They knew something they didn’t understand was going on. It was Larry who spoke. “Will them fellers be takin’ the sheep to town?” “No, Son. They’ll be takin’ them to Sydney. They’ll be slaughtered there.”

IN THE FIELD beside the old apple tree, Martha wept. She wept tears for today—for yesterday—for the whole long winter. For her whole life. When there were no tears left and the sun had given the day its last embrace, she got up, straightened her shawl, and walked slowly down to the river. On the bank, she unlaced her shoes, tied them together, and hung them around her neck. She stepped into the cool water. The sharp rocks bit into her bare feet. She didn’t feel them. On the other side, she sat down and slowly pulled her shoes back on. It was there Jennie found her.

"Cummina Hashen! I was just startin' over to yer place. Bein' ye've come to mine, all the better. What's the matter, Marthie? What's wrong? Ye sick? Ye look that white and peaked! Here. Let me help ye up to the house. The ol' man's gone off fer to see can he git a deer. We can talk it all over on a cup o' tea."

Martha didn't move.

"Willie sold the sheep," she said. "Behind me back it was—while I was bakin' him a pie—special. And me thinkin' they was saved."

Horses of the Sun

YOU WERE MORE LIKELY TO MEET SEAN walking along the road, miles from anywhere, or deep in the woods, taking a short cut. Seventy years old, he was as much a creature of the woods as a deer, a fox, or a rabbit. It wasn't that he had to walk. In his barn stood the finest pair of horses north of the Mainland.

His ghostly white skin was startling enough, so thin that the veins showed through like cobwebs on a ceiling. His long red moustache, curled and pointed, the same colour and texture as the tails of his horses, looked like the horns of a Texas steer. Two burning eyes twinkled mischievously under heavy eyebrows that hung low under the battered felt hat he wore, regardless of the seasons. In winter, a woollen scarf covered his neck and those parts left exposed by his hat. A dark ankle-length overcoat, its vintage as doubtful as its colour, covered his slightly bowed legs. In summer, the overcoat was exchanged for an old yellow raincoat.

"He must have lips," thought Mary, "though come to think of it, I've never seen them. But he must have lips to hold that old briar pipe he always carries under the brush of that moustache."

Sean wore every stitch of clothes that he owned, winter and summer—except for the old coat. It was nothing, people said, to find underneath his flannel shirt another flannel shirt; and under that, still another. Only Sean knew how many. And underneath all the shirts was that old standby, the union suit. On his feet, high black gumshoes, a full size too large—they had to accommodate all his socks—were kept tightly laced against the snow in winter, and for no reason at all in summer. People said of him: "Sean washed his feet the other day and found a pair of socks that's been missing since a year."

IT HADN'T BEEN MUCH PAST SUN-UP when Mary saw Sean strolling up the road toward the house, swinging his old lantern. She hadn't even fed the children, and Jim had left for the woods only a few minutes before. Mary was not pleased. Not because she didn't like Sean, but because he made her nervous with his everlasting monologues about fights and prizefighters. He knew the names of the fighters and the date of every fight that had ever been held, and he could describe the action as though he had been there. The gorier the better. He would chuckle to himself as he rambled. If Mary invented an excuse to leave the room, on her return she'd find that he had gone on with the story in her absence. It always worked out the same way. Mary would ask him if there was anything she could do for him, but he would tell her nothing, except that his business was with Jim. Then he'd sit down, in spite of her hints that he would find Jim just up the road or in the woods, and tell her story after story until noon when Jim came for his dinner.

Mary served dinner and watched Sean strain tea through his moustache. She sighed with relief when the men finished and Sean followed Jim outside into the yard. Men always went outside to discuss their business, if it was only to borrow a rope. Women would go into the bedroom or out to the backhouse to discuss lace for a new dress or the quality of blankets made from this year's wool.

Today, Sean's business was to ask Jim to haul wood for him the next day. He knew Jim was always ready to do a turn for a neighbour. What he didn't know was that Jim couldn't bring himself to ask for payment, and his old truck cost money to run. It used a lot of gas and oil. Jim once said to Mary, "Why doesn't Sean save all of us money and give those horses of his some exercise?"

It had been Runt—people had forgotten his proper name—who'd sold Sean the horses a few years back. Every year, as soon as the snow sloughed off in spring, Runt took to the road and started walking. His circuitous path took in from the Mainland to the tip of Cape North. A short man, he was so slight that a strong wind would blow him over—and bald, except for a few gray hairs his gnarled fingers swathed across the dome of his head. His teeth were false and ill-fitting. At mealtimes they clicked and slid around in his mouth as he ate. Everyone along his route knew that Runt got meals at mealtime and a bed at bedtime. Where beds were scarce, he'd sleep on the wooden bench in the kitchen.

Once a month, at pension time, he'd spend a drunken night—sometimes as long as a week—in whatever jail was handiest. Then, sober and broke, he'd resume his travels. He talked about nothing but horses, finding out from here and there who wanted to buy and who wanted to sell. If he knew of a horse for a prospective buyer, he'd walk any distance to fetch it. One day he decided to walk to Sean's around supper time. He knew that Sean would insist he remain the night as well. Supper over, they sat beside the fire and smoked their pipes.

"Lost our old mare today," Sean said. "She was old. Been lookin' fer her t'go, but it put us in bad shape, comin'just now with the plowin' to be done. Yer don't 'av a good horse fer sale perty reasonable, d' ye, Runty?"

"I heard of a team of chestnuts over on the Mainland. Fella

wants t'sell both, though." Runt's eyes lit up with interest. If he worked this right, he'd get a double sale.

"No use fer two," Sean said. "The other mare's all right."

"It'd be a shame to split 'em. Ye can take my word fer it," Runty added. "If ye'd see them horses, ye'd take 'em both. I could likely find somebody to take yer mare. Somebody'd be good to 'er. Any reason why ye'd want to keep 'er? These chestnuts are exactly the same size, and I've never seed anythin' so perty in a long time."

Sean sat staring at the stove, blowing black smoke from his pipe as though his life depended on it. Runt knew he had Sean thinking. Wisely, he too sat silent. Sean got up, knocked the ashes from his pipe, and ran his stubby fingers through his thin gray hair.

"What's he want?"

"Not much. Let me git 'm fer ye, then gi' me an offer. That should be good enough fer ye."

Sean nodded his head. Next morning, Runt returned the way he'd come. His feet fairly flew over the road. He knew he'd sell the pair. They'd been neglected ever since they'd been put up for sale, but Runt knew from long practice that he could paint a picture of them as they would be, after they were fed and groomed, that Sean would not be able to resist. The man was selling at a ridiculously low price, and Runt knew he stood to make a killing. In cash! For Sean was known to have cash in hoard.

Ten days later, Runt rode into Sean's yard on a chestnut mare, leading a gelding of identical size and colour. He had stopped along the way to brush and clean them as best he could. And although it was still possible to locate their ribs, they'd been grazing every night, and their flanks shone in the sunlight.

Sean lit his pipe. He waited until the tobacco glowed in the bowl before acknowledging their existence. Then, strolling over towards them, he ran his fingers over the mare's coat. He let a hand slip down a foreleg, around the fetlock, to the hoof, pressing softly on the muscle at the knee. Without taking his hand off the mare's coat, he rounded her hindquarters, examining each leg. Reaching her head, he held her still and stared into her eyes. His fingers slid down her face until they reached her mouth. Stroking her nose with his left hand, he deftly inserted the thumb and forefinger of his right hand into her mouth, forcing it open. He pulled the jaw down and inspected the teeth. Satisfied, he released her mouth. Still stroking her nose, he pressed his right forearm across her throat and pressed hard on her windpipe for several seconds. The mare did not cough, heave, or make a sound. Very gently, he released her head and moved over to the gelding, leaving his hand on the mare until the other touched the gelding, as though he feared they might vanish.

The examination over, he pushed his hand deep into a pocket and drew out a roll of notes. He paid Runt what had been asked; and standing between the heads of his horses, he led them away to the barn.

Runt made off, and once out of sight, he drew out a roll of notes and counted off eleven twenty-dollar bills and one five. These he placed in a grimy envelope. Slowly and lovingly, he then counted out three twenties, a ten, and a five, and thrust them deep into his pocket. Then, whistling, he trotted down the road to the vendor's.

LAST YEAR those precious horses had been in danger of going hungry. The crops had been hailed into the ground before the harvest, and Sean's credit with them. But eighty miles away in Sydney, Sean had a brother, a carpenter, who—it was rumoured—had money in the bank. Sean took the direct route to Sydney, ignoring the roads, preferring to face impenetrable barriers of spruce bush and hardwood undergrowth. By instinct, he kept a true course and emerged from the woods within a few miles of the city. He returned as he had gone, on foot by the same route, and arrived at Jim's house, tired, hungry, thirsty, carrying his old lantern in one hand and a maple cane in the other. He bragged about his trip, but did not mention meeting with his brother. Jim pretended not to notice the old man's weariness.

After the meal was over, Jim said, "I'm not doing anything this afternoon. I'll take ye home."

Sean got up from the table as if he were going to whirl Mary into a dance.

"Thanks, Jim," he said. "Could ye be comin' to take me t' town tomorrer? I have t' git feed fer the horses fer winter. That hailstorm drove ever'thing inta the ground. 'Bout eight be all right?"

Sean wouldn't even take his horses ten miles to haul their own feed.

That had been a year ago. Now Sean wanted help hauling wood.

"Jist a few sticks fer the fire," he said.

"I'll be over in the mornin'," said Jim, trying to hide the vexation he felt. He forgot to ask where the wood was.

GOING INTO SEAN'S HOUSE—going into the kitchen, that is, for no outsider had ever penetrated beyond the kitchen—was like going into a museum. The walls were covered with dusty odds and ends, knickknacks no other human being would consider saving or retrieving. Outdated calendars hung one upon the other everywhere. There were, of course, pictures of prizefighters, cut from papers and magazines and tacked on the wall. An old snowshoe, old boxes and crates, a three-cornered piece of broken mirror, a ragged sample of basket weaving littered the corners. Prominent on one wall a faded ribbon, tied prettily into a rosette around a badge stating, "FIRST PRIZE AWARD: The best hand-sewn lady's garment." The two red streamers that hung from the rosette showed signs of their being the favorite resting place for the flies that flew hither and thither through the room.

The Woman from Away

Although the house was Sean's, the kitchen was the domain of his foster brother Frank. Sean's old folk had taken Frank from an institution as a child, but had never bothered to adopt him legally. Frank was younger than Sean, a short bow-legged creature who would earn a second glance from no one, once they'd recovered from the shock of seeing that all the pores of his skin were stuffed with filth. A long hooked nose, slightly off centre in his wizened face, and impenetrable eyes under heavy black eyebrows made people cringe after being in his presence for more than a few minutes. He wore a pair of bibbed overalls, so dirty they might have been those he'd gotten with his full growth some forty years before. The color of the dark trousers beneath them could only be guessed. The well-worn gumshoes were tied with laces that could scarcely reach the tops; so much of their length was taken up with knots.

Today, as for a week past, Frank wore a large patch over most of his right ear. One of Sean's nephews told Jim that Frank made love to his cows and that he'd been trying to kiss one of them when she'd turned and hooked him. Mary and Jim had laughed at the time, and agreed that the nephew was just having a joke; but knowing Frank, they had to admit to the possibility of truth in the tale. Frank's ear was injured, and by a cow, as he had reported himself.

When Jim came to the door, Frank was busily wiping a cup with a square of grimy cloth.

"Is Sean in?" Jim asked.

Washing the cup made no difference to the colour or condition of Frank's hands. They stayed black with grime. Frank finished wiping the cup, wadded up the cloth as if it were a handkerchief, and stuffed it in the pocket of his overalls. The tail of it flapped against his legs as he moved.

"H-E-L-L-O J-I-M." Frank talked so slowly that even if he had anything of interest to say, his listeners would tire waiting for it. "C-O-M-E- I-N. I'-L-L G-E-T Y-O-U S-O-M-E T-E-A.

S-E-A-N J-U-S-T S-T-E-P-P-E-D O-U-T T-O F-E-E-D T-H-E H-O-R-S-E-S."

"Hello, Jim," Sean said, coming in. He spoke through toothless gums, and his words sounded like notes squeezed out of a bagpipe. "When ye've had yer tea, we'd best git started. Wood's schattered all over the place. May take a while pickin' it up."

Jim declined tea, vowing silently to get his job done quickly so that he could get back to his own house for dinner. But Sean's comment about the wood's being "schattered" was an understatement. Nowhere had it been piled. Jim slaved all morning pulling dead trees from underbrush, picking up hunks of discarded spruce here, a length of maple there. By noon, the job was only half done. There was no way to dodge Frank's dinner without insult. Jim was too hungry to plead loss of appetite. Clenching his jaw to hide his chagrin and steady his stomach, he strode down the hill to eat.

Enough potatoes for two families boiled merrily in a blackened pot on the kitchen range. The stove dominated the room. Beneath its grime and burnt-on grease splatterings, its original beauty could still be detected. An intricate maze of nickel curliques was visible and still shining in corners where the flying grease could not reach. Between the range and the cubbyhole pantry was the single under-sized window. Against the opposite wall stood a table with a chair at either end. To the right of the table and up three steps was the doorway to the floor above.

As Jim entered the kitchen, Frank was standing at the stove. Like Sean, he was small. He stretched an arm up to the warming oven, took out a frying pan, and set it on the stove top. Reaching into his pocket, he pulled out the grimy cloth and wiped the pan, before pushing it over on the heat.

Again he stretched his arm up to the warming oven and pulled out a filthy cup of dark crumb-spotted dripping. He scooped a finger-load of grease into the pan and set the cup back. He then disappeared into the pantry and returned with about a dozen eggs in a battered old quart dipper that had lost its handle. Rubbing each egg against the leg of his overalls to remove the dung, he broke six into the frying pan. Another visit to the pantry brought out a greasy bowl containing four pieces of leftover salt herring. Lifting the lid off the pan of eggs, he threw in the herring and replaced the cover.

He then set milk on the table in an old granite pitcher and surrounded it with three foggy glasses. Before Frank had loosened his grip on the handle, a big yellow cat jumped onto the table and buried its head up to the shoulders in the pitcher.

"N-I-C-E P-O-O-S-Y," crooned Frank, as he stroked the cat and went back to tend the frying pan. Frank brought the pan from the stove, wiped each plate with the same grimy cloth, and carefully arranged one piece of herring and two eggs on each. Knives and forks, the forks still bearing traces of yesterday's eggs, were carefully dusted. Then, grabbing a bowl he had obviously used for the breakfast oatmeal, he ran a finger around the rim and sucked the porridge off it. Next, he drained the potatoes, boiled in their jackets, and dumped them into the bowl, which he placed on the table. Dinner was ready!

Nine cats loomed up along the side of the table, and the yellow cat jumped into Frank's lap. Throughout the meal, Frank kept tossing morsels to the cats.

Dinner over, Sean had to care for his horses again. He invited Jim to go along. As they entered the barn, Sean, bursting with pride, stood aside to let Jim pass. Jim stopped and turned around. He was staggered. A partition from the floor to rafters divided the big red barn in two. The walls were limewashed a dazzling white that threw back the rays of the sun. Jim narrowed his eyes against the glare, and walked slowly down the centre gutter that was worn smooth by constant shovelling and brushing. On his left, a room-like unit had been boarded off. This was the rack-room. On the outside wall were large ten-penny nails driven in slantwise, and on these nails hung pieces of harness—pliable, neat and new-looking, their brass fittings polished until they shone like gold. The floor was covered with narrow pieces of hardwood that any housewife would cherish in her parlour. There was not a speck of dust to dim the grain. The air was heavy with the smell of linseed oil and leather. Against the partition dividing the barn stood two barrels with fitted lids: one was marked OATS; the other, BRAN. Beside them a ladder rose to an almost barren loft.

Jim turned and walked back toward Sean, who was standing now by the two stalls on the left. There were the horses. They were beautiful! Elegant! Sixteen hands high, their flanks shone like moonlight on mahogany. Above each stall was a sign, professionally painted in black and white, that proclaimed VICTOR to be the occupant of one stall, and VICTORIA of the other. Both horses turned at the sound of Sean's voice, bending their heads to be caressed. Sean cooed to them in the voice of a lullaby almost, while Jim watched. So these were the horses that nothing could make Sean put a harness on—that in case of fire, he would drag to safety at the risk of his own life. That's what everybody said.

"Tis a palace ye have here for 'em," said Jim. "Looks like a hospital."

"Aye," said Sean. "But I have to git feed fer 'em. Could ye be comin' fer t'take me t'town tomorrer—about eight be all right?"

Jim left the barn shaking his head.

THE DAY THE NEWS CAME, it came around noon. Sean was dead. For years it had been predicted that he would die someplace in the wilderness. It did not happen quite in that way.

Sean and Frank had been celebrating New Year's Eve at home alone. They had barely tasted their second bottle of Canadian Club (if Sean splurged, he bought the best) when the argument began. This was not unusual, and the upshot generally was that one of them walked to town and swore out a warrant for the other's arrest. Since neither would pay the fine, the offender would spend a few days at the county jail and return home chastened for a time at least.

"If either of you show up again in this court," the judge had told them not a month before, "I'm sending you both to jail!"

And now, there'd been another argument, and Sean was waiting for daybreak to start the same old journey. Frustrated from waiting the long night, he grabbed the lantern with a shaking hand, and set out for town, thirty miles away.

He got as far as his cousin Anna's, three miles up the road. "I feel a bit tired," he told her.

Anna took him in and made him lie down on the couch to rest awhile. After sleeping an hour or so, Sean rose and left. Anna watched him turn towards the town.

It wasn't until the next day, at the wake, that Mary and Joe got the whole story. When they drove into Anna's yard, there was hardly a place to leave the rig. Horses were tied to every post. Inside the house people milled about, and the rooms hummed with muted voices. Anna sat in a rocker before the kitchen fire, a soft-spoken, gentle woman with signs still of the great beauty she had been twenty years and twelve children ago. She held out a hand to Mary, so small and frail that you'd think it might break—until you remembered the fences and fences covered with washing she'd done over the years. Anna took Mary's hand and drew her close, as if she were her own.

"It was true," she said, Sean had called at her place. He was staggering, and whiter than usual. She had never known Sean to let on he felt tired or ill. She had tried to persuade him to stay, but he was so angry, so intent on swearing out a warrant for Frank's arrest that he would not. She had watched him go, climbing the hill that was part of a two-mile railroad cut. The tracks lay between the cliffs for several miles. At different times, various people had reported seeing a bright light there. That light was a forerunner they said.

"You'll see," they said, "either somethin' awful once happened down there, or somethin' will. Ye wouldn't ketch me down them tracks after dark for no money."

It was a desolate stretch, with twists and turns hardly a train's length apart. More than once the engineer had to stop the train to let a frightened fawn scamper off the track to the safety of the woods. There had been other animals not so fortunate. At the end of the cut, the welcoming valley stretched to the end of the horizon. The shallow water of the wide river twisted and turned past farms that dotted the cool green landscape. At the first farm, Anna had stood watching Sean that morning as he climbed off the tracks and up the side of the cliff. She'd seen him turn and look back. Anna had stood there with an empty pig bucket in her hand, shading her eyes against the sun. She heard the train chugging along and saw Sean's hand raised in greeting. The engine whistle blew, Anna waved her hand as she always did, then turned and went back into the house.

In the kitchen, Old Don, her father-in-law, sat in the rocker before the fire, his eyes half closed, but watching every move and hearing every word.

"That's funny," he said to Anna. "Did ye hear the train stop?"

Before Anna could reply, the whistle blew again—long urgent blasts—not ones she was used to. She knew something must be wrong. Grabbing her jacket, she flew out the door, jabbing her arms into the armholes as she went and leaving the door open behind her. She started to run, heedless of the rough ground and steep slope.

Up ahead, the train had stopped. The crew had gathered in a group, staring at something on the track. Out of breath, Anna stopped. Only the brake-man facing her noticed she was there.

"Mrs. Cameron, ye'd best not come any farther. There's been an accident."

Anna looked from one to the other. Then following their eyes, she saw Sean's hat lying on its side, between the tracks. She could see the soiled sweatband, the crown crushed and inside out. A little off to the side, laced to the top, and standing side by side, stood Sean's gumshoes. A little further up the line she could see a stockinged foot and leg, and further along, another. Anna felt the blood leave her head. She looked at the men, but they were taking no notice of her. They were looking at something else. Something lying there between the tracks, a few feet ahead of the engine. At first it looked like a bunch of ragged clothing, splashed with red paint—but the paint was moving, and the spots growing larger. The shapeless heap lay still. Anna remembered Sean, as she had last seen him waving to the train from the top of the cliff.

"Ye'd best go back, Anna. Don't look no more."

Anna shook her head. Her eyes followed the track. At the mouth of the cutting lay another object, commanding in its silence. Steadily, Anna walked toward it. The men followed her. There it lay, as though made of wax, its base cut evenly, smoothly, and cleanly across. Not one spot of blood was to be seen. It was the first time that Anna had seen that much of Sean's neck. The still white face, with its arrogantly pointed moustache, thick eyebrows, and thin sensitive nose, was all too familiar. Mottled, grey-streaked hair, released from the confinement of the old hat, fell across his forehead in long spiderlike threads. Anna didn't faint, cry out, or show any emotion. She was still staring when the men came up behind her.

Anna's story was nearly ended. "There wasn't much in his pockets," she said. "Except, of course, the old aspirin box with his gum in it." Mary knew what she meant.

"Quit the old pipe two months ago," she'd heard Sean say. "Chew gum now."

"He had a key ring with God knows what keys in it," Anna went on. "Some bills for feed for the horses and that old watch he carried all the time. It was smashed flat. They went through four shirts and three pairs of pants before they got the pocket-book he used to give such a loud snap to when he'd close it hard. Twas in the pair next to his skin. I guess they were glad when it was over. We thought he had money, but there was only three dollars and twenty-three cents on him. If he's got any money, it's hid somewhere."

"So the old watch is gone," Mary sighed. Sean had been proud of that watch, even though he couldn't tell the time. It was a big cumbersome thing on a heavy chain. Everyone had seen it at least once. No one could resist asking Sean the time, just to see him pull out his watch and turn it so its face could be seen.

"I didn't think it was that late," he'd say.

SEAN WAS WAKED ONLY ONE NIGHT. There were no relatives to come from away. Frank was the only one close to him, and Frank had never wasted affection on him.

The funeral was much larger than anyone expected. Rigs arrived from at least ten miles out of town and from all directions. Long slow processions converged on the little church.

Frank was brought along, though firm persuasion was required. He had been drinking. Learning how little there was in Sean's pocketbook, he'd gone home and out to the barn. He climbed into the loft and forked down hay for the horses until the mounds reached almost to the ceiling. Without a glance at the animals, and not bothering to water them, he went straight to the harness room. He pulled halters, collars, girths, and spangled trappings down from their nails. When he found what he was looking for, he stepped over the pieces he had dropped and went out the door.

Frank felt he'd been fooled. He'd searched everywhere for Sean's money. All right then, he'd get money anyway, in spite of Sean. Carrigan would pay twenty-two dollars for this single harness with the shiny trimming. It was only a quarter of a mile to Carrigan's.

They found Frank at Joe Mac's, just before the funeral. They held him down and shaved him, in spite of his threats and curses. Frank managed to free himself and swish the shaving cream off his face, and they didn't insist he wash his hands. One man each side of him, bolster fashion, they got him to the top step of the church and then let him shift for himself. Another pallbearer was chosen in his place.

"Had Frank found Sean's money?" people wondered. Some said Sean kept his money in that old seaman's chest of his. He had been seen buying a padlock for it. "And didn't he keep the key on the little table beside his bed?" But Frank knew all about this chest. He used to help himself from it when Sean was out of the house. And when Sean padlocked it, he simply took off the hinges and was in business again. "Heard it was Sean's money paid fer that last spree him and Red Harry was on!" The talk went on. "Sean couldn't make out how much he had, bein' he couldn't count. After that he quit usin' the chest.... A.J. said how he'd seen Sean at the Coop, buyin' a copper pot.... He'd made sure it had a tight lid.... And payin' $3.50 fer it too!"

"Well, no dish like that ever comed into the house!" Sean's closest neighbour said, shaking his head. "He musta bought it for another reason. He knowed copper wouldn't rust, or get ruined like tin if it was buried."

Red Harry was working on this too. Sean, he reasoned, would have the most of his five years pension money. Maybe not in that pot, but somewhere. Sean spent little money on anything but feed for his horses and tobacco. And he'd quit tobacco. A hundred-pound bag of flour a year, the same of oatmeal, a little salt, sugar, tea, and salt fish—only four dollars a hundred on the wharf. So there must be money somewhere.

Red Harry watched Frank throw a handful of earth on the coffin and leave the graveyard. With everyone so preoccupied, it was easy for Red to edge his way through the crowd and follow him. The young ones were dabbing their eyes; the frosty ones, loudly and piously trying to make themselves conspicuous to their Maker, were more in mourning for themselves than for Sean. Red made it to the store just behind Frank. He sat outside in his old relic of a car for a few minutes, then sauntered into the shop too.

Frank was dry, shaking dry, and the drier he got the stronger the trench-taste on his tongue. The forty cents he had was soon in the merchant's cash drawer; and Frank, with a little bottle of flavouring in his hand, went out the door, gulped its contents, and flung the bottle into the bushes. Lounging against the building, Red Harry was apparently concerned with the cigarette he was rolling.

"Well, well, Frank," he said. "Sorry for yer trouble." He nodded towards the bushes. "Did that fix yer up?"

"Hello, Red. It's too sick I am to get a cure out of one drink. You wouldn't happen to have the price of a bottle on yer, would yer?"

"Better than that!" Red Harry said, and reaching into his shirt brought out a bottle, nearly half-full of rum. "Maybe this will help." He paused. "And when you get that money o' Sean's...."

"Sean didn't have no money when they found him. He had it though, lots of it." Any sum over ten dollars was lots to Frank. "Must've put 'er ahide."

"Here, Frank." Red offered the bottle again. "Can't work on one leg." He watched Frank pull the rum down a good inch in the bottle. "Have yer looked for it any place?"

"Not yet," said Frank. "I will though, I will."

"Yer've got it comin', keepin' house for that old bugger all them years," said Red. "I'll help, if ye like. Do yer want help?"

"Yes, ye help, Red. When we git it, we'll share it. Will we go now, Red?"

THREE DAYS THEY WERE MISSING. Three days they searched. They moved every potato in the hole under the kitchen floor. Opened every drawer. Looked under every bed, and shook out their covers. They searched the attic. They found lots of things, but not the money. Pieces of an old spinning wheel. The remains of rat poison. Nothing of value. Even Red Harry was losing his enthusiasm. He was thinking of the two bottles of rum he'd wasted on Frank.

They tried under the eaves, and dug their way through old papers that went back to 1700— but found nothing. And that ghostly sound that haunted the house afterwards...was it Sean laughing at them? Or was it Sean mourning the fate of his horses?

TIME PASSED. The scandal-mongers snooped for fresh news. All fall and winter, no one thought of the horses. But when spring came, time for plowing and cultivating, the news went around. The horses had been seen up the Settlement road. Frank must have sold them on a Sunday when the whole parish was at church, during one of the thaws when no one had to stay home to keep the fire going.

"It was the young feller at old Tom Beaton's saw 'em first," Lauchie told the men hired to pick stones off the road after the grader. "The man that bought 'em had 'em hitched to the plow in the new field he's breakin'. So hard the devil himself couldn't plow it. He was givin' 'em the what for. You could hear 'im hollerin' up in Cape North."

"Somebody should report 'im. Treatin' horses like that," said one of the men.

"Good enough for 'em," said another. "They lived like kings when they was Sean's. Time they did someone some good."

"True enough," said Lauchie, "but young Beaton said their mouths was all bleedin'! Their forelegs and their chests was all splattered."

The men said nothing for a while after that.

Olive

DINNER HAD BEEN READY and waiting when Jim came in from the woods. The meal was over; he lay stretched out on the couch in the kitchen.

"Jim! Will you watch the kids? I want to run down to the school with those books." Mary cleared the table and reached for her coat. "I'll have the truck back in about ten minutes."

"Go ahead, but don't get talking an' forget I gotta be to the woods by one. Can't see why ye bother with that school secretary job anyhow, it's only bother."

"Let's not get into that again. You know why I bother. As long as our own kids are at school I want to know what's going on down there. Be right back."

As Mary turned the bend in the road she could see Olive MacLean hanging out her washing very carefully on the clothesline. Other women used fences for drying clothes and washed as infrequently as possible but Olive washed every day, sometimes twice a day. The moment she saw a spot or stain on her children's clothes, she changed them. Their pale faces were scrubbed until they glowed. They were kept so spotless that they couldn't even play comfortably. It was as though Olive was trying to wash away a guilt of her own.

Olive stood, now, her scrawny neck fitting loosely into the round collar of the coat that hung on her like a sack on a twister hanger. The material was so faded that its colour could only have been guessed. The coat had been cut to hug a figure in double-breasted elegance, but the original owner had been a heavier, much shorter woman than Olive. Here and there a button was missing. Those that remained were each so different in colour and shape that it was hard to tell which had survived the years. On Olive the sleeves were inches above her wrists, and the hem stopped far short of her gnarled knees. Her legs, shapeless as pipes and set immoderately apart, were so thin that a woman's hand could span an ankle. Her feet were at right angles to her legs, and as she walked they flopped like dories in a wild sea.

Mary knew that Olive had seen the truck and recognized the driver, though she neither turned nor gave any sign. She would have to stop. No one in the Glen ever passed a neighbour without a greeting.

"Hi!" Mary called as she switched off the ignition, "just finishing up? Nice day, your clothes should dry in no time. How have you been?"

Olive bent down without a word and picked up the herring bucket full of dry clothes.

"Don't you feel well? Can I get you something? Aspirin maybe? I've some home I'll be glad to bring you."

"ASPIRIN!" Olive's shrill voice cut the air. "Tisn't any aspirin I need. I've been near foolish...haven't slept in two nights... ever since I seen that piece ye put in the paper 'bout us."

"What piece, Olive?... I wouldn't hurt anyone...tell me what it is."

Mary slipped down from the truck and crossed the patch of trodden grass and earth to the un-painted, sagging porch.

"Why don't ye just leave us alone? Makin' a fool outta us... sayin' Dougall expected to get water on th' surface! Just like we was queer...all th' people'll be laughin' at us...."

"Where'd you hear that?" Mary's voice was rising now. "Papers aren't out yet, whoever said that told you a lie...I did mention Dougall was digging a well and that he thought he'd find water near the surface...but wasn't that what he said? Nothin' wrong with that...but you said you read it...how could you? THE PAPERS AREN'T OUT YET!"

"Well, I seen it in the paper...teacher seen it over t' the school. She thought it was so terrible she left class right there and then and came over to show me."

"Where's that paper? Let me see it. You've read it wrong. Where is it? Show me! You've both read it wrong. Let me see it."

"We don't get the paper. It was teacher's, she got it in town. People'll think we're crazy...."

"Just to mention people's names doesn't hurt them. I didn't put anything in to hurt you. Will you please stop carrying on and listen? Maybe it was in the paper the way you say, but I didn't write it that way. Please believe me?"

"Tryin' to make fools of us." Olive wasn't listening. She was shouting, in her shrill querulous voice. "Dougall was awful mad, just wait till he sees you...."

"I'm going to get that paper!" Mary turned and ran to the truck. Had there been a misprint? She drove the short distance to the school and turned in the yard. It was still lunch and Janice MacDonald, school bell in hand, stood in the door watching the children at play. Mary wasted no time coming to the point.

"I just stopped at Olive's. She jumped all over me."

"Didn't you expect it?" Janice grinned. "I knew she was laying for you."

"I feel terrible, I think she's mistaken, I did not say 'on' the ground at all. Have you got the paper? I'd like to see it for myself. Olive said you took it back."

"My paper? I don't have a paper. Did she tell you she saw it in MY paper? Why would she bring ME into this for? She's got the nerve! Just wait till school's over...bringin' me into this.... I get my paper by mail, same as you...an' they haven't come yet. When did I have time to get to town? Oh! I knew all about it. She went for me like there was a death in the family, at recess time yesterday morning. She was wild then, waving the paper in my face. Dan MacTavish was sitting there bug-eyed.... It was HIS paper. He'd brought it from town and stopped off at Olive's on the way home. She saw the paper in his pocket and asked to read it."

"What did the paper say, Janice? ON the surface or near the surface? I want to know."

"To tell you the truth, Mary, she was in such a state—and what with Dan making a jumble out of something he was trying to tell me—well, I just kept sayin' 'YES' to them both to get them out as fast as I could. Recess time was over and I didn't bother trying to get her to hold the paper still so I could see it. I don't know. The paper'll be in the mail tomorrow anyway...don't worry about it...but believe me she's going to hear from me!"

Flying stones hit the fenders as Mary kept the accelerator pedal flush with the floor all the way home. Jim stood in the door, his watch in his hand, waiting. At the sight of her face he tucked the watch into his jeans.

"What's the matter? Your face's as red as boiled lobster. What happened?"

"Oh! That Olive! She straddled me like an old wet hen... didn't even say hello...said I put something in my 'notes' about them that she didn't like."

"Oh! For Pete's sake, Mary! What in hell've ye done now!"

"Oh, SHE says that I wrote Dougall MacLean expects to find water ON the surface. I never said any such thing. I said Dougall MacLean is digging a well. That he expected to find water NEAR the surface."

"OH GOD!" Jim moaned. "Why did ye have to write about 'em at all? Mention their names even?"

"Tell me, what's so bad about that? Anyone who didn't know Dougall would think nothing of it.... I thought the ones in Boston would get a kick out of it. Everyone there takes the home papers."

"After this, don't even mention their names...no matter what!

Our own paper sh'd be in the mail t'morrow. Mebbe they've misprinted it an' ye can explain t' her."

"EXPLAIN? I explained till I was blue in the face already. She just doesn't WANT to believe me. Misprint or not, I'll not go down again and take her guff!"

"Ya know what'll happen, don't ye? Time SHE'S through talkin' everyone'll go by our house like we had the plague. Ya know how SHE IS!" Jim thundered off in the truck. Alone, Mary began to think. What makes her so touchy?

OLIVE CERTAINLY HAD A PRETTY FACE. Her fresh complexion pink and white as icing on a birthday cake. Her eyes bright blue. Her auburn curls peeped out from under a faded babushka like freshly hatched chicks. Her features so delicate—the face of a china figurine that even the shrill defiance in her voice couldn't shatter.

In spite of her anger, Mary found herself trying to make excuses for Olive. She had trials enough. Wasn't she married to Dougall? And Dougall was no prize. As cunning as a cougar, he spent most of his time lying quietly on the wooden bench in the kitchen either rolling or smoking a cigarette. He would worry as he watched Olive put the last stick of firewood in the range. Worry about who he would get to haul and cut wood this time. Then he'd go out, hitch the horse to the sleigh and drive to one of the neighbours. Most likely it would be John J. Campbell's. John J. had three young striplings, and Dougall had a way with young fellows. He had learnt long ago that by talking to them man to man, they'd be happy to do anything he asked. As long as he sat on the woodpile, or went into the woods with them and talked or listened, they would cut and gather wood for him until dark.

If the boys happened to be out on business of their own, Dougall wasn't discouraged. He'd come over and "dicker" with Jim, though a different approach had to be taken.

"How ye fixed for wood, Jim? I was thinking of gittin' a

load fer meself, ye might's well come along and we'll take one down fer ye too."

Dougall didn't fool Jim, but Jim would go along and they'd each have a load. Dougall knew he would have to split the wood for himself, but by evening one of the Campbell lads might be around. Dougall didn't dare take John J. Campbell himself. It was too soon. John J. had cut the last load from his own woods, and hauled it as well. A built-in warning system told Dougall when the limit had been reached.

Every year Dougall had the harvest all worked out from the time the seed went into the ground. This year would be Jim's. Last year had been J. J. Campbell's. Hayfork over his shoulder, cigarette hanging loosely from his lip, Dougall set out to help Jim. Jim hated to see Dougall coming. He knew that Dougall's hayfork would only serve as a leaning post while countless cigarettes were rolled and advice and orders given.

"All righttt! Now Jim." Dougall had a way of stretching out his words that always made Jim flinch. "Me hay'll be ready t'morrow. Andy, he cut 'er t'day." Andy was Dougall's brother. "Oh, yeh! Will ye bring yer pitchin' rope along...mine's busted."

As long as Jim could remember Dougall had been using that broken pitching rope as an excuse to get one neighbour or another to bring his own rope and climb to the top of the barn and affix it. Dougall had a deathly fear of heights.

"Don't you worry now. Be plenty help. Plenty. John J.'s boys'll be there 'n with yer big truck won't be a minute gittin' the hay in. Well, all right then Jim. Be expectin' ye 'bout ten? Right after the dew dries a little."

DOUGALL WASN'T MUCH TO LOOK AT, nor did he have any redeeming qualities. His head, thrust forward between narrow hunched shoulders, seemed to defy the strength of his stringy body to hold it erect. The thin, protruding lower lip never quite managed to hide his toothless gums. His teeth had rotted away slowly and painfully through the years. Like all who depend on their fellow man for existence, he made new acquaintances at the drop of a hat. His animal cunning told him that a small favour (whether wanted or unwanted) would make it impossible for the recipient to refuse him, later on. He was constantly in debt. He changed his grocery store at least three times a year. When he ran out of stores, he begged, or borrowed enough to satisfy the merchant who had been waiting the longest, then made the rounds again.

Dougall provided deer meat and game for his family. A whole puncheon of venison salted, for the winter, and another of fish. Partridge, carefully cleaned and stored, furnished rare treats and there was always fresh rabbit for a good winter stew. Dougall had a great love of hunting and fishing, in or out of season. In the hunting season, he scraped up the money for a guide's license—and many the hunter he guided went home without a lantern, a rifle, or anything else that took Dougall's fancy. Not that Dougall stole any of these things; he merely admired them or asked for them pointblank. If the hunter was not able to get a deer of his own—very often because Dougall had led them where there were none—Dougall usually had a spare carcass hanging in his barn, with a steep price tag on it.

Olive never saw a penny of Dougall's money. Beyond a few staples for the kitchen, like flour, salt, sugar and tea—candy for the children usually came after his visits to the vendor—Dougall's obligation to his family was discharged. Money in Dougall's pocket was like a crown on his head, a sceptre in his hand. He no longer needed to flatter, to speak with caution. He could say exactly what he thought about everyone and everything. It was Olive who got the lash of his tongue. This was the one way she could tell there was money around.

OLIVE'S FIRST LOVE had been a boy from the next village. They met in the city. Playing on their common heritage he had easily seduced her and as blithely disappeared when she had told him about her pregnancy. The country priest had the answer to all problems, temporal and spiritual; and now Olive, penitent and ashamed, went to her church for help.

The priest was kind. He told her about the Home for Unmarried Mothers, he even took her there himself.

"There, there!" he said, as they stood waiting on the doorstep for the bell to be answered. "Don't be afraid, my child. There's nothing to be afraid of."

"Good evening, Father," a nun said, opening the door. "Is this the young lady you called me about?" She was smiling. "Olive, isn't it?" The nun put her hand on Olive's shoulder. Her hand was warm and gentle.

"Olive, here, thinks she's alone in her trouble, Sister," the priest said. He put out his hand and clasped Olive's fingers. "Good-bye, my child, God is with you always."

"You'll soon get used to us here," Sister said as she closed the door. "Father has told me about you, so you won't be embarrassed by any questions. Girls! Girls!" she called as she led Olive into the parlour. "The girls will fill you in on our routine." Four girls trooped into the shabby parlour.

"I want you to meet Olive," Sister said. "Olive this is Sue, Jane, Theresa, and Helen. Theresa and Helen will be leaving us soon, but the rest of us will be together for some time. Theresa, you show Olive up to the room Margaret was in."

Sue and Jane had swollen bellies. Jane was pretty, she talked in a low voice but Sue didn't speak, she just smiled her welcome.

"Theresa 'n me've had our babies," Helen said as they climbed the stairs.

"Yeah!" said Theresa, "we c'n go out two nights a week now. Two weeks more and we'll have our keep all worked off—and be gone from here."

THE DORMITORY WAS A LONG ROOM, partitioned by wallboard into cubicles. Theresa took Olive's suitcase to the end cubical and dropped it beside the cot. The chest of drawers, mirror, and dresser were spotless. There was an abundant smell of antiseptic and cheap perfume.

"This is s'pose to be a room, so's we c'n have privacy," said Helen, "but if you as much as whisper Theresa 'n me c'n hear ya down the other one." They all laughed.

"You said somethin' about bein' paid up," said Olive, "what did ya mean?"

"Yisss! Paid up," said Theresa. "Ya might's well hear 'bout it now as later. If ya wants, when yer baby comes, ya c'n stay on and work to pay up yer keep an' yer doctor. Course, if yer guy comes through with th' dough...work's out! Helen'n me couldn't stick to no guy, so we work. No law sayin' ye have to but ya never know when ya might wanna come back. This place's gittin' like home t' me."

"Been here twice b'fore, she means," Helen cut in. "Me too... only just once though. I couldn't point to no guy special...'n if I stuck someone there wouldn't be a guy in the country'd look 't me agin'...be too smart. Brother! Wouldn't that be the end." They both laughed. Olive didn't see anything to laugh at.

Every evening at six o'clock there was chapel. The babies had all been fed, the cleaning, washing and ironing all done. Sue was always attentive in chapel, praying as though she was talking to a God she could see. Olive liked Sue. She liked her gentle speech. Sue didn't make jokes about the service when she got back upstairs. Jane didn't either, but she talked more; she didn't keep to herself as Sue did.

The talk after chapel opened a new world for Olive. Words like "hot" had a different meaning, but not hard to interpret. Most of the talk was about men. "Don't go into a shell," Jane warned, "or yer licked." Jane was a city girl. "I can't help seein' in yer eyes th' others talk sometimes. Some of us are different. Sue'll be crying soon. Always does. She got left. Her boy told her if she'd do it fer him she'd lay anyone and, by God, she wasn't gonna stick him! He was th' only guy, an' he knew it. The rat! I wuz engaged, goin' to be married...show you the ring someday. I keep it on a string around m' neck. Guy got killed in an accident. Don't you listen to Theresa and Helen t'morrow night, when they git in. Helen's dyin' t' git it over with too. All she talks about. To git a man. Gonna keep yer baby? I am. He'll be a part of my Dave anyway. I was crazy about Dave. I'll never git married now." Jane sighed! She didn't wait for Olive to answer her question.

Soon it was time for the lights out and there was silence.

"Hi youse! Wake up and get the news!" Olive woke instantly. "Helen an' me went to th' Red Apple. That place is always good fer a pickup. What a hunk o' muscle I got! Tall, dark an' han'some just like in the mags.... HE was standin' there just inside th' door—like he wuz waitin' fer me all the time. I made with th' eyes, an' firs' thing ye know we're havin' a drink at the bar. After a couple he says, 'Look I gotta guy over here all alone, ya don't know another bird, do ya?' That was Helen's cue, did she ever come in on the dot! Then...WOW! Ya shouldda seen th' albatross she got! Short an' fat an' waddled like a duck...how they got around them whiskers? Tell me that?"

"G'wan!" Helen giggled, "don't you gals b'lieve 'er. That wuz a MAN! Th' whiskers only made 'im more like Tarzan. Not fat, just pleasantly plump. Besides, ye can't tell a turtle by 'is shell!"

So this was what Jane had warned her about. Theresa and Helen were deliberately trying to excite the other girls, and make them conscious of their sexless lives.

"We went up on Lover's Lane—took a bottle with us."

"We really put it on fer 'em," Theresa broke in, "fought like tigers, an' all the jazz, an' laughin' up m' sleeve all th' time. I wasn't gonna come across right away an' git ditched THAT early. I ain't no fool. Fell fer that just once."

"Girls! Go to sleep." It was Sister's voice. In the darkness, no one could hear her, know how long she'd been there, how much she'd heard.

OLIVE'S LETTERS CAME from her brother Ronnie's new wife, Christina. Ronnie himself was never one to write. Olive never answered. Once or twice, overcome by homesickness, she went to the writing desk in the common room. Then she thought of Mrs. Douglas, the postmistress at home, holding up envelopes to the lamp or to the window. So Olive went on into the chapel, where she lit a candle and prayed that no one would ever find out where she was.

Olive's son was born on St. David's Day; she christened him David. She thought of his father, but only long enough to be glad she didn't have to share her baby with him.

A letter arrived with the Glen postmark. She opened it and glanced at the signature. The letter was from Dougall.

"You'd best marry me. I've got me Uncle's place now, you'll need a home. We'll fix the place up some...."

Olive threw the letter into the fire. The nerve of him to ask her to be his wife! That he should feel free to ask her to marry him! Everyone knew he had fathered his sister's son—the boy was the picture of him. Dougall—the hookworm—and a head shorter than herself! All the girls tittered behind his back. None of them would dance with him.

A second letter came. Olive read it then tore it up too and threw it into the waste paper basket. She was neither indignant nor angry.

The days passed. Olive worked, and fondled her baby. At night she lay awake and walked miles to nowhere. When Sister told her that she would have to have a lawyer if she wanted to have the child adopted, and that a lawyer would cost seventy-five dollars, Olive scarcely listened. Nothing mattered now; David was hers.

Dougall wrote again:

"Dear Olive.... You'd best make up yer mind to marry me

when ye git out and come home. I've got my Uncle's place and with a little fixing up you'll have a home. Answer rite away because Jim Douglas is home and he wants to buy the place. If you say no I'm gonna sell it to them. You've got a week to answer.—Yours Truly, Dougall MacLean."

Olive looked at the envelope. She saw it was posted in the Glen Post Office. She tore the letter across again and again until the pieces that fell into the waste paper basket were too small to tear again. If only she could go home everything would be so simple. But she couldn't do that. Could she keep her baby and work? What if her boss found out? She would be sacked right away. She couldn't. To go home—if only she could go home!

One day the postman brought another letter from Christina. "I and Ronnie will take the baby, Olive. Ron thinks he should be with his own people. Sister wrote us you called him David. It's a good name. Ron's glad. Sister said you had to stay for a while. Let us know when to come for him. When you get out you can come home with us too. Write soon. Christina."

That was the first letter Olive answered. That night she slept the whole night through. Maybe it wouldn't be so bad. She could dress the child, feed him, watch him grow. Maybe buy him little things now and then. That's all she could hope for both of them.

THE DAY CAME FOR OLIVE TO LEAVE the home. She picked up her cheap little suitcase and looked around the dormitory. "Will you write to me?" Sue begged. "You're lucky. You will see your baby every day.... M'self—I don't know what will happen to me.... Father keeps telling me how hard it'll be to keep him. Sister keeps trying to explain how much better off he would be with a father and mother. You were so comforting, Olive.... You didn't have to talk...you were just there, that was enough. Will you pray for my baby and for me? Pray God'll show us a way too?"

"Yes, Sue, I will—every night. You hev helped me too... thank you. I'll write if I can."

But Olive never did write.

Christina's first words had been, "Everyone's longin' t' see ya, Olive." Then she stood back as if looking for traces of Olive's pregnancy. "So many've asked about ye lately. Ye'll see 'em all at church t'marra, anyways."

"Welcome home, Olive!" Mrs. Douglas, all smiles and offering a welcoming hand, had been first. Head high, Olive looked neither to the right nor left. She stepped firmly on her heels straight down to her pew, only two back from the altar rail. What had she worried about? They were all the same. Nothing had changed. Right now they were all commenting on her new dress. "Look at th' style of 'er," she could almost hear them say.

These were nothing like the women the girls in the Home had talked about. They hadn't turned away when they saw her coming. Olive thought of all her talks with Jane at the Home. Jane couldn't have been wrong. But why were things so different here? Or were they? She thought of all the women kneeling around her. Mrs. Douglas. Olive had been only a child then, and memories were hazy, but there had been talk...someone had mentioned her wedding and birth announcement in the same mail from Boston.... Mrs. Douglas had run away to get married! And Mrs. John J. How well she remembered the smirks on the women's faces. The remarks. "The first can come anytime." "Didn't waste no time." Only words to her then but she knew better now. To your face they pretended nothing was wrong, but in the kitchens they would tear you apart. Maybe it was a good thing to be like Christina who didn't care what any of them said about her. But no.... She could never give them another chance like that...never. Yes, she had made a mistake, but she would never again give any of them reason to gossip about her.

DOUGALL WAITED AND WATCHED. He knew all the signs of the forest, what kind of bait the fish were taking, the antler marks on trees in the woods. He knew Olive loved to dance. He also knew that she had been to four dances since she'd come back and that no man had taken her on the floor. She had not been at the last two dances.

Then came the Sunday that the priest announced banns for Angus Beaton's daughter. The same afternoon, young Angus and a carload of friends made the rounds of all the farms inviting those they met and leaving word for any they may have missed. No one ever missed one of the Beaton dances. The Beaton family had four good fiddlers amongst them and an old piano, good food and a big barn to dance in. They made their own whiskey, which was strong and plentiful, and no one ever complained of being stinted. After two or three shots of the colourless bush Dougall forgot he couldn't dance, that he was over fifty, and without a date in his life. He even forgot about the boy up at the old homestead who looked so much like him.

"Yell hev t' take me t' git Olive now, John J.," he said to John J. Campbell. "Only take a minute." Dougall demanded, wheedled and insisted, until it was easier for John J. to give in than to listen.

RONNIE AND CHRISTINA had gone off to the dance, but Olive stayed home with the baby. She lay sleeping beside him on his pallet by the fire. The radio had signed off, it was midnight. She glanced at the clock on the shelf. Five minutes fast.... Better set it back or it would be fifteen minutes fast by morning. There was someone driving up.... She moved from the rocking chair to the window. Ronnie pushed the door open. Olive saw the deep lines between his eyes, only noticeable when he was annoyed.

"Is anything wrong?"

"Christina didn't wanna c'm home but I've got t' git up early.... T'marra harvesters'll be here. I'm goin' t' bed. Dougall's comin' in. He wants ye sh'd go t' the party. Leave David with me if ye go. I'll watch 'im."

"Cummina Hashen!" It was Dougall, pushing wide the door.

"Why'nt ye at th' dance, Olive? Ye're missin' a good one. John J.'s out there in th' car, now, waiting.... I got 'im t' take me t' git ye. Git yer clothes on, now, get a move on ye."

"But the baby...."

"Niver mind th' baby.... Ron'll take care a him."

"Look ye! It's midnight...."

"Whatssa matter wi' that? She's jist gittin' good now...last till mornin'."

"That's just it...I'm tired."

"Tired?" Dougall winked at Ron. "You git ye a taste of bush an' ye'll be wide awake."

Whatever the excuse, Dougall had an answer. In the end Olive picked up the baby and went into the front room to get ready.

AFTER THAT DOUGALL PURSUED OLIVE into the corner at every neighbour's kitchen. Molly Campbell felt sorry for Olive, yet encouraged the match. "We welcomed 'em when they had no place else t' go an' give 'em th' best room we had t'spare. I even said t' Sally not t' go near 'em...and t' keep the kids away."

Soon after the banns were published, John J. and Molly sent word around that they were giving a shower for Dougall and Olive. The shower wasn't much, as almost everyone gave money, but it provided them with something to set up house. Their first baby arrived in nine months. David remained with Ronnie and Christina. Each following year, regular as spring, a new baby joined the family. Year after year Olive watched her eldest son being dragged about the roads witnessing drunken brawls. Christina had taken to going outside the house for her fun, and David was her alibi. Year after year Olive watched her son store up memories of his foster mother and her lovers. Year by year she nursed and scrubbed her children. She had no real friends so all these things were kept locked securely inside her heart.

Yes, Olive! The first of ten children born to Thomas and

Catherine Lander. No school until she was eight because of rough weather and long distances. So many days when she had to stay at home to help her mother with the younger children, that she had trouble keeping up in class. She had been taught reading, writing, and how to figure a little by a local teacher, herself only locally taught.

When Olive's breasts began to show beneath her makeshift dresses, her father, old Thomas, sent for her. He stuffed his pipe with great deliberation, and whipped a match across his denims.

"Yer a growed woman now, Olive. Isn't it alright fer me t' be gittin' a little help...a little somethin' back...after rearin' ye all these years?" It wasn't a question. He hadn't meant it to be.

"Bernie...you know, the young fellow at the station...him and his wife'll be goin' back t' th' city in a couple of days. I'll speak to 'im t'marra...see if they got room to take ye with 'em. Ye kin stay wi' them a few days while you git yerself a little job. Start gittin' yer things t'gether.... Herself 'll give ye a hand."

Herself had cried bitterly out in the backhouse; many could only have gone behind the barn.

Who would know if her mother ever wished she had told Olive the facts of life, instead of hoping her daughter had picked up all she needed to know from the animals? For she died soon after Olive left home and old Thomas wasted no time replacing her. No longer was there a place for Olive at home. Besides, was she not a "growed woman now"?

King

SONNY WAS FOUR YEARS OLD when "King" made his appearance. King was just another day-old chick among a shipment of fifty other little chicks, who had got in with the "girls" quite by accident. When Jim, Sonny's father, found out that he was a rooster, King was immediately sentenced to the frying pan—the execution to take place when he was three months old. But that was before Sonny had anything to say about it.

It was love at first sight, and when Sonny pleaded, Jim couldn't resist.

Sonny promptly called the chick "King" and treated him accordingly. He was fed the choicest food, whether it was good for him or not. Sonny would take bites of this and that from his plate at mealtimes—and from Neeny's plate too, if she delayed with her dolls or let her attention wander from her plate. He always brought bits of paper to the table with him and when he thought his mother wasn't looking, he would collect scraps of bacon, egg, bread and butter and, under the tablecloth, wrap them up and stuff them into his pocket, until the meal was over and he could join his friend in the barn. King grew to love Sonny more every day.

By the beginning of the fall, King's feathers were a brilliant red streaked with ebony, and his head crowned with a shimmering scarlet coronet. He made his first vocal declaration of his status. That first crow was a silly kind of noise, half squeak, half high-pitched choking cackle, but King was too proud to notice. He was like a boy suddenly aware of his changing voice who hoped that by singing continually his voice would change all the sooner.

Sonny learned to crow too, and to crow better than King, so that no one could tell for sure whether it was the rooster or child who was crowing. From the moment Sonny had breakfast in the morning and went out the door, Mary knew exactly where he could be found, for he and King made a racket calling back and forth to each other.

On the first greeting of the day King would race out of the barn in a straight line for the kitchen door, his head stretched out before him, his wings spread, and calling as he ran. He did not relax his speed until he stood stiff-legged before his friend. Mary couldn't help feeling frightened as she watched him, his left leg in little flopping jigs round the little fellow; scolding mightily, until Sonny would pick him up and tuck him under his jacket. This became increasingly difficult for Sonny as King grew so much faster than he did.

Everywhere Sonny went King would follow. The two of them carried on a rooster conversation. Very soon the barn became too far away from his friend to suit King, so he took to sleeping on the fence post just under Sonny's window. Sonny thought this an ideal arrangement. Jim and Mary weren't so happy, for King would decide to check up on his friend at odd hours of the night, and crow in the loudest voice.

ONE MORNING, VERY EARLY, somewhere between three and four, Mary and Jim were awakened suddenly. King wasn't crowing. He was screaming like an old hen. A fox again!

Jim jumped into his bedside slippers and sped down the stairs in his white long-handled underwear, and out the door, not bothering to close it behind him. In less than a minute Mary found herself standing at the window. Jim was striding over the hill beyond the garden. His weird white figure appeared to be all appendages. She could hear the high-pitched single-note whistle he reserved especially for Beauty, their wise old dog. Beauty, a flash of black and white, streaked over the hill. A crescendo of vicious snarling shook the silent night. Then there was quiet. Her eyes strained through the morning dusk, Mary could see Jim moving somewhat self-consciously down the hill towards the barn. He seemed to be carrying something. The bundle fluttered and squawked. King was alive!

"Tis a good dog," Jim said, as he hastily pulled up the covers. "The rooster's all right. Shook up a little. Beauty got the fox."

Now with fear past, the vision of Jim flying over the hill in his long white underwear came back to Mary, and the bed shook with her strangled laughter.

UNTIL HIS PLUMAGE RETURNED to its former glory, King was just a trifle humbler, a trifle less loquacious, but with the return of the lustre to his coat his superiority surged. He didn't stop at just scolding, he started to chase Mary. Not while she was looking at him full in the face, admittedly, but as soon as she turned away. He would pretend to be scornfully ignoring her, and showing great interest in some imaginary object in the distance. He would go as far as turning his back on her and walking in the opposite direction. But as soon as Mary would turn towards the house he was after her. At first he stopped short, as he did when approaching Sonny, but very soon this sport became too tame for him and he started to nip at the back of her legs. Daily Mary grew more and more apprehensive, and complained to Jim. But her complaints fell on deaf ears. Jim had never seen the performance, and since Mary had no scars to prove her point, her worries were not taken seriously.

Very soon, growing bolder with the knowledge of Mary's fear, King wouldn't allow anyone, not even Jim, to touch Sonny. Not even to smooth his hair, straighten his clothes, or handle him in any way.

One day he flew at Jim and would have lost his head then

and there if Sonny hadn't been choking with laughter, thinking it all a game and great sport. Mary took to carrying a broom handle with her every time she went outdoors.

Another day, Mary was baking bread in the kitchen, Neeny was playing with her dolls in the other room, and Sonny and King were in the field at the edge of the woods—at least so Mary thought. She happened to look up—and there, through the window, she could see two little brown legs disappearing up a ladder Jim had left standing against the house. Soon the little legs disappeared out of sight above the window frame. Mary flew out of the door, and there was Sonny, the rooster in his arms, high up the ladder beside the brick flue. Mary felt frightened and furious—frightened lest the boy might fall, and furious with Jim for not removing the ladder when he had finished cleaning the flue. She knew she couldn't help Sonny down with the rooster in his arms. Afraid to startle the child, she had to content herself with standing under the ladder ready to catch him if he fell, and encourage him gently to feel carefully for each rung as he slowly descended.

"The King would have to go!" Mary decided, as she put the ladder away and hurried to the woodpile. She had almost forgotten she was in the middle of baking and needed small wood for a quick fire. Sonny and King were chattering away in rooster language, none the worse for their adventure. Mary chose three chunks from the pile and was halfway back to the house when she heard King's flying feet and flapping wings just behind her. The next minute she felt his beak snap down on her flesh just behind her knee. King had chosen the wrong time to prove his superiority.

That night Mary issued her ultimatum. This time there would be no reprieve. But the next day, as she watched the child and bird running races between the house and the barn, and Sonny laughing so hard that his little legs refused to move, Mary was sad. How could such a beautiful creature have such a diabolical nature? How could you take a loved one from a child? King was granted a stay of execution!

ALL SUMMER LONG the child and the bird played together, content and happy. Fall came and passed, and one day angry winds came chasing out of the north driving powdery white snow. For ten days Sonny frowned. King sat silently on his perch. Then the wind spent itself, and the sun shone again. Mary and Jim were considering where to start their first day of winter, but Sonny could only think of getting his clothes on and going out to see his friend. He hardly touched his breakfast that morning.

In the barn King was equally impatient, and stood waiting at the door for the moment Jim would open it. He had been crowing unceasingly since dawn. As Jim opened the door, he stepped haughtily out into the snow. After the first step he stopped, and gazed all about him. He couldn't understand what had happened to his world. Then his eyes focused on the house, the place where his friend would be. He spread his wings wide, and flapped them with exuberance. Stretching his graceful neck to its fullest extent he crowed a greeting that rang for miles across the silent white countryside.

Inside the house, Mary was trying to fasten a wiggling Sonny into a snowsuit. Sonny answered King's greeting with an equally piercing call that nearly split Mary's eardrums. With two hops Sonny was out the door. King darted towards him, disregarding all precautions. The next moment a foot went down in a drift over the drumstick, and he fell ignominiously on his side. Angrily, he put his weight on the other foot, which was still on solid ground swept bare by the eccentric wind. The buried foot was extricated. With great deliberation it was regarded. First with his head tipped to one side, then to the other. Seeing nothing wrong, he decided to peck and peck at it, first one side and then the other. At last, giving up, he tucked the injured leg among his feathers where, at least, it would be kept warm, and he stood there on one foot, with his proud head bowed.

Sonny rushed blindly towards his friend and fell headlong into a drift. He was far too concerned by his imprisonment to notice that King, having warmed his foot a little and surveyed the perilous world about him, gave one milk-curdling "Oeeeeerr-rooooo" and limped back to the barn with what little pride he could muster.

Mary saw it all. She rushed out to pull Sonny out of the drift and wipe down his clothes, and saw him tear off to the barn to join his friend. There was no one in the barn to witness their reunion, but everyone knew, by the racket, the joy and happiness they felt. They played all day. It was a happy day.

The wind came with the setting sun. Snow began to fall. The storm raged for two weeks, day and night.

Sonny, confined to the house, coaxed, pleaded and cried to be allowed to go to the barn. Mary was firm, and Sonny stayed indoors. At odd moments he'd sit preoccupied, elbows on his little table in the Christmas tree corner, his chin in his hands, listening. Once or twice, when the wind stopped to draw breath, he thought he could hear his friend calling, but the crow was so muffled and far away, he couldn't be sure.

In the barn, King, alone and cold, fluffed up the feathers he no longer felt like pruning, and mourned. Now and then he did call out, in a pitiful, humble voice, strange even for himself.

The days were cold. The nights colder. King came down from his perch only to eat, and drink the dish of warm milk Mary left for him when she had finished milking. His crown was jagged and discoloured now, and stood only half as high as before. Part of it had frozen and fallen off. His calls grew further and further apart, until at last he forgot about the summer games with his friend, as if they had only been a dream.

Mary and Jim were greatly concerned about their quiet, morose little son, and waited patiently for the storm to come to an end. It was almost like a death in the family. They whispered in their room late at night and slept little. Neeny fretted and walked about with her mouth drawn down at the corners, tears very near the surface.

THEN THE SUN SHONE AGAIN!

Mary and Jim rose early. They had noticed the change in the weather shortly past midnight, and wanted to be ready in case it would be possible to travel. The heavy wood-sleigh would have to go into service, if the change in the wind meant what they expected.

That morning, King came down from his perch as usual for his milk. Then he walked to the door, left open purposely for him. Half-heartedly, he shook his feathers, stared around, took a few uninterested pecks at the snow, and turned back into the barn. He jumped on to his perch, lifted one foot and tucked it under his feathers. There Sonny found him; head pulled in close to his body—and silent.

Sonny used every wile he could think of to persuade him to come down. Mary helped too. But King refused to play. And although he allowed the child to hold and fondle him, he wouldn't answer Sonny's greeting. Disappointed, and with chin quivering, Sonny set the bird back on the perch and, stroking him gently, said:

"G'bye, King. Why don't you answer me?"

Sonny turned and went back into the house. Mary stayed in the barn with Jim while he nailed a frame two feet square and covered it with wire. Then, with the bird squatting in the bed of hay he had placed inside, Jim carried the wire box to the henhouse. King would be warm in the henhouse, but not free. He would be well fed, but not for long.

The rest of the day was a busy one for Mary.

Jim had gone into town in the sleigh. Neeny's spirits lifted a little, in spite of Sonny's sadness. The day passed quickly. Mary even found herself singing as she went about her work, and Jim arrived home earlier than she expected. Sonny took the candy his father had brought for him, but sat quietly at the table while Neeny romped around with excitement. Then Jim took a shoe box he carried under his arm and placed it on the table. At first Sonny took no notice. Mary had her apron pulled up and rolled into a ball in her hands, as she stood watching. Then the box moved. Just a little shake, but it moved. At the same time a tiny "meeeeeew" came from inside.

Sonny was like a sphinx come to life. His eyes sparkled. He sprang to his feet. His hand fumbled with the string around the box. A little pink tongue poked out of the crack as the lid slid back. Sonny stood transfixed. Then very softly he "mewed," and giggled and pulled at the string some more. When there was a space big enough for his hand, he reached in and pulled out a blue-eyed black-and-white kitten who immediately began to sing with happiness.

"Is he mine, Daddy? Is he mine? Can I have him for all my own?"

"Of course, Sonny," said Jim. "I got him for you. You be good to him now, he's only a baby. You can't play rough with him like you did with the rooster."

"Oooooo, I won't. I won't. Oh, you're all mine. What do we care if old King won't play anymore?"

John R. and Son

~ A Novel ~

JOHN R. HAD BEEN SICK ALL WEEK but hadn't given in. Only that morning had he finally taken to his bed and allowed his son John J. to call the doctor. The doctor looked gravely over his steel-rimmed spectacles, shook his head slowly from side to side, and left muttering grimly:

"Pneumonia. I'll leave some pills but if you have anyone away, ye'd best let 'em know."

John J. drove the doctor home, stopped at a store for extra supplies for all the teas his wife, Molly, and Theresa—he always called his mother by her Christian name—would soon be making. He called at his father's sister with the news. She was his only living relative and the news spread fast.

Visitors started to arrive shortly after John J. reached home, and came in a steady flow all day. If John R. hadn't guessed how bad he was before, he knew now for certain. A ring of solemn neighbours stood around his bed. They had to stand; there were no chairs in the small room. There was no window, no furniture except for the bed with its mattress of oat straw and an upended apple box to hold the lamp. They all said the same thing:

"Ye'll feel better come morning," and went out shaking their heads.

Downstairs they stopped for tea. Their jokes and loud laughter could be heard as clearly in the sickroom as in the kitchen. But always there was the never-ending circle of faces round the old man's bed.

It was into one of these circles that John J. forced his way, paper in hand. The will was only a few scribbled lines. John J. had laboriously constructed them himself with a stub of a pencil on lined tablet paper. He looked down at his father. Old John's eyes still glowered under his heavy grey eyebrows.

"John R.," he said, "ye'd best sign the will." The old man looked at his son but didn't bat an eyelash.

"I will in the morning," he said.

"Ach! Ye'll be dead before morning." John J. forced a pencil between his father's fingers. "Ye'd best sign it now."

Old John signed without reading the paper. He knew how it was made out and was beyond caring.

"Left to you, there'll be nothing but two hundred acres o' worn-out land in the woods not worth willing." This was his only comment. John J. looked at the signature, then motioned to the two neighbours beside him to add their names before leading them back down to the kitchen.

OLD JOHN R. WAS A LITTLE MAN. Stretched out, his body ended in two mounds a good eighteen inches from the end of the bed. His wizened little face on the pillow, stubbled with grey and white whiskers, bore all the scars of a hard life and of a hard man. John R. had always expected full value for every cent. He had extracted every drop of sweat from his family, his horses and himself. In fact he had been hard on everything except the clasp of his money pouch. Although the leather had become worn and rough, the clasp was as firm as a bear trap. Old John liked to keep it closed—except when putting money in—and it was his love of money that forced the major decision in his life. His marriage.

John R. had been a normal young man with a normal young

man's appetite for sex. He carefully balanced desire against the cost of feeding and clothing a wife. He found the cost excessive, even taking into consideration the help a wife would be, working in the house and in the fields. The little Murphy girl, who had awakened John R.'s inclinations in the first place, kept making excuses to be near him and kept blinking her eyes at him. At such times John R. squirmed, put his hand in his pocket and gripped his money pouch. One evening Theresa Murphy showed up at John R.'s barn.

"Did ye see the cows, John R.?" she asked, tilting her head sideways, looking at him through sandy eyelashes. John R. looked all around, saw she was alone, then smiled. After that she came regular. John R. shaved twice a week and managed to be in the barn each day at five o'clock.

One day he was sitting on an empty nail keg, waiting, when he heard footsteps. A wide grin spread over his mean little features. He was still sitting when Theresa's father strode in, shotgun cocked and aimed straight at him. The old man's eyes were red at the rims. He waved his arms and hollered so you could hear him across the river.

"Ye son of a whore, ye knocked up my Theresa. Ye marry her, or I'll call the Mounties."

John R., hand in pocket, whined he was too poor to marry. The old man raved on unheeding.

"Ye give me three hun'red dollars, marry Theresa, or go to jail!" His voice grew louder as the argument went on.

"Don't whinney yer snivelin' nose at me. If ye want th' cream ye'd best buy the cow. What's it to be? Ye've got a choice and it best be the right one!"

Three hundred dollars was every cent John R. had. It had taken him a long time and a lot of work to save it. But jail was out of the question. Who'd feed the pigs and calves?

John R. managed to hold on to his money but he had to marry Theresa. Before most people thought proper, John R. had two extra mouths to feed and was beginning to doubt the wisdom of his decision, to regret the pleasures that had placed him in such a predicament. The second baby came as fast on the heels of the first as nature could accomplish. Theresa took the first baby into the fields and laid it in the shade while she worked. But when the second came she could no longer do her share of work. Bills gathered and tempers mounted. John R.'s pouch grew flatter and flatter. Both babies were girls. A third child was on the way. John R. announced to all who would listen that he wished he'd been born without reproductive organs. In due time the child was born—a boy. John R. made another decision. There was now a Campbell to carry his name and he was through. He packed a bag, put on his best clothes and pulled out. There was just enough money in the pouch to buy a one-way ticket to Butte, Montana, and one meal a day en route.

DURING THE FOLLOWING SIX YEARS it's doubtful whether John R. gave his family a thought. He certainly didn't write. First Theresa sold the stock until there was only one cow left and the old driving mare. The neighbours were kind. Her brother stayed with her at night and helped to milk and clean the stable. Theresa and her family lived frugally but happily. Then one morning in May, at dawn, John R. came home.

In the pre-dawn darkness the train pulled into Newport Junction. John R. groped for the soiled string hanging from his vest pocket that secured his silver watch...three-thirty! Not the best time in the world to be getting in. He took his two ragged suitcases down from the rack overhead. He managed the first easily enough, in spite of its size, for it held only dirty clothes. The second, though smaller, was heavy. He handled it carefully, for it was filled with sealed bottles he had picked up during a change of trains after crossing the border. A voice bellowed through the half-open door—"Newport Junction!" John R. stepped down on to the platform. He peered hopefully into the darkness in the direction of the naked electric light bulb that hung over the entrance to the station. A pair of nearsighted blue eyes appeared before him.

"John R. is it?" said a piping voice. "Welcome home! Harry, Harry! Look who's here? It's John R. come home!"

Soon John R. was shaking hands with blurred figures that seemed to come from nowhere. Eager hands reached for his luggage. A bottle with hardly more than a taste in it was whipped from a pocket and everyone started babbling at once.

"Take a drink, ye old son of a whore...naw, don't mind me. I don't know of a better man to give me last drink to. Do ye, boys?"

"Come on in the station, John R. Alex Mac's got the fiddle, we'll git him to play a tune for ye. It's been a long time. Six years, ain't it?"

John R. smiled. Nothing had changed. He let them welcome him. He took a bottle from his little case, broke the seal and passed it round.

"This is good!" he said, tipping the last drop from a bottle and placing it beside the other empties on the waiting room floor. "I'd best be getting out home or I won't git out at all. Know any one with a rig?"

"Red Harry here's got one," said Alex Mac. "Some rig! A Model T with a hood that folds down like a 'cordion. Will take ye anywheres, won't it, Harry? How 'bout it? We'll all go along."

There was no stopping them. They had peered over John R.'s shoulder when he had opened the little case and they knew how many bottles it still held. They knew too that John R. was tired, out of condition for marathon drinking and apprehensive about starting celebrations so far from home. Red Harry was more than willing to provide the Model T, and needed no second asking. If John R. had been piped the whole thirty miles home, it wouldn't have caused a greater stir.

THERESA LAY ON HER STRAW MATTRESS between the two small girls listening to the pre-dawn noises of the farm. She heard the old cow lowing to be milked, the rooster crowing down at the barn. She identified the soft thud beyond the partition and the whispered curse that followed. Her brother had dropped his gumshoe in the darkness. She heard little John, who shared his bed, stir, hardly conscious of his uncle's leave-taking. She could hear the kettle singing and the rattle of the dishes in the kitchen. Here and there in the gloom she could see a child's garment or one of her own hanging limply from a nail in one of the studs. A broken mirror, its jagged edges sharp, balanced precariously on three bent nails. The iron bed, bent and sagging with age, groaned, but Theresa didn't hear it, for through the small window came the sound of loud voices, fiddle music and laughter. She sat bolt upright and waited breathlessly, pinching herself to see if she was truly awake. They must be on her road and coming closer. Theresa leapt out of bed, hunted around for her clothes and ran to the window. She couldn't see anything, but the singing was growing louder and louder.... They must be on her road, and coming to the house, there was no place beyond. For a minute she stood still, unable to move; then whirling round, she ran into the next room.

"Johnnie! Johnnie! Get dressed," she cried, shaking the sleeping child. "Don't be afraid, yer father's come home!"

It only took a few minutes to get the children dressed and downstairs. Theresa went straight to the front door and peered out through the little oval window. The children huddled about her skirts too frightened to leave her. A strange throbbing silence held them clinging together, hypnotized by the racket that came nearer and nearer. Theresa looked down at their upturned faces, then turned and walked into the parlour and raised the green blind so they all could see.

Like a black beetle, turned on its back, its legs scrambling in the throes of death, the Model T inched nearer and nearer to the house. Two men were seated on the hood, their legs dangling over the side. One swayed to and fro with the fiddle under his chin squeaking out a barely recognizable reel with a bow untouched by rosin. Theresa pulled down the blind and holding the children close went out into the kitchen.

Legs, arms, bottles and fiddler spewed over the sides of the car. Led by John R., they stamped up to the door and into the kitchen. John R. stopped in the centre of the room, cast a long look around, sliding his eyes past his family to the stove, then reaching into the deep recesses of his lungs brought up a growling spit which he aimed at the firebox. As it sizzled there he acknowledged his wife's presence.

"Ye'd best git some tea," he shouted, and turning back to the men, sat down and picked up the song they were singing.

Theresa pushed the kettle over the fire and went into the pantry followed by her weeping children.

"Shhhh! Be quiet now," she whispered, "it's yer father come home. Tis best not upset 'im."

There were those who were glad of the excuse to buy a "welcoming" bottle as their price of admission to the homecoming celebrations and then stay on to help finish John R.'s supply. There were those who could smell a drink from miles off and were usually too broke to go to the vendor, but came anyway. There were five or six young bachelors (the MacTavishes and the Beatons among them) who had no responsibilities and were ready to join in the fun. Theresa moved silently from pantry to stove to table, feeding those who were still able to walk across the kitchen floor. The children were fed standing up in the pantry. The party went on for a week until the supplies ran out. Then Theresa, hands on her hips and without once looking at John R., spoke out:

"Well, if there's to be any more teas in this house, some of ye'd best be getting me something to make them with."

Once again Red Harry offered to drive to the store as well as to the vendor's free of charge. He had made the trip to the vendor's once a day all week. This time John R. went along. He returned with two huge boxes heaped with groceries as well as a brown paper bag from the vendor.

The neighbours who were sincere in welcoming John R. home stayed only an hour or so. Those with their "admission" bottles left when their contribution was finished, but the rest drank, slept, maybe ate, drank and slept until they became a grisly smelly bunch. Some made their way upstairs but couldn't get down again when nature urged. Sometimes they used beer bottles and sometimes they couldn't find anything to use, until the loft smelt of beer, stale tobacco smoke, puke, urine and there was a cloying smell of excrement, which Theresa couldn't trace. But the time had come.

Under Theresa's watchful eye, little John J. carried the bottles downstairs and out into the yard and brought back a herring bucket. Without a word Theresa took the bucket, filled it with boiling water, threw in a bar of yellow soap and half a bottle of Lysol. She could hear John R. retching outside in the yard. She watched him re-enter the kitchen, red-faced and hanging on to his stomach with both hands. He glanced at the stony face before him and slunk over to the couch without making any attempt to speak. Not only did he not say a word or offer any explanation but he made no move to get acquainted with his children who still clung to their mother's skirt. Husband and wife knew a whole new and distasteful way of life lay before them.

Theresa took the bucket and a mop and went upstairs. She swabbed the floors until the air reeked with Lysol, then marched back down to the kitchen. She went straight over to the bench, straddled her legs and with her hands on her hips looked John R. straight in the face.

"Yer room's cleaned," she said, "ye'd best get to it." Then she turned and left him. John R. looked thoughtfully at Theresa's retreating back and with his hands still on his stomach meekly went upstairs.

NEXT MORNING JOHN R. ROSE before dawn, put on a flannel shirt, gumshoes and a long-billed cap. Cursing and clattering he lit the fire, slamming down the stove lid until he woke the whole family. During the breakfast that Theresa threw on the table before him, John R. sat staring into infinity. Then he leapt to his feet, grabbed his cap and strode out of the room.

In the heat of midday the children came running into the house to report that many cows were coming over the road towards their barn. Theresa rushed to the window. Eight cows had come to a halt. Behind them stood a round-shouldered youth lazily whipping the dust with a long thin switch as if waiting for someone. He hadn't long to wait. In less than five minutes Theresa saw the old mare in the shafts of the wagon, with John R. straight and invincible at the reins. Beside him, on the buggy seat, were two boys. Wagons loaded high with supplies and machinery followed and last of all, at the end of the short rope, trotted a big black horse.

John R. had everything he needed to resume farming—even help. The youthful figures sitting beside him were two orphaned nephews of Theresa's left homeless in their early teens. John R. put them to work unloading the fertilizer, the plough, harrow, seed and the huge supply of kitchen necessities. There was salt fish, pork, corned beef, potatoes, flour, lard and a hundred pounds of ground oatmeal. Evidently John R. intended to work his men and himself with a zeal for which only stall feeding could supply enough energy.

From before sunup to dusk they worked. Fencing, plowing, fertilizing and harrowing. From the youngest child who carried drinking water to the fields, from the nephews, from his wife, John R. demanded more and more work. They all responded. All, except his son, John J. Not that John J. ever refused his father's demands; he just conveniently didn't hear, misunderstood, or forgot them. John R. had enough wisdom to know that all things have their breaking point, but there was a warning glint in Theresa's eyes when he pressed the boy. *Her* son was off limits!

FOR ELEVEN YEARS John R. sweated, drove, cursed and prospered, and fumed with frustration at his son's insolence. Not because the boy was lazy—and he *was* lazy—but because while the others worked, John J. would walk around, hands behind his back, bossing the others and showing everyone who cared to see that he, John R., the master of the house was obviously *not* the master of his own son. Theresa had beaten him.

The girls married and moved away; only the indolent John J. remained at home. For eleven years John R. had thought up scheme after scheme to make his son work for his keep. They all failed. At last he hit on a plan. He would make "bush" whiskey for sale. John J. was delegated to gather wood for the fire and to keep an eye on the still so it wouldn't get too hot and blow up during the run. John R. was only too glad to be rid of the tedious job, and John J. was delighted. During the brewing of the mash, when the still was idle, he hunted out empty bottles along the roads, in old buildings, any place where they were likely to be found. Theresa washed the bottles and helped fill them. John R. never thought to question the docility with which his wife accepted her son's new job. He didn't know that mother and son had found that by adding just enough water the finished whiskey could be stretched to fill several extra bottles. They reasoned that what John R. didn't know wouldn't hurt him. The extra bottles were kept in hiding and used to supply customers who called while John R. was out of the house. Theresa smiled now, once in a while, and John J. strutted about the farm like a bantam rooster.

Then the axe fell. The axe was Father Murphy.

All the people in the Glen knew why Father Murphy was death against stills and bush whiskey. They knew his favourite brother had bled to death in a car accident after a dance. He had died without the rites of the church. Father Murphy did penance constantly for the sins the boy carried with him to his death and it was generally believed that Father had made a vow to hunt out all blackpots and put them out of business as part of his atonement.

Father Murphy, imposing perhaps a little on his office, would question drunks in the confessional, where he had them contrite and at a disadvantage, about the men who supplied them. With this information he would round up a Mountie, take his place in the car beside the driver and go along in search of the stills. But the men who had been forced to give information hastened to warn those they had informed on, and Father Murphy always arrived too late. This is why John R. had thwarted the good priest time after time. But John R.'s luck was running out.

EVERYONE KNEW about the wedding. The whole countryside had been invited. The whiskey business would be good. Now a man named Neil Duncan went to the wedding. Dry, sick, and well hung over, he pulled himself out of bed and walked two miles to John R.'s for a cure. John R. was at home, and after a couple of drinks Neil felt better and wanted to spend the time talking, but John R. wanted to get back to the fields. Sensing this, Neil bought a bottle and shuffled down the road in search of more congenial company.

Father Murphy had been at the wedding too; he had officiated the Mass and accepted the invitation to the reception for one reason alone. At dawn, Father changed his clothes and his boots and stepped across the road to waken the Mountie. Sleepy and disgusted with many failures, the Mountie threw himself behind the wheel of his car beside the waiting priest.

They turned off the highway and along a weed-grown road, little more than a path, that led to Neil's farm; then backed into a field at a place where the house was clearly visible. The Mountie turned off the engine. They waited all morning until nearly one o'clock. Then their patience was rewarded. They saw Neil shuffling out of his front door; they saw him turn in the direction of John R.'s place. Neil was walking slowly and taking many rests.

They waited another half hour, then followed. They saw him going round the bend at John R.'s gravel pit. They decided, after consultation, not to enter John R.'s property; so they turned off the engine and waited.

Neil walked straight into the trap before he had even time to feel frightened. There was nothing he could do, with a quart bottle in his pocket. Father Murphy took his arm and the bottle, and the Mountie ordered him into the car. Neil was booked and then turned loose to appear in court. He may as well have pleaded guilty there and then, but in all fairness to John R. he had to warn him.

John R. wasn't too upset. He knew Neil would have to give the name of the supplier when questioned under oath, for even John R. didn't expect anyone to commit his immortal soul to hell by swearing falsely. He advised Neil to plead guilty and give the Mountie his name.

John R. didn't worry about anything but the fine. He would have to pay that. But as for going to jail! He had no intention of spending even an hour in jail...and he didn't. It was John J. who went to jail.

Theresa hadn't liked it when John R. ordered his son to do his time, but in her heart she knew John J. wouldn't be missed around the farm and she knew that she would have to work in the fields herself if her husband was away.

Time dragged on, but never once did John J. realize that at last his father had found a way to make him earn his keep. He resented his lost freedom; he had been secretly courting for several months and the loneliness of the jail had planted thoughts of marriage in his mind. As soon as his time was up, John J. lost no time in getting over to Molly's village. He took with him one of the last bottles of whiskey he had hidden away, as a present for her father.

The old man took the bottle John J. brought him and retired to another room, leaving the young people alone. The minute the door closed John J. came to the point.

"Are ye gonna marry me or not? I've wasted a whole year

now traipsin' back an' forth, an' if ye are not fixin' to marry me, I might as well know now, an' I'll not bother."

Now Molly had been packing a suitcase when John J. arrived. She planned to go down to the States with her sister. She didn't know what the States would be like—she was going for the fun of it. John J. wasn't at all pleased, neither was Molly's father. He liked the idea of having a son-in-law who could provide him with a bottle of whiskey.

Molly, with her suitcase packed, made her explanation and thought no more of it, but the day before she was due to leave the old man called her downstairs and instructed her to write to John J. That night everything was settled. Molly was a good-natured girl and agreed to go along with her father's wishes.

John R. was neither pleased nor displeased when he heard of the coming wedding. He just went about his work as usual, but Theresa talked of nothing else. Neither gave a thought to the ages of the young people. John J. was barely nineteen and Molly just past seventeen.

TWO DAYS BEFORE THE WEDDING an unseasonal blizzard blew itself out overnight and left the Glen covered with ten feet of snow. All plans had been made—the banns had been published, invitations were out, the reception arranged, the priest engaged and confessions attended to. Everything was in order except the licence!

Even the most optimistic couldn't believe that snowdrifts that now blocked the roads would disappear in two days, and Molly, who had been spending most of her time with the Campbells, had to get home before the wedding. Her dress was at the Campbells', its true, but there was the small matter of obtaining her parent's written consent, and the law clearly stated, "No Marriage Licence issued without written consent of parent or guardian."

The young couple set out in the sleigh. To avoid the worst of the snowdrifts they took the long way round by the highway.

Just the other side of Cromarty, they turned off along a dirt road. Two lines of fence posts stretched before them in the unmarked snow like guide posts on an airfield. After digging the mare out three times, John J. had had enough.

"Tis only foolishness chasin' back an' forth takin' chances on them roads. Jist fer a name on a paper. Who'd know th' difference anyway. Ye got any paper in yer suitcase?"

Molly's fingers, stiff with cold, wormed through her meager belongings and pulled out a small tablet with a few lined pages between the covers. She handed it to John J.

"Pencil?"

Molly dug around again and found the butt of a pencil. Using the suitcase as a table, he passed the reins to Molly and bared his reddened hands. When he had finished the letter and signed it with Molly's father's name, he read it through carefully.

"There! If anyone should say anythin', I'll jist say yer father can't write English an' I wrote it." He handed Molly the tablet then hastily snatched it back.

"Might as well git th' licence today so long as we're through town."

Once again John J. bent over the suitcase and began to write. This time the note was from his mother. He did not dare sign John R.'s name in case the old man might make trouble. Then with both notes stuck carelessly in his jacket pocket, John J. took up the reins and turned the mare around. The sun broke through the clouds just as they pulled up before the courthouse.

"Wait!" he said, and disappeared into the building. A few minutes later he came down the steps resolutely folding a white paper which he tucked into his pocket. Without even looking at Molly, he took the reins.

"Now we'll go see the priest an' git set fer the morning. If the snow's gonna hold fer tomorrow night we'll leave word at the store that the party'll be the day after."

"Yiss!" said Molly. She generally answered in words of one syllable.

The wedding was as private as a ceremony by four people could be, but the party the following night was wild. John J. made the usual earthy boasts of his prowess, much to the delight of the guests. Old men made sly references to their own virility. Old women gave Molly advice on the side. Young people hovered about the couple as if hoping in some magical way to glimpse into the marital bed. Molly blushed through it all.

Every farmer who had a still had made a special "run" for the occasion. Everyone was feeling good. Theresa, bottle in one hand and a little glass in the other, moved from one group of guests to another as long as she was able to walk; then Molly took over. The old house rocked in rhythm to the thudding of booted feet as the dancers went through the sets. The floors shivered, the rafters and the joists strained. A bedlam of shouting echoed through the valley. In the parlour, the sparse furniture was almost new. The room had only been opened twice since Theresa's own wedding and that was when the priest had called. Now, sitting in a circle, holding hands, a group was singing Gaelic songs.

John J. slipped away with his bride as soon as he could. All the beds in the house were occupied by children—the bed in the company bedroom off the parlour, all the cubicles in the men's loft and the two beds in the women's loft. Not a child woke or stirred as Molly and John J. lifted them gently and found room for them on another bed.

THE WEDDING WAS OVER. Everyone had gone except the usual handful of men who always refused to leave until they were sure that the last drop had been drunk. The family were alone at last!

Theresa took to Molly as if she were her own. Molly quietly accepted a share of the work and would have willingly taken more if Theresa had been inclined to take advantage of the girl.

Theresa was thirty-six now and looked twice her age. She was bent double from carrying buckets of water up the steep hill from the barn. Molly responded to her mother-in-law's affection and a rare friendship sprang up between the two women.

John R. made it known from the start that he had no intention of relegating himself to the rocking chair, and continued to rule the household, Molly included. John J., still reluctant to grasp responsibility or to accept his father's domination, found himself about to become the father of a child for whom he couldn't even buy a diaper.

John R.'s sharp eyes missed nothing. Since the bush whiskey business had been stopped he couldn't find a job on the farm acceptable to his son. John R. tried again. He bought a sawmill and a big truck. Now, at mealtimes John R. seemed over-talkative. Theresa's nephews, Ben and Tim, although grown men, still lived and worked on the farm. John R. directed all his talk to them, ignoring his son. They were setting up the mill, and the nephews showed a remarkable bent for machinery.

"Youse are set up, ain't yez?" said John R. "T'ink that ould motor's goin' to run 'er? Next week'll tell th' tale. If ever'think goes right along should hev a load o' timber to take t' Wrexham, come th' end o' th' week. Best try that motor this afternoon, know what's what then. Ben, ye will hev to truck th' load when we're ready." Then without apparently noticing the eagerness in John J.'s eyes, he got up, pulled his old cap down on his forehead, then pushed it back into place, hair and all, and went out.

John J. left his meal half-finished and followed his father. No one knew what passed between them. No one found out what was said; but the following week, when the big truck, piled high with freshly sawn lumber, pulled away from the mill it was John J. who sat at the wheel. John R. stood watching, a smile on his face.

At first John J. was content to make a few dollars on each trip, but soon he began to like the feel of money in his pocket. A merchant in Cromarty was only too glad to pay more to have his order delivered from Wrexham the same day and before long, John J. was carrying for anyone who would ask him and his list of customers kept growing. John R. disapproved and was about to reprimand his son but intuition warned him to be satisfied that John J. was working at all.

Molly gave birth to a son. John J. insisted that the child be called John R. after his father, as was the custom. As for the rest—they could be called One, Two, Three, Four, Five, as far as he was concerned!

It was Molly herself who was responsible for Christina coming into the house. Old Theresa was ailing and with four boys only a year apart, Molly couldn't cope with all the work. Besides, she was pregnant again. Christina, her first cousin, unmarried and a willing worker, was presently unemployed. It seemed an ideal arrangement. What Molly didn't know (although her neighbours did) was that John J. had begun to consider himself a ladies' man, and Christina's eyes were wide open to suggestions, especially after a few sips of whiskey.

"WHY DIDN'T YOU SEND FER ME sooner, ye poor dear?" Christina looked at Molly and frowned with concern. "Ye just sit down now, and I'll take over for ye. Maybe ye'd rather go up and lie down?"

Her dark eyes carried a message for John J. that had nothing to do with the words she was saying.

"Ain't that right, John J.? Shouldn't she lay down fer a while?"

"I suppose it would be all right." John J. answered as if trying to puzzle the whole thing in his mind. He had read the message in Christina's eyes.

Everyone was happy. Even John R. looked less miserable than usual. Molly spent more and more time resting. Theresa liked to have the girl lying down beside her and was glad of her presence upstairs in the loft. The children, on their own most of the time, were happy in the hastily-made teeter-totter and swings.

John J. and Christina took full advantage of every minute of their time together—in the loft, in the barn, on the side roads, during their shopping trips, just about any place where they were not likely to be discovered.

Then Ronnie showed up. No one could remember just when. Christina flirted with him a little now and then when she thought John J. wasn't looking, but never enough to give him sufficient courage to ask her out. He'd been coming for about a month when Christina, who had been silent and moody all week, went out to the barn to find John J.

"Where are the boys?" she asked.

"Th' old feller sent 'em fer a load o' firewood," said John J. "Himself cut it up on Chauncey's hill a while back. Why?"

"Just wanted to know if they was around," said Christina. "I've got something to tell you...private."

"Go ahead!" John J.'s voice was unconcerned. "No one around to hear. What is it?"

"John J., I don't know how t'say it...."

The skin on John J.'s forehead gathered into three folds above his eyes as comprehension spread across his face.

"Yea an' Hane! Ye can't be.... Are ye? Jesus Christ, what will ye do now?" John J. never fumbled for words. In his way he loved Molly, as much as he could love anything, and nothing was going to change his life.

"Ye're in it as much as me, John J.," said Christina. "Can't ye think of somethin'?"

They stood facing each other in the gutter behind the cows, each holding a bucket brimming full of milk. There were no tender little slaps now, no playful teasing common to these moments of isolation. Both were dead serious.

"I know, I know!" John J. didn't want to throw away his playmate because of a few hasty words. "Look, Christina, there's

Ronnie.... Oh, don't look like a pile of manure fell on ye. It won't make no difference between us two."

"Are ye sure, John J.? Are ye sure it won't?"

"Of course." John J.'s face relaxed. "Why should it? Ye've done a bit o' flirtin' with him already."

"Oh! John J., I never!"

"Ye didn't think I saw ye. I did though. Now tonight, when Ronnie comes, ye jist give him th' eye, like ye did me the day ye came. He'll understand."

Christina had the decency to bow her head.

"Git him to ask ye out for a walk or somethin' and make darn sure he comes back to the house responsible. You're sure now? Couldn't be ye've made a mistake? That we wouldn't hev to do all this?"

Christina gave him a lopsided smile.

"I'm sure," she said. She liked the way he'd said "we."

THAT EVENING JOHN J. WAS GAY. He even put on a wheedling voice when he asked Molly to stay down a little later than usual and make a foursome with Ronnie and Christina for a game of Forty-five. Molly blushed at the unexpected attention from her husband. They played two games and John J. walked his wife to the women's stairs, where he kissed her tenderly good night. He breathed a great sight of relief when he came back to find the kitchen empty.

Christina and Ronnie now went everywhere together. He brought her home from Mass on Sundays. After a few weeks had passed, Christina felt safe enough to tell Ronnie the same story she had told John J. Ronnie was all concern.

"It'll be all right, Christina," he said. "I'll make it all right... don't cry."

After practicing with John J., Christina did well. But things weren't so simple for Ronnie. When he got home that night, a neighbour, old MacDougall, stamped into the kitchen, fire in his eyes.

"What're ye goin' to do about it?"

"About what?" Ronnie's voice cracked like a boy soprano's.

"About Brigid! That's who. Ye fixed her. She said ye did and I know myself ye've been moonin' around the edge of the woods nights with that bunch of young smart Alecs. What's done, 's done. Are ye goin' to make it legal? Ye've got a good home here or are ye goin' to pay? Three hundred dollars right in m'hand Friday or git the licence. No one's gonna ride m'girl like a dog and git away free." When the old man paused for breath Ronnie could only say half-heartedly:

"I wasn't the only one there wuz...."

"Never mind tellin' me that stuff," the old man went on, "tryin' to worm out of it. Ye hev a home, no reason ye can't marry her."

Ronnie gave up. The old man had known what was going on when himself and the boys had waylaid the girl out walking those summer nights. Ronnie wasn't too bright but he knew a frame-up when it was as obvious as this one. He also knew that to name the other fellows was useless; he may as well shield them. Ronnie went to his best friend for advice.

John J. caught Ronnie's nod; in fact he'd been waiting for it. Christina had stayed up to tell him about their conversation when he got home from Wrexham. But John J. hadn't any way of knowing about the trap Ronnie had fallen into. The two men made an excuse to leave the kitchen and went out into the barn.

Now John J. had a natural capacity for intrigue; and intrigue held a fascination for him.

"Ronnie," he said, slapping him on the shoulder, "it's good you came to me."

"John J., you're the only friend I got. You being kind o' related to Christina an' all. Truth is, I haven't got the money to pay old Dougall, and I want to marry Christina.... She's the one I want."

"Aye, Ronnie, she's by far the best girl." John J. was sympathetic. "The other—Brigid—she's kind of light upstairs, ain't she?"

"What am I gonna do?" Ronnie was as near crying as he had ever been in his life. "What can I do?"

"Well, I ain't got much money." John J. tried to conceal his delight. "But I s'pose being it's my own niece by marriage, I might—I might be able to give ye three hundred for Dougall. But if there's any funny work 'bout Christina, I'll hev the Mounties after ye...friend or no."

"Oh, ye needn't worry 'bout Christina, John J. I wanted to marry her all the time. Ye'll never be sorry, John J. Never. Thank ye...thank ye...I'll go an' tell Christina."

"Wait!" John J. called after him. His brain was working fast now. "No need to tell Christina about Brigid. We'll jist keep it a secret between ourselves. Old Dougall ain't liable to tell. Keep th' money a secret too. Christina might t'ink she owes us, or somethin' foolish."

"Jist as you say, John J.," said Ronnie. "Can ye give me the money, Friday?"

"Yiss! Go ahead, tell Christina...she's prob'ly waiting."

John J. stayed outside awhile watching the stars and smiling to himself.

WHAT HAPPENED NEXT wasn't really John J.'s fault. He didn't like Alice. Alice was a niece of Molly's and the mother of three fatherless children. But there she was standing in the road waiting for him. He didn't want to pick her up, but she had her thumb up for a ride. She climbed over Ben and sat next to John J. in the cab. On the drive to Wrexham she said little, shook much and smelled like boiling mash. John J. stopped for lunch at a place with a big Molson's Beer sign in front. Like magic, Alice came alive. Before the first glass was before her she was coy. John J. looked at the dull brown hair—like a fork of used bedding, he thought—at the ravages of dissipation below and at the slept-in look of her soiled clothing. He twitched with disgust. That was before the beer.

She looked better and better with each succeeding drink. They reached Wrexham but Alice didn't want to get out at her destination.

"John J., I didn't wanta come here," she said. "I wuz jist sick this morning and I knew you'd be by—maybe git me a beer."

To John J.'s credit he tried half-heartedly to persuade her to get out. At last through sheer anxiety and the urgency of his business, he made the fatal mistake of giving in. Next morning, sober, his sense of smell returned, he hopped out of bed at the crack of dawn.

"Come on! We're gitting business done and I'm taking you home to yer kids where ye should be now."

They dressed—he insisted that she take a bath—and had breakfast. The business was soon attended to and John J. went to the vendor's to get a take-along package.

Safely out of town, John J., shaking a little himself, stiffened against the brake and pulled in to the side of the road.

"There's beer with the stuff in the back, but I guess we'll just do with this," he said, reaching under the seat for a brown paper bag. He broke the seal and offered Alice a bottle of cheap rum. She took a good healthy pull.

"Hummm, that's good," she said. "I wuz dry. Have one yourself." Alice handed the bottle back to John J. After a long swig he handed the bottle back to her waiting hand. Carefully she put the cork back and hid the bottle inside her coat.

"I'd best keep this. Mounties won't search a woman."

With the bottle in her charge, the cork was more often out than in, and both were high when they reached her shack.

Ben had not said a word since Alice joined them, not even at the hotel when he had to take a room on his own. Now he spoke.

"John J., I don't want to butt in or nothing, but how do you feel? Want I should drive? That barrel o' molasses in back...."

"Nothin' the matter with me, boy. I'll take her home meself.

Needn't say a word about the woman to Molly, jist get her upset. No! Needn't say a word."

Ben didn't have to be told. He knew too that John J. wouldn't let anyone touch the wheel. He crossed himself and sat quietly back in the seat. Mile after mile passed.

"Look is that bottle there somewheres," said John J. "Look in the cubbyhole." Ben couldn't find it.

"Suppose that one took the bottle along with her. Did ye see her take it, Ben?"

"I didn't see her leave it," said Ben.

"Neither did I," said John J. "Watch for a side road there. I'm goin' to pull off and git a bottle from that case in the back. Beer'd be best, anyhow. It's getting hot."

This time Ben drank as well. John J. treated each customer along the road as he delivered their order. At last there were but three orders left which had to be delivered at the village beyond the Glen. One was the molasses.

"I'll jist leave the barrel of molasses on t'night and deliver her tomorrow. Guess we'll jist shoot on home now." John J.'s eyes were beginning to blur. Ben was past caring. They pulled off the highway at the crossroads for the eight-mile ride home.

When John J. woke up he was lying in the ditch. He tried to look around but his eyes were stuck tight. He opened his hand to wipe his face and found it was sticky too. Raising the arm he had been lying on he wiped his eyes on the sleeve of his shirt; then looking around, he saw Ben beside him. He reached out and shook him.

"Ben! We dumped the molasses. Wake up!"

Ben stirred and opened his eyes.

They were lying beside the road, the dim light of the moon showed the truck on its side close by. Groceries of all description, now unrecognizable, lay strewn in a sea of molasses. John J. looked thoughtful.

"We'd best get that barrel right-side-up. Maybe there's something to be saved. Then ye'd best go fer help, Ben. Git Sandy to bring a team."

Both men were unhurt and still feeling good. John J. started to root around in the molasses.

"Wait, Ben! We'll hev a drink before you go."

John J. found three bottles, walked over to the bumper and opened two of them. He handed one to Ben.

"Bottoms up!" he said.

Ben, his best pants plastered with dirt and molasses, a bottle bulging from a pocket, went down the road and out of sight. John J. sat down, surveyed the mess and cursed.

"Three hundred dollars Ronnie wants tonight, and I haven't a hundred in my pocket. Who's goin' to pay fer the mess?" John J. talked to the night air. "Best take it home to Molly. She can maybe clean up some of the things.

"BANK! Hev to git to the bank! That son-of-a-whore of a woman! If she'd stayed where she belonged none o' this would hev happened."

THINGS DID HAPPEN VERY QUICKLY after that. John J. got three hundred dollars from the bank manager and gave the money to Ronnie. The following Sunday marriage banns were read for the first time, and when the young people came home from Mass old Theresa came downstairs for tea in honour of the occasion. She ate nothing, just sipped her tea, then rose shakily to her feet and crawled back upstairs. At dinner time Molly found her stretched out on her old straw mattress, her hands folded across her chest and smiling. She was dead.

In spite of the heat of the summer, for two days and nights people streamed in to pay their respects. A hush fell over the house. People spoke in low voices of the many kindnesses they had received from Theresa. Many eyes were moist and handkerchiefs and coat sleeves were hurriedly raised to catch tears. Clemmie Douglas who had pulled on her boots and waded the river as soon as word came, paid tribute to the dead woman as she bathed the body and dressed it in her own best dress snatched from a hanger as she left the house.

"She was a willing soul...and good. She's all right. She'll go straight to heaven...nothing was too much for her." Neighbours came in, prayed and left, staying only long enough to tell one little story of Theresa's charity. Even the men had some little memory to relate.

Because of the heat the body could not be kept longer than two days. There was no need anyway, as everyone Theresa had known in her lifetime lived in the county. After Mass the procession filed into the graveyard beside the church. Standing four or five deep, they circled the grave and listened as the priest said the final words. Misting rain was falling as the crude box was lowered into the sodden earth. When it was all over, the mourners filed out through the little gate, each one taking a last glance at the grave before going out into the road. The rain began to fall heavily now and men and women scattered to their rigs. Molly rode in John J.'s old car with Clemmie Douglas.... Molly hadn't cried or spoken, except to answer a word here and there, since she had found Theresa dead in the women's loft; and Clemmie wanted to be with her when tears would come. John J. sat straight as a lancer behind the wheel, saying nothing. Now and then he'd take his eyes from the road and glance at the sky.

"Awful day fer a funeral," said Clemmie.

"Oh, well!" John J. cocked his head. "Tis just as well. Couldn't do nothing else today anyway."

JOHN R. STARTED UP THE MILL bright and early the following day. Life went on but not as usual. Everyone missed Theresa. Molly missed her companionship. Ben and Tim grew sullen. Theresa had always slipped them tobacco from the supply that came with the groceries. Molly didn't think of them. Although Ben and Tim possessed little more than working clothes, Theresa had ordered overalls for them on her grocery list; and if John R. noticed the items he never said anything. Molly hadn't known of Theresa's thoughtfulness and even if she had, she would not have risked John R's anger. The youth, in untended clothes, were reduced to grubbing a butt here and there and grew more and more dissatisfied.

John R. was in a rage of some sort every day now. A humbler man might have admitted his loss, at least secretly, but not John R. Molly never refused the old man anything. When he asked her to sew on a button, patch an overall, or cook his eggs a little harder, she did so. But he would always have to ask. She didn't make a point of remembering his likes and dislikes.

John R. not only turned against Molly, he began hounding his son. Theresa had honoured John R.'s place in the home, putting his comfort before that of all the others. She foresaw his wants even before he did and attended to them. Children no longer sat awed in his presence but chattered and bickered unchecked when he was in the house. Now the children's plates were filled while his cup and plate stood empty. He found unmended socks among his clothes and he had to carry his own washed but unironed clothes upstairs. Molly did see that his suit was pressed, his white shirt clean and ironed at all times. She wouldn't give him an excuse to stay away from Mass. That was all. If he wanted anything else he had to ask.

John J. could think of nothing but his debt to the bank and his dependence on his father. He forgot all about Alice for a while. He had vowed after the last meeting to always leave for Wrexham before dawn, but it didn't take Alice long to find that out. The second meeting followed much the same pattern as the first except that John J., remembering the molasses, gave Alice a few dollars when they parted in lieu of any visit to the vendor.

Christina was getting big already and Molly began to count her fingers. Molly watched John J. but neither he nor Christina gave any indication that there had been more than friendship between them. Yet Molly gave up her afternoon rests and stayed down to the last in the evenings. The day Christina and Ronnie were married Molly was content.

John J. prospered but with his prosperity he grew lax. He would stop off now and then at Alice's one-room shack, partitioned by an army blanket thrown over a wire. Ben hated the long waits. He pleaded but John J. would never listen. Time came when John J. would stay all night, then blame the motor for the extra day on the road. He pocketed the extra money for room and board—and for repairs— but this was a mistake. For the first time since he had figured out the haulage business, John J. didn't brag and strut around before Molly, flashing the roll of money he'd made. Molly noticed the omission. It wasn't Christina. It must be someone else.

Molly couldn't leave the farm but she bided her time. She was no fool. It wasn't long before she noticed that John J. often mentioned her niece's name. Although Molly was suspicious, it was John J. who gave himself away. Arriving home from one of his trips (and a stopover at Alice's) filled with drink and braggadocio, he boasted not only of his success with Alice but with Christina as well. Up and down the kitchen floor he stamped, the grime on his bare ankles showing above the tops of his shoes, his trousers with every button missing, his face red, his short hair erect, smacking his sensual lips, pursed as if remembering a kiss.

"Yisss! I can git another one too, whenever I'm ready."

Molly kept her back to him, her thin lips set tight against her teeth, but she held her tongue. She finished baking, set a cheese—still John J. rambled on. She went down to the cellar for potatoes, he followed her. She went upstairs to sweep and dust. He followed but Molly would not speak.

At last he strode out and soon she heard the truck going down the road. The sound of the motor died away. Molly sat on the edge of a chair and lowered her face into her hands. Her body shook but not a tear came into her eyes. She fed the men and when John R. and Ben came in she gave them each a dish of porridge. They looked at Molly's face and the kitchen grew quiet. Long into the night, if anyone had been listening, he would have heard her voice in the room off the kitchen, built especially for her coming. He would have heard the whispered "Our Father," "Hail Mary" and the delicate clinking of touching beads.

Next morning Molly's smile came slowly, her step was heavier; but those around the table chattered as usual. John R. had had his breakfast long before. He had noticed the change in Molly and had hurried through the meal. His sharp little eyes missed nothing and in the field, seated high on the rake, he spat out his venom on the horses. Molly could have heard him from the house had she cared to listen.

Later in the day, Ronnie brought John J. home in the wagon, sick, sorry and shaking like an aspen.

Molly gave Ronnie a cup of tea, then handed one to John J. without once looking at him. Ronnie gulped his tea and said what everyone said when they had to leave immediately after receiving refreshment.

"Well, guess I'll have to do like the beggar. I've got haymakers coming."

Molly nodded. For a while John J. watched his wife as she went about her work, ignoring him, until he could stand the silence no longer.

"Molly! Molly, please...I'm awful sick. I need your help." Molly didn't speak.

"Molly! What's the old man gonna say? I turned the truck over and I'm too sick to get someone to set her back up and bring her home to the garage."

Molly gave him a scornful glance. John J. took heart.

"Please, Molly! If you'll help me I'll quit drinking. Ye'll have to help me. I'll do anything ye say."

This was the first time Molly had ever heard John J. make a promise. She could not help believing him.

"Well, all right! But all that foolish talk about women. I

knew it was Christina but I thought that was all over. Where was ye last night?"

"At Ronnie's."

"Where did ye sleep?"

"We didn't. Haven't been in bed at all. Hev you got a sip? I just can't cut her off like that. A swallow of a little something to put me on me feet to git the truck?"

""Ye'll quit your drinking if I get you well?"

"Yessss! Once I'm over this, and ye know 'tis only the drink makes me talk so foolish."

"But the women? What did ye do with the women?"

"Nothing. Molly I swear it. I wuz only trying to get you going."

Molly wanted to believe him and it didn't take John J. long to convince her. Molly strode into the pantry and came back with a small whiskey glass of rum. John J.'s eyes shone. She started giving orders and he meekly agreed to all her suggestions. He asked her advice as if only she were qualified to give it.

"Molly! How am I going to get the truck home?"

"First you'll have to get help to turn her on her wheels. Do you know if Dougall's at home?"

"Well, to tell the truth I didn't notice. He's not much good fer a job like this, Molly. But Jim Douglas has a truck. He could get her over easy." John J. was feeling his way cautiously.

"Jim! Yiss...and he's got beer too. If that's what you're wanting I'm for quitting right now. Ye have to do what I tell ye or it's no use. I'm through!"

John J. shrank into his chair and looked at her with the eyes of a hungry dog.

"Honest, Molly! Twas only the truck I was thinking of." A touch of defiance came into his voice. "Don't ye trust me? Is that it? If that's all ye think of my word, maybe it's best I don't expect ye to help me."

Molly was taken aback and quickly tried to regain her advantage.

"I just wanted to be sure. Git the wagon, we'll go after Jim Douglas."

"Hev ye got jist a little sip more to give me strength to hook her up? Me hands...." John J. stretched out his hands before her. "They're shakin' so's I couldn't get the bit in the mare's mouth. Jist a little sip...to steady 'em."

Molly went into the pantry and came out with the bottle. There was only a finger of rum left. John J. finished it off, got up, and went out to the barn.

Jim Douglas was greasing the truck when they drove up. He looked with wonder at Molly's flashing eyes. She was wearing her authority like a jewel. John J. sat hunched beside her. They went into the house. As if unable to contain her good fortune Molly hardly waited for Mary Douglas' greetings.

"John J. is going to quit drinking. He's quit already...soon's I git him over this. Tell her, John J."

Mary Douglas looked startled. She looked at John J. who sat meekly on the edge of a chair, not saying a word; but when Jim came in his eyes lit up.

"Good day!" he said, "fine weather we're havin'." When the discussion on this weather wore out, Jim's curiosity got the better of him.

"Ye've got the rig? Truck outta commission?"

"Yeah, Jim!" Molly was quick to answer. "John J. wants t'know if ye can help him get her on her wheels. He turned her over last night." John J. gave Molly's back a scowling glance.

"Went off the road between Ronnie's and Lawlor's...turned her over." Jim nodded.

"Well, ye'll be dry, I suppose. Would ye like a glass of beer? I don't know how good it is an' it's warm, but if it'll help...."

Molly didn't wait for Jim to finish.

"John J.'s quit drinkin'," she said. "He knows t'will be

hard...but I'm gonna help him. Thank ye jist the same...."

"Well, if ye have one handy," John J. butted in. "Molly gave me a sip she had in the house, but I wuz dry." John J. had a way of dragging out the word that made you feel the cotton in his mouth.

"John J. NO! Now ye promised to do as I said if I was to help ye. If ye take a beer ye can just get over by yerself." Molly was too late.

Jim had gone to the pantry and missed the last two sentences. In all innocence he handed John J. a glass of beer, unaware that he had helped shatter Molly Campbell's new-found dignity. John J. dropped his humility like a cloak, ignored his wife and went into a detailed explanation of the accident. Molly refused the cup of tea Mary offered her and went out the door. Mary watched her from the window—watched her climb into the rig and sit, slouched in the seat not bothering to grip the slackened reins or liven up the old mare, who moved off slowly, head down between the shafts, as if each step was going to be her last.

That day John R. ate his dinner in silence, lifting his head only to glare at the empty place across the table. At supper his son's place was still empty. John R., his face purple, bowed his head in hasty prayer. He tried not to raise his eyes until the meal was over. That night Molly didn't wait up for John J. She didn't even acknowledge his presence at two a.m. when he came to bed mumbling apologies.

THE NEXT MORNING John J. was shaking worse than ever. He waited until he heard the sound of the mill starting up before getting his breakfast. He wanted to make sure his father was safely out of the house. His face puffy, his hands palsied, once again he humbled himself before Molly. He took the pan from her and carried his own eggs to the table. Then in a soft voice that had always worked before, he tried to woo her all over again.

But Molly was different this morning. There was no fire in

her eyes now. Her lips were stretched thin and she didn't speak. John J. poured his tea into the saucer, swished it round once or twice and gulped it down in a single swallow. He wrapped the eggs, one at a time, round his fork and swallowed them at a single bite. When he had finished he got up. Halfway across the kitchen he stopped, turned around as if to say something. Molly hadn't time to turn away and for a moment they looked at each other in silence; then John J. turned and went out the door.

DURING THE LAST FEW DAYS John R. had driven Ben and Tim like slaves. John J. looked at the pile of lumber that had been cut, far more than he could take on a single load. Ben scowled all the way to Wrexham in spite of John J.'s ingratiating conversation and soft voice. When they stopped for tea, John J. bought tobacco, which he tossed into Ben's lap. The trip to Wrexham was monotonous and uneventful. The lumber was unloaded.

"P'raps we'd best git the things fer Aspen," he said, turning to Ben with a smile. One of his customers lived in Aspen.

"Mebbe!" said Ben, speaking for the first time; but instead of climbing into the truck he reached into the cab and pulled out his shabby little suitcase. "Ye'd best get someone to help ye load. I'll be staying here."

John J. tried to speak. His mouth flew open but the only sounds were unintelligible stutterings. His little pig's-eyes looked cold and unrelenting.

"What can ye do here?" His speech had returned as his anger mounted. His mouth twisted into a smirk. "Ye'd starve in a week."

Ben's expression did not change, so John J. changed his tactics.

"Ye'd best get back in. Is it money that's bothering ye?" John J. reached down into his pocket and pulled out a two-dollar bill.

"Here! Take this. It'll buy ye some tobacco."

Then a thought cleared his anger and a grin spread across his face.

"Ach! O'course, that's it! Would ye like to take a little trip across the tracks? Jump in. Maybe ye'll find a woman ye'll like. I'll pay and ye can keep the two dollars too."

"If I want a woman I won't have to buy her." Ben didn't try to conceal his distaste. "Go yerself if ye want, but I'm through and ye can tell that son-of-a-whore ye call your father that he's driven this man for the last time."

Ben walked away quickly as if afraid to hear John J.'s answer. Dumbfounded as he was, John J. did not fail to notice the man's straightened shoulders and the sureness of his step. He made no attempt to call him back.

JOHN R. JUNIOR, identified by all now as Johnnie John J., in sixth grade, was hastily taken from school to take Ben's place at the mill. Molly fumed and fretted, but if John J. heard her at all words meant nothing to him. If he had thought that Johnnie should stay in school (which he didn't), he was almost as terrified of his father as Molly was, and wouldn't think of crossing him. A few days later, Tim got a letter addressed to him care of the Douglases. He had known Ben wouldn't be coming back. The two had it all planned.

John J. had been afraid that Tim might desert if given the opportunity as Ben had done, so he had been taking Johnnie to Wrexham with him. He hadn't reckoned on the strength of Tim's determination. The next time gas was delivered to the mill the truck driver took away a passenger. Number two was taken out of school.

Molly had never raised her voice in protest against anything the men had ever done but this time they had gone too far.

"What in the name of God are ye two up to?" she stormed. "Colin says he'll not go back to school at all if you're going to be keeping him home every other day, and he means it. He's in Grade Six, same as Johnnie was, and he's smart. Teacher sez he's smartest in school. If ye won't do anything about it, I'm going to tell Himself." The very thought of Molly talking back to the old man had its effect.

"So what's that? Teacher says he's smart? A little reading, writing an' figgering is all that's needed around here. If he hasn't learnt that by Grade Six it's no use him goin' anymore. What does the teacher know?" John J. didn't look at Molly or he wouldn't have spoken with such confidence.

The next morning, breakfast over, Molly turned to Colin.

"Wash yerself and get yer school clothes on."

Colin looked first at his grandfather, then rose uncertainly and went over to the washbench in the corner. John R. got the bite down that was nearly choking him.

"Won't need school clothes at the mill. Don't need washing neither."

"WASH!" Molly was standing now, hands on hips and legs apart, looking the old man full in the face.

"Colin's going to school. He wants to go. I want him to go and teacher sent word he should go. Get a move on ye now."

Molly turned and walked through into her own bedroom and closed the door. Inside, she bent down to listen. She was too far away to catch all the words, as the pantry lay between the rooms, but when the voices rose she heard the old man ordering John J. to take her in hand—"teach her a woman's place." The old man said much more. She couldn't hear John J.'s voice at all. She went over to the bed and sat down to wait for him.

John J. looked at his wife as if for the first time and then started to rage. Molly waited until he stopped for breath.

"Ye'd best be figgering who yer getting for help instead of standing there wasting yer breath," said Molly. "Might be ye could keep Pat home, if he's big enough for ye. He can't do more'n write his name and isn't likely to learn, teacher says, not after four years of schooling."

"He's too small!" ranted John J. "Still, he could haul the sawdust away," he went on as if to himself.

"Yer big and strong. You go to the woods. Ye can keep Pat if ye want, though."

John J. looked at her, then strode back to the kitchen. Father and son left the house together.

John R. didn't go into the woods that morning either, but John J. who had never owned an axe of his own went into Cromarty to buy one. Pat stayed home when the mill was running, and went to school, out of the way, when the men were felling trees. This arrangement, had it not entailed John J. working himself, might have gone on indefinitely, even though the profits were smaller. One day John J. decided he had had enough. He had only been gone into the woods for about an hour when he came back and stormed into the kitchen.

"Get me some tea whilst I'm gitting me other clothes on. If I get some help right away I'll not be gone long, but if not, I can't say when I'll be back. Ye best git ready fer a boarder."

Molly lowered her head and went about preparing tea.

John J. wasn't gone long. He picked up young MacTavish at the school. Dan MacTavish was big and strong for his age. Together they went up to the MacTavish farm. Dan thought that Andy, his uncle, might come and work too. Andy agreed and soon the three went down to the mill. John J. gave them instructions and sent them off into the woods, then he went up to the house to tell Molly. The old man arrived in the kitchen just in time to hear the news. He raged. His son had usurped his throne. He had hired help without permission. That day, for the first time, John J. spoke back to his father. The men stayed and once more regular shipments of deal went to Wrexham.

ONE HEAVY MORNING IN SPRING, after the old man had been widowed for five years and his oldest grandsons were taking men's places with the work at the mill and on the farm—the eldest being fourteen—John R. came down to an empty, cold kitchen. Noisily, he got a fire going and made himself some tea. It was one of those days with promise of rain in the air that makes sleepers unaware of time. No one stirred overhead. John R. grabbed his cap and stormed out of the kitchen, slamming the door until the windows rattled. In fifteen minutes the Glen rumbled with his curses as he badgered the horses from his seat high on the plough. He cursed and ploughed and cursed for two hours as the sky darkened and the rain came closer. John R. didn't look at the sky. It was his empty stomach that finally drove him back to the house and into the still silent kitchen. It was only half-past six.

"GIT UP! Ye lazy sons of whores and earn yer keep," he raved. "I've been wearing out m'arse on the plough seat so's to keep ye from starvin' and nobody give a damn whether a man has a bit to eat himself or not. GIT UP!"

Feet thundered on to the bare boards over his head. John R. nodded, a vicious jerk of the head, and strode to the pan to wash himself. Molly had made the porridge the night before; it was heated and served with a cup of hot steaming tea in less time than seemed possible.

Breakfast over, John R. rose from the table, cap still low over his head, and left for the fields. By the time he reached the plough, cold rain splashed down in a blinding deluge, soaking him through to the skin in seconds. Tying the reins over the mare's harness, he clipped her across the rump and gave a raucous roar. The mare took off at a gallop to the barn, pulling the unwary horse still strapped to her harness along with her. Taking steps almost as long as himself, John R. was at the barn shortly behind them. He unhooked the one from the other and removed the double harness and threw it on a nail. Grabbing the mare's driving harness he pushed the wagon out into the rain and led the mare between the shafts. Without looking towards the house he put the mare into a gallop and with clothes clinging to his body, drove into the wind.

A neighbour brought John R. home that night, burning with

fever, and drunk. John J. put him to bed and left him. For four days the old man wobbled round the house finding fault with everything, his cheeks flushed, his disposition if anything worsened. Then on the fourth night he went to bed and in the morning he couldn't rise.

TWO OR THREE WEEKS after John R.'s death, Ronnie landed at the mill in his wagon looking for John J. Molly saw him from her front-door window. She watched the men gesticulating until she couldn't stand it any longer. Making sure the smallest children weren't in harm's way, she grabbed an old sweater, threw it over her shoulders and ran down the hill. Ronnie always had Christina with him when he came to get John J. to take them to town, but the baby had come three weeks ago and Christina hadn't taken him out of doors yet. The machinery at the mill stopped. Something must be wrong!

"When did it happen?"

Molly arrived just in time to hear John J. ask the question.

"Bout an hour ago," said Ronnie. "Christina found him there in the crib. He wuz sleeping when she went to feed the calves—wasn't gone more'n few minutes."

"What? Who's that?" said Molly. "Th' baby. Are ye saying the baby's dead?"

"Yeh!" Ronnie's voice quavered. Molly's face grew tender at the sorrow she saw on the face beside her.

"Only three weeks old." Ronnie cleared his throat. "Christina wants t'know if ye'll go over with her while I'm gone to tell people and to attend to things."

Molly nodded.

"Ye'll go along?" Ronnie looked at John J. "I don't know what to do. Should I git the doctor or the priest first?"

Molly didn't hear the answer. She was on her way to the house. She filled the white enamel basin with warm water; called to Sally, now twelve years old, to help her; grabbed the nearest child and started scrubbing the three youngest children while the fourth washed himself. She got clean clothes from upstairs and readied herself. She shut the draft in the range and took her little procession down the hill.

Many of the Roosters who were kin of Christina's and Molly's came back with Ronnie and John J. on the truck. The rest arrived in rigs of various descriptions. They all brought bottles of bush whiskey. Molly stayed for an hour or more getting the news from her home village. Then John J. took her and the children home. He waited while Molly baked a cake, bottled some milk, and filled a box with dishes for the teas. He went back alone.

At breakfast next morning Molly asked John J. about scratches on his face. A warning look silenced her and she waited until the older children had eaten and gone out.

"All righttt! Now how'd ye git them scratches on yer face? Go ahead."

"Christina's brother started arguing about something or other," John J. spluttered, "and the first thing I knowed they was fighting. I thought I could stop 'em.... They was hitting ever'body that came in ten feet of them. They all got into it."

John J. chuckled. Some people said that a chill would go down their spine when they heard John J. chuckle.

"Herself had to grab the box and put it in the cupboard," he said. "Some of them had brooms. Ach! They used anythin' that was loose. Yer brother threw Ronnie clean through the window. Then they all went home. About three this mornin' they come back to pay fer the window, and Christina's brother fell through the window in the kitchen and the fight started all over.... I left. They was still at it, last I seen."

"What's th' matter with them?" said Molly. "Are they crazy? What was Christina doing?" Molly drew closer to John J. and looked into his eyes. "What was Christina doing all this time?"

"I don't know," whined John J. "There was a bunch of

women in the pantry.... I suppose she was there.... Why? There wuz nothing she could do."

Molly didn't ask any further questions. She looked long and deep into his face and her lips grew taut.

THE DAY OF THE FUNERAL, while the men talked in groups in front of the church, Molly got Christina into the truck before John J. had a chance to talk to her.

"Yisss!" Christina pushed her handkerchief into her pocket. "An' if it wasn't for John J. I don't know what we'd done. He grabbed the baby fer me—I was afraid to go where they was. I wasn't drinking anything you know. John J. was jist wonderful."

"Did ye have much baking to do after I left?" Molly asked. "Did the neighbours from around bring in things?"

"Oh, yiss! They brought parcels; almost everyone had somethin'. I just don't know what all. Ye see the rest of them took over the kitchen and pantry...wouldn't leave me go near. John J. and m'self sat on the couch...he was so good. He knew I felt bad about the baby, and scared besides."

Molly smiled as Christina finished her praises of John J. The men started moving towards their rigs.

"Here comes John J. now." And turning to Christina she said, "You have your rig here, don't yer?"

It was a blatant dismissal, cold and unmistakable. Christina only smiled when John J. came up to the truck door.

"Might as well stay where you are, Christina," he said, "we'll drop you off as we go by."

"Thank ye, John J.," cooed Christina. "It's much nicer ridin' in the truck than in the wagon."

TWO WEEKS AFTER the baby's death Ronnie followed John J. out to the truck after Mass. They exchanged remarks about the weather, their health, their families and progress on their farms.

"Christina wanted me to ask if you'd be taking a load to Wrexham soon." Ronnie said, "She'd like to ride along as far as her old man's, if you don't mind taking her."

John J. eyed the cigarette in his hand, pressed the bulge in the middle; then, sticking lips out in a hissing sound, popped the cigarette between them. Taking his time, he grabbed the wheel with his left hand, straightened his long legs hard against the floorboard until his rump rose free of the seat and dug around in his pocket for a match. His hand touched a big roll of bills, nearly five hundred—the money he'd found in the old man's clothes when he died. John J. stared straight ahead, the expression on his face as innocent as a lamb's.

"Yisss...well...the saw hasn't moved, you know, since the old man died."

Ronnie scuffed a toe in the soft dirt of the churchyard and studied the miniature cloud of dust that rose. He shifted his feet, straightened his shoulders and raised his head. Then, as if in a hurry to act before his courage failed he said:

"Christina just won't listen to me. Been acting funny since the baby died. Wants I should let the farm go, drop everything and go with her. It's going to rain and I jist can't leave everything and take her over home, even if she gits mad."

"Isss that so?" John J. was thinking aloud. "There isn't a load there, but I ain't got nothing special to do tomorrow. Tell her to be over early."

John J. and Christina left just after daybreak the next morning. From her favourite place at the window in the front door Molly watched them go. Three deep lines drew her eyes closer. She didn't glance at the toddler tugging at her apron. Minutes passed before she turned, listlessly picked up the child and returned to the kitchen.

BEFORE NOON every male eye in the Glen had winked slyly and at least four women had stopped their chores to count five fingers across one hand and four across the other as they looked at the calendar on the wall.

The pair were gone for four days. Ronnie hadn't done much work after the first day. He spent most of his time on the road between John J.'s farm and his own, looking for word of Christina. Early the fifth day Molly heard the unmistakable sound of John J.'s truck and hurried to the front door. The truck was coming fast. It slowed down at the barn, turned sharp right before the big doors; then with the motor racing faster than was sensible the truck tore up the hill and stopped at the kitchen door. Molly had a good look at the occupants. Ronnie was one of them. He sat by the window. John J. was driving. And between them sat Christina, bleary-eyed, her hair matted.

Molly brushed her hand across her eyes, shivered and wrapped her arms about her chest, as if trying to warm herself. John J. came into the kitchen first. He stood in the centre of the room, an uncorked bottle of rum in the extended hand. Humming off-key he shuffled his gumshoes forward and back. Christina sat down on the wooden couch in front of the window and watched. Her glazed eyes followed every move. Ronnie stood leaning against the wall just inside the door, seeing nothing but Christina.

"Cummina Hashen!" Christina shouted and staggered to her feet. She tried to reach Molly, but Molly sidestepped deftly.

"Cummina Hashen!" she said under her breath.

"Come on, Molly!" said John J. "We'll have a drink anyway—get a glass."

"Get it yourself!" Molly almost startled herself. John J. stood dead still, lowered his head and ran his tongue over his lips. Molly went about her business getting tea.

"Ah, Molly! Don't be mad," said Ronnie, putting out a restraining arm. "Are you mad at me? Come on sit down." Ronnie was the only one who had noticed Molly's anger. He had had only a couple of drinks.

"Molly! What's wrong with you?" John J. breathed over her

shoulder. “Ye ain’t mad because I’m having a drink, are ye? Yea an’ Hane! It’s a fine thing when a man can’t have a few drinks with his friends. Come on!” His voice was low and soft now.

“Molly, take a little sip, ye’ll feel better.” He pushed the bottle under her nose. “I suppose I shouldn’t have left you so long but when I got to Christina’s her brother Tom was there, and well, we had a few drinks.”

Molly grabbed the bottle and took a long drink.

“There! Are ye satisfied? Now git out o’ my way.”

John J. put his arm around her shoulders, but Molly threw him off and turned to Ronnie. Her eyes were hard.

“Ronnie, what’s th’ matter with you? You a man? Can’t you stop your woman? Are ye blind?”

“Mind your own business,” Ronnie shouted back, but his head hung low and he didn’t meet Molly’s eyes.

Then John J. began boasting about his woman. Christina smiled idiotically and Molly’s eyes grew redder at the rims with each drink John J. forced on her. Curses and vile language cascaded from her lips like a flood in a stream. The agonies of the years broke their barriers. The children cried and tugged at her skirts. John J. laughed. Molly picked up the lamp and threw it at the wall, inches above his head; then, grabbing a chair, she started for him. John J. clenched his fists, stepped forward and landed a punch at Molly’s face. In a corner the three youngest children cowered, watching the fight with terror in their eyes. The older boys had gone out earlier in the evening and Sally, the eldest girl, was sleeping with Olive across the river. Molly, eight months pregnant, lay motionless on the floor. She didn’t see or feel the heavy gumshoe crash against her ribs once, twice, three times.

John J. walked over to the bench and sat down beside Christina. The children inched closer to their unconscious mother until they were near enough to throw themselves down beside her and nestle in her arms. Ronnie crossed over to the bench, put his hand on Christina’s shoulder and squeezed until she winced.

"Come on! We're going home."

Christina looked at him vacantly but didn't move.

"Ye'd best wait fer morning. I got no lights," said John J.

Ronnie went out alone.

"Poor babies! Poor, poor babies!" Molly whispered in her sleep.

MOLLY WOKE TO FIND JOHN J. standing over her and shaking her arm. She had been dreaming that she had a pain in her chest.

"Get up, Molly!" he cried. "The baby's crying an' well she might be after the way ye ruffled your Rooster feathers last night. Insulting the neighbours. Wouldn't be surprised if they'd never come back. Come on! Git up, I want my breakfast." He gave her a heavy push.

"I don't think I can make it to my feet. Oh! my side," Molly groaned. "What happened to my side? Did Sally get home yet?" John J. nodded.

"Good enough for ye. Ye broke the lamp in the kitchen, and a chair. Ye came at me ready to kill me. All kinds lookin' at ye. Sally's gitting me some tea like ye should be doing, instead of laying there yellin' about bein' hurted." John J.'s gumshoes flopped loosely about his feet as he strutted from the room.

After he had left the house, Sally, her eyes full of tears, knelt beside her mother.

"What did he do, Mama? Did he give ye that black eye?"

"Black eye!" Molly put her hand to her face. "Never ye worry! Git th' baby an' warm some milk. There's a pain in my chest, mebbe ye'll have to take care of things today if I can't get up. Could ye do that, Sally?"

"Yes, Mama, but what happened? When did Himself get home?"

"Get the baby first. I'll tell ye when he's fed."

Sally loved the babies and had often taken charge of them for her mother since old Theresa first took sick.

John J. didn't come back into the bedroom. He went out as soon as he'd swallowed some tea and bread. He got no porridge, as Molly hadn't made any the night before—the first time she had missed since her marriage. When all the rest were fed, the dishes washed up and the youngest child dressed, Sally went back to her mother.

"What happened?" she said.

"Sally, I don't know. Yer father says I insulted Ronnie and Christina and fought with Himself. I don't remember. He kept after me to take a drink...followed me around. He made me drink. Now I can't remember...I must've swore...pray for me Sally to get well...and for my soul. It must've been awful."

"Don't believe him, Mama."

"Sally! Don't say that." Molly winced with pain.

"I wonder what happened Christina and Ronnie? He says I insulted them, that they'll never speak to me again."

"Mama! Don't worry. Hev you forgot he was away a week nearly—with HER?"

"Run on now, Sally." Molly threw the covers back on her good side. "Put the little ones in here with me."

A FEW DAYS LATER John J. took Molly over to her home village to make her confession. She refused to go to her own parish priest. All the way to the church and back John J. preached his own sermon. Molly sat quiet, her head bowed.

John J. knew now that Molly could be aroused. He knew too that she lost her memory after a few drinks.

For almost two weeks Molly complained about the fierce pain low in her back and each day she grew bigger. It was agony for her to walk across the kitchen floor. Sally did what she could to make things easier for her mother. She was only fourteen. The new baby was due, and it was Hallowe'en!

There had been men strewn underfoot for almost two full weeks. John J. had made bush whiskey for the occasion, but the two gallons from the run had quickly disappeared. Now they were drinking bull beer, which John J. had set on the same yeast—for another run. They drank from cups, jugs, bottles, anything that came handy and would hold liquid. Molly stayed in the kitchen keeping bread to them. At first Sally tried to keep the floors swept and picked up the boots the men had kicked off and left strewn around. But the men refused to move when she tried to sweep. Many tried to embrace her.

"Let the slinks lay in the mess, I'm not even trying to sweep anymore," she said in disgust. "Don't bother with them, Mama. If John J. wants something to eat, he'll eat. We'll leave it on the table. You best lay down. Leave the bread today."

Molly shook her head. She dragged on. No one noticed her face as she took the biscuits and the bread out of the oven. John J. sent one of the smaller boys out to the barrel with his jug and when the child came back empty-handed Molly hardly noticed. The pains had started.

Those who could walk or had rigs left as soon as they heard that the barrel was empty. Only Hector Baines remained with John J. Now, Hector was a little black wiry Irishman, full of stories of his generation, the last generation and the generation before that. Like the proverbial dog, he would carry a story to your door and not leave until he had one to take away. In a single year he managed to get through more doors than anyone else in the county. He was an ideal companion for John J.

Sally gave her father a disgusted glance and went into the front of the house. She looked at the puddled floors, the broken glasses, handleless cups scattered all over the place, and crossed over to the window and looked out at the deepening dusk. She shrugged her shoulders and left everything just as it was. When she got back to the kitchen John J. and Hector were gone; so were their jugs that had stood near the stove. Sally went to find her mother.

"Are they all gone?" Molly asked. "Is Himself gone too?"

"Yeh! Him and Hector took two jugs and left."

"Where'd they go?"

"I don't know. I was in lookin' in the front room. They was gone when I got back. Why, Mama? Are ye feeling worse? Should I wrap up the flatiron for your back?"

"No! Daresn't lay still enough to get the good of it. See if there's an aspirin in that box. I s'pose not. Pat used them with his toothache last week."

Molly screamed and even Sally knew the baby was on the way.

"Mama, will I go for Mrs. Douglas?" Sally's voice was breaking with fear.

"No! We'll wait awhile yet. P'raps John J. didn't go far. I won't be for awhile. I'll let you know. Try and get the room cleaned a little for the doctor when it's time."

Molly screamed at regular intervals. The little ones clutched at Sally's skirt crying "Mama!" in shrieks that shook the girl until her hands trembled. She went into her mother's room with the children trailing after.

"Are ye all right, Mama? Is it time fer Mrs. Douglas?"

"Not yet. Put the babies in here with me while ye finish the house. Mebbe they'll fall asleep." Molly tried to smile as the little ones crawled under the covers beside her.

"There ye are now, don't be scared. I'll try not to holler so loud." But each pain got worse and the shrieks from the bedroom tore the air. The little ones cried themselves to sleep and were still sobbing when Sally carried them one by one up to her own straw mattress and laid them down.

Nearly six hours passed since John J. had gone. The screams from the bedroom grew worse and came oftener. Sally set her lips exactly as she had seen her mother do and went into the bedroom. Then, without a word to her mother she fled out of the house. Barefoot she waded the river and ran up the field to the Douglas' house on the far bank.

The Douglases were having a party.

Sally heard the laughter, fiddle music and singing as she ran up the field. Reaching the door, she knocked three times, set her mouth and straightened her dress. She heard a young man laugh. That would be Neil's laugh, she thought. He must be in the kitchen—-just under the window. That was funny. Neil always sat in the corner by the stairway in the other room when there was company. Sally had often felt his eyes follow her across the room. Sometimes she had looked his way and smiled, but more often she pretended she didn't know he was looking. Why was he in the kitchen? Sally felt a blush stealing over her face. She should have been inside too, listening to the music. She had been asked. If only John J. had stayed sober!

Sally looked down at her muddy bare feet, straightened her shoulders and was about to push open the door when Mrs. Douglas stood before her with coat thrown hastily over her head.

Mrs. Douglas took one look at the frightened girl:

"Is it your mother?" she said. Sally nodded.

"I have to go back a minute," Clemmie Douglas said. "You go on and I'll get me boots and be right over."

CLEMMIE DOUGLAS FOLLOWED Sally over the river and swept into the Campbell kitchen. Clemmie was very feminine. Frilly bows delighted her and she always wore them, even at her everyday work. Her full flabby face dropped into an undefined chin that seemed not to end but to melt away like a good intention. Its weakness denied the spiritual strength of her forehead. She tripped through the kitchen like a colt kicking up its heels. She was a perpetual adolescent, unable to cope with opposition and yet capable of forcing her will on others through sheer determination. She liked to have her virtues counted and talked about in her own presence. She came to the aid of neighbours in need as much for her own regard as for the charity of the act itself. She threw off her coat and with cold wet feet went into the bedroom where Molly lay screaming.

"How d'you feel?" she asked. "Are the pains gettin' close together?" Molly nodded and screamed again.

"Anything I can do?"

Molly shook her head, too breathless to speak.

"Be right with ye...have to get my boots off. The river went right over the top. Ye lay still now and I'll be right back." Clemmie smiled and motioned Sally to follow her.

"Have ye got a pair of the boys' heavy socks handy that I can slip on while my boots and stockin's dry?" Sally nodded. "Good! Now fill the kettle to the top and set it on the fire. Where's yer father?"

Clemmie Douglas listened until Sally came to the end of her story.

"They must've went up to the MacTavishes...won't do them no good. They're all at my place. When did they go?" The deepening lines between Clemmie's eyes showed her feelings more than any words could have done.

"If they're gone all that time they should be back soon."

Her words were no sooner said than loud voices were heard coming up the hill.

John J., his gumshoes wrapped and tied halfway down their length, was covered with mud to his waist. Hector, in the middle of one of his harangues about the lineage of some man in the Glen, was just as bad.

The men came into the kitchen without wiping their feet, each with a jug in his hand.

"Cummina Hashen, Mrs. Douglas!" Hector hollered happily. John J. didn't speak. He sat down in a chair by the oven door and pulled off his boots. Clemmie Douglas maneuvered herself into his line of vision. He took no notice of her.

"Come on Hector, let's have some of that beer since we brought it so far."

"John J., listen!" said Clemmie, wringing her hands. "Can't ye hear Molly screaming? Th' baby is ready to come. I think somethin's gone wrong. Poor soul's been hollerin' like that for hours. Ye have to get a doctor. Don't sit there, ye should be on your way now."

"Come on, Hector," said John J., as if he hadn't heard, "we'll hev a little drink anyway."

Ignoring his wife's screams and Clemmie Douglas' demands, John J. reached for the jug and took a long drink. He passed the jug to Hector who drank also. Then, startled by an agonizing cry from the bedroom, Hector jumped to his feet.

"Come on, John J., get your shoes back on. P'raps we'd best go?"

After some coaxing they got John J. moving, but not without his jug. He didn't go near the bedroom.

THE OCTOBER MUD WAS AXLE-DEEP in places and the truck had a hard time getting through. Halfway to the highway John J. had had enough and was ready to go back home without help. He had no intention of going another thirteen miles.

"Well, let's see if old Doctor Barton'll come," Hector coaxed, "he lives just over there."

"That old bastard hasn't been doctoring fer thirty years. He's older than Christ...he won't come."

But John J. drove to the doctor's house anyway.

After Hector's pounding had shaken the house, the doctor came to the door.

"I can't come," he said, "I haven't been practicing for years."

"Ye'll have to come," Hector roared, "the lady may be dyin'! Doctors are s'posed to come when they're needed, ain't they?" The old man found his insistence overwhelming and consented to go along in self-defense.

In days to come Hector told the story of the ride at every opportunity. The old doctor, well in his eighties, sat between John J. and himself in the truck, the jug of bull beer at his feet. John

J. drove like he was being pursued by a mad bull. Through the ruts, slipping and sliding over the road while Hector passed the jug back and forth in front of the doctor's face.

"Please, boys," the old doctor said, "go a little easy."

But John J. and Hector only laughed. At last they pulled up at the house.

The doctor, though more shaken than ever, went straight in the direction of the screams, calling for a basin of hot water as he passed through the kitchen. He came out of the bedroom drying his hands and shaking his head until his grey whiskers umbrellaed from his chin.

"This woman has to get to hospital right away," he said, turning to Clemmie Douglas. "There's something wrong, and there's no way I can help her. Will you get her ready right away? There's not a minute to be lost. Better take her on a mattress if you can. She can't sit up for that distance."

John J. pooh-poohed the whole thing. But Hector took the doctor's side. He coaxed and drank and coaxed again until finally John J. disappeared into the front of the house and came back with an old mattress which he threw into the back of the truck. Clemmie got Molly ready, ran over the river, changed her clothes and told her family where she was going. She also wanted another woman to come along with her—anything might happen. The first woman she saw was her daughter-in-law, Mary. Mary was glad to accompany her and in less than ten minutes the two women were back across the river.

The ride to the hospital began.

Dr. Barton braced himself for the return journey and sat, as before, between John J. and Hector. As before, the jug was passed back and forth before his face. Hector kept up a stream of profane chatter and the laughter from the cab could be heard above the roar of the engine as they sped down the road. In the back of the truck Molly lay exhausted between Clemmie Douglas and Mary, no longer able to scream out. She whimpered when

John J. hit a bump that tossed her and the mattress into the air. Mary and Mrs. Douglas took turns calling out to John J. to slow up. They only stopped once, to let the doctor off, then drove on at the same speed as before.

When they arrived at the hospital, John J. and Hector carried Molly up the stairs on the mattress—one at the head and the other at the foot. They waited at the door of the ward until the mattress was handed out to them. At the head of the long flight of stairs John J. dropped the mattress and with a kick, sent it flying to the bottom. At every bump bleached oat straw burst out of the many holes and covered the width of each tread. Laughing and enjoying the joke, John J. and Hector followed down the stairs and out to the truck.

The doctor ordered a sedative and told the nurses to give Molly a cup of tea. He said he didn't like her state of exhaustion and then added that they might hurry the delivery along with a little something that neither Clemmie nor Mary had heard of before. After the tea and sedative, Molly was wheeled into the delivery room, the doctor by her side. Soon her whimpering ceased and the strong smell of chloroform filled the hall. Clemmie and Mary, beads in hand, sat in chairs provided for them and prayed. At last they heard a wail. They looked at each other and smiled.

But the doctor didn't come out. Fifteen minutes passed.... Twenty...twenty-five. Not a sound from the delivery room except the whisk of the nurses' uniforms as they rushed in and out the door intent on their missions.

Clemmie and Mary picked up their beads once again, and their lips moved silently. Then they heard another wail, not as strong as the first, and once again they smiled.

Outside in the truck John J. and Hector had finished the contents of the jug and were asleep. Clemmie Douglas woke them.

"John J., you're the father of a fine set of twins," she said.

"That's good!" John J. answered, throwing open the cab door.

"Come on! Get in her. We'd best get under way."

"Aren't ye going to see Molly?" Clemmie's eyes widened in the light from the hospital door.

"I'll see her tomorrow," John J. answered and started up the motor. There was nothing for the women to do but get in.

JOHN J. WAS FEELING GOOD! In fact he had reached the monologue stage. A look of surprise came over his face. Molly wasn't listening. She hadn't been listening for a long time. It was the unexpected silence that made her look up. She looked in time to see John J. go out the door. She sighed and rose from the chair where she had been sitting watching the infants and punched her bread.

John J. went straight to Ronnie's. No one was in the house but Christina.

"Cummina Hashen!" said John J. "Where's Ronnie?"

"Naw! He's gone over to give a hand to the Piper today, won't be home till after supper," said Christina.

John J. was all smiles.

"Get your clothes on, we'll go for a ride. Molly's mad."

THEY DROVE STRAIGHT NORTH, not stopping until they drew up at the vendor's. John J. looked up and down the street nervously, then got out. He looked up and down the street again before leaving the building with a brown paper bag in his hand. It seemed no time at all before they were in Wrexham. John J. drove to a third-rate hotel and they went inside.

They stayed for three days, going out to eat now and then and to replenish the drink.

"Come on, we'll go git th' air," John J. said on the third day. "See if we can't find some excitement."

John J. no longer felt the need for caution in Alice's village. He drove the truck slowly down the street, then stopped, leaving the engine running. It was as though he was hoping to see Alice. He went into the vendor's and came back with his brown paper parcel with no more than a casual glance up the street to keep from getting run over. With the wine stowed away he became a different person and began talking on his favourite subject—women. Christina spoke, he didn't hear. She shook his arm, he didn't notice. He talked on and on. At last he stopped the truck in front of an unpainted shack on the outskirts of town.

"John J., what're ye stopping at Alice's for?" Christina was shouting now.

"Let's get out here." John J.'s laugh was a kind of gurgle on an indrawn breath. He got out of the cab, then glanced at Christina who hadn't moved. "Come on! Get out. I'm going in. You can suit yerself."

Just then the door of the shack flew open and Alice hurried out. She looked at the bottle and invited him in with far more hospitality than was necessary.

"Christina's with me," he said. "See if ye can get her in."

He turned and went into the shack.

The women soon followed and Alice closed the door. John J. chuckled when he looked into their eyes. He held up the bottle and picked up the monologue from the point where he had left off in the cab. Over and over again he told Alice of the stay he and Christina had had in Wrexham. Alice looked at Christina.

"Is he tellin' the truth? Did ye just come from Wrexham?"

"Of course!" Christina said haughtily, tossing her uncombed hair and smoothing her crumpled dress.

John J. sensed that he had Alice going and from now on the monologue told stories of his intimacy with her. Story after story, first about one woman and then about the other, over and over again.

"Ye may be my cousin," said Alice sneering at Christina, "but keep your pig's hands off his money. I know the likes of ye."

"Ye should!" said Christina, wobbling in her chair. "Yiss, I know you think he'll give you some of it but not if I can help it. I've been going to Wrexham with him for years. No! No no-good son-of-a-whore like you going to get what's coming to me." Then catching the tail end of some story John J. was repeating about himself and Alice, Christina stopped.

Alice stopped too.

At last they knew what John J. was up to!

John J. shuffled to and fro across the floor talking like a bad phonograph record. His big gumshoes flopped this way and that, as if in no way responsible to the long legs that connected them to his pancake rump. Above his rumpled plaid shirt sprang a deep red neck and face topped by an inch-long tuft of standing hair. He looked like a grey-crested persimmon.

The bottle was empty, the case was empty too.

"I'll go git some more," John J. said, going for his hat. Both women jumped up and followed him.

They stopped at the vendor's, then drove outside the town. John J. stopped the truck, uncorked a bottle of wine and passed it to his lady friends. Christina, on account of being the latest to accompany John J. to Wrexham, claimed priority and sat in the middle; Alice, with discontent, next to the door. Their hands shot out for the bottle at the same time and met mid-air around its neck. At the touch of Alice's fingers Christina's black eyes came alive with fury. She struck out and dashed Alice's head against the window. Alice struck back. Then the two wilted birds went at it tooth-and-nail, tearing at each other's clothing, punctuating the ripping of cloth with words of which only the Roosters knew the full meaning.

"Cut that out!" John J. commanded, the expression on his face belying his words. "Ye want I should get arrested and the whole bunch of us thrown in jail? If you are gonna fight, either get out or wait till we're a ways out of town."

John J.'s jaw now stuck out like a wedge. He brought the truck to a halt and leaning across the women he pushed the far door open.

"Get out!" he said tersely. "Yer not gonna fight in here."

He pushed Christina so hard that he shoved the two women out through the door.

Before John J. had any idea of what was happening, they were both at the door on his side of the cab. They threw open the door and yanked him out. Christina stood with a shirtsleeve in her hand while John J. took a swing at Alice who had drawn blood from his face with her jagged nails. While Alice was grovelling in the dust, he rounded on Christina. Alice picked herself up and flew, teeth bared, for his face.

From then on it was a melee, to the accompaniment of cursing and tearing cloth. It's hard to say who would have won.

It was John J. who saw him first from the corner of his eye—the blue coat and brass trimmings, the leather leggings. He looked at the concrete lines on the imperturbable face, shrugged his shoulders and drooped.

"All right, get in!" the Mountie commanded. "All three of you. Turn the truck around and head back to town. I'll blow my horn when you're to stop. And no funny work."

At the police station the captain shook his head, wrote their names and the rest of the information in his book and led them to their quarters.

A WEEK WENT BY. John J. hadn't come back and Christina was gone too. Molly knew that because Ronnie had come looking for her. Molly had run out of flour so she sent little Jimmy to a neighbour with a ten-pound lard pail "to borrow the full of it." The bread was all gone. The bottom of the sugar jar was showing as well.

"Sally, git over to Jim Douglas and tell him I want to go on a trip."

Sally put down the plate she was drying.

"A trip!" she said in amazement. "Won't he charge, Mama? Can you pay him?"

"Yer father can pay him when I get my hands on him. We hev to eat."

Molly directed Jim Douglas first to Alice's shack. No one was at home. Molly tried the door. It was open. She went in. Molly knew that two of the boys' suits had disappeared about the time John J. went on his last spree with Alice. They were brand new First Communion suits.

"I'm going to get Charlie and Angus' First Communion suits. I know where to find them."

She looked in every corner but she couldn't find what she was looking for. Then she noticed, in a corner beyond the bed, a curtain stretched across the corner. Behind it on the floor were the missing suits. Molly left the shack, climbed into the truck and carefully spread the suits across the back of the seat.

"We'll go to the store," she said, folding her hands over a shabby little purse that could have been a child's.

Molly bought twenty-five pounds of flour, two yeast cakes and ten pounds of sugar. Then, choosing carefully, ten cents worth of candy that had the most pieces for a penny.

"I'm ready, if you are," she said to Jim. "Himself'll have to pay ye—if he ever gets back," she said defiantly. "I had to have some bread for the children and the allowance wasn't enough to pay everything."

Jim knew the whole situation and was glad to be of help. As the truck stopped before the kitchen door, Sally, barefooted and dirty, ran out of the house.

"Mama, Christina's inside."

"Is she alone?" Molly glanced over Sally's shoulder. "Did John J. get home?"

"No, Mama! She says she's somethin' important to tell ye. Wouldn't tell me."

Molly went into the house.

"Cummina Hashen, Molly!" Christina said meekly. "John J.'s in jail!"

Molly pretended not to have heard.

"He was before the judge this morning," Christina went on.

"Pleaded not guilty, and they bound him over to Monday. He wants ye to get some one t'go and get the truck."

"Yisss!" Molly looked coldly at the woman. "Where's the truck?"

"In Wicker's garage—Mountie took her there."

Molly didn't answer. She went into the bedroom to change. She was gone so long that Christina fidgeted nervously.

"I'd best get going, Sally," she said. Sally didn't answer. Molly came into the kitchen the moment she heard the door close. She looked toward the empty chair and went about her work.

The next day when the bread was out of the oven and the biscuits piled high to cool in the pantry, Molly folded her apron and told Sally to call the boys in.

"Yer father's in jail," she said to the four spindly youths before her. "He wants us to bring the truck home. If Sally keeps the babies, I'd best be going along. We'll have to have money for groceries. Get yerselves ready," she said, waving away their questions.

"IS THIS WHERE WE GO?" Molly asked as they stood before the Mounties' office.

None of them knew. Molly went in.

"I want to take John J. Campbell's truck home," she said to the Mounties behind the desk.

"John J. Campbell's," the officer drawled. "Hmmm! Would that be the John J. Campbell we picked up with two women? What kind of truck is it? Who are you?"

"I'm his wife," said Molly. "It's a Fargo truck. Just what did he get in jail for?"

"It says here"—the Mountie slowly turned the page—"the truck was stopped in the middle of the road, stopping traffic. The three of them were fighting inside the truck when the officer first saw them. Then as he watched, it says, they all got out and the two women were fighting with each other as well as with him.

His shirt was almost torn off and he was bleeding around the face like he'd been cut."

"Was he hurt?" asked Molly quickly.

"Naw! Twas just a few scratches. They bleed bad about the head, you know. The women's dress was torn and their hair all mussed up." The Mountie chuckled, but sobered quickly at the sight of Molly's face.

"You say you're his wife?"

"Yiss, and these are his boys," said Molly. "What's the charges, and can I see him myself?"

"Yes, you can see him. There's a whole list of charges. If he gets a lawyer it's possible some can be dropped. As it is he's charged with operating a vehicle under the influence of liquor. Creating a public nuisance. Fighting. Disturbing the peace and resisting an officer."

"What y'do with the women?" Molly asked.

"One of them, an Alice something or other...I just forgot, we just say 'Alice' when she comes in. We all know her, she's here so often."

"Never mind," said Molly quickly, "I know her."

"Well!" The officer stopped looking for Alice's record and went on. "We kept her, got ten days, she put up a fight. The other, Christina, we let go in court this morning. She pleaded guilty to drunkenness. Your husband paid the ten-dollar fine. I don't know where she went."

"When's John J. Campbell's trial?" Molly asked.

"Monday!"

Molly nodded. "Now can I talk to him?"

The officer nodded and led her and the boys down to the cells.

"Oh, Molly, Molly! Yer must believe me!" John J. tried to take her hand. "I'm an innocent man." Then turning to the Mountie he whimpered, "Sir, would ye give m'wife a hundred dollars of my money. She'll have to hev it to feed the children."

"I'll get the paper for you to sign," the officer said and left the family alone.

"Molly, it ain't so bad as it looks, ye know." John J. tried to laugh. "If ye'll just quit standing there staring out the window, I'll tell ye just what did happen."

Molly turned and stood waiting.

"Honest, Molly! I went over to see Ronnie about something and Christina told me he was at the Piper's and wouldn't be home till after supper...said she needed things from the store; she didn't know what to do with Ronnie gone and no one to take her. That's how it started...Molly? Are ye lissenin'?"

Molly gave no sign, just stood staring at him.

"I can see there's no talkin' to ye." John J. shook his head in sorrow. "Ye just don't want to believe me...but ye'll have to believe there was nothing wrong...we was just drinking. Ye know I don't care for anyone but ye. I know I talk foolish just to get ye going...to see how mad will ye get, but that's all it is, ye know that. Come over closer to the bars and give me a kiss so's I know yer m'girl again."

Molly accepted the noisy smack on the side of the cheek and stepped back just as the Mountie came through the door.

The boys, slouching against the bars, chewing spruce gum as fast as their gums could go, stopped to sneer. John J. looked from one to the other and put his hand up to his grey chest and began twisting the lock of hair round between his thumb and forefinger.

"Take the truck home," he said at last. "Johnnie here can drive it. Get the groceries and Molly, please come to court, Monday. If ye come the lawyers says there's a good chance for me to get off easy."

Molly looked at him, signed the paper the Mountie had brought, took the bills, counted them and snapped her little purse shut.

"Well, good-bye then!" she said simply. The boys followed her out of the cell.

Before Molly left town she went into the beauty parlour and made an appointment for a permanent wave—on Monday. As soon as they got home all the boys learned to drive the truck. They took turns running up and down the roads.

On Monday, Johnnie drove his mother into town to get her permanent. John J. got sixty days, lost his license and paid a fine that took nearly all his money he had left in the Mountie's office.

THE OLDER BOYS HARDLY KNEW what to do with their new-found freedom. For a whole week they drove the truck constantly, then idleness got boring. There was nothing to do but sit around and chew spruce gum. Then, one evening Johnnie let the front legs of the chair he was sitting on down on the floor with a bang.

"What's the matter with us anyways? We've got the mill. The old feller's away. We could take some deal to Wrexham—maybe get a car of our own, eh?"

"Yiss!" Molly nodded her head. "That would be all right."

The boys went to work and cut the logs. Everyone helped, even Sally. Johnnie who had used the saw now and then when his father had been "nervous" did the sawing. Some of the boards weren't so straight and maybe they brought less than was paid for first-class lumber but the boys had more than enough money for a car. It was the first time they had money of their own to spend. Molly beamed with pride—her smiles came often now.

The boys went to fetch John J. home in the car. John J. was dumbfounded. He opened his mouth to speak but closed it again without saying a word. He looked the car over, asked a few questions; and then as if this sort of thing happened every day of the week, he opened the door and got in.

"Well, get in," he said, "let's see how she runs."

They took John J. to the vendor and he was full and happy before he saw Molly.

The next day was different. Molly had John J. in the porch

giving him a haircut. He picked up the corner of Molly's old dress that was pinned around his neck to keep the hairs from getting inside his underwear and wiped his eyes. John J. was allergic to alcohol and every time he sobered up his eyes ran for a day or two. He was sober now and unwell.

"Fine woman ye are," he said, "wouldn't even come to court to help her husband. Where was ye anyway?"

"I was at the beauty parlour," Molly answered flatly.

"Beauty parlour!" John J. roared, turning round in his chair.

"If ye'd keep yer prick where it's s'posed to be ye wouldn't have been in jail," Molly answered hotly. "Let the whore was with ye go to court with ye."

John J. didn't say a word. He turned around and let her finish his hair.

FROM THEN ON he drove the boys unmercifully. He took a load to Wrexham every week. He insisted that Johnnie drive. Johnnie went and reported everything that happened to his mother and what little respect he had for his father was lost. He told his brothers and they grew more and more rebellious. They put up with it all summer because they had the car and had started going to dances. Now and then, when John J. was away, they got a few days work on the roads and the money kept them in gas and there was enough left to buy a bottle from the bootlegger, who drove into the yard at the dances with his truck loaded with watered rum in pint bottles. He didn't ask anyone's age. Molly talked to them severely about drinking but they paid no attention.

Winter came and the roads closed. The boys were broke and restless. There was no freedom anymore. John J. drove them into the woods all week and when Friday came the big saw was started and the logs sawn into boards. The boys loaded the truck while John J. stood, hands behind his back, watching. The two boys younger than Sally hitched up the horses to a homemade wooden plough and carried shovels and an axe; they drove ahead to open a track for the truck. The wooden plough was only of use where there were no drifts, so when John J. pulled out the truck all five boys had to accompany it to the end of the Glen road. At every drift the boys would take their shovels and try to dig a way through while John J. sat in the cab rolling cigarettes. Sometimes it took a whole day to reach the highway. If they were lucky the municipal plough might have come by; if not, then Colin and Pat would have to go and search for the driver. The trip was long and cold; the boys savage; but they feared the lashing their father would give them in the barn.

One day Johnnie spoke out.

"Mama!" he said, "we're thinking of going away."

"All of ye?" She looked at each face in turn. "What're ye telling me? Himself can't get the hay in alone and the grain?"

"Let him pay someone for a change," said Johnnie, "we haven't had five cents all winter. We do all the work and he goes on a spree with the money. We don't git no clothes, shoes maybe, when he gits ashamed in front of neighbours when our toes comes through, or overalls when our tails is showing, that's all. If ye didn't give us tobacco we wouldn't even have smokes. He takes all the money and rolls it up and shows off."

"Yeh!" said Colin, the silent one. "If there's anyone around at all he has to play the big shot—on OUR MONEY. Some big shot! Anyway it was us earned it for him."

"Yisss!" Molly looked from one to the other. "I see you have made up your mind. Yez'll have to stay for now though, and go after the hayin'. If ye don't Himself will have me and the little one in the field."

"Ye wouldn't have t'go," Johnnie said slowly.

"Yiss!" said Molly, as she picked up one of the twins, "we'd hev to go, or he'd git drunk and leave the cows to starve all winter and him telling the neighbours it was yer fault."

"I s'pose," said Johnnie, unable to hide his disappointment.

He never disobeyed his mother.

"If I have to stay, I'm going to work at Lawlor's," said Colin. "Himself can say whatever he's a notion to but he won't use the harness on me no more—on any of us." He looked at his brothers for affirmation. "We made our minds up to that. If he starts anything we're all going to take a hand and he'll pay for every licking he ever gave any of us."

The others nodded.

"All right, Colie!" Molly looked at her son with pride. "It's best ye work. Yell need the money. I'd be worried if ye didn't hev a copper, leaving."

"O.K.!" they said, almost at the same time.

"We don't like to leave ye, Mama," Johnnie went on, "ye know that. An' we'll send ye money as we get work."

Molly smiled.

HAYING TIME CAME. The boys fixed the barn with less care than in former years but John J. didn't notice. When the pitching rope was in place and the old hay seed shoveled from the floor, they ducked out the back of the barn and went off towards the river out of sight.

Being in an affluent mood the week before, John J. had hired a tractor to mow his hay but this morning when the man and the tractor showed up at the crowing of Sally's bantam rooster, it was a sick, dry and ill-tempered John J. that rubbed his flat pocket and cursed himself.

"Four boys and two horses idle!" he muttered under his breath, and looking around he saw the boys leaning against the side of the barn, each with a straw in his mouth, all grinning. John J. spat vigorously, turned and walked off to show the driver which field to mow first.

"Bumper crop of oats yer gonna get there," the fellow said.

"If the hail stays away," John J. grunted, "and the wind."

John J. had built a covered porch on his house and placed a wooden bench along the wall opposite the door. From this seat he could see almost the whole farm without moving. He headed for the seat now. It wasn't long before a shadow fell across the ground in front of him. John J. wasn't surprised to see Dougall.

"Hev a seat," he said, patting the bench beside him.

Dougall sat down and smiled, ready for what he was so sure would happen. He had risen a full half hour earlier than usual and walked to John J.'s to be on hand. He even brought his hay fork so his intentions would seem good.

"How're ye today, John J.?" Dougall asked.

John J. shook his head silently.

"Pretty rough, eh?" Dougall, with his cigarette hanging from his lips started rooting in his bib-overalls pocket and took out a crumpled two-dollar bill.

"Look, John J.! I got one two-dollar bill. I'll get a bottle of wine for the cure if ye'll furnish the rig. Won't take a minute."

"I'll see if I can drive," said John J., standing up. "Should be able to get that far." He led Dougall to the truck.

The bootlegger lived three miles from John J.'s farm and the men should have been back easily within the hour, but after two drinks they were all set for the day.

"Might's well keep north," said John J., pushing down on the throttle. "Yiss, that's what we'll do."

IT WAS WELL PAST THE DINNER HOUR. The boys were impatient to be on their way. The hay had been raked, turned and gathered; only John J. held up the operation.

"Come on!" said Johnnie; "we've wasted time enough. Himself might be gone a week. Git the horses harnessed, Pat. I'll pull the rack up to the barn. Colie, ye get the hay forks and throw 'em on the rack."

Soon the first load was stacked in the barn and the hayrack almost empty for the second time.

"How's it down there?" Johnnie called down from the loft. "Can we git her up in one fork?"

"More'n enough for one load and not enough for two," Danny answered.

"Can ye get her all on one fork?"

"Yeah!"

"What th' hell! The rope's new an' we've got a double team. Put her on, Danny, let's get her up and get through."

Now, the team was a horse and a mare. The horse a good two hands higher than the little mare, lurched ahead, before Colie gave the command, pulling the mare along the first couple of steps. When the mare got the command she strained forward and the rope snapped. The load fell with a thud that nearly went through the bottom of the hayrack.

Before the boys could get the fork out of the hay John J. drove up. He saw it all. His face red and distorted with fury, his grey crest bobbing forward and back, his hands opening and clenching, he stood like a madman. He was not only furious but three-quarters drunk. The boys braced themselves. In the past, John J. had laced them with a piece of harness or anything handy to his reach. But today there was something about the boys, their lopsided smiles, their mocking attitudes that warned him that times had changed. Johnnie held one end of the frayed rope and looked at John J. towering above him.

"We think p'raps ye'd best get somebody else to finish the hay. That's it, ain't it, Danny? Pat?" Johnnie looked at his brothers. John J.'s hands clenched tight at his side, moved towards the boys as if to snatch the rope and throttle them. Then suddenly the rage seemed to melt away leaving his face wreathed in smiles.

"Ye couldn't leave me now, could ye?" he wheedled. "Everyone's at their own hay. I'll go out t'town and get a new rope. Be back b'fore you fellers get the next load on."

Johnnie wasn't listening.

Leaving the horses harnessed and standing where they were,

he strolled off up the hill to the house.

"What's th' matter?" Molly said when he came into the kitchen. "What's he done now?"

"We busted his damn pitchin' rope," said Johnnie. "All the hay'll have to be pitched by hand now. Pat went after Colie; we'll be leaving right away. If the old man had stayed away we'd have gone for Jim Douglas' pitchin' rope and finished up. He's been to the vendor and to hell with him!"

"Are yez all going?" Molly asked. "Colie too?"

"Yiss! The old man ain't gonna take his hangovers out on us boys no more."

At that moment John J. stalked into the kitchen.

"Come into the room," he said, without looking at his sons. "I want to hev a word with ye."

Johnnie followed his father into the parlour.

"Well!" said Johnnie, lowering himself into the nearest chair.

"Is this the way yez are going to treat me when I'm after feeding and putting clothes on yer backs all them years?" John J. moaned.

"Wuz'n't ye put the clothes on our backs," Johnnie answered. "It was Grandpa took care of all of us—yerself and Mama too."

"Mebbe!" said John J. tersely.

"And it was Ben and Tim did all the work when Grandpa couldn't go no more. YE DIDN'T," said Johnnie.

"It's been twenty years since then," John J. raved.

"We wez earning all we ever got long before they left. Ye never give us nothin'. It wuz us supporting you. Yeh! even to the wine ye bought yer whores."

John J. raved, threw his hands into the air, walked the floor for fully fifteen minutes. Never before had he been so frustrated. He went out into the kitchen to find Molly.

"Did yer know about this?" he fumed.

"Know about what?" asked Molly innocently.

"The boys. They've quit me, and after all I done for 'em. First they bust me pitchin' rope I paid six dollars for only the other day. Nothing but foolishness, carelessness—must've done it on purpose. Now they say they're going away."

"It's yer own fault." Molly had caught courage from the boys.

"Ye won't leave them use the new truck, and them after buying it fer ye, ye might say. Young boys like a dollar to spend once in a while. Ye go away fer a week and come home hollering they ain't done nothin' right. Ye don't leave 'em right food to eat. Yisss! ye only have yerself to blame."

John J. was beaten. He paced a couple of turns across the floor, then straightened up a little and went back to Johnnie in the parlour.

"Ye heven't any money to go, Johnnie," he said, "tell ye what I'll do. Ye fellers help me get in the hay and give me time to git out and we'll all go."

"Oh yeh!" said Johnnie disrespectfully, grabbing time to get the offer straight in his mind. This was the last thing he expected from his father. "There'll be the grain after that, and all the time we're waiting the milking and everything else to do."

"No! No!" said John J. He was getting carried away himself now.

"We'll turn all the cows into the grain so they'll be handy. Yer mother'll milk th' ones that have too much to let go dry, and the two with the new calves...well, we'll put the calves on them and let them go with the rest. I'll pay the gas an' oil fer yer car and get new tires fer the trip. I'll even pay the expenses."

John J. had made his point and Johnnie looked thoughtful.

"Well, I don't know," Johnnie said, "I'll have to ask the rest."

THE DAY OF JOHN J.'S AUCTION came round. It was harvest time. One or two industrious farmers had risen before dawn to get the cuttings into the barns before going to the auction. The fields in the Glen were idle under the blistering sun. Mowing machines, hayrakes and wagons stood unattended in the fields. Everyone was going to the auction.

"I'd go if I was dead!" Lauchie MacTavish said the night before, and he spoke for them all.

The auctioneer was a stranger; not more than a handful of people knew the man, but his speech and dress were unmistakable. He was a man from the county. Now and then he raised his long-billed cap and brushed the moisture from his forehead. A thin, weathered neck bobbed in and out of his rumpled plaid collar like a chicken looking for worms. The maple branch he carried—more often in the air, pointing out this and that—served as a cane. A splotch of brown liquid spewed from his toothless gums and when he spat it shot out over the projecting hook of his chin, barely missing the end of his nose. As he gazed out over the crowd standing in a circle around him, he kept changing his cane from one hand to the other.

Satisfied that he had their attention, he started chanting about the serviceability of a badly cracked hammer that John J. was holding aloft, although all could see that the handle was ready to split on the next job.

In front of the circle Dougall MacDougall stood rolling a cigarette. Lauchie MacTavish was the first to notice him. Curious to see who had bid for the hammer, he strained on tiptoe to see over the heads of the crowd.

"That was Dougall! Look at him...biddin' like he had his pockets full, and him without a copper."

The men laughed, unaware of the part Dougall was playing. Bidding was slow at first. No man seemed anxious to part with his money. The boys dragged one piece of harness after another out of the barn door and threw them in a heap before the auctioneer. In silent supplication John J. stepped up to the pile and held up what was left of a halter. It's roughened surface, bent rein-rings, and the place where Pat had punched a nail through and bent it over to hold the headstrap together, looked like something even the rats had left behind. Danny drew Colin aside.

"Look at that halter. Never looked so bad when we was using it. The other stuff too...do yer see it?"

"Yeh!" said Colin, "did you see that Dougall? Just raised the fifty-cent bid to a dollar, like he had bills in every pocket. What's the idea? If the ole man keeps that feller in there we won't be after going no place. Himself'll still be broke and all the junk'll be left with him."

Colin kicked viciously at a dried horse apple and sent it sailing through the air. The boys glanced over at their father and saw his long jaw muscle popping in and out like he was making bubbles in his cheeks.

"He's looking fer something he ain't seeing," said Danny. "His face looks like a piece of fresh meat in a lime pit."

"Over there!" said Colin, pointing up the hill towards the wood behind the house. "Hector Baines and the jug coming outta the woods. What ye s'pose kept him so long? No wonder the ole man's jaw wuz bobbing."

John J. had seen Hector too. He drew a deep breath of relief.

John J. and his helpers had finished the two-gallon of bush whiskey made especially for the auction several days ago and there had been no time for the yeast to finish working in the new batch. The liquid Hector was handing round now was thick and yellow but none the less potent, although it didn't look fit to drink. John J. motioned to Colin to bring out the horses.

Colin led the mare into the center of the ring and the bidding started. She was a good steady animal, if a little old. The kind of horse a farmer finds useful—gentle with children. Someone made a fair offer. Dougall concentrating on the cigarette he was rolling either didn't notice John J.'s head bobbing furiously or chose to disregard it. He raised the bid again and it was once too often.

"Sold!" said the auctioneer, hardly able to hide his disapproval. "To the man rolling himself a smoke."

DANNY LED THE BIG HORSE into the ring and as soon as he could reach his father's outstretched hand, gave him the rope. The brown gelding, fourteen hands high, stood tense, ears flat against his head, nostrils flaring. His wide breast indicated stamina and staying power, the qualities responsible for the satanic gleam in his eyes. The boys always had to work in relays to catch him in the field and long before they could trap him they were tired and furious. Once caught, they tied him to a post or anything strong enough to hold him and flogged him unmercifully. He was beyond being fooled any longer. Even his own oat box wouldn't tempt him. He bit, kicked, reared up on his hind legs and tried to trample anyone who came under him. Dougall's was the only bid.

John J. and the auctioneer led the crowd over to the field by the barn that had been fenced off for a day. One by one the boys led out the cows.

"Sold!" the auctioneer's voice rang out, time and time again, "to the gent over by the fence." The cows weren't going for the right price. John J. had overvalued his animals; they were all small and odd-shaped, the result of inbreeding. John J. had never gone outside his herd for sires. Each year he saved a calf for the purposes. Colin brought a little brown cow into the ring. The heifer, two years old and pot-bellied with calf, looked little more than a yearling. The auctioneer looked the animal over, then with a hand across his mouth, whispered to John J. Anyone in the crowd could read what he was saying.

"Ach! What's the difference?" replied John J. "If they can't see fer themselves that she's a runt, that she's no business being with calf at all, at her age, that's their hard luck. Let them make beef with her, if no one wants a calf that small. It's not for ye to be worrying about. Ye jist sell her. That's yer job. She should bring hundred an' seventy-five anyways."

John J. snapped his fingers. The auctioneer shrugged his shoulders.

"Here ye are folks, look at this nice little heifer, only two years old, and havin' her first calf come October. Ain't she a nice one, though? Seventy-five, I'm bid...should be worth a hundred and twenty-five. Look at them horns—smooth as silk, not a wrinkle in 'em," and then in a loud whisper—"Wish I could say the same of m'own." The auctioneer smiled his approval at the laughter that followed.

"Sold!" he said at last, to Dougall MacDougall.

Lauchie looked at Dougall who never raised his head from the cigarette he was still rolling, and nudged Jim.

"Dougall's getting hisself a cheap herd."

The sale of the sheep finished everything outside, and all that was left now was to sell the household effects. But instead of leading the way into the house John J. stood looking toward the barn and the pens. He wasn't a happy man.

"Cummina Hashen!"

John J. felt a hand on his shoulder and whirled around. It was one of the Beavers. No one bothered to learn their first names, there were so many of them. All the Beavers had long prominent front teeth; but the comparison did not end with their teeth. They were also clannish and industrious. When a young Beaver married, the clan to a man went into the woods, cut, hewed and sneaked out logs for a cabin. They built it and furnished it with rough homemade furniture. After a few days the groom joined the others in the fields. Each family had its own farm, yet all worked together at harvest time or whenever a member of the family required extra help.

"Yiss?" hissed John J., his jaw muscle working furiously.

"That brown gelding of yers; hev ye auctioned him yet? I just got here; broke a shaft...."

"What makes ye ask?" John J.'s eyes were as bright as newly minted coins.

"If ye wouldn't be askin' too much fer him I thought mebbe... my boy Angus' banns has been published two times now; he don't hev a horse and we want to give him one."

"Well, now, this is an auction."

John J. reached out and catching the auctioneer by the shoulder swung him round. "We can't set a price on him, can we?" Then without waiting for an answer, "Mebbe we could bring him out again, the...no one wuz around time he was up. Couldn't git a right bid, so I kept him." John J. nodded thoughtfully. "Yiss, that's what we'd best do—we'll put him up again."

The three started down the hill to the barn again, drawing the crowd behind them like a magnet. Joe Beaton laughed. Someone else laughed and soon everyone was laughing. The contents of Hector's little brown jug were beginning to take effect. The Beaver bought the horse at a good price and John J., taking advantage of the crowd's good humour, ordered the boys to bring out all the harness and the cows "sold" to Dougall.

The women were in the kitchen taking tea and exchanging everyday news. Molly served like a queen handing out citations. She was dressed for the occasion. She held her head high; her lips were drawn tight. It seemed of little importance that her black sequinned dress was too short, too youthful, that her distended stomach raised the hemline above her knee and that there were two grease spots on the skirt. Dung encrusted the heels of her brown oxfords and the lipstick spilled over her lips like a wave on dry sand.

"Excuse me," said Molly, as she grabbed the empty water bucket and left the kitchen. She saw the gelding come out for auction and she saw the bundle of dollar bills in John J.'s pocket.

"Yer man's after sprouting money from every pocket like rye grass in a turnip patch," someone shouted. "Ye'd best keep an eye on him."

"What good'd that do?" Molly didn't smile; her answer was barely audible and she kept on her way down the slope until she reached the well. At the barrel trap she dipped her bucket deep and raised it overflowing. Her shoulders sagged as she plodded back up the hill unmindful of the water splattering on her dress and on her shoes. Although the hill was steep she did not falter until she reached the kitchen door and closed it behind her.

By five o'clock the men had completely forgotten about the value of clear skies for harvesting and of the day's work they had lost. The harness, the cows and machinery that had been knocked down to Dougall when bidding was cold went exceptionally well the second time around. Dougall was nowhere to be seen. John J. didn't need him any more.

There were now two jugs going the rounds. People were buying things they couldn't possibly use and everyone knew what was going on as item after item came up. John J. strode four steps to the left and four to the right, smoking furiously. He caught sight of Johnnie leaning against the barn and motioned him over. Johnnie listened attentively, nodded his head and disappeared round the corner of the barn. Soon he was back pulling a creaking old two-wheel cart that hadn't been seen before. It creaked and groaned and the wheels threatened to go in opposite directions with every revolution. Johnnie threw down the shafts before his father. The auctioneer stopped chanting and stared open-mouthed. John J. raised his hand and whispered. The auctioneer nodded.

"This...." He paused so long that people began to fidget. "Everyone knows how handy a cart is around the farm." He paused again. "With a little soakin' the cracks in the wheels will tighten up." Finding himself speechless for the first time since he started his trade he could only say, "What am I offered?"

Someone got the cart for a few cents. Then the bidding started on an ancient barrel churn worked by a foot pedal, that was as leaky as a sieve. Lauchie MacTavish made the first bid. Waves of laughter echoed across the Glen. Only the women who'd come to find the cause of the merriment looked grim.

The crowd moved into the house. All that could be hauled into the kitchen was piled into the middle of the floor. Metal tables with legs wired together. Chairs with rungs missing; a cheap white medicine cabinet smeared with crayons; a table that sagged in the middle. All were sold with no trouble at all and the prices were good. Charlie Lawlor bought a spinning wheel, and his saintly wife, standing next to Clemmie Douglas, whispered, "He can keep it." Joe Beaton, a bachelor, who used only the kitchen of his house, bought a three-piece chesterfield set for almost full price.

THEN IT WAS ALL OVER.

Those who sat on chairs already sold got up; some put on sweaters against the chill of the evening. The auctioneer went about shaking hands with new acquaintances and everyone was nosily minding his own business when John J., shirt and trouser pockets bulging with dollar bills, pushed his way through the crowd, yelling for them all to sit down again. In his hand John J. carried a rusty old kerosene lantern all crooked and bent in some encounter with a cow.

"Don't go...don't go yit," John J. yelled. "There's still this lantern!" He pushed the lantern into the auctioneer's hand. The chant began and ended abruptly with "Fifty cents," and without looking at John J. the auctioneer walked out and down the hill to the barn. The auction was over.

It didn't seem as if John J. was ever going to pull himself together. The boys watched and waited. He had Pat in the kitchen now, coaxing him to drive him to the vendor again for the fourth time.

Johnnie whispered, "If Pat goes for him again, we'll just pull out and leave them all."

"Leave Pat to come with Himself?" Colin asked, unable to believe that his brother could make such a suggestion.

"Why not? If he's crazy enough to let the old feller talk him into going for more liquor?"

"What yer s'pose the old lady thinks about going?" Danny asked.

"She just sits and looks out across the field like she was seeing something out there and if I say anything she just nods her head up and down and says 'never mind.'"

For a moment the brothers were silent.

"On this trip the old bastard might be after going to that slut and blow the whole frigging auction money and none of us will get to go at all. We ain't got any money. What we should'a did was go when Colie had his pay for haymakin'."

The boys were standing outside the kitchen window.

"Shhh!" whispered Danny, who had his ear to the window and could hear what was going on.

"Come on, it's all right, Pat's coming."

Johnnie motioned towards the barn and started walking down the hill. The others followed at his heels.

"Is Pat coming yet?" he said without stopping or looking over his shoulder. Pat ran and caught up with them.

"The old man nearly cried when I told him if he wanted a cure he could get it himself," said Pat, catching his breath. "Said he'd start tomorrow, same old go-ahead, said he wuz too nervous to drive. Then I told him that us guys wuz going today whether he did or not. That lit a fire under his arse, started him beggin' fer help t'load up."

"Get the truck before he changes his mind again. Mebbe we can get going by noon," said Colin.

"Mama followed me to the door and said to hurry, there's nothing to eat here," said Pat.

MANY SAW THEM PARKED in front of the vendor's. The boy's car and John J.'s truck behind it. Everything had been thrown in, helter-skelter; there was no way of knowing what had fallen off or what would go next.

No one in the county saw John J. Campbell or his family

again for many years.

Women remembered Molly, sitting proud and upright, looking straight ahead between the heads of the children on her knee. “Them that goes away come back driving big new cars.” Maybe her John J. would do the same.

They were on their way to Ontario.

Family History–Tessie's Story

I HAVE OFTEN MARVELLED at fate which could bring out of a family of shanty Irish...a real fighting woman and a saint like my mother.

Only in the United States could she have mated with a nephew of Edmund D. Rose and the son of Henry Rice of Michigan, heir to Lord Rice of some place back in Ireland. The Lord part of my family were dull, but the Weavers from which I sprung up were something else again.

John Weaver, emigrant from Ireland, small, bearded and docile, was swooped into marriage by an amazon from Dublin named Nancy Good. Swooped is the word, because poor John was strung up and manoeuvred for the rest of his days.

Nancy was a huge woman, black-haired and buxom. She ruled with an iron hand and a clenched fist. She gave birth to two boys and a girl before the North could declare war on the South—a bare three years. And she didn't stop with Phil, Jacob and Mary; she was heavy with Ollie when John got word that he was drafted to serve with the northern troops.

Nancy hit the ceiling!

Up in Indiana where they had settled, there were no slaves except poor John and even poor John hadn't an inkling of whether the war was right or not. He hadn't had time to think about it.

Nancy knew that for two hundred dollars John could stay home and pay a neighbour to do the fighting. Nancy made the deal and John, who would have enjoyed getting away, stayed home.

The war did not get near the Weavers' farm; there were no fought battles, but bushwhackers were thick. Every morning John took the milk cows into the woods and hid them.

But the day came when Nancy wasn't able to manoeuvre Uncle Sam any more. John had no money, and even if there had been money no one had the courage to take it. So John went to war leaving Nancy with four children and John Jr. in her belly.

Diphtheria rampaged, Ollie and the baby John came down with the dread disease. Nancy pulled them through and when John crawled home from war, their pallid faces bore the traces of their brush with death. Nancy ruled that the two boys were excused from every chore, "them being sickly."

Young Mary, kind and warm-hearted like her father, fitted in with housekeeping regulations as soon as she could make a biscuit and rub a handkerchief on a board. Nancy quit work and sat back to a full time of bossing. Jacob and Phil were like Old John, so their lot was work; and that left Ollie and John Jr. to their leisure. John Jr. was the instigator, Ollie the follower, and Phil and Jacob were enough like their father in every way to divide the Weavers' house between the workers and the fighters. The other two, urged on by the family clannish-ness jammed into them by Nancy from birth, couldn't let John Jr. get whipped by any outsider. This, oftener than not, left costly damage in its wake, which Nancy enjoyed as much in the retelling as the boys involved in the incident.

THE DAY CAME, HOWEVER, when the rest of the village clanned up against the entire Weaver family and gave them a deadline to vacate their holdings! At the same time as the family prepared their wagons for the trail westward they were joined by Otto Guenther, a lad from Pennsylvania, who had been placed on a neighbouring farm by brutal relatives when his parents died. There were two wagons. Jacob and Ollie had married and their families occupied one wagon. The old folks, Granma Nancy, Old John, Phil and Mary travelled in the second.

At nightfall when they ringed the wagons, and Paw and the boys were busy setting up the big tent, Mary took a bucket and went down to the river. Of all the young men, it was Otto Guenther who always got there first. I've no way of knowing how they finally got the nerve to speak but love speaks its own language.

Before the train crossed the Ohio line Mary and Otto were married. Even then Otto might not have found the words to propose, but a preacher and his wife, travelling with the train, helped the courtship along. The minister caught Mary and Otto whispering together at the end of John's wagon.

"Come around early in the morning.... No need putting it off," he said.

"Puttin' what off?" asked Otto. Mary blushed.

"Gettin' married. You was thinkin' of gettin' married, wasn't ye?"

Otto peeked up from under the bowed eyelashes and stuttered:

"Yes...eer...I dunno...I didn't ask her."

Mary slipped her hand under his arm, and Otto's head sprang up like a sprung window shade.

"Yes!" he shouted.

Every mother of the wagon train looked over; you could have heard a pin drop.

DOWN INTO KANSAS THEY WENT and made camp right outside Dodge City. Mary was showing by now and they had moved away from Paw and Nancy's wagon to Jacob and Ollie's, but Maw Nancy took care to see that Mary took care of the wagon she had left and its people. Otto became very concerned that Mary had so much work in her condition, he wanted to speak to Maw

Nancy, but Mary wouldn't let him. She knew that her Otto was no match for battling Nancy.

"We'll stop before long, Otto," she whispered. "We'll build away from the rest...I can hardly wait. Promise you'll not talk up to 'er." He promised.

After supper Phil and John Jr. rode off to Dodge City. Phil had married a nice little girl on the way but when the day dawned she hadn't slept a wink. No one had told her about the scrapes and the fights of the Weaver boys. Everyone on the wagon train had been strangers from the start, so no one knew the Weavers and even if they had they would hardly have talked.

"That poor darling," whispered Mary to her Otto that night under the stars, "why didn't ye tell her, before she married 'im?"

"Mary, I couldn't. He's your brother, and she looked to me like she wouldn't believe me nohow." Mary hugged Otto a little closer and said a little breathless prayer of thanksgiving for the gentle man He'd sent her.

The wagon train passed through Dodge City and the next morning continued into the wild and bare land near the Oklahoma territory. Old Nancy, weary and bad tempered—she had lain awake waiting; the night before too, although she hadn't told anyone—shouted to Old John who walked beside the wagon.

"Pull up there. I ain't goin' another step. Me ass is near wored off me now...bouncin' and jostlin' fer near nine months. We're gettin' too fur away from civilization. We gits out here an' we can do our tradin' in Dodge City. How's that ground there, John?"

Old John had the wagon pulled out of line, and he kicked a clod from the ground, stooped down and crumbled it through his fingers as only a man who loves the earth can. He did not answer.

"Good. Hain't it?" Nancy asked, her eyes screwed up watching and reading the look on the little man's face.

"We'll settle here where there's trees enough to build.... Pitch th' tent fer now.... You Jacob, Phil! Give him a hand." She pulled herself over the side of the wagon and got down to oversee.

Paw staked out some land for themselves, and a plot for each of the boys. John Jr. spent most nights in Dodge City. Mary gave birth to a little girl, whom old Nancy insisted they call Nancy. Crops were in, and cabins built. It was time for fencing. John Jr., as usual ready and willing to get away from work, offered to go into Dodge City for nails.

He came home next day with Laura. He had been seeing her in the saloon where she worked, and had married her.

Marriage kept John Jr. home only as long as it took for the newness of marriage to wear off. He and Phil began to go to Dodge City every night. Every night they had fights...fist fights. Laura tried hard to be a good wife to John, but John didn't appreciate her. He was, after all, used to being the main event whenever at home.

THE LITTLE CLAN WAS SETTLED IN nicely. Most of the cattle had survived the drive from Indiana, had reproduced, and now there was plenty for all the families. John Jr. did not work but he shared in everything. The others carried him along uncomplaining.

Two winters passed, and it was spring. Paw was in the field plowing, and each boy was doing his own job, yet all were thinking of John. He hadn't come home the night before. Old Nancy came out of the cabin like a storm, lifted her foghorn voice and called them all in for a powwow.

"John's in trouble.... He'd be home b'now if he wasn't.... Phil, I want you should ride into Dodge.... You go with him, Ollie.... Git John and if you find he's hurt...give them devils as done it a damn good pounding."

They brought John home astride his horse, but with his head so far down they couldn't see his face. Nancy screamed and lumbered out to meet them.

"Johnny...Johnny.... Oh! my baby, what have them devils done to ye? Here let me see ye." She held his head tenderly and his ear hanging by the skin fell on her arm. You could hear her curse clear over to John's cabin and Laura came running out. She took John home, soothing him like a baby. She boiled a needle and spool of white thread on the old wood stove. Then, telling John Jr. to lay still, sewed his ear back on.

All the clan had gathered in the little cabin and waited silently for the story. When he had been cleaned of the blood and had a big slug of whiskey inside, he talked.

"Phil.... Ye gotta go back with me next Monday.... They knocked me down and busted me ribs.... I know they're busted... and that Red Glass-man chewed off my ear while three of the sons of bitches held me.... I told 'em I'd be back when the sides were evener...you guys.... I'll have to go."

No one said no.

John Jr. laid up for five days. Laura was happy. She waited on him hand and foot. Then on the sixth day, against her pleading, John Jr. took a lunch, mounted his horse and rode off into the hills.

He wasn't back Sunday night and he didn't come back Monday morning.

Old Nancy called the boys into her cabin.

"John's gone. Must be hidin' out.... Never seen the day I thought one of MY boys be a coward.... We can't let them get away with it. You boys gonna let people in Dodge say the Weavers is cowards?"

The boys' wives looked from one to the other. Ollie's wife was pregnant, and Phil's wife was pretty sure she was. Phil's wife looked at her little girl. Her eyes filled with tears. They all marched out solemnly.

"We'll wait one hour more," Phil said, "then we'll go.... If John hain't come by then...."

"He ain't comin'," said Old John. The first he'd dared open

his mouth. "He's done gone to the hills to hide out. Got enough fightin'."

"Why you!" Old Nancy tried to grab the old man, but he did not wait for her reaction.

Old Nancy was the only one to watch the boys out of sight. She stood at the road and waved.

ALSO AVAILABLE FROM
Breton Books

The Cabot Trail in Black & White

collected & edited by RONALD CAPLAN

HEARTBREAKING AND TRIUMPHANT, a collection of stories and photographs in stark black and white, as we rarely see the Trail or its people and, in many cases, as we will likely never see them again. From over 25 years of *Cape Breton's Magazine*, these are pieces of life along a trace of road that became the highway–the Cabot Trail.

8.5 X 11 • 150 PHOTOS • 144 PAGES • ISBN 1-895415-99-3

Cape Breton Highlands National Park

A PARK LOVER'S COMPANION

by CLARENCE BARRETT

FOR BOTH HIKER AND ARMCHAIR TRAVELLER, this excellent guide brings us northern Cape Breton in all seasons, both on and off trail. This noted naturalist, photographer, and "near-legendary" outdoorsman shares his lifelong love, respect, and enthusiasm for the rich landscape and lore of the Highlands.

35 COLOUR PHOTOS • DRAWINGS • MAPS • 176 PAGES

ISBN 1-895415-62-4

As True As I'm Sittin' Here

200 CAPE BRETON STORIES

edited by BRIAN SUTCLIFFE & RONALD CAPLAN

COLLECTED BY ARCHIE NEIL CHISHOLM—laughs, comebacks, ghosts, fairies, put-downs, and all-round wit—from Dan Angus Beaton, Jim St. Clair, Sid Timmons, Hector Doink MacDonald, Annie the Tailor MacPhee, Alex John MacIsaac, Paddy MacDonald, and many more.

Stories that shorten the road, lighten the work, and fill pauses between tunes, from kitchens and living rooms throughout Cape Breton Island.

220 PAGES • $22.50 • ISBN 1-895415-58-6

Rita Joe: For the Children

by RITA JOE • woodcuts by BURLAND MURPHY

STRONG, ENCOURAGING POEMS, by the Order of Canada recipient from Eskasoni First Nation. With the young person in mind–down-to-earth and often humorous–these poems tell stories of Mi'kmaw life, and of the concrete and spiritual world of this courageous elder. Illustrated with powerful, tender wildlife woodcuts.

38 POEMS • 52 PAGES • ISBN 1-895415-98-5

Breton Books

Wreck Cove, Cape Breton, Nova Scotia B0C 1H0

bretonbooks@ns.sympatico.ca • 1-800-565-5140

www.capebretonbooks.com

ALSO AVAILABLE FROM
Breton Books

Rise Again! Book One
The Story of Cape Breton Island
by ROBERT J. MORGAN

HERE IS BOOK ONE of Bob Morgan's readable and informative history of Cape Breton Island.

Rise Again! takes you from our geological roots through Mi'kmaw life, and the building of French Louisbourg–the island's First Economic Boom–and the Colony of Cape Breton. An accessible and lasting achievement.

232 PAGES • PHOTOS • ISBN 1-895415-81-0

Rise Again! Book Two
The Story of Cape Breton Island
by ROBERT J. MORGAN

FROM 1900 TO TODAY the story continues with industrialization, as coal mines are consolidated and the steel plants rise, calling rural Cape Breton and the wider world to the wage paying industrial east. *Rise Again! Book 2* takes you through two World Wars, the Mi'kmaw battle for cultural survival, and preservation of Scottish, Acadian and Irish life–as today's Cape Bretoner emerges.

288 PAGES • PHOTOS • ISBN 1-895415-85-3

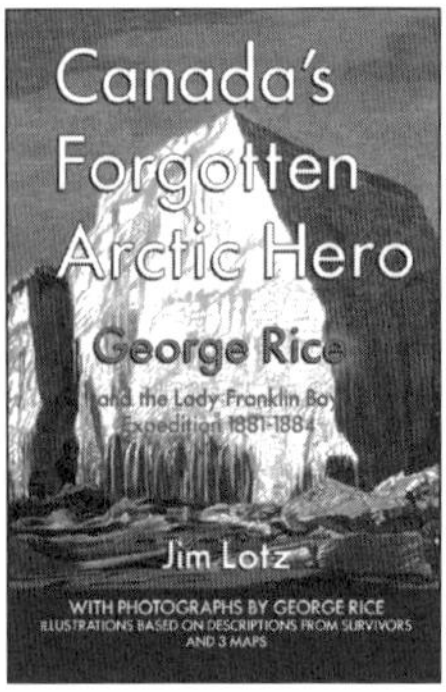

Canada's Forgotten Arctic Hero
George Rice
and the Lady Franklin Bay Expedition 1881-1884
by JIM LOTZ

THE TERRIFIC TRUE ADVENTURE of an unjustly forgotten Cape Bretoner –Canada's first photographer of the High Arctic. The "indefatigable" George Rice emerged a leader on an American Arctic expedition, and died a hero searching for food for his starving comrades. This gripping and painful story is told through George Rice's previously unpublished diaries. Packed with humour, pathos, and magnificent description, this book is a powerful historic and literary event–masterfully presented by Jim Lotz.

208 PAGES • ISBN 1-895415-94-2

BLAST!
CAPE BRETON COAL MINE DISASTERS
by RENNIE MACKENZIE

A MONUMENT TO COURAGE and achievement, BLAST! tells the stories of all 18 major disasters in Cape Breton's coal mining history. The author brings his coal miner's eye and heart to these painful, often staggering stories of tragedies that resulted in three or more deaths–from the first boiler explosion in 1877 to the last methane disaster in 1979.

192 PAGES • ISBN 1-895415-79-9

Breton Books
Wreck Cove, Cape Breton, Nova Scotia B0C 1H0
bretonbooks@ns.sympatico.ca • 1-800-565-5140
www.capebretonbooks.com